The Lions of the Lord
A Tale of the Old West

by

Harry Leon Wilson

Double 9
BOOKS

The Lions of the Lord
A Tale of the Old West
by Harry Leon Wilson

ISBN: 978-93-63054-35-6

Published by

DOUBLE 9 BOOKS

2/13-B, Ansari Road
Daryaganj, New Delhi – 110002
info@double9books.com
www.double9books.com
Tel. 011-40042856

ABOUT THE AUTHOR

Harry Leon Wilson, an American novelist and dramatist, is best known for his novels Ruggles of Red Gap and Merton of the Movies. Bunker Bean, another of his works, contributed to the popularity of the term "flapper". Harry Leon Wilson was born in Oregon, Illinois, to Samuel and Adeline. His father was a newspaper publisher, so Harry learnt to set type at a young age. He attended public schools and enjoyed reading Bret Harte and Mark Twain. He acquired shorthand and secretarial abilities. Wilson left his family at the age of 16 and worked as a stenographer for the Union Pacific Railroad in Topeka, Kansas, Omaha, Nebraska, and Denver, Colorado before moving to California in 1887. Puck magazine approved Wilson's article "The Elusive Dollar Bill" in December of 1886. He continued to contribute to Puck, eventually becoming assistant editor in 1892. Henry Cuyler Bunner died in 1896, and Wilson took over as editor. Wilbertine Nesselrode Teters Worden was Wilson's first wife, and they married in 1898. The marriage terminated in divorce in 1900. In 1902, he married Rose Cecil O'Neill Latham. O'Neill and Wilson worked together at Puck, and she illustrated four of his novels. They separated in 1907. Wilson's black and white pit bull dog, Sprangle, was the inspiration for Rose O'Neill's biscuit porcelain Kewpie dog figure, known as the "Kewpiedoodle dog" and sold internationally by importer George Borgfeldt.

CONTENTS

FOREWORD

In the days of '49 seven trails led from our Western frontier into the Wonderland that lay far out under the setting sun and called to the restless. Each of the seven had been blazed mile by mile through the mighty romance of an empire's founding. Some of them for long stretches are now overgrown by the herbage of the plain; some have faded back into the desert they lined; and more than one has been shod with steel. But along them all flit and brood the memory-ghosts of old, rich-coloured days. To the shout of teamster, the yell of savage, the creaking of tented ox-cart, and the rattle of the swifter mail-coach, there go dim shapes of those who had thrilled to that call of the West;—strong, brave men with the far look in their eyes, with those magic rude tools of the pioneer, the rifle and the axe; women, too, equally heroic, of a stock, fearless, ready, and staunch, bearing their sons and daughters in fortitude; raising them to fear God, to love their country,—and to labour. From the edge of our Republic these valiant ones toiled into the dump of prairie and mountain to live the raw new days and weld them to our history; to win fertile acres from the wilderness and charm the desert to blossoming. And the time of these days and these people, with their tragedies and their comedies, was a time of epic splendour;—more vital with the stuff and colour of life, I think, than any since the stubborn gray earth out there was made to yield its treasure.

Of these seven historic highways the one richest in story is the old Salt Lake Trail: this because at its western end was woven a romance within a romance;—a drama of human passions, of love and hate, of high faith and low, of the beautiful and the ugly, of truth and lies; yet with certain fine fidelities under it all; a drama so close-knit, so amazingly true, that one who had lightly designed to make a tale there was dismayed by fact. So much more thrilling was it than any fiction he might have imagined, so more than human had been the cunning of the Master Dramatist, that the little make-believe he was pondering seemed clumsy and poor, and he turned from it to try to tell what had really been.

In this story, then, the things that are strangest have most of truth. The make-believe is hardly more than a cement to join the queerly wrought stones of fact that were found ready. For, if the writer has now and again had to divine certain things that did not show,—yet must have been,—surely these are not less than truth. One of these deductions is the Lute of the Holy Ghost who came in the end to be the Little Man of Sorrows: who loved a woman, a child, and his God, but sinned through pride of soul;—whose life, indeed, was a poem of sin and retribution. Yet not less true was he than the Lion of the Lord, the Archer of Paradise, the Wild Ram of the Mountains, or the gaunt, gray woman whom hurt love had crazed. For even now, as the tale is done, comes a dry little note in the daily press telling how such a one actually did the other day a certain brave, great thing it had seemed the imagined one must be driven to do. Only he and I, perhaps, will be conscious of the struggle back of that which was printed; but at least we two shall know that the Little Man of Sorrows is true, even though the cross where he fled to say his last prayer in the body has long since fallen and its bars crumbled to desert dust.

Yet there are others still living in a certain valley of the mountains who will know why the soul-proud youth came to bend under invisible burdens, and why he feared, as an angel of vengeance, that early cowboy with the yellow hair, who came singing down from the high divide into Amalon where a girl was waiting in her dream of a single love; others who, to this day, will do not more than whisper with averted faces of the crime that brought a curse upon the land; who still live in terror of shapes that shuffle furtively behind them, fumbling sometimes at their shoulders with weak hands, striving ever to come in front and turn upon them. But these will know only one side of the Little Man of Sorrows who was first the Lute of the Holy Ghost in the Poet's roster of titles: since they have lacked his courage to try the great issue with their God.

New York City, May 1st, 1903.

Chapter I
The Dead City

The city without life lay handsomely along a river in the early sunlight of a September morning. Death had seemingly not been long upon it, nor had it made any scar. No breach or rent or disorder or sign of violence could be seen. The long, shaded streets breathed the still airs of utter peace and quiet. From the half-circle around which the broad river bent its moody current, the neat houses, set in cool, green gardens, were terraced up the high hill, and from the summit of this a stately marble temple, glittering of newness, towered far above them in placid benediction.

Mile after mile the streets lay silent, along the river-front, up to the hilltop, and beyond into the level; no sound nor motion nor sign of life throughout their length. And when they had run their length, and the outlying fields were reached, there, too, was the same brooding spell as the land stretched away in the hush and haze. The yellow grain, heavy-headed with richness, lay beaten down and rotting, for there were no reapers. The city, it seemed, had died calmly, painlessly, drowsily, as if overcome by sleep.

From a skiff in mid-river, a young man rowing toward the dead city rested on his oars and looked over his shoulder to the temple on the hilltop. There was something very boyish in the reverent eagerness with which his dark eyes rested upon the pile, tracing the splendid lines from its broad, gray base to its lofty spire, radiant with white and gold. As he looked long and intently, the colour of new life flushed into a face that was pinched and drawn. With fresh resolution, he bent again to his oars, noting with a quick eye that the current had carried him far down-stream while he stopped to look upon the holy edifice.

Landing presently at the wharf, he was stunned by the hush of the streets. This was not like the city of twenty thousand people he had left three months before. In blank bewilderment he stood, turning to each quarter for some solution of the mystery. Perceiving at length that there was really no life either way along the river, he started wonderingly up a street that led from the waterside,—a street which, when he had last walked it, was quickening with the rush of a mighty commerce.

Soon his expression of wonder was darkened by a shade of anxiety. There was an unnerving quality in the trance-like stillness; and the mystery of it pricked him to forebodings. He was now passing empty workshops, hesitating at door after door with ever-mounting alarm. Then he began to call, but the sound of his voice served only to aggravate the silence.

Growing bolder, he tried some of the doors and found them to yield, letting him into a kind of smothered, troubled quietness even more oppressive than that outside. He passed an empty ropewalk, the hemp strewn untidily about, as if the workers had left hurriedly. He peered curiously at idle looms and deserted spinning-wheels—deserted apparently but the instant before he came. It seemed as if the people were fled maliciously just in front, to leave him in this fearfullest of all solitudes. He wondered if he did not hear their quick, furtive steps, and see the vanishing shadows of them.

He entered a carpenter's shop. On the bench was an unfinished door, a plane left where it had been shoved half the length of its edge, the fresh pine shaving still curling over the side. He left with an uncanny feeling that the carpenter, breathing softly, had watched him from some hiding-place, and would now come stealthily out to push his plane again.

He turned into a baker's shop and saw freshly chopped kindling piled against the oven, and dough actually on the kneading-tray. In a tanner's vat he found fresh bark. In a blacksmith's shop he entered next the fire was out, but there was coal heaped beside the forge, with the ladling-pool and the crooked water-horn, and on the anvil was a horseshoe that had cooled before it was finished.

With something akin to terror, he now turned from this street of shops into one of those with the pleasant dwellings, eager to find something alive, even a dog to bark an alarm. He entered one of the gardens, clicking the gate-latch loudly after him, but no one challenged. He drew a drink from the well with its loud-rattling chain and clumsy, water-sodden bucket, but no one called. At the door of the house he whistled, stamped, pounded, and at last flung it open with all the noise he could make. Still his hungry ears fed on nothing but sinister echoes, the barren husks of his own clamour. There was no curt voice of a man, no quick, questioning tread of a woman. There were dead white ashes on the hearth, and the silence was grimly kept by the dumb household gods.

His nervousness increased. So vividly did his memory people the streets and shops and houses that the air was vibrant with sound,—low-toned conversations, shouts, calls, laughter, the voices of children, the creaking of wagons, pounding hammers, the clangour of many works; yet all muffled away from him, as if coming from some phantom-land. His eyes, too, were kept darting from side to side by vague forms that flitted privily near by, around corners, behind him, lurking always a little beyond his eyes, turn them quickly as he would. Now, facing the street, he shouted, again and again, from sheer nervousness; but the echoes came back alone.

He recalled a favourite day-dream of boyhood,—a dream in which he became the sole person in the world, wandering with royal liberty through strange cities, with no voice to chide or forbid, free to choose and partake, as would a prince, of all the wonders and delights that boyhood can picture; his own master and the master of all the marvels and treasures of earth. This was like the dream come true; but it distressed him. It was necessary to find the people at once. He had a feeling that his instant duty was to break some malign spell that lay upon the place—or upon himself. For one of them was surely bewitched.

Out he strode to the middle of the street, between two rows of yellowing maples, and there he shouted again and still more loudly to evoke some shape or sound of life, sending a full, high, ringing call up the empty thoroughfare. Between the shouts he scanned the near-by houses intently.

At last, half-way up the next block, even as his lungs filled for another peal, he thought his eyes caught for a short half-second the mere thin shadow of a skulking figure. It had seemed to pass through a grape arbour that all but shielded from the street a house slightly more pretentious than its neighbours. He ran toward the spot, calling as he went. But when he had vaulted over the low fence, run across the garden and around the end of the arbour, dense with the green leaves and clusters of purple grapes, the space in front of the house was bare. If more than a trick-phantom of his eye had been there, it had vanished.

He stood gazing blankly at the front door of the house. Was it fancy that he had heard it shut a second before he came? that his nerves still responded to the shock of its closing? He had already imagined so many noises of the kind, so many misty shapes fleeing before him with little soft rustlings, so many whispers at his back and hushed cries behind the closed doors. Yet this door had seemed to shut more tangibly, with a warmer promise of life. He went quickly up the three wooden steps, turned the knob, and pushed it open—very softly this time. No one appeared. But, as he stood on the threshold, while the pupils of his eyes dilated to the gloom of the hall into which he looked, his ears seemed to detect somewhere in the house a muffled footfall and the sound of another door closed softly.

He stepped inside and called. There was no answer, but above his head a board creaked. He started up the stairs in front of him, and, as he did so, he seemed to hear cautious steps across a bare floor above. He stopped climbing; the steps ceased. He started up, and the steps came again. He knew now they came from a room at the head of the stairs. He bounded up the remaining steps and pushed open the door with a loud "Halloo!"

The room was empty. Yet across it there was the indefinable trail of a presence,—an odour, a vibration, he knew not what,—and where a bar of sunlight cut the gloom under a half-raised curtain, he saw the motes in the air all astir. Opposite the door he had opened was another, leading, apparently, to a room at the back of the house. From behind it, he could have sworn came the sounds of a stealthily moved body and softened breathing. A presence, unseen but felt, was all about. Not without effort did he conquer the impulse to look behind him at every breath.

Determined to be no longer eluded, he crossed the room on tiptoe and gently tried the opposite door. It was locked. As he leaned against it, almost in a terror of suspense, he knew he heard again those little seemings of a presence a door's thickness away. He did not hesitate. Still holding the turned knob in his hand, he quickly crouched back and brought his flexed shoulder heavily against the door. It flew open with a breaking sound, and, with a little gasp of triumph, he was in the room to confront its unknown occupant.

To his dismay, he saw no one. He peered in bewilderment to the farther side of the room, where light struggled dimly in at the sides of a curtained window. There was no sound, and yet he could acutely feel that presence; insistently his nerves tingled the warning of another's nearness. Leaning forward, still peering to sound the dim corners of the room, he called out again.

Then, from behind the door he had opened, a staggering blow was dealt him, and, before he could recover, or had done more than blindly crook one arm protectingly before his face, he was borne heavily to the floor, writhing in a grasp that centered all its crushing power about his throat.

Chapter II
The Wild Ram of the Mountains

Slight though his figure was, it was lithe and active and well-muscled, and he knew as they struggled that his assailant was possessed of no greater advantage than had lain in his point of attack. In strength, apparently, they were well-matched. Twice they rolled over on the carpeted floor, and then, despite the big, bony hands pressing about his throat, he turned his burden under him, and all but loosened the killing clutch. This brought them close to the window, but again he was swiftly drawn underneath. Then, as he felt his head must burst and his senses were failing from the deadly grip at his throat, his feet caught in the folds of the heavy curtain, and brought it down upon them in a cloud of dust.

As the light flooded in, he saw the truth, even before his now panting and sneezing antagonist did. Releasing the pressure from his throat with a sudden access of strength born of the new knowledge, he managed to gasp, though thickly and with pain, as they still strove:

"Seth Wright—wait—let go—wait, Seth—I'm Joel—Joel Rae!"

He managed it with difficulty.

"Joel Rae—Rae—Rae—don't you see?"

He felt the other's tension relax. With many a panting, puffing "Hey!" and "What's that now?" he was loosed, and drew himself up into a chair by the saving window. His assailant, a hale, genial-faced man of forty, sat on the floor where the revelation of his victim's identity had overtaken him. He was breathing hard and feeling tenderly of his neck. This was ruffled ornamentally by a style of whisker much in vogue at the time. It had proved, however, but an inferior defense against the onslaught of the younger man in his frantic efforts to save his own neck.

They looked at each other in panting amazement, until the older man recovered his breath, and spoke:

"Gosh and all beeswax! The Wild Ram of the Mountains a-settin' on the Lute of the Holy Ghost's stomach a-chokin' him to death. My sakes!

I'm a-pantin' like a tuckered hound—a-thinkin' he was a cussed milishy mobocrat come to spoil his household!"

The younger man was now able to speak, albeit his breathing was still heavy and the marks of the struggle plain upon him.

"What does it mean, Brother Wright—all this? Where are the Saints we left here—why is the city deserted—and why this—this?"

He shook back the thick, brown hair that fell to his shoulders, tenderly rubbed the livid fingerprints at his throat, and readjusted the collar of his blue flannel shirt.

"Thought you was a milishy man, I tell you, from the careless way you hollered—one of Brockman's devils come back a-snoopin', and I didn't crave trouble, but when I saw the Lord appeared to reely want me to cope with the powers of darkness, why, I jest gritted into you for the consolation of Israel. You'd 'a' got your come-uppance, too, if you'd 'a' been a mobber. You was nigh a-ceasin' to breathe, Joel Rae. In another minute I wouldn't 'a' give the ashes of a rye-straw for your part in the tree of life!"

"Yes, yes, man, but go back a little. Where are our people, the sick, the old, and the poor, that we had to leave till now? Tell me, quick."

The older man sprang up, the late struggle driven from his mind, his face scowling. He turned upon his questioner.

"Does my fury swell up in me? No wonder! And you hain't guessed why? Well, them pitiful remnant of Saints, the sick, the old, the poor, waitin' to be helped yender to winter quarters, has been throwed out into that there slough acrost the river, six hundred and forty of 'em."

"When we were keeping faith by going?"

"What does a mobocrat care for faith-keepin'? Have you brought back the wagons?"

"Yes; they'll reach the other side to-night. I came ahead and made the lower crossing. I've seen nothing and heard nothing. Go on—tell me—talk, man!"

"Talk?—yes, I'll talk! We've had mobs and the very scum of hell to boil over here. This is Saturday, the 19th, ain't it? Well, Brockman marched against this stronghold of Israel jest a week ago, with eight hundred men. They had cannons and demanded surrender. We was a scant two hundred fightin' men, and the only artillery we had was what we made ourselves. We broke up an old steamboat shaft and bored out the pieces so's they'd take a six-pound shot—but we wasn't goin' to give up. We'd learned our lesson about mobocrat milishies. Well, Brockman, when he got our defy, sent out his Warsaw riflemen as flankers on the right and left, put the Lima Guards to our front with one cannon, and marched his main body through that corn-field and orchard to the south of here to the city lines. Then we had it hot. Brockman shot away all his cannon-balls—he had sixty-one—and drew back while he sent to Quincy for more. He'd killed three of our men. Sunday and Monday we swopped a few shots. And then Tuesday, along comes a committee of a hundred to negotiate peace. Well, Wednesday evening they signed terms, spite of all I could do. I'd 'a' fought till the white crows come a-cawin', but the rest of 'em wasn't so het up with the Holy Ghost, I reckon. Anyway, they signed. The terms wasn't reely set till Thursday morning, but we knew they would be, and so all Wednesday night we was movin' acrost the river, and it kept up all next day,—day before yesterday. You'd ought to 'a' been here then; you wouldn't wonder at my comin' down on you like a thousand of brick jest now, takin' you for a mobocrat. You'd 'a' seen families druv right out of their homes, with no horses, tents, money, nor a day's provisions,—jest a little foolish household stuff they could carry in their hands,—sick men and women carried on beds, mothers luggin' babies and leadin' children. My sakes! but I did want to run some bullets and fill my old horn with powder for the consolation of Israel! They're lyin' out over there in the slough now, as many as ain't gone to glory. It made me jest plumb murderous!"

The younger man uttered a sharp cry of anguish. "What, oh, what has been our sin, that we must be proved again? Why have we got to be chastened?"

"Then Brockman's force marched in Thursday afternoon, and hell was let loose. His devils have plundered the town, thrown out the bedridden that jest couldn't move, thrown their goods out after 'em, burned, murdered, tore up. You come up from the river, and you ain't seen that yet—they ain't touched the lower part of town—and now they're bunkin' in the temple, defacin' it, defilin' it,—that place we built to be a house of rest for the Lord when he cometh again. They drove me acrost the river yesterday, and promised to shoot me if I dast show myself again. I sneaked over in a skiff last night and got here to get my two pistols and some money and trinkets we'd hid out. I was goin' to cross again to-night and wait for you and the wagons."

"My God! and this is the nineteenth century in a land of liberty!"

"State of Illinois, U.S.A., September 19, 1846—but what of that? We're the Lord's chosen, and over yender is a generation of vipers warned to flee from the wrath to come. But they won't flee, and so we're outcasts for the present, driven forth like snakes. The best American blood is in our veins.

We're Plymouth Rock stock, the best New England graft; the fathers of nine tenths of us was at Bunker Hill or Valley Forge or Yorktown, but what of that, I ask you?"

The speaker became oratorical as his rage grew.

"What did Matty Van Buren say to Sidney Rigdon and Elias Higbee when they laid our cause before him at Washington after our Missouri persecutions—when the wicked hatred of them Missourians had as a besom of fire swept before it into exile the whipped and plundered Saints of Jackson County? Well, he said: 'Gentlemen, your cause is just, but I can do nothing for you.' That's what a President of the United States said to descendants of *Mayflower* crossers who'd been foully dealt with, and been druv from their substance and their homes, their wheat burned in the stack and in the shock, and themselves butchered or put into the wilderness. And now the Lord's word to this people is to gether out again."

The younger man had listened in deep dejection.

"Yes, it's to be the old story. I saw it coming. The Lord is proving us again. But surely this will be the last. He will not again put us through fire and blood."

He paused, and for a moment his quick brown eyes looked far away.

"And yet, do you know, Bishop, I've thought that he might mean us to save ourselves against this Gentile persecution. Sometimes I find it hard to control myself."

The Bishop grinned appreciatively.

"So I heer'd. The Lute of the Holy Ghost got too rambunctious back in the States on the subject of our wrongs. And so they called you back from your mission?"

"They said I must learn to school myself; that I might hurt the cause by my ill-tempered zeal—and yet I brought in many—"

"I don't blame you. I got in trouble the first and only mission I went on, and the first time I preached, at that. When I said, 'Joseph was ordained by Peter, James, and John,' a drunken wag in the audience got up and called me a damned liar. I started for him. I never reached him, but I reached the end of my mission right there. The Twelve decided I was usefuller here at home. They said I hadn't got enough of the Lord's humility for outside work. That was why they put me at the head of—that little organisation I wanted you to join last spring. And it's done good work, too. You'll join now fast enough, I guess. You begin to see the need of such doin's. I can give you the oath any time."

"No, Bishop, I didn't mean that kind of resistance. It sounded too practical for me; I'm still satisfied to be the Lute of the Holy Ghost."

"You can be a Son of Dan, too."

"Not yet, not yet. We must still be a little meek in the face of Heaven."

"You're in a mighty poor place to practise meekness. What'd you cross the river for, anyway?"

"Why, for father and mother, of course. They must be safe at Green Plains. Can I get out there without trouble?"

The Bishop sneered.

"Be meek, will you? Well, mosey out to Green Plains and begin there. It's a *burned* plains you'll find, and Lima and Morley all the same, and Bear Creek. The mobbers started out from Warsaw, and burned all in their way, Morley first, then Green Plains, Bear Creek, and Lima. They'd set fire to the houses and drive the folks in ahead. They killed Ed Durfee at Morley for talkin' back to 'em."

"But father and mother, surely—"

"Your pa and ma was druv in here with the rest, like cattle to the slaughter."

"You don't mean to say they're over there on the river bank?"

"Now, they are a kind of a mystery about that—why they wa'n't throwed out with the rest. Your ma's sick abed—she ain't ever been peart since the night your pa's house was fired and they had to walk in—but that ain't the reason they wa'n't throwed out. They put out others sicker. They flung families where every one was sick out into that slough. I guess what's left of 'em wouldn't be a supper-spell for a bunch of long-billed mosquitoes. But one of them milishy captains was certainly partial to your folks for some reason. They was let to stay in Phin Daggin's house till you come."

"And Prudence—the Corsons—Miss Prudence Corson?"

"Oh, ho! So she's the one, is she? Now that reminds me, mebbe I can guess the cute of that captain's partiality. That girl's been kind of lookin' after your pa and ma, and that same milishy captain's been kind of lookin' after the girl. She got him to let her folks go to Springfield."

"But that's the wrong way."

"Well, now, I don't want to spleen, but I never did believe Vince Corson was anything more'n a hickory Saint—and there's been a lot of talk—but you get yours from the girl. If I ain't been misled, she's got some ready for you."

"Bishop, will there be a way for us to get into the temple, for her to be sealed to me? I've looked forward to that, you know. It would be hard to miss it."

"The mob's got the temple, even if you got the girl. There's a verse writ in charcoal on the portal:—

"'Large house, tall steeple,
Silly priests, deluded people.'

"That's how it is for the temple, and the mob's bunked there. But the girl may have changed her mind, too."

The young man's expression became wistful and gentle, yet serenely sure.

"I guess you never knew Prudence at all well," he said. "But come, can't we go to them? Isn't Phin Daggin's house near?"

"You may git there all right. But I don't want *my* part taken out of the tree of life jest yet. I ain't aimin' to show myself none. Hark!"

From outside came the measured, swinging tramp of men.

"Come see how the Lord is proving us—and step light."

They tiptoed through the other rooms to the front of the house.

"There's a peek-hole I made this morning—take it. I'll make me one here. Don't move the curtain."

They put their eyes to the holes and were still. The quick, rhythmic, scuffling tread of feet drew nearer, and a company of armed men marched by with bayonets fixed. The captain, a handsome, soldierly young fellow, glanced keenly from right to left at the houses along the line of march.

"We're all right," said the Bishop, in low tones. "The cusses have been here once—unless they happened to see us. They're startin' in now down on the flat to make sure no poor sick critter is left in bed in any of them houses. Now's your chance if you want to git up to Daggin's. Go out the back way, follow up the alleys, and go in at the back when you git there. But remember, 'Dan shall be a serpent by the way, an adder in the path that biteth the horse heels, so that his rider shall fall backward!' In Clay County we had to eat up the last mule from the tips of his ears to the end of the fly-whipper. Now we got to pass through the pinches again. We can't stand it for ever."

"The spirit may move us against it, Brother Seth."

"I wish to hell it would!" replied the Bishop.

Chapter III
The Lute of the Holy Ghost Breaks His Fast

In his cautious approach to the Daggin house, he came upon her unawares—a slight, slender, shapely thing of pink and golden flame, as she poised where the sun came full upon her. One hand clutched her flowing blue skirts snugly about her ankles; the other opened coaxingly to a kitten crouched to spring on the limb of an apple-tree above her. The head was thrown back, the vivid lips were parted, and he heard her laugh low to herself. Near by was a towering rose-bush, from which she had broken the last red rose, large, full, and lush, its petals already loosened. Now she wrenched away a handful of these, and flung them upward at the watchful kitten. The scarlet flecks drifted back around her and upon her. Like little red butterflies hovering in golden sunlight, they lodged in her many-braided yellow hair, or fluttered down the long curls that hung in front of her ears. She laughed again under the caressing shower. Then she tore away the remaining petals and tossed them up with an elf-like daintiness, not at the crouched and expectant kitten this time, but so that the whole red rain floated tenderly down upon her upturned face and into the folds of the white kerchief crossed upon her breast. She waited for the last feathery petal. Her hidden lover saw it lodge in the little hollow at the base of her bare, curved throat. He could hold no longer.

Stepping from the covert that had shielded him, he called softly to her.

"Prudence—Prue!"

She had reached again for the kitten, but at the sound of his low, vigorous note, she turned quickly toward him, colouring with a glow that spread from the corner of the crossed kerchief up to the yellow hair above her brow. She answered with quick breaths.

"Joel—Joel—Joel!"

She laughed aloud, clapping her small hands, and he ran to her—over beds of marigolds, heartsease, and lady's-slippers, through a row of drowsy-looking, heavy-headed dahlias, and past other withering flowers, all but choked out by the rank garden growths of late summer. Then his arms opened and seemed to swallow the leaping little figure, though his kisses fell with hardly more weight upon the yielded face than had the rose-petals a moment since, so tenderly mindful was his ardour. She submitted, a little as the pampered kitten had before submitted to her own pettings.

"You dear old sobersides, you—how gaunt and careworn you look, and how hungry, and what wild eyes you have to frighten one with! At first I thought you were a crazy man."

He held her face up to his eager eyes, having no words to say, overcome by the joy that surged through him like a mighty rush of waters. In the moment's glorious certainty he rested until she stirred nervously under his devouring look, and spoke.

"Come, kiss me now and let me go."

He kissed her eyes so that she shut them; then he kissed her lips—long—letting her go at last, grudgingly, fearfully, unsatisfied.

"You scare me when you look that way. You mustn't be so fierce."

"I told him he didn't know you."

"Who didn't know me, sir?"

"A man who said I wasn't sure of you."

"So you *are* sure of me, are you, Mr. Preacherman? Is it because we've been sweethearts since so long? But remember you've been much away. I've seen you—let me count—but one little time of two weeks in three years. You *would* go on that horrid mission."

"Is not religion made up of obedience, let life or death come?"

"Is there no room for loving one's sweetheart in it?"

"One must obey, and I am a better man for having denied myself and gone. I can love you better. I have been taught to think of others. I was sent to open up the gospel in the Eastern States because I had been endowed with almost the open vision. It was my call to help in the setting up of the Messiah's latter-day kingdom. Besides, we may never question the commands of the holy priesthood, even if our wicked hearts rebel in secret."

"If you had questioned the right person sharply enough, you might have had an answer as to why you were sent."

"What do you mean? How could I have questioned? How could I have rebelled against the stepping-stone of my exaltation?"

His face relaxed a little, and he concluded almost quizzically:

"Was not Satan hurled from high heaven for resisting authority?"

She pouted, caught him by the lapels of his coat and prettily tried to shake him.

"There—horrid!—you're preaching again. Please remember you're not on mission now. Indeed, sir, you were called back for being too—too—why, do you know, even old Elder Munsel, 'Fire-brand Munsel,' they call him, said you were too fanatical."

His face grew serious.

"I'm glad to be called back to you, at any rate,—and yet, think of all those poor benighted infidels who believe there are no longer revelations nor prophecies nor gifts nor healings nor speaking with tongues,—this miserable generation so blind in these last days when the time of God's wrath is at hand. Oh, I burn in my heart for them, night after night, suffering for the tortures that must come upon them—thrice direful because they have rejected the message of Moroni and trampled upon the priesthood of high heaven, butchering the Saints of the Most High, and hunting the prophets of God like Ahab of old."

"Oh, dear, please stop it! You sound like swearing!" Her two hands were closing her ears in a pretty pretense.

He seemed hardly to hear her, but went on excitedly:

"Yet I have done what man could do. I am never done doing. I would gladly give my body to be burned a thousand times if it would avail to save them into the Kingdom. I have preached the word tirelessly—fanatically, they say—but only as it burned in my bones. I have told them of visions, dreams, revelations, miracles, and all the mercies of this last dispensation. And I have prayed and fasted. Just now coming from winter quarters, when I could not preach, I held twelve fasts and twelve vigils. You will say it has weakened me, but it has weakened only the bonds that the flesh puts upon the spirit. Even so, I fell short of my vision—my tabernacle of flesh must have been too much profaned, though how I cannot dream—believe me, I have kept myself as high and clean as I knew. Yet there was promise. For only last night at the river bank, the spirit came partially upon me. I was taken with a faintness, and I heard above my head a sound like the rustling of silken robes, and the spirit of God hovered over me, so that I could feel its radiance. All in good time, then, it shall dwell within me, so that I may know a way to save the worthy."

He grasped her wrist and bent eagerly forward, with the same wild look in his eyes that had before disquieted her.

"Mark what I say now—I shall do great works for this generation; I am strangely favoured of God; I have felt the spirit quicken wondrously within me, and I know the Lord works not in vain; what great wonder of grace I shall do, what miracle of salvation, I know not, but remember, it shall be transcendent; tell it to no one, but I know in my inner secret heart it shall be a greater work than man hath yet done."

He stopped and drew himself up, shaking his head, as if to shrug off the spell of his own feeling.

"Now, now! stop it at once, and come to the house. I've been tending your father and mother, and I'm going to tend you. What you need directly is food. Your look may be holy, but I prefer full cheeks. Not another word until you have eaten every crumb I put before you."

With an air of captor, daintily fierce, she led him toward the house and up to the door, which she pushed open before him.

"Come softly, your mother may be still asleep—no, your father is talking—listen!"

A querulous voice, rough with strong feeling, came from the inner room.

"Here, I tell you, is the prophecy of Joseph to prove it, away back in 1832: 'Verily thus saith the Lord concerning the wars that will shortly come to pass, beginning at the rebellion of South Carolina, which will terminate in the death and misery of many souls. The days will come that war will be poured out upon all nations, beginning at that place; for behold, the Southern States shall be divided against the Northern States, and the Southern States will call on other nations, even the nation of Great Britain, as it is called.' Now will you doubt again, mother? For persecuting the Saints of the most high God, this republic shall be dashed to pieces like a potter's vessel. But we shall be safe. The Lord will gather Israel home to the chambers of the mountains against the day of wrath that is coming on the Gentile world. For all flesh hath corrupted itself on the face of the earth, but the Saints shall possess a purified land, upon which there shall be no curse when the Lord cometh. Then shall the heavens open—"

He broke off, for the girl came leading in the son, who, as soon as he saw the white-haired old man with his open book, sitting beside the wasted woman on the bed, flew to them with a glad cry.

They embraced him and smoothed and patted him, tremulously, feebly, with broken thanks for his safe return. The mother at last fell back upon her pillow, her eyes shining with the joy of a great relief, while the father was seized with a fit of coughing that cruelly racked his gaunt frame and left him weak but smiling.

The girl had been placing food upon the table.

"Come, Joel," she urged, "you must eat—we have all breakfasted, so you must sit alone, but we shall watch you."

She pushed him into the chair and filled his plate, in spite of his protests.

"Not another word until you have eaten it all."

"The very sight of it is enough. I am not hungry."

But she coaxed and commanded, with her hands upon his shoulders, and he let himself be persuaded to taste the bread and meat. After a few mouthfuls, taken with obvious disrelish, she detected the awakening fervour of a famished man, and knew she would have to urge no more.

As the son ate, the girl busied herself at the mother's pillow, while the father talked and ruminated by intervals,—a text, a word of cheer to the wasted mother, incidents of old days, memories of early revivals. In 1828, he had hailed Dylkes, the "Leatherwood God," as the real Messiah. Then he had been successively a Freewill Baptist, a Winebrennerian, a Universalist, a Disciple, and finally an eloquent and moving preacher in the Church of Jesus Christ of Latter-day Saints. Now he was a wild-eyed old dreamer with a high, narrow forehead depressed at the temples, enfeebled, living much in the past. Once his voice would be low, as if he spoke only to himself; again it would rise in warning to an evil generation.

"The end of the world is at hand, laddie," he began, after looking fondly at his son for a time. "Joseph said there are those now living who shall not taste of death till Jesus comes. And then, oh, then—the great white day! There is strong delusion among the wicked in the day in which we live, but the seed of Abraham, the royal seed, the blessed seed of the Lord, shall be told off to its separate glory. The Lord will spread the curtains of Zion and gather it out to the fat valleys of Ephraim, and there, with resurrected bodies it shall possess the purified earth. I shall be away for a time before then, laddie—and the dear mother here. Our crowns have been earned and will not long be withheld. But you will be there for the glory of it, and who more deserves it?"

"I pray to be made worthy of the exaltation, Father."

"You are, laddie. The word and the light came to me when I preached another faith—for the spirit of Thomas Campbell had aforetime moved me— but you, laddie, you have been bred in the word and the truth. The Lord, as a mark of his favour, has kept you from the contamination of doubters, infidels, heretics, and apostates. You have been educated under the care of the priesthood, close here in Nauvoo the Beautiful, and who could more deserve the fulness of thrones, dominions, and of power—who of all those whose number the after-time shall unfold?"

He turned appealingly to the mother, whose fevered eyes rested fondly upon her boy as she nodded confirmation of the words.

"Did he not march all the way from Kirtland to Missouri with us in '34—the youngest soldier in the whole army of Zion? How old, laddie?— twelve, was it?—so he marched a hundred miles for every one of his little years—and so valiant—none more so—begging us to hasten and give battle so he could fight upon the Lord's side. Twelve hundred miles he walked to put back in their homes the persecuted Saints of Jackson County. But, ah! There he saw liberty strangled in her sanctuary. Do you mind, laddie, how in '38 we were driven by the mob from Jackson across the river into Clay County? how they ran off our cattle, stole our grain? how your poor old mother's mother died from exposure that night in the rain and sleet? how we lived on mast and corn, the winter, in tents and a few dugouts and rickety huts—we who had the keys of St. Peter and the gifts of the apostolic age? Do you mind the sackings and burnings at Adam-Ondi-Ahman? Do you mind the wife of Joseph's brother, Don Carlos, she that was made by the soldiers to wade Grand River with two helpless babes in her arms? They would not even let her warm herself, before she started, at the flames of her own hut they had fired. And, laddie, you mind Haun's mill. Ah, the bloody day!—you were there, and one other, the sister, happy, beautiful as her in the Song of Songs, when the brutes came—"

"Don't, father—stop there—you are making my throat shut against the food."

"Then you came to Far West in time to see Joseph and his brethren sold to the mobocrats by that devil's traitor, Hinkle,—you saw the fleeing Saints ⌐forced to leave their all, hunted out of Missouri into Illinois—their houses burned, the cattle stolen, their wives and daughters—"

"Don't, father! Be quiet again. You and mother must be fit for our journey, as fit as we younger folk."

He glanced fondly across the table, where the girl had leaned her chin in her hands to watch him, speculatively. She avoided his eyes.

"Yes, yes," assented the old man, "and you know of our persecutions here—how we had to finish the temple with our arms by our sides, even as the faithful finished the walls of Jerusalem—and how we were driven out by night—"

"Quiet, father!"

"Yes, yes. Ah, this gathering out! How far shall we go, laddie?"

"Four hundred miles to winter quarters. From there no one yet knows,—a thousand, maybe two thousand."

"Aye, to the Rockies or beyond, even to the Pacific. Joseph prophesied it—where we shall be left in peace until the great day."

The young man glanced quickly up.

"Or have time to grow mighty, if we should not be let alone. Surely this is the last time the Lord would have us meek under the mob."

"Ho, ho! As you were twelve years ago, trudging by my side, valiant to fight if the Lord but wills it! But have no fear, boy. This time we go far beyond all that may tempt the spoiler. We go into the desert, where no humans are but the wretched red Lamanites; no beasts but the wild ones of four feet to hunger for our flesh; no verdure, no nourishment to sustain us save the manna from on high,—a region of unknown perils and unnamed deserts. Truly we make the supreme test. I do not overcolour it. Prudence, hand me yonder scrap-book, there on the secretary. Here I shall read you the words of no less a one than Senator Daniel Webster on the floor of the Senate but a few months agone. He spoke on the proposal to fix a mail-route from Missouri to the mouth of the Columbia River in that far-off land. Hear this great man who knows whereof he speaks. He is very bitter. 'What do we want with this vast, worthless area—this region of savages and wild beasts, of deserts, of shifting sands and whirlwinds of dust, of cactus and prairie-dogs? To what use could we ever hope to put these great deserts or those endless mountain ranges, impenetrable and covered to their very base with eternal snows? What can we ever hope to do with that Western coast, a coast of three thousand miles, rock-bound, cheerless, uninviting, and not a harbour on it. Mr. President, I will never vote one cent from the public treasury to place the Pacific Coast one inch nearer to Boston than it now is!'"

The girl had been making little impatient flights about the room, as if awaiting an opportunity to interrupt the old man's harangue, but even as she paused to speak, he began again:

"There, laddie, do you hear him?—arid deserts, shifting sand, snow and ice, wild beasts and wilder men—that is where Israel of the last days shall be hidden to wait for the second coming of God's Christ. There, having received our washings and anointings in the temple of God on earth, we shall wait unmolested, and spread the curtains of Zion in due circumspection. And what a migration to be recorded in another sacred history ages hence! Surely the blood of our martyred Prophet hath not smoked to heaven in vain. Where is there a parallel to this hegira? They from Egypt went from a heathen land, a land of idolatry, to a fertile home chosen for them by the Lord. But we go from a fair, smiling land of plenty and pretended Christianity into the burning desert. They have driven us to the edge; now they drive us in. But God works his way among the peoples of earth, and we are strong. Who knows but that we shall in our march throw up a highway of holiness to the rising generation? So let us round up our backs to the burden!"

"Amen!" replied the young man fervently, as he rose from the table.

"And now we must be about our preparations for the journey. The time is short—who is that?"

He sprang to the door. Outside, quick steps were heard approaching. The girl, who had risen in some confusion, stood blushing and embarrassed before him. The mother rose feebly on her elbow to reassure him.

"'Tis Captain Girnway, laddie. Have no alarm—he has befriended us. But for him we should have been put out two days ago, without shelter and without care. He let us be housed here until you should come."

There was a knock at the door, but Joel stood with his back to it. The words of Seth Wright were running roughshod through his mind. He looked sharply at Prudence.

"A mobocrat—our enemy—and you have taken favours from him—a minion of the devil?—shame!"

The girl looked up.

"He was kind; you don't realise that he has probably saved their lives. Indeed, you must let him in and thank him."

"Not I!"

The mother interposed hurriedly.

"Yes, yes, laddie! You know not how high-handed they have been. They expelled all but us, and some they have maltreated shamefully. This one has been kind to us. Open the door."

"I dare not face him—I may not contain myself!"

The knock was repeated more loudly. The girl went up to him and put her hands on his shoulders to draw him away.

"Be reasonable," she pleaded, in low tones, "and above all, be polite to him."

She put him gently aside and drew back the door. On the threshold smiled the young captain he had watched from the window that morning, marching at the head of his company. His cap was doffed, and his left hand rested easily on the hilt of his sword. He stepped inside as one sure of his welcome.

"Good morning, Miss Prudence, good morning, Mr. Rae, good morning, madam—good morning—"

He looked questioningly at the stranger. Prudence stepped forward.

"This is Joel Rae, Captain Girnway."

They bowed, somewhat stiffly. Each was dark. Each had a face to attract women. But the captain was at peace with the world, neatly uniformed, well-fed, clean-shaven, smiling, pleasant to look upon, while the other was unshaven, hollow-cheeked, gaunt, roughly dressed, a thing that had been hunted and was now under ban. Each was at once sensible of the contrast between them, and each was at once affected by it: the captain to a greater jauntiness, a more effusive affability; the other to a stonier sternness.

"I am glad to know you have come, Mr. Rae. Your people have worried a little, owing to the unfortunate circumstances in which they have been placed."

"I—I am obliged to you, sir, in their behalf, for your kindness to my father and mother and to Miss Corson here."

"You are a thousand times welcome, sir. Can you tell me when you will wish to cross the river?"

"At the very earliest moment that God and the mob will let us. To-morrow morning, I hope."

"This has not been agreeable to me, believe me—"

"Far less so to us, you may be sure; but we shall be content again when we can get away from all your whiggery, democratism, devilism, mobism!"

He spoke with rising tones, and the other flushed noticeably about the temples.

"Have your wagons ready to-morrow morning, then, Mr. Rae—at eight? Very well, I shall see that you are protected to the ferry. There has been so much of that tone of talk, sir, that some of our men have resented it."

He turned pleasantly to Prudence.

"And you, Miss Prudence, you will be leaving Nauvoo for Springfield, I suppose. As you go by Carthage, I shall wish to escort you that far myself, to make sure of your safety."

The lover turned fiercely, seizing the girl's wrist and drawing her toward him before she could answer.

"Her goal is Zion, not Babylon, sir—remember *that!*"

She stepped hastily between them.

"We will talk of that to-morrow, Captain," she said, quickly, and added, "You may leave us now for we have much to do here in making ready for the start."

"Until to-morrow morning, then, at eight."

He bowed low over the hand she gave him, gracefully saluted the others, and was gone.

"HER GOAL IS ZION, NOT BABYLON, SIR—REMEMBER *THAT!*"

Chapter IV
A Fair Apostate

She stood flushed and quick-breathing when the door had shut, he bending toward her with dark inquiry in his eyes. Before she spoke, he divined that under her nervousness some resolution lay stubbornly fixed.

"Let us speak alone," she said, in a low voice. Then, to the old people, "Joel and I will go into the garden awhile to talk. Be patient."

"Not for long, dear; our eyes are aching for him."

"Only a little while," and she smiled back at them. She went ahead through the door by which they had first entered, and out into the garden at the back of the house. He remembered, as he followed her, that since he had arrived that morning she had always been leading him, directing him as if to a certain end, with the air of meaning presently to say something of moment to him.

They went past the rose-bush near which she had stood when he first saw her, and down a walk through borders of marigolds. She picked one of the flowers and fixed it in his coat.

"You are much too savage—you need a posy to soften you. There! Now come to this seat."

She led him to a rustic double chair under the heavily fruited boughs of an apple-tree, and made him sit down. She began with a vivacious playfulness, poorly assumed, to hide her real feeling.

"Now, sobersides, it must end—this foolishness of yours—"

She stopped, waiting for some question of his to help her. But he said nothing, though she could feel the burning of his eyes upon her.

"This superstitious folly, you know," she blurted out, looking up at him in sudden desperation.

"Tell me what you mean—you must know I'm impatient."

She essayed to be playful again, pouting her dimpled face near to his that he might kiss her. But he did not seem to see. He only waited.

"Well—this religion—this Mormonism—"

She shot one swift look at him, then went on quickly.

"My people have left the church, and—I—too—they found things in Joseph Smith's teachings that seemed bad to them. They went to Springfield. I would have gone, too, but I told them I wanted first to see you and—and see if you would not come with us—at least for awhile, not taking the poor old father and mother through all that wretchedness. They consented to let me stay with your parents on condition that Captain Girnway would protect them and me. He—he—is very kind—and had known us since last winter and had seen me—us—several times. I hadn't the heart to tell your father; he was so set on going to the new Zion, but you *will* come, won't you?"

"Wait a moment!" He put a hand upon her arm as if to arrest her speech. "You daze me. Let me think." She looked up at him, wondering at his face, for it showed strength and bitterness and gentleness all in one look—and he was suffering. She put her hand upon his, from an instinct of pity. The touch recalled him.

"Now—for the beginning." He spoke with aroused energy, a little wistful smile softening the strain of his face. "You were wise to give me food, else I couldn't have solved this mystery. To the beginning, then: You, Prudence Corson, betrothed to me these three years and more; you have been buried in the waters of baptism and had your washings and anointings in the temple of the most high God. Is it not so? Your eyes were anointed that they might be quick to see, your ears that they might be apt at hearing, your mouth that you might with wisdom speak the words of eternal life, and your feet that they might be swift to run in the ways of the Lord. You accepted thereby the truth that the angel of God had delivered to Joseph Smith the sealing keys of power. You accepted the glorious articles of the new covenant. You were about to be sealed up to me for time and eternity. Now—I am lost—what is it?—your father and mother have left the church, and because of what?"

"Because of bad things, because of this doctrine they practise—this wickedness of spiritual wives, plural wives. Think of it, Joel—that if I were your wife you might take another."

"I need not think of it. Surely you know my love. You know I could not do that. Indeed I have heard at last that this doctrine so long gossiped of is a true one. But I have been away and am not yet learned in its mysteries. But this much I do know—and it is the very corner-stone of my life: Peter, James, and John ordained Joseph Smith here on this earth, and Joseph ordained the twelve. All other churches have been established by the wisdom or folly of man. Ours is the only one on earth established by direct revelation from God. It has a priesthood, and that priesthood is a power we must reverence and obey, no matter what may be its commands. When the truth is taught me of this doctrine you speak of, I shall see it to be right for those to whom it is ordained. And meantime, outside of my own little life—my love for you, which would be always single—I can't measure the revealed will of God with my little moral foot-rule. Joseph was endowed with the open vision. He saw God face to face and heard His voice. Can the standards of society in its present corruption measure and pass upon the revelations of so white-souled a man?"

"I believe he was not white-souled," she replied, in a kind, animated way, as one who was bent upon saving him from error. "I told you I knew why you were sent away on mission. It was because you were my accepted lover—and your white-souled Joseph Smith wanted me for himself."

"I can't believe it—you couldn't know such a thing"—his faith made a brave rally—"but even so, if he sought you, why, the more honour to you—and to me, if you still clung to me."

"Listen. I was afraid to tell you before—ashamed—but I told my people. It's three years ago. I was seventeen. It was just after we had become engaged. My people were then strong in the faith, as you know. One morning after you had left for the East, Brigham Young and Heber Kimball came to our house for me. They said the Prophet had long known me by sight, and wished to talk with me. Would I go with them to visit him and he would bless and counsel me? Of course I was flattered. I put on my prettiest frock and fetchingest bonnet and set off with them, after mamma had said yes. On the way they kept asking me if I was willing to do all the Prophet required. I said I was sure of it, thinking they meant to be good and worshipful. Then they would ask if I was ready to take counsel, and they said, 'Many things are revealed unto us in these last days that the world would scoff at,' but that it had been given to them to know all the mysteries of the Kingdom. Then they said, 'You will see Joseph and he will tell you what you are to do.'"

He was listening with a serious, confident eagerness, as if he knew she could say nothing to dim the Prophet's lustre.

"When we reached the building where Joseph's store was, they led me up-stairs to a small room and sent down to the store for the Prophet. When he came up they introduced me and left me alone in the little room with him. Their actions had seemed queer to me, but I remembered that this man had talked face to face with God, so I tried to feel better. But all at once he stood before me and asked me to be his wife. Think of it! I was so frightened!

I dared not say no, he looked at me so—I can't tell you how; but I said it would not be lawful. He said, 'Yes, Prudence, I have had a revelation from God that it is lawful and right for a man to have as many wives as he wants—for as it was in the days of Abraham, so it shall be in these days. Accept me and I shall take you straight to the celestial Kingdom. Brother Brigham will marry us here, right now, and you can go home to-night and keep it secret from your parents if you like.' Then I said, 'But I am betrothed to Joel Rae, the son of Giles Rae, who is away on mission.' 'I know that,' he said—'I sent him away, and anyway you will be safer to marry me. You will then be absolutely sure of your celestial reward, for in the next world, you know, I am to have powers, thrones, and dominions, while Brother Joel is very young and has not been tried in the Kingdom. He may fall away and then you would be lost.'"

The man in him now was struggling with his faith, and he seemed about to interrupt her, but she went on excitedly.

"I said I would not want to do anything of the kind without deliberation. He urged me to have it over, trying to kiss me, and saying he knew it would be right before God; that if there was any sin in it he would take it upon himself. He said, 'You know I have the keys of the Kingdom, and whatever I bind on earth is bound in heaven. Come,' he said, 'nothing ventured, nothing gained. Let me call Brother Brigham to seal us, and you shall be a star in my crown for ever.'

"Then I broke down and cried, for I was so afraid, and he put his arms around me, but I pushed away, and after awhile I coaxed him to give me until the next Sabbath to think it over, promising on my life to say not one word to any person. I never let him see me alone again, you may be sure, and at last when other awful tales were told about him here, of wickedness and his drunkenness—he told in the pulpit that he had been drunk, and that he did it to keep them from worshipping him as a God—I saw he was a bad, common man, and I told my people everything, and soon my father was denounced for an apostate. Now, sir, what do you say?"

When she finished he was silent for a time. Then he spoke, very gently, but with undaunted firmness.

"Prudence, dearest, I have told you that this doctrine is new to me. I do not yet know its justification. But that I shall see it to be sanctified after they have taught me, this I know as certainly as I know that Joseph Smith dug up the golden plates of Mormon and Moroni on the hill of Cumorah when the angel of the Lord moved him. It will be sanctified for those who choose it, I mean. You know I could never choose it for myself. But as for others, I must not question. I know only too well that eternal salvation for me depends upon my accepting manfully and unquestioningly the authority of the temple priesthood."

"But I know Joseph was not a good man—and they tell such absurd stories about the miracles the Elders pretend to work."

"I believe with all my heart Joseph was good; but even if not—we have never pretended that he was anything more than a prophet of God. And was not Moses a murderer when God called him to be a prophet? And as for miracles, all religions have them—why not ours? Your people were Methodists before Joseph baptised them. Didn't Wesley work miracles? Didn't a cloud temper the sun in answer to his prayer? Wasn't his horse cured of a lameness by his faith? Didn't he lay hands upon the blind Catholic girl so that she saw plainly when her eyes rested upon the New Testament and became blind again when she took up the mass book? Are those stories absurd? My father himself saw Joseph cast a devil out of Newell Knight."

"And this awful journey into a horrid desert. Why must you go? Surely there are other ways of salvation." She hesitated a moment. "I have been told that going to heaven is like going to mill. If your wheat is good, the miller will never ask which way you came."

"Child, child, some one has tampered with you."

She retorted quickly.

"He did not tamper, he has never sought to—he was all kindness."

She stopped, her short upper lip holding its incautious mate a prisoner. She blushed furiously under the sudden blaze of his eyes.

"So it's true, what Seth Wright hinted at? To think that you, of all people—my sweetheart—gone over—won over by a cursed mobocrat—a fiend with the blood of our people wet on his hands! Listen, Prue; I'm going into the desert. Even though you beg me to stay, you must have known—perhaps you hoped—that I would go. There are many reasons why I must. For one, there are six hundred and forty poor hunted wretches over there on the river bank, sick, cold, wet, starving, but enduring it all to the death for their faith in Joseph Smith. They could have kept their comfortable homes here and their substance, simply by renouncing him—they are all voluntary exiles—they have only to say 'I do not believe Joseph Smith was a prophet of God,' and these same Gentiles will receive them with open arms, give them clothing, food, and shelter, put them again in possession of their own. But they are lying out over there, fever-stricken, starving, chilled, all because they will not deny their faith. Shall I be a craven, then, who have scarcely ever wanted for food or shelter, and probably shall not? Of course you don't love me or you couldn't ask me to do that. Those faithful wretched ones are waiting over there for me to guide them on toward a spot that will probably be still more desolate. They could find their way, almost, by the trail of graves we left last spring, but they need my strength and my spirit, and I am going. I am going, too, for my own salvation. I would suffer anything for you, but by going I may save us both. Listen, child; God is going to make a short work on earth. We shall both see the end of this reign of sin. It is well if you take wheat to the mill, but what if you fetch the miller chaff instead?"

She made a little protesting move with her hands, and would have spoken, but he was not done.

"Now, listen further. You heard my father tell how I have seen this people driven and persecuted since I was a boy. That, if nothing else, would take me away from these accursed States and their mobs. Hatred of them has been bred into my marrow. I know them for the most part to be unregenerate and doomed, but even if it were otherwise—if they had the true light—none the less would I be glad to go, because of what they have done to us and to me and to mine. Oh, in the night I hear such cries of butchered mothers with their babes, and see the flames of the little cabins—hear the shots and the ribaldry and the cursings. My father spoke to you of Haun's mill,—that massacre back in Missouri. That was eight years ago. I was a boy of sixteen and my sister was a year older. She had been left in my care while father and mother went on to Far West. You have seen the portrait of her that mother has. You know how delicately flower-like her beauty was, how like a lily, with a purity and an innocence to disarm any villainy. Thirty families had halted at the mill the day before, the mob checking their advance at that point. All was quiet until about four in the afternoon. We were camped on either side of Shoal Creek. Children were playing freely about while their mothers and fathers worked at the little affairs of a pilgrimage like that. Most of them had then been three months on the road, enduring incredible hardships for the sake of their religion—for him you believe to be a bad, common man. But they felt secure now because one of the militia captains, officious like your captain here, had given them assurance the day before that they would be protected from all harm. I was helping Brother Joseph Young to repair his wagon when I glanced up to the opposite side of Shoal Creek and saw a large company of armed and mounted men coming toward our peaceful group at full speed. One of our number, seeing that they were many and that we were unarmed, ran out and cried, 'Peace!' but they came upon us and fired their volley. Men, women, and little children fell under it. Those surviving fled to the blacksmith's shop for shelter—huddling inside like frightened sheep. But there were wide cracks between the logs, and up to these the mob went, putting their guns through to do their work at leisure. Then the plundering began—plundering and worse."

He stopped, trembling, and she put out her hand to him in sympathy. When he had regained control of himself, he continued.

"At the first volley I had hurried sister to a place of concealment in the underbrush, and she, hearing them search for the survivors after the shooting was over, thought we were discovered, and sprang up to run further. One of them saw her and shot. She fell half-fainting with a bullet through her arm, and then half a dozen of them gathered quickly about her. I ran to them, screaming and striking out with my fists, but the devil was in them, and she, poor blossom, lay there helpless, calling 'Boy, boy, boy!' as she had always called me since we were babies together. Must I tell you the rest?—must I tell you—how those devils—"

"Don't, don't! Oh, *no*!"

"I thought I must die! They held me there—"

He had gripped one of her wrists until she cried out in pain and he released it.

"But the sight must have given me a man's strength, for my struggles became so troublesome that one of them—I have always been grateful for it—clubbed his musket and dealt me a blow that left me senseless. It was dark when I came to, but I lay there until morning, unable to do more than crawl. When the light came I found the poor little sister there near where they had dragged us both, and she was *alive*. Can you realise how awful that was—that she had lived through it? God be thanked, she died before the day was out.

"After that the other mutilated bodies, the plundered wagons, all seemed less horrible to me. My heart had been seared over. They had killed twenty of the Saints, and the most of them we hurried to throw into a well, fearful that the soldiers of Governor Boggs would come back at any moment to strip and hack them. O God! and now you have gone over to one of them!"

"Joel,—dear, *dear* Joel!—indeed I pity and sympathise—and care for—but I cannot go—even after all you say. And don't you see it will always be so! My father says the priesthood will always be in trouble if it sets itself above the United States. Dear Joel, I can't go, indeed I *can't* go!"

He spoke more softly now.

"Thank God I don't realise it yet—I mean, that we must part. You tell me so and I hear you and my mind knows, but my heart hasn't sensed it yet—I can feel it now going stupidly along singing its old happy song of hope and gladness, while all this is going on here outside. But soon the big hurt will come. Oh, Prue—Prue, girl!—can't you think what it will mean to me? Don't you know how I shall sicken for the sight of you, and my ears will listen for you! Prudence, Prue, darling—yet I must not be womanish! I have a big work to do. I have known it with a new clearness since that radiance rested above my head last night. The truth burns in me like a fire. Your going can't take that from me. It must be I was not meant to have you. With you perhaps I could not have had a heart single to God's work. He permitted me to love you so I could be tried and proved."

He looked at her fondly, and she could see striving and trembling in his eyes a great desire to crush her in his arms, yet he fought it down, and continued more calmly.

"But indeed I must be favoured more than common, to deserve that so great a hurt be put upon me, and I shall not be found wanting. I shall never wed any woman but you, though, dear. If not you, never any other."

He stood up.

"I must go in to them now. There must be work to do against the start to-morrow."

"Joel!"

"May the Lord deafen my ears to you, darling!" and squaring his shoulders resolutely away from her, he left her on the seat and went in.

The old man looked up from his Bible as his son entered.

"It's sore sad, laddie, we can't have the temple for your sealing-vows."

"Prudence will not be sealed to me, father." He spoke dazedly, as if another like the morning's blow had been dealt him. "I—I am already sealed to the Spirit for time and eternity."

"Was it Prudence's doings?" asked his mother, quickly.

"Yes; she has left the church with her people."

The long-faced, narrow-browed old man raised one hand solemnly.

"Then let her be banished from Israel and not numbered in the books of the offspring of Abraham! And let her be delivered over to the buffetings of Satan in the flesh!"

Chapter V
Giles Rae Beautifies His Inheritance

By eight o'clock the next morning, out under a cloudy sky, the Raes were ready and eager for their start to the new Jerusalem. Even the sick woman's face wore a kind of soft and faded radiance in the excitement of going. On her mattress, she had been tenderly installed in one of the two covered wagons that carried their household goods. The wagon in which she lay was to be taken across the river by Seth Wright,—for the moment no Wild Ram of the Mountains, but a soft-cooing dove of peace. Permission had been granted him by Brockman to recross the river on some needful errands; and, having once proved the extreme sensitiveness, not to say irritability, of those in temporary command, he was now resolved to give as little éclat as possible to certain superior aspects of his own sanctity. He spoke low and deferentially, and his mien was that of a modest, retiring man who secretly thought ill of himself.

He mounted the wagon in which the sick woman lay, sat well back under the bowed cover, clucked low to the horses, and drove off toward the ferry. If discreet behaviour on his part could ensure it there would be no conflict provoked with superior numbers; with numbers, moreover, composed of violent-tempered and unprincipled persecutors who were already acting with but the merest shadow of legal authority.

On the seat of the second wagon, whip in hand, was perched Giles Rae, his coat buttoned warmly to the chin. He was slight and feeble to the eye, yet he had been fired to new life by the certainty that now they were to leave the territory of the persecuting Gentiles for a land to be the Saints' very own. His son stood at the wheel, giving him final directions. At the gate was Prudence Corson, gowned for travel, reticule in hand, her prettiness shadowed, under the scoop of her bonnet, the toe of one trim little boot meditatively rolling a pebble over the ground.

"Drive slowly, Daddy. Likely I shall overtake you before you reach the ferry. I want but a word yet with Prudence; though"—he glanced over at the bowed head of the girl—"no matter if I linger a little, since Brother Seth will cross first and we must wait until the boat comes back. Some of our people will be at the ferry to look after you,—and be careful to have no words with any of the mob—no matter what insult they may offer. You're feeling strong, aren't you?"

"Ay, laddie, that I am! Strong as an ox! The very thought of being free out of this Babylon has exalted me in spirit and body. Think of it, boy! Soon we shall be even beyond the limits of the United States—in a foreign land out there to the west, where these bloodthirsty ones can no longer reach us. Thank God they're like all snakes—they can't jump beyond their own length!"

He leaned out of the wagon to shake a bloodless, trembling fist toward the temple where the soldiers had made their barracks.

"Now let great and grievous judgments, desolations, by famine, sword, and pestilence come upon you, generation of vipers!"

He cracked the whip, the horses took their load at his cheery call, and as the wagon rolled away they heard him singing:—

"Lo, the Gentile chain is broken!
Freedom's banner waves on high!"

They watched him until the wagon swung around into the street that fell away to the ferry. Then they faced each other, and he stepped to her side as she leaned lightly on the gate.

"Prue, dear," he said, softly, "it's going hard with me. God must indeed have a great work reserved for me to try me with such a sacrifice—so much pain where I could least endure it. I prayed all the night to be kept firm, for there are two ways open—one right and one wrong; but I cannot sell my soul so early. That's why I wanted to say the last good-bye out here. I was afraid to say it in there—I am so weak for you, Prue—I ache so for you in all this trouble—why, if I could feel your hands in my hair, I'd laugh at it all—I'm so *weak* for you, dearest."

She tossed her yellow head ever so slightly, and turned the scoop of her bonnet a little away from his pain-lighted face.

"I am not complimented, though—you care more for your religion than for me."

He looked at her hungrily.

"No, you are wrong there—I don't separate you at all—I couldn't—you and my religion are one—but, if I must, I can love you in spirit as I worship my God in spirit—"

"If it will satisfy you, very well!"

"My reward will come—I shall do a great work, I shall have a Witness from the sky. Who am I that I should have thought to win a crown without taking up a cross?"

"I am sorry for you."

"Oh, Prue, there must be a way to save the souls of such as you, even in their blindness. Would God make a flower like you, only to let it be lost? There must be a way. I shall pray until I force it from the secret heavens."

"My soul will be very well, sir!" she retorted, with a distinct trace of asperity. "I am not a heathen, I'd thank you to remember—and when I'm a wife I shall be my husband's only wife—"

He winced in acutest pain.

"You have no right to taunt me so. Else you can't know what you have meant to me. Oh, you were all the world, child—you, of your own dear self—you would have been all the wives in the world to me—there are many, many of you, and all in a heavenly one—"

"Oh, forgive me, dearest," she cried, and put out a little gloved hand to comfort him. "I know, I know—all the sweetness and goodness of your love, believe me. See, I have kept always by me the little Bible you gave me on my birthday—I have treasured it, and I know it has made me a better girl, because it makes me always think of your goodness—but I couldn't have gone there, Joel—and it does seem as if you need not have gone—and that marrying is so odious—"

"You shall see how little you had to fear of that doctrine which God has seen fit to reveal to these good men. I tell you now, Prue, I shall wed no woman but you. Nor am I giving you up. Don't think it. I am doing my duty and trusting God to bring you to me. I know He will do it—I tell you there is the spirit of some strange, awful strength in me, which tells me to ask what I will and it shall be given—to seek to do anything, how great or hard soever, and a giant's, a god's strength will rest in me. And so I know you will come. You will always think of me so,—waiting for you—somehow, somewhere. Every day you must think it, at any idle moment when I come to your mind; every night when you waken in the dark and silence, you must think, 'Wherever he is, he is waiting for me, perhaps awake as I am now, praying, with a power that will surely draw me.' You will come somehow. Perhaps, when I reach winter quarters, you will have changed your mind. One never knows how God may fashion these little providences. But He will bring you safe to me out of that Gentile perdition. Remember, child, God has set his hand in these last days to save the human family from the ruins of the fall, and some way, He alone knows how, you will come to me and find me waiting."

"As if you needed to wait for me when I am here now ready for you, willing to be taken!"

"Don't, don't, dear! There are two of me now, and one can't stand the pain. There is a man in me, sworn to do a man's work like a man, and duty to God and the priesthood has big chains around his heart dragging it across the river. But, low, now—there is a little, forlorn boy in me, too—a poor, crying, whimpering, babyish little boy, who dreamed of you and longed for you and was promised you, and who will never get well of losing you. Oh, I know it well enough—his tears will never dry, his heart will always have a big hurt in it—and your face will always be so fresh and clear in it!"

He put his hands on her shoulders and looked down into the face under the bonnet.

"Let me make sure I shall lose no look of you, from little tilted chin, and lips of scarlet thread, and little teeth like grains of rice, and eyes into which I used to wander and wonder so far—"

She looked past him and stepped back.

"Captain Girnway is coming for me—yonder, away down the street. He takes me to Carthage."

His face hardened as he looked over his shoulder.

"I shall never wed any woman but you. Can you feel as deeply as that? Will you wed no man but me?"

She fluttered the cherry ribbons on the bonnet and fixed a stray curl in front of one ear.

"Have you a right to ask that? I might wait a time for you to come back—to your senses and to me, but—"

"Good-bye, darling!".

"What, will you go that way—not kiss me? He is still two blocks away."

"I am so weak for you, sweet—the little boy in me is crying for you, but he must not have what he wants. What he wants would leave his heart rebellious and not perfect with the Lord. It's best not," he continued, with an effort at a smile and in a steadier tone. "It would mean so much to me— oh, so very much to me—and so very little to you—and that's no real kiss. I'd rather remember none of that kind—and don't think I was churlish—it's only because the little boy—I will go after my father now, and God bless you!"

He turned away. A few paces on he met Captain Girnway, jaunty, debonair, smiling, handsome in his brass-buttoned uniform of the Carthage Grays.

"I have just left the ferry, Mr. Rae. The wagon with your mother has gone over. The other had not yet come down. Some of the men appear to be a little rough this morning. Your people are apt to provoke them by being too outspoken, but I left special orders for the good treatment of yourself and outfit."

With a half-smothered "thank you," he passed on, not trusting himself to say more to one who was not only the enemy of his people, but bent, seemingly, on deluding a young woman to the loss of her soul. He heard their voices in cheerful greeting, but did not turn back. With eyes to the front and shoulders squared he kept stiffly on his way through the silent, deserted streets to the ferry.

Fifteen minutes' walk brought him to the now busy waterside. The ferry, a flat boat propelled by long oars, was landing when he came into view, and he saw his father's wagon driven on. He sped down the hill, pushed through the crowd of soldiers standing about, and hurried forward on the boat to let the old man know he had come. But on the seat was another than his father. He recognised the man, and called to him.

"What are you doing there, Brother Keaton? Where's my father?"

The man had shrunk back under the wagon-cover, having seemingly been frightened by the soldiers.

"I've taken your father's place, Brother Rae."

"Did he cross with Brother Wright?"

"Yes—he—" The man hesitated. Then came an interruption from the shore.

"Come, clear the gangway there so we can load! Here are some more of the damned rats we've hunted out of their holes!"

The speaker made a half-playful lunge with his bayonet at a gaunt, yellow-faced spectre of a man who staggered on to the boat with a child in his arms wrapped in a tattered blue quilt. A gust of the chilly wind picked his shapeless, loose-fitting hat off as he leaped to avoid the bayonet-point, and his head was seen to be shaven. The crowd on the bank laughed loud at his clumsiness and at his grotesque head. Joel Rae ran to help him forward on the boat.

"Thank you, Brother—I'm just up from the fever-bed—they shaved my head for it—and so I lost my hat—thank you—here we shall be warm if only the sun comes out."

Joel went back to help on others who came, a feeble, bedraggled dozen or so that had clung despairingly to their only shelter until they were driven out.

"You can stay here in safety, you know, if you renounce Joseph Smith and his works—they will give you food and shelter." He repeated it to each little group of the dispirited wretches as they staggered past him, but they replied staunchly by word or look, and one man, in the throes of a chill, swung his cap and uttered a feeble "Hurrah for the new Zion!"

When they were all on with their meagre belongings, he called again to the man in the wagon.

"Brother Keaton, my father went across, did he?"

Several of the men on shore answered him.

"Yes"—"Old white-whiskered death's-head went over the river"—"Over here"—"A sassy old codger he was"—"He got his needings, too"—"Got his needings—"

They cast off the line and the oars began to dip.

"And you'll get your needings, too, if you come back, remember that! That's the last of you, and we'll have no more vermin like you. Now see what old Joe Smith, the white-hat prophet, can do for you in the Indian territory!"

He stood at the stern of the boat, shivering as he looked at the current, swift, cold, and gray under the sunless sky. He feared some indignity had been offered to his father. They had looked at one another queerly when they answered his questions. He went forward to the wagon again.

"Brother Keaton, you're sure my father is all right?"

"I am sure he's all right, Brother Rae."

Content with this, at last, he watched the farther flat shore of the Mississippi, with its low fringe of green along the edge, where they were to land and be at last out of the mob's reach. He repeated his father's words: "Thank God, they're like all snakes; they can't jump beyond their own length."

The confusion of landing and the preparations for an immediate start drove for the time all other thoughts from his mind. It had been determined to get the little band at once out of the marshy spot where the camp had been made. The teams were soon hitched, the wagons loaded, and the train ready to move. He surveyed it, a hundred poor wagons, many of them without cover, loaded to the full with such nondescript belongings as a house-dwelling people, suddenly put out on the open road, would hurriedly snatch as they fled. And the people made his heart ache, even to the deadening of his own sorrow, as he noted their wobegoneness. For these were the sick, the infirm, the poor, the inefficient, who had been unable for one reason or another to migrate with the main body of the Saints earlier in the season. Many of them were now racked by fever from sleeping on the damp ground. These bade fair not to outlast some of the lumbering carts that threatened at every rough spot to jolt apart.

Yet the line bravely formed to the order of Seth Wright as captain, and the march began. Looking back, he saw peaceful Nauvoo, its houses and gardens, softened by the cloudy sky and the autumn haze, clustering under the shelter of their temple spire,—their temple and their houses, of which they were now despoiled by a mob's fury. Ahead he saw the road to the West, a hard road, as he knew,—one he could not hope they should cross without leaving more graves by the way; but Zion was at the end.

The wagons and carts creaked and strained and rattled under their swaying loads, and the line gradually defined itself along the road from the confused jumble at the camp. He remembered his father again now, and hurried forward to assure himself that all was right. As he overtook along the way the stumbling ones obliged to walk, he tried to cheer them.

"Only a short march to-day, brothers. Our camp is at Sugar Creek, nine miles—so take your time this first day."

Near the head of the train were his own two wagons, and beside the first walked Seth Wright and Keaton, in low, earnest converse. As he came up to them the Bishop spoke.

"I got Wes' and Alec Gregg to drive awhile so we could stretch our legs." But then came a quick change of tone, as they halted by the road.

"Joel, there's no use beatin' about the bush—them devils at the ferry jest now drowned your pa."

He went cold all over. Keaton, looking sympathetic but frightened, spoke next.

"You ought to thank me, Brother Rae, for not telling you on the other side, when you asked me. I knew better. Because, why? Because I knew you'd fly off the handle and get yourself killed, and then your ma'd be left all alone, that's why, now—and prob'ly they'd 'a' wound up by dumping the whole passle of us bag and baggage into the stream. And it wa'n't any use, your father bein' dead and gone."

The Bishop took up the burden, slapping him cordially on the back.

"Come, come,—hearten up, now! Your pa's been made a martyr—he's beautified his inheritance in Zion—whinin' won't do no good."

He drew himself up with a shrug, as if to throw off an invisible burden, and answered, calmly:

"I'm not whining, Bishop. Perhaps you were right not to tell me over there, Keaton. I'd have made trouble for you all." He smiled painfully in his effort to control himself. "Were you there, Bishop?"

"No, I'd already gone acrost. Keaton here saw it."

Keaton took up the tale.

"I was there when the old gentleman drove down singing, 'Lo, the Gentile chain is broken.' He was awful chipper. Then one of 'em called him old Father Time, and he answered back. I disremember what, but, any way, one word fired another until they was cussin' Giles Rae up hill and down dale, and instead of keepin' his head shet like he had ought to have done, he was prophesyin' curses, desolations, famines, and pestilences on 'em all, and callin' 'em enemies of Christ. He was sassy—I can't deny that—and that's where he wa'n't wise. Some of the mobocrats was drunk and some was mad; they was all in their high-heeled boots one way or another, and he enraged 'em more. So he says, finally, 'The Jews fell,' he says, 'because they wouldn't receive their Messiah, the Shiloh, the Saviour. They wet their hands,' he says, 'in the best blood that had flowed through the lineage of Judah, and they had to pay the cost. And so will you cowards of Illinois,' he says, 'have to pay the penalty for sheddin' the blood of Joseph Smith, the best blood that has flowed since the Lord's Christ,' he says. 'The wrath of God,' he says, 'will abide upon you.' The old gentleman was a powerful denouncer when he was in the spirit of it—"

"Come, come, Keaton, hurry, for God's sake—get on!"

"And he made 'em so mad, a-settin' up there so peart and brave before 'em, givin' 'em as good as they sent—givin' 'em hell right to their faces, you might say, that at last they made for him, some of them that you could see had been puttin' a new faucet into the cider barrel. I saw they meant to do him a mischief—but Lord! what could I do against fifty, being then in the midst of a chill? Well, they drug him off the seat, and said, 'Now, you old rat, own up that Holy Joe was a danged fraud;' or something like that. But he was that sanctified and stubborn—'Better to suffer stripes for the testimony of Christ,' he says, 'than to fall by the sin of denial!' Then they drug him to the bank, one on each side, and says, 'We baptise you in the holy name of Brockman,' and in they dumped him—backwards, mind you! I saw then they was in a slippery place where it was deep and the current awful strong. But they hauled him out, and says again, 'Do you renounce Holy Joe Smith and all his works?' The poor old fellow couldn't talk a word for the chill, but he shook his head like sixty—as stubborn as you'd wish. So they said, 'Damn you! here's another, then. We baptise you in the name of James K. Polk, President of the United States!' and in they threw him again. Whether they done it on purpose or not, I wouldn't like to say, but that time his coat collar slipped out of their hands and down he went. He came up ten feet down-stream and quite a ways out, and they hooted at him. I seen him come up once after that, and then they see he couldn't swim a stroke, but little they cared. And I never saw him again. I jest took hold of the team and drove it on the boat, scared to death for what you'd do when you come,—so I kept still and they kept still. But remember, it's only another debt the blood of the Gentiles will have to pay—"

"Either here on earth or in hell," said the Bishop.

"And the soul of your poor pa is now warm and dry and happy in the presence of his Lord God."

Chapter VI
The Lute of the Holy Ghost
Is Further Chastened

Listening to Keaton's tale, he had dimly seen the caravan of hunted creatures crawl past him over the fading green of the prairie; the wagons with their bowed white covers; a heavy cart, jolting, creaking, lumbering mysteriously along, a sick driver hidden somewhere back under its makeshift cover of torn counterpanes; a battered carriage, reminiscent of past luxury, drawn by oxen; more wagons, some without covers; a two-wheeled cart, designed in the ingenuity of desperation, laden with meal-sacks, a bundle of bedding, a sleeping child, and drawn by a little dry-dugged heifer; then more wagons with stooping figures trudging doggedly beside them, here a man, there a woman leading a child. He saw them as shapes floating by in a dream, blurred and inconsequent. But between himself and the train, more clearly outlined to his gaze, he saw the worn face of his father tossed on the cold, dark waters, being swept down by the stream, the weak old hands clutching for some support in the muddy current, the white head with the chin held up sinking lower at each failure, then at last going under, gulping, to leave a little row of bubbles down the stream.

In a craze of rage and grief he turned toward the river, when he heard the sharp voice of the Bishop calling him back.

"It ain't any use, Joel."

"Couldn't we find his body?"

"Not a chance in a thousand. It was carried down by the current. It would mean days and mebbe weeks. Besides, we need you here. Here's your duty. Sakes alive! If we only had about twenty minutes with them cusses like it was in the old days! When you're ready to be a Son of Dan you'll know what I mean. But never mind, we'll see the day yet when Israel will be the head and not the tail."

"My mother? Has any one told her?"

"Wal, now, I'm right sorry about that, but it got out before you come over. Tarlton McKenny's boy, Nephi, rowed over in a skiff and brought the news, and some of the women went and tattled it to your ma. I guess it upset her considerable. You go up and see her."

He ran forward toward the head of the train, hearing as he went words of sympathy hurried to him by those he passed. Mounting the wagon, he climbed over the seat to where his mother lay. She seemed to sleep in spite of the jolting. The driver called back to him:

"She took on terrible for a spell, Brother Rae. She's only jest now got herself pacified."

He put his hand on her forehead and found it burning. She stirred and moaned and muttered disjointed sentences. He heard his father's name, his sister's, and his own, and he knew she was delirious. He eased her bed as well as he could, and made a place for himself beside her where he could sit and take one of the pale, thin hands between his own and try to endow her with some of his abundant life. He stayed by her until their camping-place was reached.

Once for a moment she opened her eyes with what seemed to him a more than normal clearness and understanding and memory in them. Though she looked at him long without speaking, she seemed to say all there was to say, so that the brief span was full of anguish for him. He sighed with relief when the consciousness faded again from her look, and she fell to babbling once more of some long gone day in her girlhood.

When the wagon halted he was called outside by the driver, who wished instructions regarding the camp to be made. A few moments later he was back, and raised the side of the wagon cover to let in the light. The look on her face alarmed him. It seemed to tell unmistakably that the great change was near. Already she looked moribund. An irregular gasping for breath, an occasional delirious mutter, were the only signs of life. She was too weak to show restlessness. Her pinched and faded face was covered with tiny cold beads. The pupils of her eyes were strangely dilated, and the eyes themselves were glazed. There was no pulse at her wrist, and from her heart only the faintest beating could be heard. In quick terror he called to a boy working at a wagon near by.

"Go for Bishop Wright and tell him to bring that apothecary with him."

The two came up briskly a few moments later, and he stood aside for them in an agony of suspense. The Bishop turned toward him after a long look into the wagon.

"She's gone to be with your pa, Joel. You can't do anything—only remember they're both happy now for bein' together."

It made little stir in the busy encampment. There had been other deaths while they lay out on the marshy river flats. Others of the sorry band were now sick unto death, and many more would die on the long march across the Iowa prairie, dropping out one by one of fever, starvation, exposure. He stood helpless in this chaos of woe, shut up within himself, knowing not where to turn.

Some women came presently from the other wagons to prepare the body for burial. He watched them dumbly, from a maze of incredulity, feeling that some wretched pretense was being acted before him.

The Bishop and Keaton came up. They brought with them the makeshift coffin. They had cut a log, split it, and stripped off its bark in two half-cylinders. They led him to the other side of the wagon, out of sight. Then they placed the strips of bark around the body, bound them with hickory withes, and over the rough surface the women made a little show of black cloth.

For the burial they could do no more than consign the body to one of the waves in the great billowy land sea about them. They had no tombstone, nor were there even rocks to make a simple cairn. He saw them bury her, and thought there was little to choose between hers and the grave of his father, whose body was being now carried noiselessly down in the bed of the river. The general locality would be kept by landmarks, by the bearing of valley bends, headlands, or the fork and angles of constant streams. But the spot itself would in a few weeks be lost.

When the last office had been performed, the prayer said, a psalm sung, and the black dirt thrown in, they waited by him in sympathy. His feeling was that they had done a monstrous thing; that the mother he had known was somewhere alive and well. He stood a moment so, watching the sun sink below the far rim of the prairie while the white moon swung into sight in the east. Then the Bishop led him gently by the arm to his own camp.

There cheer abounded. They had a huge camp-fire tended by the Bishop's numerous children. Near by was a smaller fire over which the good man's four wives, able-bodied, glowing, and cordial, cooked the supper. In little ways they sought to lighten his sorrow or to put his mind away from it. To this end the Bishop contributed by pouring him drink from a large brown jug.

"Not that I approve of it, boy, but it'll hearten you,—some of the best peach brandy I ever sniffed. I got it at the still-house last week for use in time of trouble,—and this here time is *it*."

He drank the fiery stuff from the gourd in which it was given him, and choked until they brought him water. But presently the warmth stole along his cold, dead nerves so that he became intensely alive from head to foot, and strangely exalted. And when they offered him food he ate eagerly and talked. It seemed to him there had been a thousand matters that he had long wished to speak of; matters of moment in which he felt deeply; yet on which he had strangely neglected to touch till now.

He talked long with the Bishop when the women had climbed into their wagon for the night. He amazed that good man by asking him if the Lord would not be pleased to have them, now, as they were, go back to Nauvoo and descend upon the Gentiles to smite them. The Bishop counselled him to have patience.

"What could we do how with these few old fusees and cheap arms that we managed to smuggle across—to say nothing of half of us being down sick?"

"But we are Israel, and surely Israel's God—"

"The Lord had His chance the other day if He'd wanted it, when they took the town. No, Joel, He means us to gether out and become strong enough to beat 'em in our own might. But you *wait*; our day will come, and all the more credit to us then for doin' it ourselves. Then we'll consecrate the herds and flocks of the Gentile and his store and basket, his gold and silver, and his myrrh and frankincense. But for the present—well, we got to be politic and kind of modest about such doin's. The big Fan, the Sons of Dan, done good work in Missouri and better in Nauvoo, and it'll do still better where we're goin'. But we must be patient. Only next time we'll get to work quicker. If the Gentiles had been seen to quicker in Nauvoo, Joseph would be with us now. We learned our lesson there. Now the Lord has unfurled a Standard of Zion for the gathering of Israel, and this time we'll fix the Gentiles early."

"Amen! Brother Seth."

A look of deep hatred had clouded the older man's face as he spoke. He continued.

"Let the wrath of God abide upon 'em, and remember that we're bein' tried and proved for a purpose. And we got to be more practical. You been too theoretical yourself and too high-flyin' in your notions. The Kingdom ain't to be set up on earth by faith alone. The Lord has got to have *works*, like I told you about the other day."

"You were right, Bishop, I need to be more practical. The olive-branch and not the sword would Ephraim extend to Japheth, but if—"

"If Japheth don't toe the mark the Lord's will must be worked upon him."

"So be it, Brother Seth! I am ready now to be a Son of Dan."

The Bishop rose from in front of their fire and looked about. No one was near. Here and there a fire blazed, and the embers of many more could be seen dying out in the distance. The nearest camp was that of the fever-stricken man who had fled on to the boat that morning with his child in his arms. They could see his shaven head in the firelight, and a woman hovering over him as he lay on the ground with a tattered quilt fixed over him in lieu of a tent. From another group came the strains of an accordion and the chorus of a hymn.

"That's right," said the Bishop. "I knew you'd come to it. I saw that long ago. Brother Brigham saw it, too. We knew you could be relied on. You want the oath, do you?"

"Yes, yes, Brother Seth. I was ready for it this morning when they told me about father."

"Hold up your right hand and repeat after me:

"'In the name of Jesus Christ, the Son of God, I do covenant and agree to support the first Presidency of the Church of Jesus Christ of Latter-day Saints, in all things right or wrong; I will faithfully guard them and report to them the acts of all men as far as in my power lies; I will assist in executing all the decrees of the first President, Patriarch, or President of the Twelve, and I will cause all who speak evil of the Presidency or Heads of the Church to die the death of dissenters or apostates, unless they speedily confess and repent, for pestilence, persecution, and death shall follow the enemies of Zion. I will be a swift herald of salvation and messenger of peace to the Saints, and I will never make known the secret purposes of this Society called the Sons of Dan, my life being the forfeiture in a fire of burning tar and brimstone. So help me God and keep me steadfast.'"

He repeated the words without hesitation, with fervour in his voice, and the light of a holy and implacable zeal in his face.

"Now I'll give you the blessing, too. Wait till I get my bottle of oil."

He stepped to the nearest wagon, felt under the cover, and came back with a small bottle in his hand.

"Stand jest here—so—now!"

They stood at the edge of the wavering firelight, and he put his hand on the other's head.

"'In the name of Jesus Christ, the Son of God, and by the authority of the Holy Priesthood, the first President, Patriarch, and High Priest of the Church of Jesus Christ of Latter-day Saints, representing the first, second, and third Gods in Heaven, the Father, Son, and Holy Ghost, I do now anoint you with holy consecrated oil, and by the imposition of my hands do ordain and set you apart for the holy calling whereunto you are called; that you may consecrate the riches of the Gentiles to the House of Israel, bring swift destruction upon apostate sinners, and execute the decrees of Heaven without fear of what man can do with you. So mote it be. Amen.'

"There, boy, if I ain't mistaken, that's the best work for Zion that I done for some time. Now be off to your rest!"

"Good night, Bishop, and thank you for being kind to me! The Church Poet called me the Lute of the Holy Ghost, but I feel to-night, that I must be another Lion of the Lord. Good night!"

He went out of the firelight and stumbled through the dark to his own wagons. But when he came to them he could not stop. Under all the exhilaration he had been conscious of the great pain within him, drugged for the moment, but never wholly stifled. Now the stimulus of the drink had gone, and the pain had awakened to be his master.

He went past the wagons and out on to the prairie that stretched away, a sea of silvery gray in the moonlight. As he walked, the whole stupendous load of sorrow settled upon him. His breath caught and his eyes burned with the tears that lay behind them. He walked faster to flee from it, but it came upon him more heavily until it made a breaking load,—the loss of his sister by worse than death, his father and mother driven out at night and their home burned, his father killed by a mob whose aim had lacked even the dignity of the murderer's—for they had seemingly intended but a brutal piece of horse-play; his mother dead from exposure due to Gentile persecutions; the girl he had loved taken from him by Gentile persuasions. If only she had been left him so that now he could put his head down upon her shoulder, slight as that shoulder was, and feel the supreme soothing of a woman's touch; if only the hurts had not all come at once! The pain sickened him. He was far out on the prairie now, away from the sleeping encampment, and he threw himself down to give way to his grief. Almost silently he wept, yet with sobs that choked him and cramped him from head to foot. He called to his mother and to his father and to the sister who had gone before them, crying their names over and over in the night. But under all his sorrow he felt as great a rage against the Gentile nation that had driven them into the wilderness.

When the spasm of grief had passed, he still lay there a long time. Then becoming chilled he walked again over the prairie, watching the moon go down and darkness come to make the stars brighter, and then the day show gray in the east. And as he walked against his sorrow, the burden of his thought came to be: "God has tried me more than most men; therefore he expects more of me; and my reward shall be greater. New visions shall be given to me, and a new power, and this poor, hunted, plundered remnant of Israel shall find me their staff. Much has been taken from me, but much will be given unto me."

And under this ran a minor strain born of the rage that still burned within him:

"But, oh, the day of wrath that shall dawn on yonder Gentiles!"

So did he chasten himself through the night; and when the morning came he took his place in the train, strangely exalted by this new sense of the singular favour that was to be conferred upon him.

For seven weeks the little caravan crept over the prairies of Iowa, and day after day his conviction strengthened that he had been chosen for large works. In this fervour he cheered the sick and the weak of the party by picturing for them a great day to come when the Lord should exalt the valleys of humility and abase the mountains of Gentile pride; when the Saints should have their reward, and retribution should descend upon the wicked nation they were leaving behind. Scourges, afflictions, and depredations by fire, famine, and the tyrant's hand he besought them to regard as marks of Heaven's especial favour.

The company came to look upon him as its cloud by day and its pillar of fire by night. Old women—mothers in Israel—lavished attentions upon him as a motherless boy; young women smiled at him with soft pity, and were meek and hushed when he spoke. And the men believed that the things he told them concerning their great day to come were true revelations from God. They did not hesitate to agree with the good Bishop Wright, who declared in words of pointed admiration, "When that young man gets all het up with the Holy Ghost, the Angel of the Lord jest *has* to give down!"

Chapter VII
Some Inner Mysteries Are Expounded

The hosts of Israel had been forced to tarry for the winter on the banks of the Missouri. A few were on the east side at Council Bluffs on the land of the Pottawattamie Indians. Across the river on the land of the Omahas the greater part of the force had settled at what was known as Winter Quarters. Here in huts of logs, turf, and other primitive materials, their town had been laid out with streets and byways, a large council-house, a mill, a stockade, and blockhouses. The Indians had received them with great friendliness, feeling with them a common cause of grievance, since the heavy hand of the Gentile had pushed them also to this bleak frontier.

To this settlement early in November came the last train from Nauvoo, its members wearied and wasted by the long march, but staunch in their faith and with hope undimmed. It was told in after years how there had leaped from the van of this train a very earnest young man, who had at once sought an audience with Brigham Young and certain other members of the Twelve who had chanced to be present at the train's arrival; and how, being closeted with these, he had eagerly inquired if it might not be the will of the Lord that they should go no farther into the wilderness, but stand their ground and give battle to the Gentiles forthwith. He made the proposal as one who had a flawless faith that the God of Battles would be with them, and he appeared to believe that something might be done that very day to force the matter to an issue. When he had made his proposal, he waited in a modest attitude to hear their views of it. To his chagrin, all but two of those who had listened laughed. One of these two, Bishop Snow,—a man of holy aspect whom the Church Poet had felicitously entitled the Entablature of Truth,—had looked at him searchingly, then put his hand upon his own head and shaken it hopelessly to the others.

The other who had not laughed was Brigham himself. For to this great man had been given the gift to look upon men and to know in one slow sweep of his wonderful eyes all their strength and all their weakness. He had listened with close attention to the remarkable plan suggested by this fiery young zealot, and he studied him now with a gaze that was kind. A noticeable result of this attitude of Brigham's was that those who had laughed became more or less awkwardly silent, while the Entablature of Truth, in the midst of his pantomime, froze into amazement.

"We'd better consider that a little," said Brigham, finally. "You can talk it over with me tonight. But first you go get your stuff unloaded and get kind of settled. There's a cabin just beyond my two up the street here that you can move into." He put his large hand kindly on the other's shoulder. "Now run and get fixed and come to my house for supper along about dark."

Somewhat cooled by the laughter of the others, but flattered by this consideration from the Prophet, the young man had gone thoughtfully out to his wagons and driven on to the cabin indicated.

"I *did* think he was plumb crazy," said Bishop Snow, doubtfully, as if the reasons for changing his mind were even yet less than compelling.

"He *ain't* crazy," said Brigham. "All that's the matter with him, he's got more faith than the whole pack of us put together. You just remember he ain't like us. We was all converted after we got our second teeth, while he's had it from the cradle up. He's the first one we've caught young. He's what the priesthood can turn out when they get a full swing with the rising generation. We got to remember that. We old birds had to learn to crow in middle life. These young ones will crow stronger; they'll out-crow us. But all the better for that. They'll be mighty brash at first, but all they need is to be held in a little, and then they'll be a power in the Kingdom."

"Well, of course you're right, Brother Brigham, but that boy certainly needs a check-rein and a curb-bit right now," said Snow.

"He'll have his needings," answered Brigham, shortly, and the informal council dispersed.

Brigham talked to him late that night, advancing many cogent reasons why it should be unwise to make war at once upon the nation of Gentiles to the east. Of these reasons the one that had greatest weight with his listener was the assurance that such a course would not at present be pleasing in the sight of God. To others, touching upon the matter of superior forces they might have to contend with, he was loftily inattentive.

Having made this much clear, Brigham went on in his fatherly way to impress him anew with the sinfulness of all temporal governments outside the Church of Jesus Christ of Latter-day Saints. Again he learned from the lips of authority that any people presuming to govern themselves by laws of their own making and officers of their own appointing, are in wicked rebellion against the Kingdom of God; that for seventeen hundred years the nations of the Western Hemisphere have been destitute of this Kingdom and destitute of all legal government; and that the Lord was now about to rend all earthly governments, to cast down thrones, overthrow nations, and make a way for the establishment of the everlasting Kingdom, to which all others would have to yield, or be prostrated never more to rise. Thus was the rebuff of the afternoon gracefully atoned for.

From matters of civil government the talk ranged to affairs domestic.

"Tell me," said the young man, "the truth of this new order of celestial marriage." And Brigham had become animated at once.

"Yes," he said, "when the family organisation was revealed from Heaven, and Joseph began on the right and the left to add to his family, oh, dear, what a quaking there was in Israel! But there it was, plain enough. When you have received your endowments, keys, blessings, all the tokens, signs, and every preparatory ordinance that can be given to a man for his entrance through the celestial gate, then you can see it."

He gazed a moment into the fire of hickory logs before which they sat, and then went on, more confidentially:

"Now you take that promise to Abraham—'Lift up your eyes and behold the stars. So shall thy seed be as numberless as the stars. Go to the seashore and look at the sand, and behold the smallness of the particles thereof'—I am giving you the gist of the Lord's words, you understand—'and then realise that your seed shall be as numberless as those sands.' Now think for a minute how many particles there are, say in a cubit foot of sand—about one thousand million particles. Think of that! In eight thousand years, if the inhabitants of earth increased one trillion a century, three cubic yards of sand would still contain more particles than there would be people on the whole globe. Yet there you got the promise of the Lord in black and white. Now how was Abraham to manage to get a foundation laid for this mighty kingdom? Was he to get it all through one wife? Don't you see how ridiculous that is? Sarah saw it, and Sarah knew that unless seed was raised to Abraham he would come short of his glory. So what did Sarah do? She gave Abraham a certain woman whose name was Hagar, and by her a seed was to be raised up unto him. And was that all? No. We read of his wife Keturah, and also of a plurality of wives which he had in the sight and favour of God, and from whom he raised up many sons. There, then, was a foundation laid for the fulfilment of that grand promise concerning his seed."

He peered again into the fire, and added, by way of clenching his argument: "I guess it would have been rather slow-going, if the Lord had confined Abraham to one wife, like some of these narrow, contracted nations of modern Christianity. You see, they don't know that a man's posterity in this world is to constitute his glory and kingdom and dominion in the world to come, and they don't know, either, that there are thousands of choice spirits in the spirit world waiting to tabernacle in the flesh. Of course, there are lots of these things that you ain't ready to hear yet, but now you know that polygamy is necessary for our exaltation to the fulness of the Lord's glory in the eternal world, and after you study it you'll like the doctrine. I do; I can swallow it without greasing *my* mouth!"

He prayed that night to be made "holy as Thy servant Brigham is holy; to hear Thy voice as he hears it; to be made as wise as he, as true as he, even as another Lion of the Lord, so that I may be a rod and staff and comforter to these buffeted children of Thine."

His prayer also touched on one of the matters of their talk. "But, O Lord, teach me to be content without thrones and dominion in Thy Kingdom if to gain these I must have many wives. Teach me to abase myself, to be a servant, a lowly sweeper in the temple of the Most High, for I would rather be lowly with her I love than exalted to any place whatsoever with many. Keep in my sinful heart the face of her who has left me to dwell among the Gentiles, whose hair is melted gold, whose eyes are azure deep as the sky, and whose arms once opened warm for me. Guard her especially, O Lord, while she must company with Gentiles, for she is not wonted to their wiles; and in Thine own good time bring her head unharmed to its home on Thy servant's breast."

He fasted often, that winter, waiting and watching for his great Witness—something that should testify to his mortal eyes the direct favour of Heaven. He fasted and kept vigils and studied the mysteries; for now he was among the favoured to whom light had been given in abundance—men at whose feet he was eager to sit. He learned of baptism for the dead; of the Godship of Adam, and his plurality of wives; of the laws of adoption and the process by which the Saints were to people, and be Gods to, earths yet formless.

There was much work out of doors to be done, and of this he performed his share, working side by side with the tireless Brigham. But there were late afternoons and long evenings in which he sat with the Prophet to his great advantage. For, strangely enough, the two men, so unlike, were drawn closely together—Brigham Young, the broad-headed, square-chinned buttress of physical vitality, the full-blooded, clarion-voiced Lion of the Lord, self-contained, watchful, radiating the power that men feel and obey without knowing why, and Joel Rae, of the long, narrow, delicately featured face, sensitive, nervous, glowing with a spiritual zeal, the Lute of the Holy Ghost, whose veins ran fire instead of blood. One born to command, to domineer; the other to believe, to worship, and to obey. For the younger man it was a winter of limitless aspiration and chastening discipline. In spite of the great sorrows that weighed upon him, the sudden sweeping away of those he had held most dear and the blasting of his love hopes, he remembered it through all the eventful years that followed as a time of strange happiness. Memories of it came gratefully to him even on the awful day when at last his Witness came; when, as he lay fainting in the desert, driven thence by his sin, the heavens unfolded and a vision was vouchsafed him;—when the foundations of his world were shattered, the tables of the law destroyed, and but one little feather saved to his famished soul from the wings of the dove of truth. After all these years, the memory of this winter was a spot of joy that never failed to glow when he recalled it.

At night he went to his bunk in the little straw-roofed hut and fell asleep to the howling of the wolves, his mind cradled in the thought of his mission. He had a part in the great work of bringing into harmony the labours of the prophets and apostles of all ages. In due time, by the especial favour of Heaven, he would be wrapped in a sea of vision, shown an eternity of knowledge, and be intrusted with singular powers. And he was content to wait out the days in which he must school, chasten, and prove himself.

"You have built me up," he confided to Brigham, one day. "I feel to rejoice in my strength." And Brigham was highly pleased.

"That's good, Brother Joel. The host of Israel will soon be on the move, and I shouldn't wonder if the Lord had a great work for you. I can see places where you'll be just the tool he needs. I mistrust we sha'n't have everything peaceful even now. The priest in the pulpit is thorning the politician against us, gouging him from underneath—he'd never dare do it openly, for our Elders could crimson his face with shame—and the minions of the mob may be after us again. If they do, I can see where you will be a tower of strength in your own way."

"It's all of my life, Brother Brigham."

"I believe it. I guess the time has come to make you an Elder."

And so on a late winter afternoon in the quiet of the Council-House, Joel Rae was ordained an Elder after the order of Melchisedek; with power to preach and administer in all the ordinances of the Church, to lay on hands, to confirm all baptised persons, to anoint the afflicted with oil, and to seal upon them the blessings of health.

In his hard, narrow bed that night, where the cold came through the unchinked logs and the wind brought him the wailing of the wolves, he prayed that he might not be too much elated by this extraordinary distinction.

Chapter VIII
A Revelation from the Lord and
a Toast from Brigham

From his little one-roomed cabin, dark, smoky, littered with hay, old blankets, and skins, he heard excited voices outside, one early morning in January. He opened the door and found a group of men discussing a miracle that had been wrought overnight. The Lord had spoken to Brigham and word had come to Zion to move toward the west.

He hurried over to Brigham's house and by that good man was shown the word of the Lord as it had been written down from his lips. With emotions of reverential awe he read the inspired document.

"The Word and Will of the Lord Concerning the Camp of Israel in its Journeyings to the West." Such was its title.

"Let all the people," it began, "of the Church of Jesus Christ of Latter-day Saints, be organised into companies with a covenant and a promise to keep all the statutes of the Lord our God.

"Let the companies be organised with captains of hundreds and captains of fifties and captains of tens, with a President and Counsellor at their head under the direction of the Twelve Apostles.

"Let each company provide itself with all the teams, wagons, provisions, and all other necessaries for the journey.

"Let every man use all of his influence and property to remove this people to the place where the Lord shall locate a stake of Zion, and let them share equally in taking the poor, the widows, and the fatherless, so that their cries come not up into the ears of the Lord against His people.

"And if ye do this with a pure heart, with all faithfulness, ye shall be blessed in your flocks and in your herds and in your fields and in your families. For I am the Lord your God, even the God of your fathers, the God of Abraham, Isaac, and of Jacob. I am He who led the children of Israel out of the land of Egypt, and my arm is stretched out in these last days to save my people of Israel.

"Fear not thine enemies, for they are in my hands, and I will do my pleasure with them.

"My people must be tried in all things, that they may be worthy to receive the glory that I have in store for them, even the glory of Zion; and he that will not receive chastisement is not worthy of my Kingdom. So no more at present. Amen and Amen!"

This was what he had longed for each winter night when he had seen the sun go down,—the word of the Lord to follow that sun on over the rim into the pathless wilderness, infested by savage tribes and ravenous beasts, abounding in terrors unknown. There was an adventure worth while in the sight of God. It had never ceased to thrill him since he first heard it broached,—the mad plan of a handful of persecuted believers, setting out from civilisation to found Zion in the wilderness,—to go forth a thousand miles from Christendom with nothing but stout arms and a very living faith in the God of Israel, and in Joseph Smith as his prophet, meeting death in famine, plagues, and fevers, freezing in the snows of the mountains, thirsting to death on the burning deserts, being devoured by ravening beasts or tortured to death by the sinful Lamanites; but persisting through it all with dauntless courage to a final triumph so glorious that the very Gods would be compelled to applaud the spectacle of their devoted heroism.

And now he was face to face with the awful, the glorious, the divinely ordained fact. It was like standing before the Throne of Grace itself. Out over that western skyline was a spot, now hidden and defended by all the powers of Satan, where the Ten Tribes would be restored, where Zion would be rebuilt, where Christ would reign personally on earth a thousand years, and from whence the earth would be renewed and receive again its paradisiac glory. The thought overwhelmed.

"If we could only start at once!" he said to Bishop Wright, who had read the revelation with him. But the canny Bishop's religious zeal was henceforth to be tempered by the wisdom of the children of darkness.

"No more travelling in this kind of a time for the Saints," the Bishop replied. "We got our full of that when we first left Nauvoo. We had to scrape snow from the ground and set up tents when it was fifteen or twenty below zero, and nine children born one night in that weather. Of course it was better than staying at Nauvoo to be shot; but no one is going to shoot us here, so here we'll tarry till grass grows and water runs."

"But there was a chance to show devotion, Brother Seth. Think how precious it must have been in the sight of the Lord."

"Well, the Lord knows we're devoted now, so we'll wait till it fairs up. We'll have Zion built in good time and a good gospel fence built around it, elk-high and bull-tight, like we used to say in Missouri. But it's a long ways over yender, and while I ain't ever had any revelations myself, I'm pretty sure the Lord means to have me toler'bly well fed, and my back kept bone-dry on the way. And we got to have fat horses and fat cattle, not these bony critters with no juice in 'em. Did you hear what Brother Heber got off the other day? He butchered a beef and was sawing it up when Brother Brigham passed by. 'Looks hard, Brother Heber,' says Brother Brigham. 'Hard, Brother Brigham? Why, I've had to grease the saw to make it work!' Yes, sir, had to grease his saw to make it work through that bony old heifer. Now we already passed through enough pinches not to go out lookin' for 'em any more. Why, I tell you, young man, if I knew any place where the pinches was at, you'd see me comin' the other way like a bat out of hell!"

And so the ardent young Elder was compelled to curb his spirit until the time when grass should grow and water run. Yet he was not alone in feeling this impatience for the start. Through all the settlement had thrilled a response to the Lord's word as revealed to his servant Brigham. The God of Israel was to be with them on the march, and old and young were alike impatient.

Early in April the life began to stir more briskly in the great camp that sprawled along either side of the swollen, muddy river. From dawn to dark each day the hills echoed with the noise of many works, the streets were alive with men and women going and coming on endless errands, and with excited children playing at games inspired by the occasion. Wagons were mended and loaded with provisions and tools, oxen shod, ox-bows renewed, guns put in order, bullets moulded, and the thousand details perfected of a migration so hazardous. They were busy, noisy, excited, happy days.

At last, in the middle of April, the signs were seen to be right. Grass grew and water ran, and their part, allotted by the Lord, was to brave the dangers of that forbidding land that lay under the western sun. Then came a day of farewells and merry-making. In the afternoon, the day being mild and sunny, there was a dance in the bowery,—a great arbour made of poles and brush and wattling. Here, where the ground had been trodden firm, the age and maturity as well as the youth and beauty of Israel gathered in such poor festal array as they had been able to save from their ravaged stores.

The Twelve Apostles led off in a double cotillion, to the moving strains of a violin and horn, the lively jingle of a string of sleigh-bells, and the genial snoring of a tambourine. Then came dextrous displays in the dances of our forbears, who followed the fiddle to the Fox-chase Inn or Garden of Gray's

Ferry. There were French Fours, Copenhagen jigs, Virginia reels,—spirited figures blithely stepped. And the grave-faced, square-jawed Elders seemed as eager as the unthinking youths and maidens to throw off for the moment the burden of their cares.

From midday until the April sun dipped below the sharp skyline of the Omaha hills, the modest revel endured. Then silence was called by a grim-faced, hard-voiced Elder, who announced:

"The Lute of the Holy Ghost will now say a word of farewell from our pioneers to those who must stay behind."

He stood before them erect, brave, confident; and the fire of his faith warmed his voice into their hearts.

"Children of Israel, we are going into the wilderness to lay the foundations of a temple to the most high God, so that when his Son, our elder Brother, shall come on earth again, He may have a place where He can lay His head and spend, not only a night or a day, but rest until He can say, 'I am satisfied!'—a place, too, where you can obtain the ordinances of salvation for yourselves, your living, and your dead. Let your prayers go with us. We have been thrust out of Babylon, but to our eternal salvation. We care no more for persecution than for the whistle of the north wind, the croaking of the crane that flies over our heads, or the crackling of thorns under a pot. True, some of our dearest, our best-loved, have dropped by the way; they have fallen asleep, but what of that?—and who cares? It is as well to live as to die, or to die as to live—as well to sleep as to be awake. It is all one. They have only gone a little before us; and we shall soon strike hands with them across those poor, mean, empty graves back there on the forlorn prairies of Iowa. For you must let me clench this God's truth into your minds; that you stand now in your last lot, in the end of your days when the Son of Man cometh again. Afflictions shall be sent to humble and to prove you, but oh! stand fast to your teachings so that not one of you may be lost. May sinners in Zion become afraid henceforth, and fearfulness surprise the hypocrite from this hour! And now may the favour and blessing of God be manifest upon you while we are absent from one another!"

When the fervent amens had died away they sang the farewell hymn:—

"Thrones shall totter, Babel fall,
Satan reign no more at all;

"Saints shall gain the victory,
Truth prevail o'er land and sea;

"Gentile tyrants sink to hell;
Now's the day of Israel."

The words of the young Elder were felt to be highly consoling; but a toast given by Brigham that night was longer talked of. It was at a farewell party at the house of Bishop Wright. On the hay-covered floor of the banquet-room, amid the lights of many candles hung from the ceiling and about the walls in their candelabra of hollowed turnips, the great man had been pleased to prophesy blessings profusely upon the assembled guests.

"I am awful proud," he began, "of the way the Lord has favoured us. I am proud all the time of his Elders, his servants, and his handmaids. And when they do well I am prouder still. I don't know but I'll get so proud that I'll be four or five times prouder than I am now. As I once said to Sidney Rigdon, our boat is an old snag boat and has never been out of Snag-harbour. But it will root up the snags, run them down, split them, and scatter them to the four quarters. Our ship is the old ship of Zion; and nothing that runs foul of her can withstand her shock and fury."

Then had followed the toast, which was long remembered for its dauntless spirit.

"Here's wishing that all the mobocrats of the nineteenth century were in the middle of the sea, in a stone canoe, with an iron paddle; that a shark would swallow the canoe, and the shark be thrust into the nethermost part of hell, with the door locked, the key lost, and a blind man looking for it!"

Chapter IX
Into the Wilderness

Onto the West at last to build the house of God in the mountains. On to what Daniel Webster had lately styled "a region of savages and wild beasts, of deserts, of shifting sands and whirlwinds of dust, of cactus and prairie-dogs."

The little band of pioneers chosen to break a way for the main body of the Saints consisted of a hundred and forty-three men, three women, and two children. They were to travel in seventy-three wagons, drawn by horses and oxen. They knew not where they were to stop, but they were men of eager initiative, fearless and determined; and their consolation was that, while their exodus into the desert meant hardship and grievous suffering, it also promised them freedom from Gentile interference. It was not a fat land into which they were venturing; but at least it was a land without a past, lying clean as it came from the hand of its maker, where they could be free to worship God without fearing the narrow judgment of the frivolous. Instructed in the sacred mysteries revealed to Joseph Smith through the magic light of the Urim and Thummim, and sustained by the divine message engraved on the golden plates he had dug up from the hill of Cumorah, they were now ready to feel their way across the continent and blaze a trail to the new Jerusalem.

They went in military style with due precautions against surprise by the Lamanites—the wretched red remnant of Abraham's seed—that swarmed on every side.

Brigham Young was lieutenant-general; Stephen Markham was colonel; the redoubtable John Pack was first major, and Shadrach Roundy, second. There were two captains of hundreds and fourteen captains of tens. The orders of the lieutenant-general required each man to walk constantly beside his wagon, leaving it only by his officer's commands. To make the force compact, the wagons were to move two abreast where they could. Every man was to keep his weapons loaded. If the gun was a caplock, the cap was to be taken off and a piece of leather put on to exclude moisture and dirt; if a flintlock, the filling was to be taken out and the pan filled with tow or cotton.

Their march was not only cautious but orderly. At five A.M. the bugle sounded for rising, two hours being allowed for prayers and breakfast. At night each man had to retire to his wagon for prayer at eight-thirty, and to rest at nine. If they camped by a river they drew the wagons into a semicircle with the river at its base. Other times the wagons made a circle, a fore-wheel of one touching a rear wheel of the next, thus providing a corral for the stock. In such manner was the wisdom of the Lord concerning this hegira supplemented in detail by the worldly forethought of his servant Brigham.

They started along the north bank of the Platte River under the auspicious shine of an April sun. A better route was along the south bank where grass was more plentiful and the Indians less troublesome. But along the south bank parties of migrating Gentiles might also be met, and these sons of perdition were to be avoided at any cost—"at least for the present," said Brigham, in tones of sage significance.

And so for two hundred miles they broke a new way over the plains, to be known years after as "the old Mormon trail," to be broadened later by the gold-seekers of forty-nine, and still later to be shod with steel, when the miracle of a railway was worked in the desert.

To Joel Rae, Elder after the order of Melchisedek, unsullied product of the temple priesthood, it was a time of wondrous soul-growth. In that mysterious realm of pathless deserts, of illimitable prairies and boundless plains, of nameless rivers and colossal hills, a land of dreams, of romance, of marvellous adventure, he felt strange powers growing within him. It seemed that in such a place the one who opened his soul to heaven must become endowed with all those singular gifts he had longed for. He looked confidently forward to the time when they should regard him as a man who could work miracles.

At the head of Grand Island they came to vast herds of buffalo—restless brown seas of humped, shaggy backs and fiercely lowered heads. In their first efforts to slay these they shot them full in the forehead, and were dismayed to find that their bullets rebounded harmlessly. They solved the mystery later, discovering the hide on the skull of a dead bull to be an inch thick and covered with a mat of gnarled hair in itself almost a shield against bullets. Joel Rae, with the divine right of youth, drew for them from this circumstance an instructive parallel.

So was the head of their own church protected against Gentile shafts by the hide of righteousness and the matted hair of faith.

The Indians killed buffalo by riding close and striking them with an arrow at the base of the spine; whereupon the beast would fall paralysed, to be hamstrung at leisure. Only by some such infernal strategy, the young Elder assured them, could the Gentiles ever henceforth cast them down.

For many days their way lay through these herds of buffalo—herds so far-reaching that none could count their numbers or even see their farther line, lost in the distance over the swell of the plains. Often their way was barred until a herd would pass, making the earth tremble, and with a noise like muffled thunder. They waited gladly, feeling that these were obstacles on the way to Zion.

Thus far it had been a land of moderate plenty, one in which they were, at least, not compelled to look to Heaven for manna. Besides the buffalo which the hunters learned to kill, they found deer, antelope, great flocks of geese and splendid bronzed wild turkeys. Even the truculent grizzly came to be numbered among their trophies.

Day after day marched the bearded host,—farmers with ploughs, mechanics with tools, builders, craftsmen, woodsmen, all the needed factors of a colony, led by the greatest coloniser of modern times, their one great aim being to make ready some spot in the wilderness for the second advent of the Messiah. All about them was the prairie, its long grass gently billowed by the spring breeze. On the far right, blue in the haze, was a continuous range of lofty bluffs. On the left the waters of the Platte, muddied by the spring freshets, flowed over beds of quicksand between groves of cottonwood that pleasantly fringed its banks. The hard labour and the constant care demanded by the dangers that surrounded them prevented any from feeling the monotony of the landscape.

Besides the regular trials of the march there were wagons to be "snaked" across the streams, tires to be reset and yokes to be mended at each "lay-by," strayed stock to be hunted, and a thousand contingencies sufficient to drive from their minds all but the one thought that they had been thrown forth from a Christian land for the offence of worshipping God according to the dictates of their own consciences.

Joel Rae, walking beside his wagon, meditated chiefly upon the manner in which his Witness would first manifest itself. The wonder came, in a way, while he thus meditated. Late one afternoon the scouts thrown in advance came hurrying back to report a large band of Indians strung out in battle array a few miles ahead. The wagons were at once formed five abreast, their one cannon was wheeled to the front, and the company advanced in close formation. Perceiving these aggressive manoeuvres, the Indians seemed to change their plan and, instead of coming on to attack, were seen to be setting fire to the prairie.

The result might well have been disastrous, as the wind was blowing toward the train. Joel Rae saw it; saw that the time had come for a miracle if the little company of Saints was to be saved a serious rebuff. He quickly entered his wagon and began to pray. He prayed that the Lord might avert this calamity and permit the handful of faithful ones to proceed in peace to fashion His temple on earth.

When he began to pray there had been outside a woful confusion of sounds,—scared and plunging horses, bellowing oxen, excited men shouting to the stock and to one another, the barking of dogs and the rattling of the wagons. Through this din he prayed, scarcely hearing his own voice, yet feeling within himself the faith that he knew must prevail. And then as he prayed he became conscious that these noises had subsided to a wonderful silence. A moment this lasted, and then he heard it broken by a mighty shout of gladness, followed by excited calls from one man to another.

He looked out in calm certainty to observe in what manner the Lord had consented to answer his petition. He saw that the wind had veered and, even as he looked, large drops of rain came pounding musically upon his wagon-cover. Far in front of them a long, low line of flame was crawling to the west, while above it lurid clouds of smoke rolled away from them. In another moment the full force of the shower was upon them from a sky that half an hour before had been cloudless. Far off to the right scurried the Indians, their feathery figures lying low upon the backs of their small ponies. His heart swelled within him, and he fell again to his knees with many earnest words of thanksgiving for the intercession.

They at once made camp for the night, and by Brigham's fire later in the evening Joel Rae confided the truth of his miracle to that good man, taking care not to utter the words with any delight or pride in himself. He considered that Brigham was unduly surprised by the occurrence; almost displeased in fact; showing a tendency to attribute the day's good fortune to phenomena wholly natural. Although the miracle had seemed to him a small, simple thing, he now felt a little ashamed of his performance. He was pleased to note, however, that Brigham became more gracious to him after a short period of reflection. He praised him indeed for the merit which he seemed to have gained in the Lord's sight; taking occasion to remind him, however, that he, Brigham, had meant to produce the same effects by a prayer of his own in due time to save the train from destruction; that he had chosen to wait, however, in order to try the faith of the Saints.

"As a matter of fact, Brother Joel," he concluded, "I don't know as there is any limit to the power with which the Lord has blessed me. I tell you I feel equal to any miracle—even to raising the dead, I sometimes think—I feel that fired up with the Holy Ghost!"

"I am sure you will do even that, Brother Brigham." And the young man's eyes swam with mingled gratitude and admiration. He resolved in his wagon that night, that when the time came for another miracle, he would not selfishly usurp the honour of performing it. He would not again forestall the able Brigham.

By the first of June they had wormed their way over five hundred miles of plain to the trading post of Fort Laramie. Here they were at last forced to cross the Platte and to take up their march along the Oregon trail. They were now in the land of alkaline deserts, of sage-brush and greasewood, of sad, bleak, deadly stretches; a land where the favour of Heaven might have to be called upon if they were to survive. Yet it was a land not without inspiration,—a land of immense distances, of long, dim perspectives, and of dreamy visions in the far, vague haze. In such a land, thought Joel Rae, the spirit of the Lord must draw closer to the children of earth. In such a land no miracle should be too difficult. And so it came that he was presently enabled to put in Brigham's way the opportunity of performing a work of mercy which he himself would have been glad to do, but for the fear of affronting the Prophet.

A band of mounted Sioux had met them one day with friendly advances and stopped to trade. Among the gaudy warriors Joel Rae's attention was called to a boy who had lost an arm. He made inquiries, and found him to be the son of the chief. The chief himself made it plain to Joel that the young man had lost his arm ten moons before in a combat with a grizzly bear. Whereupon the young Elder cordially bade the chief bring his crippled son to their own great chief, who would, by the gracious power of God, miraculously restore the missing member.

A few moments later the three were before Brigham, who was standing by his wagon; Joel Rae, glowing with a glad and confident serenity; the tawny chief with his sable braids falling each side of his painted face, gay in his head-dress of dyed eagle plumes, his buckskin shirt jewelled with blue beads and elk's teeth, warlike with his bow and steel-pointed arrows; and the young man, but little less ornate than his splendid father, stoical, yet scarce able to subdue the flash of hope in his eyes as he looked up to the great white chief.

Brigham looked at them questioningly. Joel announced their errand.

"It's a rare opportunity, Brother Brigham, to bring light to these wretched Lamanites. This boy had his arm torn off a year ago in a fight with a grizzly. You know you told me that day I brought the rain-storm that you could well-nigh raise the dead, so this will be easy for you."

Brigham still looked puzzled, so the young man added with a flash of enthusiasm: "Restore this poor creature's arm and the noise of the miracle will go all through these tribes;" he paused expectantly.

It is the mark of true greatness that it may never be found unprepared. Now and again it may be made to temporise for a moment, cunningly adopting one expedient or another to hide its unreadiness—but never more than briefly.

Brigham had looked slowly from the speaker to the Indians and slowly back again. Then he surveyed several bystanders who had been attracted to the group, and his eyelids were seen to work rapidly, as if in sympathetic pace with his thoughts. Then all at once he faced Joel.

"Brother Rae, have you reflected about this?"

"Why—Brother Brigham—no—not reflected—perhaps if we both prayed with hearts full of faith, the Lord might—"

"Brother Rae!"

There was sternness in the voice now, and the young man trembled before the Lion of the Lord.

"You mistake me. I guess I'm a good enough servant of the Lord, so my own prayer would restore this arm without any of your help; yes, I guess the Lord and me could do it without *you*—if we thought it was best. Now pay attention. Do you believe in the resurrection of the body?"

"I do, Brother Brigham, and of course I didn't mean to"—he was blushing now.

"Do you believe the day of judgment is at hand?"

"I do."

"How near?"

"You and our priests and Elders say it will come in 1870."

"Correct! How many years is that from now?"

"Twenty-three, Brother Brigham."

"Yes, twenty-three. Now then, how many years are there to be after that?"

"How many—surely an eternity!"

"More than twenty-three years, then—much more?"

"Eternity means endless time."

"Oh, it does, does it?"

There had been gradually sounding in his voice a ring of triumph which now became distinct.

"Well, then, answer me this—and remember it shall be as you say to the best of my influence with the Lord—you shall be responsible for this poor remnant of the seed of Cain. Now, don't be rash! Is it better for this poor creature to continue with his one arm here for the twenty-three years the world is to endure, and then pass on to eternity where he will have his two arms forever; or, do you want me to renew his arm now and let him go through eternity a freak, a monstrosity? Do you want him to suffer a little inconvenience these few days he has here, or do you want him to go through an endless hereafter with *three arms*?"

The young man gazed at him blankly with a dropped jaw.

"Come, what do you say? I'm full of faith. Shall I—"

"No—no, Brother Brigham; don't—for God's sake, don't! Of course he would be resurrected with three arms. You think of everything, Brother Brigham!"

The Indians had meanwhile been growing puzzled and impatient. He now motioned them to follow him.

By dint of many crude efforts in the sign language and an earnest use of the few words known to both, he succeeded, after a long time, in putting the facts before the chief and his son; They, after an animated conversation, succeeded with much use of the sign language in conveying to Joel Rae the information that the young man was not at all dismayed by the prospect of having three arms during the next life. He gathered, indeed, that both father and son would be rather elated than otherwise by this circumstance, seeming to suspect that the extra member must confer superior prowess and high distinction upon its possessor.

But he shook his head with much determination, and refused to take them again before the great white chief. The thought troubled him exceedingly and would not be gone—yet he knew not how to account for it—that Brigham would not receive this novel view of the matter with any cordiality.

When they were camped that night, Brigham made a suggestion to him.

"Brother Rae, it ain't just the best plan in the world to come on a man sudden that way for so downright a miracle. A man can't be always fired up with the Holy Ghost, with all the cares of this train on his mind. You come and have a private talk with me beforehand after this, when you got a miracle you want done."

He prayed more fervently than ever that night to be made "wise and good like thy servant Brigham"—also for the gift of tongues to come upon him so that he might instruct the Indians in the threefold character of the Godhead and in other matters pertaining to their salvation.

Chapter X
The Promised Land

So far on their march the Lord had protected them from all but ordinary hardships. True, some members of the company had suffered from a fever which they attributed to the clouds of dust that enveloped the column of wagons when in motion, and to the great change of temperature from day to night. Again, the most of them were for many weeks without bread, saving for the sick the little flour they had and subsisting upon the meat provided by the hunters. Before reaching Fort Laramie, too, their stock had become weakened for want of food; an extended drought, the vast herds of buffalo, and the Indian fires having combined to destroy the pasturage.

This weakness of the animals made the march for many days not more than five or six miles a day. At the last they had fed to the stock not only all their grain but the most of their crackers and other breadstuffs. But these were slight matters to a persecuted people gathering out of Babylon.

Late in June they reached the South Pass. For many hundred miles they had been climbing the backbone of the continent. Now they had reached the summit, the dividing ridge between streams that flowed to the Atlantic and streams that flowed to the Pacific. From the level prairies they had toiled up into the fearsome Rockies where bleak, grim crags lowered upon them from afar, and distant summits glistening with snow warned them of the perils ahead.

Through all this time of marching the place where they should pitch the tent of Israel was not fixed upon. When Brigham was questioned around the camp-fire at night, his only reply was that he would know the site of their new home when he saw it. And it came to be told among the men that he had beheld in vision a tent settling down from heaven and resting over a certain spot; and that a voice had said to him, "Here is the place where my people Israel shall pitch their tents and spread wide the curtains of Zion!" It was enough. He would recognise the spot when they reached it.

From the trappers, scouts, and guides encountered along the road they had received much advice as to eligible locations; and while this was various as to sites recommended, the opinion had been unanimous that the Salt Lake Valley was impossible. It was, they were told, sandy, barren, rainless, destitute of timber and vegetation, infested with hordes of hungry crickets, and roamed over by bands of the most savage Indians. In short, no colony could endure there.

One by one the trappers they met voiced this opinion. There was Bordeaux, the grizzled old Frenchman, clad in ragged buckskin; Moses Harris; "Pegleg" Smith, whose habit of profanity was shocking; Miles Goodyear, fresh from captivity among the Blackfeet; and James Bridger. The latter had discovered Great Salt Lake twenty-five years before, and was especially vehement in his condemnation of the valley. They had halted a day at his "fort," two adjoining log houses with dirt roofs, surrounded by a high stockade of logs, and built on one of several small islands formed by the branches of Black's Fork. Here they had found the old trapper amid a score of nondescript human beings, white men, Indian women, and half-breed children.

Bridger had told them very concisely that he would pay them a thousand dollars for the first ear of corn raised in Salt Lake Valley. It is true that Bridger seemed to have become pessimistic in many matters. For one, the West was becoming overcrowded and the price of furs was falling at a rate to alarm the most conservative trapper. He referred feelingly to the good old days when one got ten dollars a pound for prime beaver skins in St. Louis; but "now it's a skin for a plug of tobacco, and three for a cup of powder, and other fancies in the same proportion." And so, had his testimony been unsupported, they might have suspected he was underestimating the advantages of the Salt Lake Valley. But, corroborated as he had been by his brother trappers, they began to descend the western slope of the Rockies strong in the opinion that this same Salt Lake Valley was the land that had been chosen for them by the Lord.

They dared not, indeed, go to a fertile land, for there the Gentiles would be tempted to follow them—with the old bloody end. Only in a desert such as these men had described the Salt Lake Valley to be could they hope for peace. From Fort Bridger, then, their route bent to the southwest along the rocky spurs of the Uintah Mountains, whose snow-clad tops gleamed a bluish white in the July sun.

By the middle of July the vanguard of the company began the descent of Echo Cañon,—a narrow slit cut straight down a thousand feet into the red sandstone,—the pass which a handful of them was to hold a few years later against a whole army of the hated Gentiles.

The hardest part of their journey was still before them. Their road had now to be made as they went, lying wholly among the mountains. Lofty hills, deep ravines with jagged sides, forbidding cañons, all but impassable streams, rock-bound and brush-choked,—up and down, through or over all these obstacles they had now to force a passage, cutting here, digging there; now double-locking the wheels of their wagons to prevent their crashing down some steep incline; now putting five teams to one load to haul it up the rock-strewn side of some water-way.

From Echo Cañon they went down the Weber, then toward East Cañon, a dozen of the bearded host going forward with spades and axes as sappers. Sometimes they made a mile in five hours; sometimes they were less lucky. But at length they were fighting their way up the choked East Cañon, starting fierce gray wolves from their lairs in the rocks and hearing at every rod of their hard-fought way the swift and unnerving song of the coiled rattlesnake.

Eight fearful miles they toiled through this gash in the mountain; then over another summit,—Big Mountain; down this dangerous slide, all wheels double-locked, on to the summit of another lofty hill,—Little Mountain; and abruptly down again into the rocky gorge afterwards to become historic as Immigration Cañon.

Following down this gorge, never doubting they should come at last to their haven, they found its mouth to be impassable. Rocks, brush, and timber choked the way. Crossing to the south side, they went sheerly up the steep hill—so steep that it was all but impossible for the straining animals to drag up the heavy wagons, and so narrow that a false step might have dashed wagon and team half a thousand feet on to the rocks below.

But at last they stood on the summit,—and broke into shouts of rapture as they looked. For the wilderness home of Israel had been found. Far and wide below them stretched their promised land,—a broad, open valley hemmed in by high mountains that lay cold and far and still in the blue haze. Some of these had slept since the world began under their canopies of snow, and these flashed a sunlit glory into the eager eyes of the pilgrims. Others reared bare, scathed peaks above slopes that were shaggy with timber. And out in front lay the wondrous lake,—a shield of deepest glittering turquois held to the dull, gray breast of the valley.

Again and again they cried out, "Hosanna to God and the Lamb!" and many of the bearded host shed tears, for the hardships of the way had weakened them.

Then Brigham came, lying pale and wasted in his wagon, and when they saw him gaze long, and heard him finally say, "Enough—drive on!" they knew that on this morning of July 24, 1847, they had found the spot where in vision he had seen the tent of the Lord come down to earth.

Joel Rae had waited with a beating heart for Brigham's word of confirmation, and when he heard it his soul was filled to overflowing. He knew that here the open vision would enfold him; here the angel of the Lord would come to him fetching his great Witness. Here he would rise to immeasurable zeniths of spirituality. And here his people would become a mighty people of the Lord. He foresaw the hundred unwalled cities that Brigham was to found, and the green gardens that were to make the now desert valley a fit setting for the temple of God. Here was a stricken Rachel, a barren Sarah to be transformed by the touch of the Saints to a mother of many children. Here would the lambs of the Lord be safe at last from the Gentile wolves—safe for a time at least, until so long as it might take the Lions of the Lord to come to their growth. And that was to be no indefinite period; for had not Brigham just said, with a snap of his great jaws and a cold flash of his blue eyes, "Let us alone ten years here, and we'll ask no odds of Uncle Sam or the Devil!"

There on the summit they knelt to entreat the mercy of God upon the land. The next day, by their leader's direction, they consecrated the valley to the Lord, and planted six acres of potatoes.

Chapter XI
Another Miracle and a Temptation in the Wilderness

The floor of the valley was an arid waste, flat and treeless, a far sweep of gray and gold, of sage-brush spangled with sunflowers, patched here and there with glistening beds of salt and soda, or pools of the deadly alkali. Here crawled the lizard and the rattlesnake; and there was no music to the desolation save the petulant chirp of the cricket. At the sides an occasional stream tumbled out of the mountains to be all but drunk away at once by the thirsty sands. Along the banks of these was the only green to be found, sparse fringes of willow and wild rose. On the borders of the valley, where the steeps arose, were little patches of purple and dusty brown, oak-bush, squaw-berry, a few dwarfed cedars, and other scant growths. At long intervals could be found a marsh of wire-grass, or a few acres of withered bunch-grass. But these served only to emphasise the prevailing desert tones.

The sun-baked earth was so hard that it broke their ploughs when they tried to turn it. Not until they had spread water upon it from the river they had named Jordan could the ploughs be used. Such was the new Canaan, the land held in reserve by the Lord for His chosen people since the foundations of the world were laid.

Dreary though it was, they were elated. Had not a Moses led them out of bondage up into this chamber of the mountains against the day of wrath that was to consume the Gentile world? And would he not smite the rocks for water? Would he not also be a Joshua to sit in judgment and divide to Israel his inheritance?

They waited not nor demurred, but fell to work. Within a week they had explored the valley and its cañons, made a road to the timber eight miles away, built a saw-pit, sawed lumber for a skiff, ploughed, planted, and irrigated half a hundred acres of the parched soil, and begun the erection of many dwellings, some of logs, some of adobes. Ground had also been chosen and consecrated by Brigham, whereon, in due time, they would build up their temple to the God of Jacob.

Meantime, they would continue to gather out of Babylon. During the late summer and fall many wagons arrived from the Missouri, so that by the beginning of winter their number was nearly two thousand. They lived rudely, a lucky few in the huts they had built; more in tents and wagon-boxes. Nor did they fail to thank Providence for the mild winter vouchsafed to them during this unprotected period, permitting them not only to survive, but to continue their labours—of logging, home-building, the making of rough furniture, and the repairing of wagons and tools.

When the early spring came they were again quickly at the land with their seeds. Over five thousand acres were sown to needful produce. When this began to sprout with every promise of a full harvest, their joy was boundless; for their stock of breadstuffs and provisions had fallen low during the winter, and could not last later than harvest-time, even with rigid economy.

But early in June, in the full flush of this springtide of promise, it appeared that the Lord was minded to chasten them. For into their broad, green fields came the ravenous crickets in wide, black streams down the mountain sides. Over the growing grain they spread as a pall, and the tender sprouts were consumed to the ground. In their track they left no stalk nor growing blade.

Starvation now faced the Saints. In their panic they sought to fight the all-devouring pest. While some went wildly through the fields killing the crickets, others ran trenches and tried to drown them. Still others beat them back with sticks and brooms, or burned them by fires set in the fields. But against the oncoming horde these efforts were unavailing. Where hundreds were destroyed hundreds of thousands appeared.

Despair seized the Saints, the bitter despair of a cheated, famished people—deluded even by their God. In their shorn fields they wept and cursed, knowing at last they could not stay the pest.

Then into the fields came Joel Rae, rebuking the frenzied men and women. The light of a high faith was upon him as he called out to them:

"Have I not preached to you all winter the way to salvation in times like this? Does faith mean one thing in my mouth and another thing here? Why waste yourselves with those foolish tricks of fire and water? They only make you forget Jehovah—you fools—you poor, blind fools—to palter so!"

He raised his voice, and the wondering group about him grew large.

"Down, down on your knees and pray—pray—pray! I tell you the Lord shall *not* suffer you to perish!"

Then, as but one or two obeyed him—

"So your hearts have been hardened? Then my own prayer shall save you!"

Down he knelt in the midst of the group, while they instinctively drew back from him on all sides. But as his voice rose, a voice that had never failed to move them, they, too, began to kneel, at first those near him, then others back of them, until a hundred knelt about him.

He had not observed them, but with eyes closed he prayed on, pouring out his heart in penitent supplication.

"These people are but little children, after all, seeing not, groping blindly, attempting weakly, blundering always, yet never faltering in love for Thee. Now I, Thy servant, humble and lowly, from whom Thou hast already taken in hardest ways all that his heart held dear, who will to-day give his body to be crucified, if need be, for this people—I implore Thee to save these blundering children now, in this very moment. I ask nothing for myself but that—"

As his words rang out, there had been quick, low, startled murmurs from the kneeling group about him; and now loud shouts interrupted his prayer. He opened his eyes. From off toward the lake great flocks of gulls had appeared, whitening the sky, and now dulling all other sounds with the beating of their wings and their high, plaintive cries. Quickly they settled upon the fields in swirling drifts, so that the land all about lay white as with snow.

A groan went up,—"They will finish what the crickets have left."

He had risen to his feet, looking intently. Then he gave an exultant shout.

"No! No!—they are eating only the *crickets*!—the white birds are devouring the black pests; the hosts of heaven and hell have met, and the powers of light have triumphed once more over darkness! *Pray*—pray now with all your hearts in thanksgiving for this mercy!"

And again they knelt, many with streaming eyes, while he led them in a prayer of gratitude for this wondrous miracle.

All day long the white birds fed upon the crickets, and when they left at night the harvest had been saved. Thus had Heaven vouchsafed a second miracle to the Lute of the Holy Ghost. It is small wonder then if his views of the esteem in which he was held by that power were now greatly enlarged.

In August, thanks to the Heaven-sent gulls, they were able to celebrate with a feast their first "Harvest Home." In the centre of the big stockade a bowery was built, and under its shade tables were spread and richly laden with the first fruits their labours had won from the desert,—white bread and golden butter, green corn, watermelons, and many varieties of vegetables. Hoisted on poles for exhibition were immense sheaves of wheat, rye, barley, and oats, coaxed from the arid level with the water they had cunningly spread upon it.

There were prayers and public thanksgiving, songs and speeches and dancing. It was the flush of their first triumph over the desert. Until nightfall the festival lasted, and at its close Elder Rae stood up to address them on the subject of their past trials and present blessings. The silence was instant, and the faces were all turned eagerly upon him, for it was beginning to be suspected that he had more than even priestly power.

"To-day," he said, "the favour and blessing of God have been manifest upon us. But let us not forget our debts and duties in this feasting of the flesh. Afflictions are necessary to humble and prove us, and we shall have them as often as they are needed. Oh, never doubt it! I have, indeed, but one fear concerning this people in the valleys of the mountains—but one trembling fear in the nerves of my spirit—and that is lest we do not live the religion we profess. If we will only cleave to that faith in our practise, I tell you we are at the defiance of all hell. But if we transgress the law God has given us, and trample His mercies, blessings, and ordinances under our feet, treating them with the indifference I have thought some occasionally do, not realising their sins, I tell you that in consequence we shall be overcome, and the Lord will let us be again smitten and scattered. Take it to heart. May the God of heaven fill you with the Holy Ghost and give you light and joy in His Kingdom."

When he was done many pressed forward to take his hand, the young and the old, for they had both learned to reverence him.

Near the outer edge of the throng was a red-lipped Juno, superbly rounded, who had gleaned in the fields until she was all a Gipsy brown, and her movements of a Gipsy grace in their freeness. She did not greet the young Elder as did the others, seeming, indeed, to be unconscious of his presence. Yet she lingered near as they scattered off into the dusk, in little groups or one by one; and still she stood there when all were gone, now venturing just a glance at him from deep gray eyes set under black brows, turning her splendid head a little to bring him into view. He saw the figure and came forward, peeringly.

"Mara Cavan—yes, yes, so it is!" He took her hand, somewhat timidly, an observer would have said. "Your father is not able to be out? I shall walk down with you to see him—if you're ready now."

She had been standing much like a statue, in guarded restraint, but at his words and the touch of his hand she seemed to melt and flow into eager acquiescence, murmuring some hurried little words of thanks for her father, and stepping by his side with eyes down.

They went out into the soft summer night, past the open doors where rejoicing groups still lingered, the young standing, the old sitting in chairs by the doors of their huts. Then they were out of the stockade and off toward the southern end of the settlement. A big, golden moon had come up over the jagged edge of the eastern hills,—a moon that left the valley in a mystic sheen of gold and blue, and threw their shadows madly into one as they walked. They heard the drowsy chirp of the cricket, now harmless, and the low cry of an owl. They felt the languorous warmth of the night, spiced with a hint of chilliness, and they felt each other near. They had felt this nearness before. One of them had learned to fear it, to tremble for himself at the thought of it. The other had learned to dream of it, and to long for it, and to wonder why it should be denied.

Now, as they stepped side by side, their hands brushed together, and he caught hers in his grasp, turning to look full upon her. Her ecstasy was poignant; she trembled in her walk. But she looked straight ahead,—waiting. To both of them it seemed that the earth rocked under their feet. He looked long at her profile, softened in the magic light. She felt his eyes upon her, and still she waited, in a trembling ecstasy, stepping closely by his side. She felt him draw a long breath, and then another, quickly,—and then he spoke.

In words that were well-chosen but somewhat hurried, he proceeded to instruct her in the threefold character of the Godhead. The voice at first was not like his own, but as he went on it grew steadier. After she drew her hand gently out of his, which she presently did, it seemed to regain its normal pitch and calmness.

He saw her to the door of the cabin on the outskirts of the settlement, and there he spoke a few words of cheer to her ailing father.

Then he was off into the desert, pacing swiftly into the grim, sandy solitude beyond the farthest cabin light and the bark of the outmost watch-dog. Feverishly he walked, and far, until at last, as if naught in himself could avail, he threw himself to the ground and prayed.

"Keep me *good*! Keep me to my vows! Help me till my own strength grows, for I am weak and wanting. Let me endure the pain until this wicked fire within me hath burned itself out. Keep me for *her*!"

Back where the houses were, in the shadow of one of them, was the flushed, full-breathing woman, hurt but dumb, wondering, in her bruised tenderness, why it must be so.

Still farther back, inside the stockade, where the gossiping groups yet lingered, they were saying it was strange that Elder Rae waited so long to take him a wife or two.

Chapter XII
A Fight for Life

The stream of Saints to the Great Basin had become well-nigh continuous—Saints of all degrees of prosperity, from Parley Pratt, the Archer of Paradise, with his wealth of wives, wagons, and cattle, to Barney Bigler, unblessed with wives or herds, who put his earthly goods on a wheelbarrow, and, to the everlasting glory of God, trundled it from the Missouri River to the valley of the Great Salt Lake. Train after train set out for the new Zion with faith that God would drop manna before them.

Each train was a little migrating State in itself. And never was the natural readiness of the American pioneer more luminously displayed. At every halt of the wagons a shoemaker would be seen searching for a lapstone; a gunsmith would be mending a rifle, and weavers would be at their wheels or looms. The women early discovered that the jolting wagons would churn their cream to butter; and for bread, very soon after the halt was made, the oven hollowed out of the hillside was heated, and the dough, already raised, was in to bake. One mother in Israel brought proudly to the Lake a piece of cloth, the wool for which she had sheared, dyed, spun, and woven during her march.

Nor did the marches ever cease to be fraught with peril and, hardship. There were tempests, droughts, famines, stampedes of the stock, prairie fires, and Indian forays. Hundreds of miles across the plain and through the mountains the Indians would trail after them, like sharks in the wake of a ship, tirelessly watching, waiting for the right moment to stampede the stock, to fire the prairie, or to descend upon stragglers.

One by one the trains worked down into the valley, the tired Saints making fresh their covenants by rebaptism as they came. In the waters of the River Jordan, Joel Rae made hundreds to be renewed in the Kingdom, swearing them to obey Brigham, the Lord's anointed, in all his orders, spiritual or temporal, and the priesthood or either of them, and all church authorities in like manner; to regard this obligation as superior to all laws of the United States and all earthly laws whatsoever; to cherish enmity against the government of the United States, that the blood of Joseph Smith and the

Apostles slain in that generation might be avenged; and to keep the matter of this oath a profound secret then and forever. And from these waters of baptism the purified Saints went to their inheritances in Zion—took their humble places, and began to sweat and bleed in the upbuilding of the new Jerusalem.

"*I'M* THE ONE WILL HAVE TO BE CAUGHT"

From a high, tented wagon in one such train, creaking its rough way down Emigration Cañon, with straining oxen and tired but eager people, there had leaped one late afternoon the girl whose eyes were to call to him so potently,—incomparable eyes, large and deep, of a velvety grayness, under black brows splendidly bent. Nor had the eyes alone voiced that call to his starved senses. He had caught the free, fearless confidence of her leap over the wheel, and her graceful abandon as she stood there, finely erect and full-curved, her head with its Greek lines thrown well back, and her strong hands raised to readjust the dusky hair that tumbled about her head like a storm-cloud.

Men from the train were all about, and others from the settlement, and these spoke to her, some in serious greeting, some with jesting words. She returned it all in good part without embarrassment,—even the sally of the winking wag who called out, "Now then, Mara Cavan! Here we are, and a girl like yourself ought to catch an Elder, at the very lowest."

She laughed with easy good-nature, still fumbling in the dusk of blown hair at the back of her head, showing a full-lipped mouth, beautifully large, with strong-looking, white teeth. "I'll catch never a one myself, if you please, Nathan Tanner! I'll do no catching at *all*, now! *I'm* the one will have to be caught!"

Her voice was a contralto, with the little hint of roughness that made it warm and richly golden; that made it fall, indeed, upon the ears of the listening Elder like a cathedral chime calling him to forget all and worship— forget all but that he was five and twenty with the hot blood surging and crowding and crying out in his veins.

Now, having a little subdued the tossing storm-cloud of hair, she stood with one hand upon her hip and the other shading her eyes, looking intently into the streets of the new settlement. And again there was bantering jest from the men about, and the ready, careless response from her, with gestures of an impishly reckless unconcern, of a full readiness to give and take in easy good-fellowship. But then, in the very midst of a light response to one of the bantering men, her gray eyes met for the first time the very living look of the young Elder standing near. She was at once confused, breaking off her speech with an awkward laugh, and looking down. But, his eyes keeping steadily upon her, she, as if defiantly, returned his look for a fluttering second, trying to make her eyes survey him slowly from head to foot with her late cool carelessness; but she had to let them fall again, and he saw the colour come under the clear skin.

He knew by these tokens that he possessed a power over this splendid woman that none of the other men could wield,—she had lowered her eyes to no other but him—and all the man in him sang exultantly under the knowledge. He greeted her father, the little Seumas Cavan of indomitable spirit, fresh, for all his march of a thousand miles, and he welcomed them both to Zion. Again and again while he talked to them he caught quick glances from the wonderful eyes;—glances of interest, of inquiry,—now of half-hearted defiance, now of wondering submission.

The succeeding months had been a time of struggle with him—a struggle to maintain his character of Elder after the Order of Melchisedek in the full gaze of those velvety gray eyes, and in the light of her reckless, full-lipped smile; to present to the temptress a shield of austere piety which her softest glances should not avail to melt. For something in her manner told him that she divined all his weakness; that, if she acknowledged his power over her, she recognised her own power over him, a power equal to and justly balancing the other. Even when he discoursed from the pulpit, his glance would fasten upon hers, as if there were but the one face before him instead of a thousand, and he knew that she mocked him in her heart; knew she divined there was that within him which strongly would have had her and himself far away—alone.

Nor was the girl's own mind all of a piece. For, if she flaunted herself before him, as if with an impish resolve to be his undoing, there were still times when he awed her by his words of fire, and by his high, determined stand in some circle to which she knew she could never mount. That night when he walked with her in the moonlight, she knew he had trembled on the edge of the gulf fixed so mysteriously between them. She had even felt herself leaning over to draw him down with her own warm arms; and then all at once he had strangely moved away, widening this mysterious gulf that always separated them, leaving her solitary, hurt, and wondering. She could not understand it. Life called through them so strongly. How could he breast the mighty rush? And why, why must it be so?

During the winter that now came upon them, it became even a greater wonder to her; for it was a time when all of them were drawn closer in a common suffering—a time of dark days which she felt they might have lightened for each other, and a time when she knew that more than ever she drew him.

For hardly had the feast of the Harvest Home gone by when food once more became scarce. The heaven-sent gulls had, after all, saved but half a crop. Drought and early frost had diminished this; and those who came in from the East came all too trustingly with empty meal-sacks.

By the beginning of winter there were five thousand people in the valley to be fed with miraculous loaves and fishes. Half of these were without decent shelter, dwelling under wagon-covers or in flimsy tents, and forced much of the time to be without fuel; for wood had to be hauled through the snow from the distant cañons, and so was precious stuff. For three months the cutting winds came down from the north, and the pitiless winter snows raged about them. An inventory was early taken of the food-stuffs, and thereafter rations were issued alike to all, whether rich or poor. Otherwise many of the latter must have perished. It was a time of hard expedients, such as men are content to face only for the love of God. They ranged the hills and benches to dig sego and thistle roots, and in the last days of winter many took the rawhides from their roofs, boiling and eating them. When spring came, they watched hungrily for the first green vegetation, which they gathered and cooked. Truly it seemed they had stopped in a desert as cruel in its way as the human foes from whom they had fled.

It was now that the genius of their leader showed. He was no longer Brigham Young, the preacher, but a father in Israel to his starving children.

When prayers availed not for a miracle, his indomitable spirit saved them. Starvation was upon them and nakedness to the blast; yet when they desponded or complained, the Lion of the Lord was there to check them. He scolded, pleaded, threatened, roared prophecies, and overcame them, silencing every murmur. He made them work, and worked himself, a daily example before them of tireless energy. He told them what to do, and how, both for their material salvation and their spiritual; when to haul wood, and how to distinguish between false and true spirits; how to thatch roofs and in what manner the resurrection would occur; how to cook thistle roots to best advantage, and how God was man made perfect; he reminded them of the day of wrath, and told them mirthful anecdotes to make them laugh. He pictured God's anger upon the sinful, and encouraged them to dance and to make merry; instructed them in the mysteries of the Kingdom and instigated theatrical performances to distract their minds. He was bland and bullying by turns; affable and gruff; jocose and solemn—always what he thought their fainting spirits needed. He was feared and loved—feared first. They learned to dread the iron of his hand and the steel of his heart—the dauntless spirit of him that left them no longer their own masters, yet kept them loving their bondage. Through the dreadful cold and famine, the five thousand of them ceased not to pray nor lost their faith—their great faith that they had been especially favoured of God and were at the last to be saved alone from the wreck of the world.

The efforts of Brigham to put heart into the people were ably seconded by Joel Rae. He was loved like Brigham, but not feared. He preached like Brigham submission to the divine will as interpreted by the priesthood, but he was more extravagant than Brigham in his promises of blessings in store for them. He never resorted to vagueness in his pictures of what the Lord was about to do for them. He was literal and circumstantial to a degree that made Brigham and the older men in authority sometimes writhe in public and chide him in private. They were appalled at the sweeping victories he promised the Saints over the hated Gentiles at an early day. They suggested, too, that the Lord might withhold an abundance from them for a few years until He had more thoroughly tried them. But their counsel seemed only to inflame him to fresh absurdities. In the very days of their greatest scarcity that winter, when almost every man was dressed in skins, and the daily fare was thistle roots, he declared to them at a Sunday service:

"A time of plenty is at hand—of great plenty. I cannot tell you how I know these things. I do not know how they come to me. I pray—and they come to life in my spirit; that is how I have found this fact: in less than a year States-goods of all needed kinds will be sold here cheaper than they can be bought in Eastern cities. You shall have an abundance at prices that will amaze you."

And the people thrilled to hear him, partaking of his faith, remembering the gulls that ate the crickets, and the rain and wind that came to save the pioneer train from fire. To the leaders such prophesying was merely reckless, inviting further chastisements from heaven, and calculated to cause a loss of faith in the priesthood.

And yet, wild as it was, they saw this latter prophecy fulfilled; for now, so soon after the birth of this new empire, while it suffered and grew weak and bade fair to perish in its cradle of faith, there was made for it a golden spoon of plenty.

Over across the mountains the year before, on the decayed granite bed-rock of the tail-race at the mill of one Sutter, a man had picked up a few particles of gold, the largest as big as grains of wheat. The news of the wonder had spread to the East, and now came frenzied hordes of gold-seekers. The valley of the mountains where the Saints had hoped to hide was directly in their path, and there they stopped their richly laden trains to rest and to renew their supplies.

The harvest of '49 was bountiful in all the valley; and thus was the wild prophecy of Joel Rae made sober truth. Many of the gold-seekers had loaded their wagons with merchandise for the mining' camps; but in their haste to be at the golden hills, they now sold it at a sacrifice in order to lighten their loads. The movement across the Sierras became a wild race; clothing, provisions, tools, and arms—things most needful to the half-clad, half-starved community on the shores of the lake—were bartered to them at less than half-price for fresh horses and light wagons. Where a twenty-five dollar pack-mule was sold for two hundred dollars, a set of joiner's tools that had cost a hundred dollars back in St. Louis would be bought for twenty-five.

The next year the gain to the Saints was even greater, as the tide of gold-seekers rose. Early that summer they sold flour to the oncoming legions for a dollar a pound, taking their pay in the supplies they most needed on almost their own terms.

Thus was the valley of the mountains a little fattened, and thus was Joel Rae exalted in the sight of men as one to whom the secrets of heaven might at any time be unfolded. But the potent hand of Brigham was still needed to hold the Saints in their place and in their faith.

Many would have joined the rush for sudden riches. A few did so. Brigham issued a mild warning, in which such persons were described as "gainsayers in behalf of Mammon." They were warned, also, that the valley of the Sacramento was unhealthful, and that, in any event, "the true use of gold is for paving streets, covering houses, and making culinary dishes; and when the Saints shall have preached the gospel, raised grain, and built cities enough, the Lord will open up the way for a supply of gold to the satisfaction of his people."

A few greed-stung Saints persisted in leaving in the face of this friendly admonition. Then the Lion of the Lord roared: "Let such men remember that they are not wanted in our midst. Let them leave their carcasses where they do their work. We want not our burying-grounds polluted with such hypocrites. Let the souls of them go down to hell, poverty-stricken and naked, and lie there until they are burned out like an old pipe!" The defections ceased from that moment, and Zion was preserved intact. Brigham was satisfied. If he could hold them together under the alluring tales of gold-finds that were brought over the mountains, he had no longer any fear that they might fall away under mere physical hardship. And he held them,—the supreme test of his power over the bodies and minds of his people.

This passing of the gold-seekers was not, however, a blessing without drawbacks. For the Saints had hoped to wax strong unobserved, unmolested, forgotten, in this mountain retreat. But now obscurity could no longer be their lot. The hated Gentiles had again to be reckoned with.

First, the United States had expanded on the west to include their territory—the fruit of the Mexican War—the poor bleak desert they were making to blossom. Next, the government at Washington had sent to construe and administer their laws men who were aliens from the Commonwealth of Israel. True, Millard Fillmore had appointed Brigham governor of the new Territory—but there were chief justices and associate justices, secretaries, attorneys, marshals, and Indian agents from the wicked and benighted East; men who frankly disbelieved that the voice of Brigham was as the voice of God, and who did not hesitate to let their heresy be known. A stream of these came and went—trouble-mongers who despised and insulted the Saints, and returned to Washington with calumnies on their lips. It was true that Brigham had continued, as was right, to be the only power in the Territory; but the narrow-minded appointees of the Federal government persisted in misconstruing this circumstance; refusing to look upon it as the just mark of Heaven's favour, and declaring it to be the arrogance of a mere civil usurper.

Under such provocation Joel Rae longed more than ever to be a Lion of the Lord, for those above him in the Church endured too easily, he considered, the indignities that were put upon them by these evil-minded Gentile politicians. He would have rejected them forthwith, as he believed the Lord would have had them do,—nay, as he believed the Lord would sooner or later punish them for not doing. He would have thrust them into the desert, and called upon the Lord for strength to meet the storm that would doubtless be raised by such a course. He was impatient when the older men cautioned moderation and the petty wiles of diplomacy. Yet he was not altogether discouraged; for even they lost patience at times, and were almost as outspoken as he could have wished.

Even Brigham, on one notable occasion, had thrilled him, when in the tabernacle he had bearded Brocchus and left him white and cowering before all the people, trembling for his life,—Brocchus, the unworthy Associate Justice, who had derided their faith, insulted their prophet, and slandered their women. How he rejoiced in that moment when Brigham for once lost his temper and let his eyes flash their hate upon the frightened official.

"But you," Brigham had roared, "standing there white and shaking at the hornets' nest you have stirred up—you are a coward—and that is why you praise men that are not cowards—why you praise Zachary Taylor!"

Brigham had a little time before declared that Zachary Taylor was dead and in hell, and that he, Brigham, was glad of it.

"President Taylor you can't praise," he had gone on to the gradually whitening Brocchus. "What was he? A mere soldier with regular army buttons on—no better to go at the head of troops than a dozen men I could pick up between Leavenworth and Laramie. As to what you have intimated about our morals—you miserable cringing coward, you—I won't notice it except to make my personal request of every brother and husband present not to give your back what your impudence deserves. You talk of things you have on hearsay since you came among us. I'll talk of hearsay, then—the hearsay that you are mad and will go home because we can't make it worth your while to stay. What it would satisfy you to get out of us it wouldn't be hard to tell; but I know it's more than you'll get. We don't want you. You are such a baby-calf that we would have to sugar your soap to coax you to wash yourself on Saturday night. Go home to your mammy, straightaway, and the sooner the better."

This was the manner, thought Joel Rae, that Federal officials should be treated when they were out of sympathy with Zion—though he thought he might perhaps have chosen words that would be more dignified had the task been entrusted to him. He told Brigham his satisfaction with the address when the excited congregation had dispersed, and the alarmed Brocchus had gone.

"That is the course we must take, Brother Brigham—do more of it. Unless we take our stand now against aggression, the Lord will surely smite us again with famine and pestilence." And Brigham had answered, in the tones of a man who knows, "Wait just a little!"

But there came famine upon them again; in punishment, declared Joel Rae, for their ungodly temporising with the minions of the United States government. In '54 the grasshoppers ate their growing crops. In '55 they came again with insatiate maws—and on what they left the drought and frost worked their malignant spells. The following winter great numbers of their cattle and sheep perished on the range in the heavy snows.

The spring of '56 found them again digging roots and resorting to all the old pitiful makeshifts of famine.

"This," declared Joel Rae, to the starving people, "is a judgment of Heaven upon us for permitting Gentile aggression. It is meant to clench into our minds the God's truth that we must stand by our faith with the arms of war if need be."

"Brother Rae is just a little mite soul-proud," Brigham thereupon confided to his counsellors, "and I wouldn't wonder if the Lord would be glad to see some of it taken out of him. Anyway, I've got a job for him that will just about do it."

Chapter XIII
Joel Rae Is Treated for Pride of Soul

Brigham sent for him the next day and did him the honour to entrust to him an important mission. He was to go back to the Missouri River and bring on one of the hand-cart parties that were to leave there that summer. The three years of famine had left the Saints in the valley poor, so that the immigration fund was depleted. The oncoming Saints, therefore, who were not able to pay their own way, were this summer, instead of riding in ox-carts, to walk across the plains and mountains, and push their belongings before them in hand-carts. It had become Brigham's pet scheme, and the Lord had revealed to him that it would work out auspiciously. Joel prepared to obey, though it was not without aversion that he went again to the edge of the Gentile country.

He was full of bitterness while he was obliged to tarry on the banks of the Missouri. The hatred of those who had persecuted him and his people, bred into him from boyhood, flashed up in his heart with more fire than ever. Even when a late comer from Nauvoo told him that Prudence Corson had married Captain Girnway of the Carthage Grays, two years after the exodus from Nauvoo, his first feeling was one of blazing anger against the mobocrats rather than regret for his lost love.

"They moved down to Jackson County, Missouri, too," concluded his informant, thus adding to the flame. They had gone to set up their home in the very Zion that the Gentiles with so much bloodshed had wrested from the Saints.

Even when the first anger cooled and he could face the thing calmly in all its deeper aspects, he was still very bitter. While he had stanchly kept himself for her, cherishing with a single heart all the old memories of her dearness, she had been a wife these seven years,—the wife, moreover, of a mob-leader whose minions had put them out of their home, and then wantonly tossed his father like a dead branch into the waters. She had loved this uniformed murderer—his little Prue—perhaps borne him children, while he, Joel Rae, had been all too scrupulously true to her memory, fighting against even the pleased look at a woman; fighting—only the One above could know with what desperate valour—against the warm-hearted girl with the gray eyes and the red lips, who laughed in her knowledge that she drew him—fighting her away for a sentimental figment, until she had married another.

Now when he might have let himself turn to her, his heart freed of the image of that yellow-haired girl so long cherished, this other was the wife of Elder Pixley—the fifth wife—and an unloving wife as he knew.

She had sought him before the marriage, and there had been some wholly frank and simple talk between them. It had ended by his advising her to marry Elder Pixley so that she might be saved into the Kingdom, and by her replying, with the old reckless laugh, a little dry and strained, and with the wonderful gray eyes full upon him,—"Oh, I'll marry him! Small difference to me what man of them I marry at all,—now!"

And while he, by a mighty effort, had held down his arms and let her turn away, the woman for whose memory he did it was the wife of an enemy, caring nothing for his fidelity, sure to feel not more than amused pity for him should she ever know of it. Surely, it had been a brave struggle—for nothing.

But again the saving thought came that he was being tried for a purpose, for some great work. And now it seemed that the time of it must be near. As to what it was there could be little question: it must be to free his people forever from Gentile aggression or interference. Everything pointed to that. He was to be entrusted with great powers, and be made a Lion of the Lord to lead them to their rightful glory.

He was eager to be back to the mountains where he could fitly receive this new power, and becomingly make it known that he had been chosen of Heaven to free them forever from the harassing Gentile. He felt instinctively that a climax was close at hand—some dread moment of turning that would try the faith of the Saints once for all—try his own faith as well, and at last bring his great Witness before him, if his soul should survive the perilous ordeal. For he had never ceased to wait for this heavenly Witness— something he needed—he knew not what—some great want of his soul unsatisfied despite all the teachings of the temple priesthood. The hunger gnawed in his heart,—a hunger that only his Witness could feed.

When the hand-cart party came in across the prairies of Iowa he made all haste to be off with it to the valley of the Lake. Several such parties had left the Missouri earlier in the season. His own was to be the last. There were six hundred of them, young and old, men, women, and children. Their carts moved on two light wheels with two projecting shafts of hickory joined by a cross-piece. He was indignant to learn that the Gentiles along the route of their march across Iowa had tried to beguile these people from their faith. And even while they were in camp on the Missouri there were still ungodly ones to warn them that they were incurring grave dangers by starting across the plains so late in the season.

With rare fervour he rallied the company from these attacks, pointed out the divine source of the hand-cart plan, prophesied blessings and abundance upon them for their faith in starting, and dwelt warningly upon the sin they would be guilty of should they disobey their leader and refuse to start.

They responded bravely, and by the middle of August all was ready for the march. He divided them into hundreds, allotting to each hundred five tents, twenty hand-carts, and one wagon, drawn by three yokes of oxen, to carry the tents and provisions. Families with more young men than were needed to push their own carts helped families not so well provided; but many carts had to be pushed by young girls and women.

He put the company on rations at the time of starting; ten ounces of flour to each adult, four ounces to children, with bacon, sugar, coffee, and rice served occasionally; for he had been unable to obtain a full supply of provisions. Even in the first days of the march some of the men would eat their day's allowance for breakfast, depending on the generosity of settlers by the way, so long as there were any, for what food they had until another morning. They were sternly rebuked by their leader for thus, without shame, eating the bread of ungodliness.

Their first trouble after leaving the Missouri was with the carts; their construction in all its details had been dictated from on high, but the dust of the parched prairie sifted into the wooden hubs, and ground the axles so that they broke.-This caused delay for repairs, and as there was no axle grease, many of them, hungry as they were, used their scanty allowance of bacon to grease the wheels.

Yet in spite of these hardships they were cheerful, and in the early days of the march they sang with spirit, to the tune of "A Little More Cider," the hymn of the hand-cart written by one of their number:

"Hurrah for the Camp of Israel! Hurrah for the hand-cart scheme! Hurrah, hurrah! 'tis better far Than the wagon and ox-team. "Oh, our faith goes with the hand-carts, And they have our hearts' best love; 'Tis a novel mode of travelling Designed by the Gods above. "And Brigham's their executive, He told us their design; And the Saints are proudly marching on Along the hand-cart line. "Who cares to go with the wagons? Not we who are free and strong. Our faith and arms with a right good will Shall push our carts along."

At Wood River the plains seethed with buffalo, a frightened herd of which one night caused a stampede of their cattle. After that the frail carts had to relieve the wagons of a part of their loads, in order that the remaining animals could draw them, each cart taking on a hundred more pounds.

Thus, overworked and insufficiently fed, they pushed valiantly on under burning suns, climbing the hills and wading the streams with their burdens, the vigorous in the van. For a mile behind the train straggled the lame and the sick. Here would be an aged sire in Israel walking painfully, supported by a son or daughter; there a mother carrying a child at her breast, with others holding by her skirts; a few went on crutches.

As they toiled painfully forward in this wise, they were heartened by a visit from a number of Elders who overtook them in returning to the valley. These good men counselled them to be faithful, prayerful, and obedient to their leader in all things, prophesying that they should reach Zion in safety,—that though it might storm on their right and on their left, the Lord would open their way before them. They cried "Amen!" to this, and, at the request of the Elders, killed one of their few remaining cattle for them, cheering them as they drove on in the morning in their carriages.

They took up the march with new courage; but then in a few days came a new danger to threaten them,—the cold. A rule made by Brigham had limited each cart's outfit of clothing and bedding to seventeen pounds. This had now become insufficient. As they advanced up the Sweetwater, the mountains on either side took on snow. Frequent wading of the streams chilled them. Morning would find them numb, haggard, spiritless, unfitted for the march of the day.

A week of this cold weather, lack of food, and overwork produced their effect. The old and the weak became too feeble to walk; then they began to die, peacefully, smoothly, as a lamp ceases to burn when the oil is gone. At first the deaths occurred irregularly; then they were frequent; soon it was rarely that they left a camp-ground without burying one or more of their number.

Nor was death long confined to the old and the infirm. Young men, strong at the start, worn out now by the rigours of the march, began to drop. A father would pull his cart all day, perhaps with his children in it, and die at night when camp was reached. Each day lessened their number.

But they died full of faith, murmuring little, and having for their chief regret, apparently, that they must be left on the plains or mountains, instead of resting in the consecrated ground of Zion—this, and that they must die without looking upon the face of their prophet, seer, and revelator.

Their leader cheered them as best he could. He was at first puzzled at the severity of their hardships in the face of past prophecies. But light at last came to him. He stopped one day to comfort a wan, weak man who had halted in dejection by the road.

"You have had trouble?" he asked him, and the man had answered, wearily:

"No, not what you could call trouble. When we left Florence my mother could walk eighteen or twenty miles a day. She did it for weeks. But then she wore out, and I had to haul her in my cart; but it was only for three days. She gave up and died before we started out, the morning of the fourth day. We buried her by the roadside without a coffin—that was hard, to put her old, gray head right down into the ground with no protection. It made us mourn, for she had always been such a good friend. Then we went on a few days, and my sister gave out. I carried her in the cart a few days, but she died too. Then my youngest child, Ephraim, died. Then I fell sick myself, and my wife has pushed the cart with me in it for two days. She looked so tired to-day that I got out to rest her. But we don't call it trouble, only for the cold—my wife has a chill every time she has to wade one of those icy streams. She's not very used to rough life."

As he listened to the man's tale, the truth came to him in a great light. Famine not sufficing, the Lord was sending this further affliction upon them. He was going to goad them into asserting and maintaining their independence of his enemies, the Gentiles. The inspiration of this thought nerved him anew. Though they all died, to the last child, he would live to carry back to Zion the message that now burned within him. They had temporised with the Gentile and had grown lax among themselves. They must be aroused to repentance, and God would save him to do the work.

So, when the snow came at last, the final touch of hardship, driving furiously about the unprotected women and children, putting wild fear into the heart of every man, he remained calm and sure and defiant. The next morning the snow lay heavily about them, and they had to dig through it to bury five of their number in one grave. The morning before, they had issued their last ration of flour. Now he divided among the company a little hard bread they had kept, and waited in the snow, for they could travel no further without food.

One of their number was sent ahead to bring aid. After a day in which they ate nothing, supplies reached them from the valley; but now they were so weakened that food could not fortify them against the extreme cold that had set in. They wrapped themselves in their few poor quilts, and struggled bravely on into a white, stinging fog of snow. Each morning there were more and more of them to bury. And even the burial was a mockery, for wolves were digging at the graves almost before the last debilitated straggler had left the camping-place. The heavy snows continued, but movement was necessary. Into the white jaws of the beautiful, merciless demon they went.

Among the papers of a man he helped to bury, Joel Rae found a journal that the dead man had kept until within a few days of his death. By the light of his last candle he read it until late into the night.

"The weather grew colder each day; and many got their feet so badly frozen that they could not walk and had to be lifted from place to place. Some got their fingers frozen; others their ears; and one woman lost her sight by the frost. These severities of the weather also increased our number of deaths, so that we buried several each day.

"The day we crossed the Rocky Ridge it was snowing a little—the wind hard from the northwest, and blowing so keenly that it almost pierced us through. We had to wrap ourselves closely in blankets, quilts, or whatever else we could get, to keep from freezing. Elder Rae this day appointed me to bring up the rear. My duty was to stay behind everything and see that nobody was left along the road. I had to bury a man who had died in my hundred, and I finished doing so after the company had started. In about half an hour I set out on foot alone to do my duty as rear-guard to the camp. The ascent of the ridge commenced soon after leaving camp, and I had not gone far up it before I overtook the carts that the folks could not pull through the snow, here about knee-deep. I helped them along, and we soon overtook another. By all hands getting to one cart we could travel; so we moved one of the carts a few rods, and then went back and brought up the others. After moving in this way for awhile, we overtook other carts at different points of the hill, until we had six carts, not one of which could be moved by the parties owning it. I put our collective strength to three carts at a time, took them a short distance, and then brought up the other three. Thus by travelling over the hill three times—twice forward and once back—I succeeded after hours of toil in bringing my little company to the summit. The carts were then trotted on gaily down-hill, the intense cold stirring us to action.

"One or two parties who were with these carts gave up entirely, and but for the fact that we overtook one of our ox-teams that had been detained on the road, they must have perished on the Rocky Ridge. One old man named James, a farmer from Gloucestershire, who had a large family, and who had worked very hard all the way, I found sitting by the roadside unable to pull his cart any farther. I could not get him into the wagon, as it was already overcrowded. He had a shotgun, which he had brought from England, and which had been a great blessing to him and his family, for he was a good shot, and often had a mess of sage-hens or rabbits for his family. I took the gun from his cart, put a bundle on the end of it, placed it on his shoulder, and started him out with his little boy, twelve years old. His wife and two daughters, older than the boy, took the cart along finely after reaching the summit.

"We travelled along with the ox-team and overtook others, all so laden with the sick and helpless that they moved very slowly. The oxen had almost given out. Some of our folks with carts went ahead of the team, for where the roads were good they could out-travel oxen; but we constantly overtook stragglers, some with carts, some without, who had been unable to keep pace with the body of the company. We struggled along in this weary way until after dark, and by this time our rear numbered three wagons, eight hand-carts, and nearly forty persons.

"With the wagons were Millen Atwood, Levi Savage, and William Woodward, captains of hundreds, faithful men who had worked all the way. We finally came to a stream of water which was frozen over. We could not see where the company had crossed. If at the point where we struck the creek, then it had frozen over since they passed it. We started one team across, but the oxen broke through the ice, and would not go over. No amount of shouting and whipping could induce them to stir an inch. We were afraid to try the other teams, for even could they cross, we could not leave the one in the creek and go on.

"There was no wood in the vicinity, so we could make no fire, and we were uncertain what to do. We did not know the distance to the camp, but supposed it to be three or four miles. After consulting about it, we resolved that some one should go on foot to the camp to inform the captain of our situation. I was selected to perform the duty, and I set out with all speed. In crossing the creek I slipped through the ice and got my feet wet, my boots being nearly worn out. I had not gone far when I saw some one sitting by the roadside. I stopped to see who it was, and discovered the old man, James, and his little boy. The poor old man was quite worn out.

"I got him to his feet and had him lean on me, and he walked a little distance, but not very far. I partly dragged, partly carried, him a short distance farther, but he was quite helpless, and my strength failed me. Being obliged to leave him to go forward on my own errand, I put down a quilt I had wrapped around me, rolled him in it, and told the little boy to walk up and down by his father, and on no account to sit down, or he would be frozen to death. He asked me very bravely why God or Brigham Young had not sent us some food or blankets.

"I again set out for the camp, running all the way and frequently falling down, for there were many obstructions and holes in the road. My boots were frozen stiff, so that I had not the free use of my feet, and it was only by rapid motion that I kept them from being badly frozen. As it was, both feet have been nipped.

"After some time, I came in sight of the camp-fires, which encouraged me. As I neared the camp, I frequently overtook stragglers on foot, all pressing forward slowly. I stopped to speak to each one, cautioning them all against resting, as they would surely freeze to death. Finally, about eleven P.M., I reached the camp almost exhausted. I had exerted myself very much during the day, and had not eaten anything since breakfast. I reported to Elder Rae the situation of the folks behind. He immediately got up some horses, and the boys from the valley started back about midnight to help the ox-teams in. The night was very severe, and many of the animals were frozen. It was five A.M. before the last team reached the camp.

"I told my companions about the old man James and his little boy. They found the little fellow keeping faithful watch over his father, who lay sleeping in my quilt just as I left him. They lifted him into a wagon, still alive, but in a sort of stupor, and he died just as they got him up by the fire. His last words were an inquiry as to the safety of his shotgun.

"There were so many dead and dying that it was decided to lay by for the day. In the forenoon I was appointed to go around the camp and collect the dead. I took with me two young men to assist me in the sad task, and we collected together, of all ages and both sexes, thirteen corpses, all stiffly frozen. We had a large square hole dug, in which we buried these thirteen people, three or four abreast and three deep. When they did not fit in, we put one or two crosswise at the head or feet of the others. We covered them with willows and then with the earth. When we buried these thirteen people, some of their relatives refused to attend the services. They manifested an utter indifference about it. The numbness and cold in their physical natures seemed to have reached the soul, and to have crushed out natural feeling and affection. Had I not myself witnessed it, I could not have believed that suffering could produce such terrible results. But so it was. Two others died during the day, and we buried them in the same big grave, making fifteen in all. Even so it has been better for them than to stay where their souls would have been among the rejected at the day of resurrection.

"But for Elder Rae, our leader, we should all have perished by now. He is at times severe and stern with those who falter, but only for their good. He is all along the line, helping the women, who well-nigh worship him, and urging on the men. He cheers us by prophesying that we shall soon prevail over all conditions and all our enemies. I think he must never sleep and never eat. At all hours of the night he is awake. As to eating, a girl in our hundred, Fidelia, daughter of Jabez Merrismith, who has been much attracted by him and stays near him when she can, called him aside the other day, so she has told me, and gave him a biscuit—*soaked, perfectly soaked, with bacon grease.* She had saved it for many days. He took it and thanked her, but later she saw him giving it to the wife of Henry Glines, who is hauling Henry and the two babies in the cart. She taxed him with not eating it himself; but he told her that she had given him more than bread, which was the power to *give* bread. The *giving* happiness, he told her, is always a little more than the *taking* happiness, even when we are starving. He says the one kind of happiness always keeps a little ahead of the other."

December 1st, the remnant of the caravan reached the city of the Saints. Of six hundred setting out from the Missouri River, over one quarter had died by the way.

And to Joel Rae had now come another mission,—one that would not let him wait, for the spirit was moving him strangely and strongly,—a mission of reformation.

Chapter XIV
How the Saints Were Brought to Repentance

He put his torch to the tinder of irreligion at the first Sunday meeting after his return. There were no premonitions, no warnings, no signs.

A few of the Elders had preceded him to rejoice at the escape of the last hand-cart party from death in the mountains; and Brigham, after giving the newcomers some practical hints about their shelter during the winter now upon them, had invited Elder Rae to address the congregation.

He arose and came uncertainly forward, apparently weak, able hardly to stand without leaning upon the desk in front of him; his face waxen and drawn, hollowed at the cheeks and temples, his long hands thin to transparency. Life was betrayed in him only by the eyes. These burned darkly, far back under his brows, and flashed fiercely, as his glance darted swiftly from side to side.

At first he spoke weakly and slowly, his opening words almost inaudible, so that the throng of people before him leaned forward in sympathetic intentness, and silence became absolute in the great hall except for the high quavering of his tones. But then came a miracle of reinvigoration. Little by little his voice swelled until it was full, sonorous, richly warm and compelling, the words pouring from him with a fluency that enchained. Little by little his leaning, drooping posture of weakness became one of towering strength, the head flung back, the gestures free and potent. Little by little his burning eyes seemed to send their flash and glow through all his body, so that he became a creature of life and fire.

They heard each word now, but still they leaned forward as when he spoke at first, inaudibly—caught thrilled and breathless in his spell, even to the Elders, Priests, and Apostles sitting near him. Nor was his manner alone impressive. His words were new. He was calling them sinners and covenant-breakers, guilty of pride, covetousness, contention, lying, stealing, moral uncleanness—and launching upon them the curse of Israel's God unless they should repent.

"It has been told you again and again," he thundered, "that if you wish to be great in the Kingdom of God you must be good. It has been told you many times, and now I burn the words once more into the bones of your soul, that in this kingdom which the great Elohim has again set up on earth, no man, no woman, can become great without being good, without being true to his integrity, faithful to his trust, full of charity and good works.

"Hear it now: if you do not order your lives to do all the good you can, if you are false to one trust, you shall be stripped naked before Jehovah of all your anticipations of greatness. And you have failed in your work; you have been false to your trust; you have been lax and wicked, and you have temporised, nay, affiliated with Gentiles. I have asked myself if this, after all, may not have been the chief cause of God's present wrath upon us. The flesh is weak. I have had my own hours of wrestling with Satan. We all know his cunning to take shapes that most weaken, beguile, and unman us, and small wonder if many of us succumb. But this other sin is wilful. Not only have Gentile officers, Federal officers, come among us and been let to insult, abuse, calumniate, and to trample upon our most sacred ordinances, but we have consorted, traded, and held relations with the Gentiles that pass by us. You have the term 'winter Mormons,' a generation of vipers who come here, marry your daughters in the fall, rest with you during the winter, and pass on to the gold fields in the spring, never to return. You, yourselves, coined the Godless phrase. But how can you utter it without crimson faces? I tell you now, God is to make a short work upon this earth. His lines are being drawn, and many of you before me will be left outside. The curtains of Zion have been spread, but you are gone beyond their folds. You are no longer numbered in the household of faith. For your weak souls the sealing keys of power have been delivered in vain. You have become waymarks to the kingdom of folly. This is truth I tell you. It has been frozen and starved into me, but it will be burned into you. For your sins, the road between here and the Missouri River is a road between two lines of graves. For your sins, from the little band I have just brought in, one hundred and fifty faithful ones fell asleep by the wayside, and their bodies went to be gnawed by the wolves. How long shall others die for you? Forever, think you? No! Your last day is come. Repent, confess your sins in all haste, be buried again in the waters of baptism, then cast out the Gentile, and throw off his yoke,—and thereafter walk in trembling all your days,—for your wickedness has been great."

Such was the opening gun in what became known as the "reformation." The conditions had been ripe for it, and in that very moment a fever of repentance spread through the two thousand people who had cowered under his words. Alike with the people below, the leaders about him had been fired with his spirit, and when he sat down each of them arose in turn and echoed his words, denouncing the people for their sins and exhorting them to repentance.

After another hour of this excitement, priests and people became alike demoralised, and the meeting broke up in a confusion of terror.

As the doors of the tabernacle flew open, and the Saints pushed out of that stifling atmosphere of denunciation, a cry came to the lips of the dozen that first escaped:

"To the river—the waters of baptism!"

The words were being taken up by others until the cry had run back through the crowd to the leaders, still talking in excited groups about the pulpit. These comprehended when they heard it, and straightway a line of conscience-stricken Saints was headed toward the river.

There in the icy Jordan, on that chill December afternoon, when the snows lay thick on the ground, the leaders stood and buried the sinful ones anew in the cleansing waters. From the sinners themselves came cries of self-accusation; from the crowd on the banks came the strains of hymns to fortify them for the icy ordeal and the public confession.

There in the freezing current stood Joel Rae until long after the December sun had gone below the Oquirrh hills, performing his office of baptism, and reviving hope in those his words had smitten with fear.

His strength already depleted by the long march with the hand-cart party and by the exhausting strain of the day, he was early chilled by the water into which he plunged the repentant sinners. For the last hour that he stood in the stream, his whole body was numb; he had ceased to feel life in his feet, and his arms worked with a mechanical stiffness like the arms of some automaton over which his mind had control.

For there was no numbness as yet in his mind. It was wonderfully clear and active. He had begun a great work. His words had been words of fire, and the flames of them had spread so that in a little while every sinner in Zion should burn in them and be purified. Even the leaders—a great wave of exultation surged through him at this thought—even Brigham had felt the glow, and henceforth would be a fiercer Lion of the Lord to resist the Godless Gentile.

Long after sensation had left his body his thoughts were rushing in this fever of realisation, while his chilled hands made new in the Kingdom such sinners as came there repenting.

Not until night fell did the hymns cease and the crowd dwindle away. The air grew colder, and he began to feel pain again, the water cutting against his legs like a blade. Little groups were now hurrying off in the darkness, and the last Saint he had baptised was standing for the moment, chill and dripping, on the bank.

Seeing there was no one else to come, he staggered out of the stream where he had stood for three hours, finding his feet curiously clumsy and uncontrollable. Below him in the stream another Elder still waited to baptise a man and woman; but those who had been above him in the river were gone, and his own work was done.

He ascended the bank, and stood looking back at the Elder who remained in the stream. This man was now coming out of the water, having performed his office for the last one who waited. He called to Joel Rae:

"Don't stand there, Brother Rae. Hurry and get to your fire and your warm drink and your supper, or you'll be bed-fast with the chills."

"It has been a glorious day, Brother Maltby!"

"Truly, a great work has been begun, thanks to you—but hurry, man! you are freezing. Get to your fireside. We can't lose you now."

With a parting word he turned and set off down the dark street, walking unsteadily through the snow, for his feet had to be tossed ahead of him, and he could not always do it accurately. And the cold, now that he was out of the water, came more keenly upon him, only it seemed to burn him through and through with a white heat. He felt his arms stiffening in his wet sleeves, and his knees grow weak. He staggered on past a row of cabins, from which the light of fires shone out on the snow. At almost every step he stumbled out of the narrow path that had been trodden.

"To your own fireside." He recalled the words of Elder Maltby, and remembered his own lone, dark cabin, himself perhaps without strength to build a fire or to get food, perhaps without even strength to reach the place, for he felt weaker now, all at once, and put his hand out to support himself against the fence.

He had been hearing footsteps behind him, creaking rapidly over the packed snow-path. He might have to ask for help to reach his home. Even as the steps came close, he felt himself swaying. He leaned over on the fence, but to his amazement that swayed, too, and threw him back. Then he felt himself falling toward the street; but the creaking steps ceased, now by his side, and he felt under him something soft but firm—something that did not sway as the fence had unaccountably done. With his balance thus regained, he discovered the thing that held him to be a woman's arm. A woman's face looked close into his, and then she spoke.

"You are so cold. I knew you would be. And I waited—I wanted to do for you—let me!"

At once there came back to him the vision of a white-faced woman in the crowd along the river bank, staring at him out of deep, gray eyes under heavy, black brows.

"Mara—Mara!"

"Yes, yes—you are so cold!"

"But you must not stand so close—see, I am wet—you will be chilled!"

"But *you* are already chilled; your clothes are freezing on you; and you were falling just now. Can you walk?"

"Yes—yes—my house is yonder."

"I know; it's far; it's beyond the square. You must come with me."

"But your house is still farther!"

She had started him now, with a firm grasp of his arm, walking beside him in the deep snow, and trying to keep him in the narrow path.

"No—I am staying here with Hubert Plimon's two babies, while the mother has gone to Provo where Hubert lies sick. See—the light there. Come with me—here's the gate—you shall be warmed."

Slowly and with many stumblings, leaning upon her strong arm, he made his way to the cabin door. She pushed it open before him and he felt the great warm breath of the room rush out upon him. Then he was inside, swaying again uncertainly upon his feet. In the hovering light that came from the fireplace he saw the bed in the far corner where the two small children were sleeping, saw Mara with her back to the door, facing him breathlessly, saw the heavy shadows all about; but he was conscious of hardly more than the vast heavenly warmth that rolled out from the fire and enfolded him and made him drunk.

Again he would have fallen, but she steadied him down on to a wide couch covered with buffalo robes, beside the big fireplace; and here he fell at once into a stupor. She drew out the couch so that it caught more of the heat, pulled off the water-soaked boots and the stiffened coat, wrapped him in a blanket which she warmed before the fire, and covered him still again with one of the buffalo robes.

She went then to bring food and to make a hot drink, which she strengthened with brandy poured from a little silver flask.

Presently she aroused him to drink the hot liquor, and then, after another blank of stupor, she aroused him again, to eat. He could take but little of the food, but called for more of the drink, and felt the soul of it thrill along his frozen nerves until they awoke, sharpened, alert, and eager. He lay so, with closed eyes a little time, floating in an ecstasy that seemed to be half stupor and half of keenest sensibility. Then he opened his eyes. She was kneeling by the couch on which he lay. He felt her soft, quick breathing, and noted the unnatural shining of her eyes and lips where the firelight fell upon them. All at once he threw out his arms and drew her to him with such a shuddering rush of power that she cried aloud in quick alarm—but the cry was smothered under his kisses.

For ages the transport seemed to endure, the little world of his senses whirling madly through an illimitable space of sensuous light, his lips melting upon hers, his neck bending in the circle of pulsing warmth that her soft arms wove about it, his own arms crushing to his breast with frenzied fervour the whole yielding splendour of her womanhood. A moment so, then he fell back upon the couch, all his body quivering under the ecstasy from her parted lips, his triumphant senses rioting insolently through the gray, cold garden of his vows.

She drew a little back, her hands resting on his shoulders, and he saw again the firelight shining in her eyes and upon her lips. Yet the eyes were now lighted with a strange, sad reluctance, even while the mutinous lips opened their inciting welcome.

He was floating—floating midway between a cold, bleak heaven of denial and a luring hell of consent; floating recklessly, as if careless to which his soul should go.

His gaze was once more upon her face, and now, in a curiously cool little second of observation, he saw mirrored there the same conflicting duality that he knew raged within himself. In her eyes glowed the pure flame of fear and protest—but on her mad lips was the curl of provocation. And as the man in him had waited carelessly, in a sensuous luxury of unconcern, for his soul to go where it might—far up or far down—so now the woman waited before him in an incurious, unbiassed calm—the clear eyes with their grave, stern "No!"—the parted lips all but shuddering out their "Yes!"

Still he looked and still the leaning woman waited—waited to welcome with impartial fervour the angel or the devil that might come forth.

And then, as he lay so, there started with electric quickness, from some sudden coldness of recollection, the image of Prue. Sharp and vivid it shone from this chill of truth like a glittering star from the clean winter sky outside. Prue was before him with the tender blue of her eyes and the fleecy gold of her hair and her joy of a child—her little figure shrugging and nestling in his arms in happy faith—calling as she had called to him that morning—"*Joel*—*Joel*—*Joel!*"

He shivered in this flood of cold, relentless light, yet unflinchingly did he keep his face turned full upon the truth it revealed.

And this was now more than the image of the sweetheart he had sworn to cherish—it was also the image of himself vowed to his great mission. He knew that upon neither of these could he suffer a blemish to come if he would not be forever in agony. With appalling clearness the thing was lined out before him.

The woman at his side stirred and his eyes were again upon her. At once she saw the truth in them. Her parted lips came together in a straight line, shutting the red fulness determinedly in. Then there shone from her eyes a glad, sweet welcome to the angel that had issued.

His arms seemed to sicken, falling limply from her. She arose without speaking, and busied herself a little apart, her back to him.

He sat up on the couch, looking about the little room curiously, as one recovering consciousness in strange surroundings. Then he began slowly to pull on the wet boots that she had placed near the fire.

When he stood up, put on his coat, and reached for his hat, she came up to him, hesitating, timid.

"You are so cold! If you would only stay here—I am afraid you will be sick."

He answered very gently:

"It is better to go. I am strong again, now."

"I would—I would not be near you—and I am afraid for you to go out again in the cold."

He smiled a little. "*Nothing* can hurt me now—I am strong."

He opened the door, breathing his fill of the icy air that rushed in. He stepped outside, then turned to her. She stood in the doorway, the light from the room melting the darkness about them.

They looked long at each other. Then in a sudden impulse of gratitude, of generous feeling toward her, he put out his arm and drew her to him. She was cold, impassive. He bent over and lightly kissed her closed, unresponding lips. As he drew away, her hand caught his wrist for a second.

"I'm *glad!*" she said.

He tried to answer, but could only say, "Good night, Mara!"

Then he turned, drew the wide collar of his coat well up, and went down the narrow path through the snow. She stood, framed in the light of the doorway, leaning out to look after him until he was lost in the darkness.

As she stepped back and closed the door, a man, who had halted by a tree in front of the next house when the door first opened, walked on again.

It had been a great day, but, for one cause or another, it came near to being one of the last days of the man who had made it great.

Late the next afternoon, Joel Rae was found in his cabin by a messenger from Brigham. He had presumably lain there unattended since the night before, and now he was delirious and sick unto death; raving of the sins of the Saints, and of his great work of reformation. So tenderly sympathetic was his mind, said those who came to care for him, that in his delirium he ranked himself among the lowest of sinners in Zion, imploring them to take him out and bury him in the waters of baptism so that he might again be worthy to preach them the Word of God.

He was at once given every care, and for six weeks was not left alone night or day; the good mothers in Israel vying with each other in kindly offices for the sick Elder, and the men praying daily that he might not be taken so soon after his great work had begun.

The fifth wife of Elder Pixley came once to sit by his bedside, but when she heard him rave of some great sin that lay black upon his soul, beseeching forgiveness for it while the tears rained down his fevered face, she had professed that his suffering sickened her so she could not stay. Thereafter she had contented herself with inquiring at his door each day—until the day when they told her that the sickness was broken; that he was again rational and doubtless would soon be well. After that she went no more; which was not unnatural, for Elder Pixley was about to return from his three years' mission abroad, and there was much to do in the community-house in preparation for the master's coming.

But the long sickness of the young Elder did not in any manner stay the great movement he had inaugurated. From that first Sunday the reformation spread until it had reached every corner of the new Zion. The leaders took up the accusing cry,—the Elders, Bishops, High Priests, and Counsellors. Missionaries were appointed for the outlying settlements, and meetings were held daily in every center, with a general renewing of covenants.

Brigham, who had warmly seconded Joel Rae's opening discourse, was now, not unnaturally, the leader of the reformation, and in his preaching to the Saints while Joel Rae lay sick he committed no faults of vagueness. For profane swearing he rebuked his people: "You Elders in Israel will go to the

cañons for wood, get a little brush-whipped, and then curse and swear—
damn and curse your oxen and swear by Him who created you. You rip and
curse as bad as any pirates ever did!"

For the sin of cattle-stealing he denounced them. A fence high enough
to keep out cattle-thieves, he told them, must be high enough to keep out
the Devil.

Sometimes his grievance would have a personal basis, as when he
told them: "I have gone to work and made roads to the cañon for wood;
and I have cut wood down and piled it up, and then I have not got it. I
wonder if any of you can say as much about the wood I have left there. I
could tell stories of Elders that found and took my wood that should make
professional thieves blush. And again I have proof to show that Bishops
have taken thousands of pounds of wheat in tithing which they have never
reported to the general tithing-office,—proof that they stole the wheat to let
their friends speculate upon."

Under this very pointed denunciation many of the flock complained
bitterly. But Brigham only increased the flow of his wrath upon them. "You
need," said he, "to have it rain pitchforks, tines downward, from this pulpit,
Sunday after Sunday."

Still there were rebellious Saints to object, and, as Brigham drew the
lines of his wrath tighter, these became more prominent in the community.
When they voiced their discontent, they angered the priesthood. But when
they indicated their purpose to leave the valley, as many soon did, they gave
alarm. An exodus must be prevented at any cost, and so the priesthood let it
be known that migrations from the valley would be considered as nothing
less than apostasy. In Brigham's own words: "The moment a person decides
to leave this people, he is cut off from every object that is desirable in time
or eternity. Every possession and object of affection will be taken from those
who forsake the truth, and their identity will eventually cease."

But, as the reform wave swept on, it became apparent that these words
had been considered merely figurative by many who were about to seek
homes outside the valley. From every side news came privately that this
family or that was preparing to leave.

And so it came about that the first Sunday Joel Rae was able to walk
to the tabernacle, still weak and wasted and trembling, he heard a sermon
from Brigham which made him question his own soul in an agony of terror.
For, on this day, was boldly preached, for the first time in Zion, something
which had never before been more than whispered among the highest
elect,—the doctrine of blood-atonement—of human sacrifice.

"I am preaching St. Paul, this morning," began Brigham, easily. "Hebrews, Chapter ix., and Verse 22: 'And almost all things are by the law purged with blood; and without shedding of blood is no remission.' Also, and more especially, first Corinthians, Chapter v., Verse 5: 'To deliver such an one unto Satan for the destruction of the flesh, that the spirit may be saved in the day of the Lord Jesus.' Remember these words of Paul's. The time has come when justice will be laid to the line and righteousness to the plummet; when we shall take the old broadsword, and ask, 'Are you for God?' And if you are not heartily on the Lord's side, you will be hewn down."

There was a rustling movement in the throng before him, and he paused until it subsided.

"I tell you there are men and women amongst you who ought to come and ask me to select a place and appoint a committee to shed their blood. Only in that way can they be saved, for water will not do. Their sins are too deep for that. I repeat—there are covenant-breakers here, and we need a place set apart and men designated to shed their blood for their own salvation. If any of you ask, do I mean you, I answer yes. We have tried long enough with you, and now I shall let the sword of the Almighty be unsheathed, not only in words but in deed. I tell you there are sins for which men cannot otherwise receive forgiveness in this world nor in the world to come; and if you guilty ones had your eyes opened to your true condition, you would be willing to have your blood spilt upon the ground that the smoke thereof might go up to heaven for your sins. I know when you hear this talk about cutting people off from the earth you will consider it strong doctrine; but it is to save them, and not destroy them. Take a person in this congregation who knows the principles of that kind of life and sees the beauties of eternity before him compared with the vain and foolish things of the world—and suppose he is overtaken in a gross fault which he knows will rob him of that exaltation which he desires and which he now cannot obtain without the shedding of his blood; and suppose he knows that by having his blood shed he will atone for that sin and be saved and exalted with the Gods. Is there a man or woman here but would say, 'Save me—shed my blood, that I may be exalted.' And how many of you love your neighbour well enough to save him in that way? That is what Christ meant by loving our neighbours as ourselves. I could refer you to plenty of instances where men have been righteously slain to atone for their sin; I have seen scores and hundreds of people for whom there would have been a chance in the last day if their lives had been taken and their blood spilt upon the ground as a smoking incense to the Almighty, but who are now angels to the Devil because it was not done. The weakness and ignorance of the nations forbids this law being in full and open force; yet, remember, if our neighbour needs help we must help him. If his soul is in danger we must save it.

"Now as to our enemies—apostates and Gentiles—the tree that brings not forth good fruit shall be hewn down. 'What,' you ask, 'do you believe that people would do right to put these traitors to death?' Yes! What does the United States government do with traitors? Examine the doings of earthly governments on this point and you will find but one practise universal. A word to the wise is enough; just remember that there are sins that the blood of a lamb, of a calf, or of a turtle-dove, cannot remit."

Under this discourse Joel Rae sat terrified, with a bloodless face, cowering as he had made others to cower six weeks before. The words seemed to carry his own preaching to its rightful conclusion; but now how changed was his world!—a whirling, sickening chaos of sin and remorse.

As he listened to Brigham's words, picturing the blood of the sinner smoking on the ground, his thoughts fled back to that night, that night of wondrous light and warmth, the last he could remember before the great blank came.

Now the voice of Brigham came to him again: "And almost all things are by the law purged with blood; and without shedding of blood is no remission!"

Then the service ended, and he saw Bishop Wright pushing toward him through the crowd.

"Well, well, Brother Rae you do look peaked, for sure! But you'll pick up fast enough, and just in time, too. Lord! what won't Brother Brigham do when the Holy Ghost gets a strangle-holt on him? Now, then," he added, in a lower tone, "if I ain't mistaken, there's going to be some work for the Sons of Dan!"

Chapter XV
How the Souls of Apostates Were Saved

The Wild Ram of the Mountains had spoken truly; there was work at hand for the Sons of Dan. When his Witness at last came to Joel Rae, he tried vainly to recall the working of his mind at this time; to remember where he had made the great turn—where he had faced about. For, once, he knew, he had been headed the way he wished to go, a long, plain road, reaching straight toward the point whither all the aspirations of his soul urged him.

And then, all in a day or in a night, though he had seen never a turn in the road, though he had gone a true and straight course, suddenly he had looked up to find he was headed the opposite way. After facing his goal so long, he was now going from it—and never a turn! It was the wretched paradox of a dream.

The day after Brigham's sermon on blood-atonement, there had been a meeting in the Historian's office, presided over by Brigham. And here for the first time Joel Rae found he was no longer looked upon as one too radical. Somewhat dazedly, too, he realised at this close range the severely practical aspects of much that he had taught in theory. It was strange, almost unnerving, to behold his own teachings naked of their pulpit rhetoric; to find his long-cherished ideals materialised by literal-minded, practiced men.

He heard again the oath he had sworn, back on the river-flat: "*I will assist in executing all the decrees of the First President, Patriarch, or President of the Twelve, and I will cause all who speak evil of the Presidency or Heads of the Church to die the death of dissenters or apostates*—" And then he had heard the business of the meeting discussed. Decisions were reached swiftly, and orders given in words that were few and plain. Even had these orders been repugnant to him, they were not to be questioned; they came from an infallible priesthood, obedience to which was the first essential to his soul's salvation; and they came again from the head of an organisation to which he was bound by every oath he had been taught to hold sacred. But, while they left him dazed, disconcerted, and puzzled, he was by no means certain that they were repugnant. They were but the legitimate extension of his teachings since childhood, and of his own preaching.

In custody at Kayesville, twenty-five miles north of Salt Lake City, were six men who had been arrested by church authority while on their way east from California. They were suspected of being federal spies. The night following the meeting which Joel Rae had attended, these prisoners were attacked while they slept. Two were killed at once; two more after a brief struggle; and the remaining two the following day, after they had been pursued through the night. The capable Bishop Wright declared in confidence to Joel Rae that it reminded him of old days at Nauvoo.

The same week was saved Rosmas Anderson, who had incurred rejection from Israel and eternal wrath by his misbehaviour. Becoming submissive to the decree of the Church, when it was made known to him by certain men who came in the night, it was believed that his atonement would suffice to place him once more in the household of faith. He had asked but half a day to prepare for the solemn ceremony. His wife, regretful but firm in the faith, had provided clean garments for her sinful husband, and the appointed executioners dug his grave. They went for him at midnight. By the side of the grave they had let him kneel and pray. His throat had then been cut by a deft hand, and he was held so that his blood ran into the grave, thus consummating the sacrifice to the God of Israel. The widow, obeying priestly instructions, announced that her husband had gone to California.

Then the soul of William Parrish at Springville was saved to eternal glory; also the soul of his son, Beason. For both of these sinful ones were on the verge of apostasy; had plotted, indeed, and made secret preparations to leave the valley, all of which were discovered by church emissaries, fortunately for the eternal welfare of the two most concerned. Yet a few years later, when the hated Gentiles had gained some shadow of authority in the new Zion, their minions were especially bitter as to this feat of mercy, seeking, indeed, to indict the performers of it.

As to various persons who met death while leaving the valley, opinion was divided on the question of their ultimate salvation. For it was announced concerning these, as their bodies were discovered from time to time, that the Indians had killed them. This being true, they had died in apostasy, and their rejection from the Kingdom was assured. Yet after awhile the Saints at large took hope touching the souls of these; for Bishop Wright, the excellent and able Wild Ram of the Mountains, took occasion to remark one Sabbath in the course of an address delivered in the tabernacle: "And it amazes me, brethren, to note how the spirit has been poured out on the Lamanites. It really does seem as if an Injun jest naturally hates an apostate, and it beats me how they can tell 'em the minute they try to sneak out of this valley of the Lord. They must lie out in them hills jest a-waiting for apostates; and they won't have anything else; they never touch the faithful. You wouldn't think they had so much fine feeling to look at 'em. You wouldn't suspect they was so sensitive, and almost bigoted, you might say. But there it is—and I don't believe the critters will let many of these vile apostates get beyond the rocky walls of Zion." Those who could listen between the words began to suspect that the souls of such apostates had been duly saved.

Yet one apostate the very next day was rash enough to controvert the Bishop's views. To a group of men in the public street at high noon and in a loud voice he declared his intention of leaving for California, and he spoke evil of the Church.

"I tell you," he said, in tones of some excitement, "men are murdered here. Their murder is planned by Bishops, Priests, Elders, and Apostles, by the President and his Counsellors, and then it is done by men they send to do it. Their laying it on to the Indians don't fool me a minute. That's the kind of a church this is, and you don't ketch me staying in it any longer!"

Trees had been early planted in the new settlement, and owing to the care bestowed upon them by the thrifty colonists, many were now matured. From a stout limb of one of these the speaker was found hanging the following morning. A coroner's jury hastily summoned from among the Saints found that he had committed suicide.

Another whose soul was irrevocably lost was Frederick Loba, who had refused to take more than one wife in spite of the most explicit advice from his superiors that he could attain to but little glory either in this world or that to come with less than three. He crowned his offense by speaking disrespectfully of Brigham Young. Orders were issued to save his soul; but before his tabernacle could be seized by those who would have saved him, the wretched man had taken his one wife and fled to the mountains. There they wandered many days in the most inclement weather, lost, famished, and several times but narrowly escaping the little band that had been sent in pursuit of them; whose members would, had they been permitted, not only have terminated their bodily suffering, but saved their souls to a worthy place in the life to come. As it was, they wandered a distance of three hundred miles, and three days after their last food was eaten, the man carrying the woman in his arms the last six miles, they reached a camp of the Snake Indians. These, not sharing with their Utah brethren the prejudice against apostates, gave them a friendly welcome, and guided them to Fort Laramie, thereby destroying for the unhappy man and his wife their last chance of coming forth in the final resurrection. But few at this time were so unlucky as this pair; for judgment had begun at the house of the Lord, and Israel was attentively at work.

It was now that Joel Rae became conscious that he was facing directly away from the glory he had so long sought and suffered for. Though as yet no blood for Israel had been shed in his actual presence, he had attended the meetings of the Sons of Dan, and was kept aware of their operations. It seemed to him in after years that his faculties had at this time been in trance.

He was seized at length with an impulse to be away from it all. As the days went by with their tragedies, he became half wild with restlessness and a strange fear of himself. In spite of his lifelong training, he knew there was wrong in the air. He could not question the decrees of the priesthood, but this much became clear to him,—that only one thing could carry with it more possibilities of evil than this course of the Church toward dissenters— and that was to doubt that Brigham Young's voice was as the voice of God. Not yet could he bring himself to this. But the unreasoning desire to be away became so strong that he knew he must yield to it.

Turning this in his mind one day he met a brother Elder, a man full of zeal who had lately returned from a mission abroad. There had been, he said, a great outpouring of the spirit in Wales.

"And what a glorious day has dawned here," he continued. "Thank God, there is a way to save the souls of the blind! That reminds me—have you heard of the saving work Brother Pixley was obliged to do?"

"Brother Pixley?—no." He heard his own voice tremble, in spite of his effort at self-control. The other became more confidential, stepping closer and speaking low.

"Of course, it ain't to be talked of freely, but you have a right to know, for was it not your own preaching that led to this glorious reformation? You see, Brother Pixley came back with me, after doing great works abroad. Naturally, he came full of love for his wives. But he had been here only a few days when he became convinced that one of them had forgotten him; something in her manner made him suspect it, for she was a woman of singularly open, almost recklessly open, nature. Then a good neighbour came and told him that one night, while on his way for the doctor, he had seen this woman take leave of her lover—had seen the man, whom he could not recognise, embrace her at parting. He taxed her with this, and she at once confessed, though protesting that she had not sinned, save in spirit. You can imagine his grief, Brother Rae, for he had loved the woman. Well, after taking counsel from Brigham, he talked the matter over with her very calmly, telling her that unless her blood smoked upon the ground, she would be cast aside in eternity. She really had spiritual aspirations, it seems, for she consented to meet the ordeal. Then, of course, it was necessary to learn from her the name of the man—and when all was ready for the sacrifice, Brother Pixley commanded her to make it known."

"Tell me which of Brother Pixley's wives it was." He could feel the little cool beads of sweat upon his forehead.

"The fifth, did I not say? But to his amazement and chagrin, she refused to give him the name of the man, and he had no way of learning it otherwise, since there was no one he could suspect. He pointed out to her that not even her blood could save her should she die shielding him. But she declared that he was a good man, and that rather than bring disgrace upon him she would die—would even lose her soul; that in truth she did not care to live, since she loved him so that living away from him was worse than death. I have said she was a woman of a large nature, somewhat reckless and generous, and her mistaken notion of loyalty led her to persist in spite of all the threats and entreaties of her distressed husband. She even smiled when she told him that she would rather die than live away from this unknown man, smiled in a way that must have enraged him—since he had never won that kind of love from her for himself—for then he let her meet the sacrifice without further talk. He drew her on to his knee, kissed her for the last time, then held her head back—and the thing was done. How sad it is that she did not make a full confession. Then, by her willing sacrifice, she would have gone direct to the circle of the Gods and Goddesses; but now, dying as she did, her soul must be lost—"

"Which wife did you say—"

"The fifth—she that was Mara Cavan—but, dear me, Brother Rae! you should not be out so soon! Why, man, you're weak as a cat! Come, I'll walk with you as far as your house, and you must lie abed again until you are stronger. I can understand how you wished to be up as soon as possible; how proud you must feel that your preaching has led to this glorious awakening and made it possible to save the souls of many sinful ones—but you must be careful not to overtax yourself."

Four days later, a white-faced young Elder applied to Brigham for permission to go to the settlements on the south. He professed to be sick, to have suffered a relapse owing to incautious exposure so soon after his long illness. He seemed, indeed, not only to be weak, but to be much distressed and torn in his mind.

Brigham was gracious enough to accord the desired permission, adding that the young Elder could preach the revived gospel and rebaptise on his way south, thus combining work with recreation. He was also good enough to volunteer some advice.

"What ails you mostly, Brother Joel, is your single state. What you need is wives. You've been here ten years now, and it's high time. You're given to brooding over things that are other people's to brood on, and then, you're naturally soul-proud. Now, a few wives will humble you and make you more reasonable, like the rest of us. I don't want to be too downright with you, like I am with some of the others, because I've always had a special kind of feeling for you, and so I've let you go on. But you think it over, and talk to me about it when you come back. It's high time you was building up your thrones and dominions in the Kingdom."

He started south the next day, riding down between the two mountain ranges that bordered the valley, stopping at each settlement, breathing more freely, resting more easily, as each day took him farther away. Yet, when he closed his eyes, there, like an echo, was the vision of a woman's face with shining eyes and lips, — a vision that after a few seconds was washed away by a great wave of blood.

But after a few days, certain bits of news caught up with him that happily drove this thing from his sight for a time by stirring within him all his old dread of Gentile persecution.

First he heard that Parley Pratt, the Archer of Paradise and one of the Twelve Apostles, had been foully murdered back in Arkansas while seeking to carry to their mother the children of his ninth wife. The father of these children, so his informant reported, had waylaid and shot him.

Then came rumours of a large wagon-train going south through Utah on its way to California. Reports said it was composed chiefly of Missourians, some of whom were said to be boasting that they had helped to expel the Saints from Jackson County in that State. Also in this train were reported to be several men from Arkansas who had been implicated in the assassination of Apostle Pratt.

But news of the crowning infamy reached him the following day, — news that had put out all thought of his great sin and his bloody secret, news of a thing so monstrous that he was unable to give it credence until it had been confirmed by other comers from the north. President Buchanan, inspired by tales that had reached him of various deeds growing out of the reformation, and by the treatment which various Federal officers were said to have received, had decided that rebellion existed in the Territory of Utah. He had appointed a successor to Brigham Young as governor, so the report ran, and ordered an army to march to Salt Lake City for the alleged purpose of installing the new executive.

Three days later all doubt of the truth of this story was banished. Word then came that Brigham was about to declare martial law, and that he had promised that Buchanan's army should never enter the valley.

Now his heart beat high again, with something of the old swift fervour. The Gentile yoke was at last to be thrown off. War would come, and the Lord would surely hold them safe while they melted away the Gentile hosts.

He reached the settlement of Parowan that night, and when they told him there that the wagon-train coming south—their ancient enemies who had plundered and butchered them in Jackson County—was to be cut off before it left the basin, it seemed but right to him, the just vengeance of Heaven upon their one-time despoilers, and a fitting first act in the war-drama that was now to be played.

Once more the mob was marching upon them to despoil and murder and put them into the wilderness. But now God had nerved and strengthened them to defend the walls of Zion, even against a mighty nation. And as a token of His favour and His wish, here was a company of their bitterest foes delivered into their hands. Beside the picture was another; he saw his sister, the slight, fair girl, in the grasp of the fiends at Haun's Mill; the face of his father tossing on the muddy current and sucked under to the river-bottom; and the rough bark cylinder, festooned with black cloth, holding the worn form of the mother whose breast had nursed him.

When he started he had felt that he could never again preach while that secret lay upon him,—that he could no longer rebuke sinners honestly,—but this matter of war was different.

He preached a moving sermon that day from a text of Samuel: "As thy sword hath made women childless, so shall thy mother be childless among women." And when he was done the congregation had made the little dimly lighted meeting-house at Parowan ring with a favourite hymn:—

"Up, awake, ye defenders of Zion!
The foe's at the door of your homes;
Let each heart be the heart of a lion,
Unyielding and proud as he roams.
Remember the wrongs of Missouri,
Remember the fate of Nauvoo!
When the God-hating foe is before ye,
Stand firm and be faithful and true."

Chapter XVI
The Order from Headquarters

He left Parowan the next morning to preach at one of the little settlements to the east. He was gone three days. When he came back they told him that the train of Missourians had passed through Parowan and on to the south. He attended a military council held that evening in the meeting-house. Three days of reflection, while it had not cooled the anger he felt toward these members of the mob that had so brutally wronged his people, had slightly cooled his ardour for aggressive warfare.

It was rather a relief to know that he was not in a position of military authority; to feel that this matter of cutting off a wagon-train was in the hands of men who could do no wrong. The men who composed the council he knew to be under the immediate guidance of the Lord. Their names and offices made this certain. There was George A. Smith, First Counsellor to Brigham, representing as such the second person of the Trinity, and also one of the Twelve Apostles. There was Isaac Haight, President of the Cedar City Stake of Zion and High Priest of Southern Utah; there were Colonel Dame, President of the Parowan Stake of Zion, Philip Klingensmith, Bishop from Cedar City, and John Doyle Lee, Brigham's most trusted lieutenant in the south, a major of militia, probate judge, member of the Legislature, President of Civil Affairs at Harmony, and farmer to the Indians under Brigham.

When a call to arms came as a result of this council, and an official decree was made known that the obnoxious emigrant train was to be cut off, he could not but feel that the deed had heavenly sanction. As to worldly regularity, the proceeding seemed to be equally faultless. The call was a regular military call by the superior officers to the subordinate officers and privates of the regiment, commanding them to muster, armed and equipped as directed by law, and prepared for field operations. Back of the local militia officers was his Excellency, Brigham Young, not only the vicar of God on earth but governor of Utah and commander-in-chief of the militia. It seemed, indeed, a foretaste of those glorious campaigns long promised them, when they should go through the land of the Gentiles "like a lion among the flocks of sheep, cutting down, breaking in pieces, with none to deliver, leaving the land desolate."

The following Tuesday he continued south to Cedar City, the most populous of the southern settlements. Here he learned of the campaign's progress. Brigham's courier had preceded the train on its way south, bearing written orders to the faithful to hold no dealings with its people; to sell them neither forage for their stock nor food for themselves. They had, it was reported, been much distressed as a result of this order, and their stock was greatly weakened. At Cedar City, it being feared that they might for want of supplies be forced to halt permanently so near the settlement that it would be inconvenient to destroy them, they were permitted to buy fifty bushels of wheat and to have it and some corn the Indians had sold them ground at the mill of Major Lee.

As Joel's informant, the fiery Bishop Klingensmith, remarked, this was not so generous as it seemed, since, while it would serve to decoy them on their way toward San Bernardino, they would never get out of the valley with it. The train had started on, but the animals were so weak that three days had been required to reach Iron Creek, twenty miles beyond, and two more days to reach Mountain Meadows, fifteen miles further south.

Here at daybreak the morning before, Klingensmith told him, a band of Piede Indians, under Lee's direction, had attacked the train, killing and wounding a number of the men. It had been hoped, explained Klingensmith, that the train would be destroyed at once by the Indians, thus avoiding any call upon the militia; but the emigrants had behaved with such effectiveness that the Indians were unable to complete the task. They had corralled their wagons, dug a rifle-pit in the center, and returned the fire, killing one Indian and wounding two of the chiefs. The siege was being continued.

The misgiving that this tale caused Joel Rae he put down to unmanly weakness—and to an unfamiliarity with military affairs. A sight of the order in Brigham's writing for the train's extermination would have set his mind wholly at rest; but though he had not been granted this, he was assured that such an order existed, and with this he was obliged to be content. He knew, indeed, that an order from Brigham, either oral or written, must have come; otherwise the local authorities would never have dared to proceed. They were not the men to act without orders in a matter so grave after the years in which Brigham had preached his right to dictate, direct, and control the affairs of his people from the building of the temple "down to the ribbons a woman should wear, or the setting up of a stocking."

Late on the following day, Wednesday, while they were anxiously waiting for news, a messenger from Lee came with a call for reinforcements.

The Indians, although there were three hundred of them, had been unable to prevail over the little entrenched band of Gentiles. Ten minutes after the messenger's arrival, the militia, which had been waiting under arms, set out for the scene in wagons. From Cedar City went every able-bodied man but two.

Joel Rae was with them, wondering why he went. He wanted not to go. He preferred that news of the approaching victory should be brought to him; yet invisible hands had forced him, even while it seemed that frenzied voices—voices without sound—warned him back.

The ride was long, but not long enough for his mind to clear. It was still clouded with doubts and questionings and fears when they at last saw the flaring of many fires with figures loitering or moving busily about them. As they came nearer, a strange, rhythmic throbbing crept to his ears; nearer still, he resolved it into the slow, regular beatings of a flat-toned drum. The measure, deliberate, incessant, changeless,—the same tones, the same intervals,—worked upon his strained nerves, at first soothingly and then as a pleasant stimulant.

The wagons now pulled up near the largest camp fire, and the arrivals were greeted by a dozen or so of the Saints, who, with Major Lee, had been directing and helping the Indians in their assaults upon the enemy. Several of these had disguised themselves as Indians for the better deception of the besieged.

At the right of their camp went the long line of the Indians' fires. From far down this line came a low ringing chant and the strangely insistent drum-beats.

"They're mourning old Chief Moqueetus," explained Lee. "He fell asleep before the fire just about dark, while his corn and potatoes were cooking, and he had a bad nightmare. The old fellow woke up screaming that he had his double-hands full of blood, and he grabbed his gun and was up on top of the hill firing down before he was really awake, I guess. Anyway, one of the cusses got him—like as not the same one that did this to-day while I was peeking at them," and he showed them a bullet-hole in his hat.

At fires near by the Indians were broiling beef cut from animals they had slaughtered belonging to the wagon-train. Still others were cutting the hides into strips to be made into lariats. As far down as the line could be seen, there were dusky figures darting in and out of the firelight.

A council was at once called of the Presidents, Bishops, Elders, High Priests, and the officers of the militia who were present. Bishop Klingensmith bared his massive head in the firelight and opened the council with prayer, invoking the aid of God to guide them aright. Then Major Higbee, presiding as chairman, announced the orders under which they were assembled and under which the train had been attacked.

"It is ordered from headquarters that this party must be used up, except such as are too young to tell tales. We got to do it. They been acting terrible mean ever since we wouldn't sell them anything. If we let them go on now, they been making their brag that they'll raise a force in California and come back and wipe us out—and Johnston's army already marching on us from the east. Are we going to submit again to what we got in Missouri and in Illinois? No! Everybody is agreed about that. Now the Indians have failed to do it like we thought they would, so we got to finish it up, that's all."

Joel Rae spoke for the first time.

"You say except such as are too young to tell tales, Brother Higbee; what does that mean?"

"Why, all but the very smallest children, of course."

"Are there children here?"

Lee answered:

"Oh, a fair sprinkling—about what you'd look for in a train of a hundred and thirty people. The boys got two of the kids yesterday; the fools had dressed them up in white dresses and sent them out with a bucket for water. You can see their bodies lying over there this side of the spring."

"And there are women?" he asked, feeling a great sickness come upon him.

"Plenty of them," answered Klingensmith, "some mighty fine women, too; I could see one yesterday, a monstrous fine figure and hair shiny like a crow's wing, and a little one, powerful pretty, and one kind of between the two—it's a shame we can't keep some of them, but orders is orders!"

"These women must be killed, too?"

"That's the orders from headquarters, Brother Rae."

"From the military headquarters at Parowan, or from the spiritual headquarters at Salt Lake?"

"Better not inquire how far back that order started, Brother Rae—not of me, anyway."

"But women and children—"

"The great Elohim has spoken from the heavens, Brother Rae—that's enough for me. I can't put my human standards against the revealed will of God."

"But women and children—" He repeated the words as if he sought to comprehend them. He seemed like a man with defective sight who has come suddenly against a wall that he had thought far off. Higbee now addressed him.

"Brother Rae, in religion you have to eat the bran along with the flour. Did you suppose we were going to milk the Gentiles and not ever shed any blood?"

"But innocent blood—"

"There ain't a drop of innocent blood in the whole damned train. And what are you, to be questioning this way about orders from on high? I've heard you preach many a time about the sin of such doings as that. You preach in the pulpit about stubborn clay in the hands of the potter having to be put through the mill again, and now that you're out here in the field, seems to me you get limber like a tallowed rag when an order comes along."

"Defenseless women and little children—" He was still trying to regain his lost equilibrium. Lee now interposed.

"Yes, Brother Rae, as defenseless as that pretty sister of yours was in the woods there, that afternoon at Haun's Mill."

The reminder silenced him for the moment. When he could listen again, he heard them canvassing a plan of attack that should succeed without endangering any of their own numbers. He walked away from the group to see if alone, out of the tumult and torrent of lies and half-truths, he could not fetch some one great unmistakable truth which he felt instinctively was there.

And then his ears responded again to the slow chant and the constant measured beat of the flat-toned, vibrant drum. Something in its rhythm searched and penetrated and swayed and seemed to overwhelm him. It came as the measured, insistent beat of fate itself, relentless, inexorable; and all the time it was stirring in him vague, latent instincts of savagery. He wished it would stop, so that he might reason, yet dreaded that it might stop at any moment. Fascinated by the weird rhythm and the hollow beat, he could not summon the will to go beyond its sway.

He walked about the fires or lingered by the groups in consultation until the first signs of dawn. Then he climbed the low, rocky hill to the east and peered over the top, the drum-beats still pulsing through him, still coercing him. As the light grew, he could make out the details of the scene below. He was looking down into a narrow valley running north and south, formed by two ranges of rugged, rocky hills five hundred yards or so apart. To the north this valley widened; to the south it narrowed until it became a mere gap leading out into the desert.

Directly below him, half-way between the ranges of hills, was a circle of covered wagons wheel to wheel. In the center of this a pit had been dug, and here the besieged were finding such protection as they could from the rifle-fire that came down from the hills on either side. Even now he could see Indians lying in watch for any who might attempt to escape. The camp had been attacked on Monday morning after the wagons had moved a hundred yards away from the spring. It was now Friday. For four days, therefore, with only what water they could bring by dashes to the spring under fire, they had held their own in the pit.

When it grew still lighter he descried, out on his left near the spring, two spots of white close together, and remembered Lee's tale the night before of the two little girls sent for water.

At that instant, the chanting and the beat of the drum stopped, and in the silence a flood of light seemed to shine in upon his mind, showing him in something of its true aspect the thing they were about to do. Not clearly did he see it, for he was still torn and dazed—and not in its real proportions, moreover; for he saw it against the background of his teaching from the cradle; the murder of their Prophet, the persecution of the Saints, the outrages put upon his own family, the fate of his sister, the murder of his father, and the death of his mother; the coming of an army upon them now to repeat these persecutions; the reported offenses of this particular lot of Gentiles. And then, too, he saw it against his own flawless faith in the authority of the priesthood, his implicit belief that whatsoever they ordered was to be obeyed as the literal command of God, his unshaken conviction that to disobey the priesthood was to commit the unforgivable sin of blasphemy against the Holy Ghost. "If you trifle with the commands of any of the priesthood," he himself had preached but a few days before, "you are trifling with Brigham; if you trifle with Brigham, you are trifling with God; and if you do that, you will trifle yourselves down to hell."

Yet as he looked upon the doomed camp, lying still and quiet in the gray light,—in spite of breeding, training, habit of thought, and passionate belief, he felt the horror of it, and a hope came to him out of that horror. He hurried down the hill and searched among the groups of Indians until he found Lee.

"Major, isn't there a chance that Brother Brigham didn't order this?"

"Brother Rae, no one has said he did—it wouldn't be just wise."

"But *did* he—has any one seen the written order or heard who brought the oral order?"

"Brother Rae, look here, now—you know Brother Brigham. You know his authority, and you know Dame and Haight. You know they wouldn't either of them dare do as much as take another wife without asking Brigham first. Well, then, do you reckon they'd dare order this militia around in this reckless way to cut off a hundred and thirty people unless they had mighty good reason to know he wanted it?"

He stood before Lee with bent head; the hope had died. Lee went on:

"And look here, Elder, just as a friendly hint, I wouldn't do any more of this sentimental talk. Why, in the last six months I've known men to get blood-atoned for less than you've said."

He saw they were holding another council. Bishop Klingensmith again led in prayer. He prayed for revelation, for the gifts of the spirit for each of them, and for every order of the priesthood; that they might prevail over the army marching against them; that Israel might grow and multiply and cover the earth with cities and become a people so great that no man could number them; and that the especial favour of Heaven might attend them on their righteous smiting of the Gentile host now delivered over to them by an all-wise Jehovah.

The plan of assault was now again rehearsed, and its details communicated to their Indian allies. By ten o'clock all was ready.

Chapter XVII
The Meadow Shambles

They chose William Bateman to go forward with a flag of truce. He was short and plump, with a full, round, ingenuous face. He was chosen, so said Klingensmith, for his plausible ways. He could look right at you when he said anything; and the moment needed a man of this talent. He was to enter the camp and say to the people that the Mormons had come to save them; that on giving up their arms they would be safely conducted to Cedar City, there to await a proper time for continuing their journey.

From the hill to the west of the besieged camp they watched the plausible Bateman with his flag of truce meet one of the emigrants who came out, also with a white flag, and saw them stand talking a little time. Bateman then came back around the end of the hill that separated the two camps. His proposal had been gratefully accepted. The besieged emigrants were in desperate straits; their dead were unburied in the narrow enclosure, and they were suffering greatly for want of water.

Major Higbee, in command of the militia, now directed Lee to enter the camp and see that the plan was carried out. With him went two men with wagons. Lee was to have them load their weapons into one wagon, to separate the adults from the children and wounded, who were to be put into the other, and then march the party out.

As Lee approached the corral its occupants swarmed out to meet him, — gaunt men, unkempt women and children, with the look of hunted animals in their eyes. Some of the men cheered feebly; some were silent and plainly distrustful. But the women laughed and wept for joy as they crowded about their deliverer; and wide-eyed children stared at him in a friendly way, understanding but little of it all except that the newcomer was a desirable person.

It took Lee but a little time to overcome the hesitation of the few suspicious ones. The plan he proposed was too plainly their only way of escape from a terrible death. Their animals had been shot down or run off so that they could neither advance nor retreat. Their ammunition was almost gone, so that they could not give battle. And, lastly, their provisions were low, with no chance to replenish them; for on the south was the most to be dreaded of all American deserts, while on the north they had for some reason unknown to themselves been unable to buy of the abundance through which they passed.

Arrangements for the departure were quickly completed under Lee's supervision. In one wagon were piled the guns and pistols of the emigrants, together with half a dozen men who had been wounded in the four days' fighting. In the other wagon a score of the smaller children were placed, some with tear-stained faces, some crying, and some gravely apprehensive. At Lee's command the two wagons moved forward. After these the women followed, marching singly or in pairs; some with little bundles of their most precious belongings; some carrying babes too young to be sent ahead in the wagon. A few had kept even their older children to walk beside them, fearing some evil—they knew not what.

One such, a young woman near the last of the line, was leading by the hand a little girl of three or four, while on her left there marched a sturdy, pink-faced boy of seven or eight, whose almost white hair and eyebrows gave him a look of fright which his demeanour belied. The woman, looking anxiously back over her shoulder to the line of men, spoke warningly to the boy as the line moved slowly forward.

"Take her other hand, and stay close. I'm afraid something will happen—that man who came is not an honest man. I tried to tell them, but they wouldn't believe me. Keep her hand in yours, and if anything does happen, run right back there and try to find her father. Remember now, just as if she were your own little sister."

The boy answered stoutly, with shrewd glances about for possible danger.

"Of course I'll stay by her. I wouldn't run away. If I'd only had a gun," he continued, in tones of regretful enthusiasm, "I know I could have shot some of those Indians—but these, what do you call them?—Mormons—they'll keep the Indians away now."

"But remember—don't leave my child, for I'm afraid—something warns me."

Farther back the others had now fallen in, so that the whole company was in motion. The two wagons were in the lead; then came the women; and some distance back of these trailed the line of men.

When the latter reached the place where the column of militia stood drawn up in line by the roadside, they swung their hats and cheered their deliverers; again and again the cheers rang in tones that were full of gratitude. As they passed on, an armed Mormon stepped to the side of each man and walked with him, thus convincing the last doubter of their sincerity in wishing to guard them from any unexpected attack by the Indians.

In such fashion marched the long, loosely extended line until the rear had gone some two hundred yards away from the circle of wagons. At the head, the two wagons containing the children and wounded had now fallen out of sight over a gentle rise to the north. The women also were well ahead, passing at that moment through a lane of low cedars that grew close to the road on either side. The men were now stepping briskly, sure at last of the honesty of their rescuers.

Then, while all promised fair, a call came from the head of the line of men,—a clear, high call of command that rang to the very rear of the column:

"Israel, do your duty!"

Before the faces of the marching men had even shown surprise or questioning, each Mormon had turned and shot the man who walked beside him. The same instant brought piercing screams from the column of women ahead; for the signal had been given while they were in the lane of cedars where the Indian allies of the Saints had been ambushed. Shots and screams echoed and reëchoed across the narrow valley, and clouds of smoke, pearl gray in the morning sun, floated near the ground.

The plan of attack had been well laid for quick success. Most of the men had fallen at the first volley, either killed or wounded. Here and there along the all but prostrate line would be seen a struggling pair, or one of the emigrants running toward cover under a fire that always brought him low before he reached it.

On the women, too, the quick attack had been almost instantly successful. The first great volume of mad shrieks had quickly died low as if the victims were being smothered; and now could be heard only the single scream of some woman caught in flight,—short, despairing screams, and others that seemed to be cut short—strangled at their height.

Joel Rae found himself on the line after the first volley, drawn by some dread power he could not resist. Yet one look had been enough. He shut his eyes to the writhing forms, the jets of flame spitting through the fog of smoke, and turned to flee.

Then in an instant—how it had come about he never knew—he was struggling with a man who shouted his name and cursed him,—a dark man with blood streaming from a wound in his throat. He defended himself easily, feeling his assailant's strength already waning. Time after time the man called him by name and cursed him, now in low tones, as they swayed.

Then the Saint whose allotted victim this man had been, having reloaded his pistol, ran up, held it close to his head, fired, and ran back to the line.

He felt the man's grasp of his shoulders relax, and his body grow suddenly limp, as if boneless. He let it down to the ground, looking at last full upon the face. At first glance it told him nothing. Then a faint sense of its familiarity pushed up through many old memories. Sometime, somewhere, he had known the face.

The dying man opened his eyes wide, not seeing, but convulsively, and then he felt himself enlightened by something in their dark colour,—something in the line of the brow under the black hair;—a face was brought back to him, the handsome face of the jaunty militia captain at Nauvoo, the man who had helped expel his people, who had patronised them with his airs of protector,—the man who had—

It did not come to him until that instant—this man was Girnway. In the flash of awful comprehension he dropped, a sickened and nerveless heap, beside the dead man, turning his head on the ground, and feeling for any sign of life at his heart.

Forward there, where the yells of the Indians had all but replaced the screams of frantic women—butchered already perhaps, subjected to he knew not what infamy at the hands of savage or Saint—was the yellow-haired, pink-faced girl he had loved and kept so long imaged in his heart; yet she might have escaped, she might still live—she might even not have been in the party.

He sprang up and found himself facing a white-haired boy, who held a little crying girl by a tight grasp of her arm, and who eyed him aggressively.

"What did you hurt Prudence's father for? He was a good man. Did you shoot him?"

He seized the boy roughly by the shoulder.

"Prudence—Prudence—where is she?"

"Here."

He looked down at the little girl, who still cried. Even in that glance he saw her mother's prettiness, her pink and white daintiness, and the yellow shine of her hair.

"Her mother, then,—quick!"

The boy pointed ahead.

"Up there—she told me to take care of Prudence, and when the Indians came out she made me run back here to look for him." He pointed to the still figure on the ground before them. And then, making a brave effort to keep back the tears:

"If I had a gun I'd shoot some Indians;—I'd shoot you, too—you killed him. When I grow up to be a man, I'll have a gun and come here—"

He had the child in his arms, and called to the boy:

"Come, fast now! Go as near as you can to where you left her."

They ran forward through the gray smoke, stepping over and around bodies as they went. When they reached the first of the women he would have stopped to search, but the boy led him on, pointing. And then, half-way up the line, a little to the right of the road, at the edge of the cedars, his eye caught the glimpse of a great mass of yellow hair on the ground. She seemed to have been only wounded, for, as he looked, she was up on her knees striving to stand.

He ran faster, leaving the boy behind now, but while he was still far off, he saw an Indian, knife in hand, run to her and strike her down. Then before he had divined the intent, the savage had gathered the long hair into his left hand, made a swift circling of the knife with his right,—and the thing was done before his eyes. He screamed in terror as he ran, and now he was near enough to be heard. The Indian at his cry arose and for one long second shook, almost in his face as he came running up, the long, shining, yellow hair with the gory patch at the end. Before his staring eyes, the hair was twisting, writhing, and undulating,—like a golden flame licking the bronzed arm that held it. And then, as he reached the spot, the Indian, with a long yell of delight and a final flourish of his trophy, ran off to other prizes.

He stood a moment, breathless and faint, looking with fearful eyes down at the little, limp, still figure at his feet. One slender, bare arm was flung out as if she had grasped at the whole big earth in her last agony.

The spell of fear was broken by the boy, who came trotting up. He had given way to his tears now, and was crying loudly from fright. Joel made him take the little girl and sit under a cedar out of sight of the spot.

Chapter XVIII
In the Dark of the Aftermath

He was never able to recall the events of that day, or of the months following, in anything like their proper sequence. The effort to do so brought a pain shooting through his head. Up to the moment when the yellow hair had waved in his face, everything had kept a ghastly distinctness. He remembered each instant and each emotion. After that all was dark confusion, with only here and there a detached, inconsequent memory of appalling vividness.

He could remember that he had buried her on the other side of the hill where a gnarled cedar grew at the foot of a ledge of sandstone, using a spade that an Indian had brought him from the deserted camp. By her side he had found the scattered contents of the little bundle she had carried,—a small Bible, a locket, a worn gold bracelet, and a picture of herself as he had known her, a half-faded daguerreotype set in a gilt oval, in a square rubber case that shut with a snap. The little limp-backed Bible had lain flung open on the ground in the midst of the other trinkets. He remembered picking these things up and retying them in the blue silk handkerchief, and then he had twice driven away an Indian who, finding no other life, came up to kill the two children huddled at the foot of the cedar.

He recalled that he had at some time passed the two wagons; one of them was full of children, some crying, some strangely quiet and observant. The other contained the wounded men whom Lee and the two drivers had dispatched where they lay.

He remembered the scene close about him where many of the women and older children had fallen under knife and tomahawk. At intervals had come a long-drawn scream, terrifying in its shrillness, from some woman struggling with Saint or savage.

Later he remembered becoming aware that the bodies were being stripped and plundered; of seeing Lee holding his big white hat for valuables, while half a dozen men searched pockets and stripped off clothing. The picture of the naked bodies of a dozen well-grown children tangled in one heap stayed with him.

Still later, when the last body had been stripped and the smaller treasures collected, he had known that these and the stock and wagons were being divided between the Mormons and the Indians; a conflict with these allies being barely averted, the Indians accusing the Saints of withholding more than their share of the plunder.

After the division was made he knew that the Saints had all been called together to take an oath that the thing should be kept secret. He knew, too, that he had gone over the spot that night, the moon lighting the naked forms strewn about. Many of them lay in attitudes strangely lifelike,—here one resting its head upon its arm, there a white face falling easily back as if it looked up at the stars. He could not recall why he had gone back, unless to be sure that he had made the grave under the cedar secure from the wolves.

Some of the men had camped on the spot. Others had gone to Hamblin's ranch, near the Meadows, where the children were taken. He had sent the boy there with them, and he could recall distinctly the struggle he had with the little fellow; for the boy had wished not to be taken from the girl, and had fought valiantly with fists and feet and his sharp little teeth. The little girl with her mother's bundle he had taken to another ranch farther south in the Pine Mountains. He told the woman the child was his own, and that she was to be kept until he came again.

Where he slept that night, or whether he slept at all, he never knew. But he had been back on the ground in the morning with the others who came to bury the naked bodies. He had seen heaps of them piled in little depressions and the dirt thrown loosely over them, and he remembered that the wolves were at them all a day later.

Then Dame and Haight and others of high standing in the Church had come to look over the spot and there another oath of secrecy was taken. Any informer was to be "sent over the rim of the basin"—except that one of their number was to make a full report to the President at Salt Lake City. Klingensmith was then chosen by vote to take charge of the goods for the benefit of the Church. Klingensmith, Haight, and Higbee, he recalled, had later driven two hundred head of the cattle to Salt Lake City and sold them. Klingensmith, too, had put the clothing taken from the bodies, blood-stained, shredded by bullets and knives, into the cellar of the tithing office at Cedar City. Here there had been, a few weeks later, a public auction of the property taken, the Bishop, who presided as auctioneer, facetiously styling it "plunder taken at the siege of Sebastopol." The clothing, however, with the telltale marks upon it, was reserved from the auction and sold privately from the tithing office. Many stout wagons and valuable pieces of equipment had thus been cheaply secured by the Saints round about Cedar City.

He knew that the surviving children, seventeen in number, had been "sold out" to Saints in and about Cedar City, Harmony, and Painter's Creek, who would later present bills for their keep.

He knew that Lee, whom the Bishops had promised a crown of glory for his work that day, had gone to Salt Lake City and made a confidential report to Brigham; that Brigham had at first professed to regard the occurrence as unfortunate for the Church, though admitting that no innocent blood had been shed; that he had sworn Lee never to tell the story again to any person, instructing him to make a written report of the affair to himself, as Indian agent, charging the deed to the Indians. He was said to have added on this point, after a period of reflection, "Only Indians, John, don't save even the little children." He was reported to have told Lee further, on the following day, that he had asked God to take the vision from his sight if the killing had been a righteous thing, and that God had done so, thus proving the deed in the sight of heaven to have been a just vengeance upon those who had once made war upon the Saints in Missouri.

With these and with many another disjointed memory of the day Joel Rae was cursed; of how Hamblin the following spring had gathered a hundred and twenty skulls on the ground where the wolves had left them, and buried them again; of how an officer from Camp Floyd had built a cairn on the spot and erected a huge cross to the memory of the slain; of how the thing became so dire in the minds of those who had done it, that more than one man lost his reason, and two were known to have killed themselves to be rid of the death-cries of women.

But the clearest of all among the memories of the day itself was the prayer offered up as they stood amid the heaps of fresh earth, after they had sworn the oath of secrecy; how God had been thanked for delivering the enemy into their hands, and how new faith and better works were promised to Him for this proof of His favour.

The memory of this prayer stayed with him many years: "Bless Brother Brigham—bless him; may the heavens be opened unto him, and angels visit and instruct him. Clothe him with power to defend Thy people and to overthrow all who may rise against us. Bless him in his basket and in his store; multiply and increase him in wives, children, flocks and herds, houses and lands. Make him very great to be a lawgiver and God to Thy people, and to command them in all things whatsoever in the future as in the past."

Nor did he forget that, soon after he had listened to this prayer, and the forces had dispersed, he had made two discoveries;—first, that his hair was whitening; second, that he could not be alone at night and keep his reason.

Chapter XIX
The Host of Israel Goes forth to Battle

He went north in answer to the call for soldiers. He went gladly. It promised activity—and company.

A score of them left Cedar City with much warlike talk, with many ringing prophecies of confusion to the army now marching against them, and to the man who had sent it. They cited Fremont, Presidential candidate of the newly organised Republican party the year before, with his catch phrase, "The abolition of slavery and polygamy, the twin relics of barbarism." Fremont had been defeated. And there was Stephen A. Douglas, once their staunch friend and advocate in Illinois; but the year before he had turned against them, styling polygamy "the loathsome ulcer of the body politic," asserting that the people of Utah were bound by oath to recognise only the authority of Brigham Young; that they were forming alliances with Indians and organising Danite bands to rob and murder American citizens; and urging a rigid investigation into these enormities. For this slander Brigham had hurled upon him the anathema of the priesthood, in consequence of which Douglas had failed to secure even a nomination for the high office which he sought.

And now Buchanan was in a way to draw upon himself that retribution which must ever descend upon the foes of Israel. Brigham was at last to unleash the dogs of war. They recalled his saying when they came into the valley, "If they will let us alone for ten years, we will ask no odds of Uncle Sam or the Devil." The ten years had passed and the Devil was taking them at their word. One of them recalled the prophecy of another inspired leader, Parley Pratt, the Archer of Paradise: "Within ten years from now the people of this country who are not Mormons will be entirely subdued by the Latter-day Saints or swept from the face of the earth; and if this prophecy fails, then you may know the Book of Mormon is not true."

Their great day was surely at hand. Their God of Battles reigned. All through the Territory the leaders preached, prayed, and taught nothing but war; the poets made songs only of war; and the people sang only these.

Public works and private were alike suspended, save the manufacture of new arms, the repairing of old, and the sharpening of sabers and bayonets.

On the way, to fire their ardour, they were met by Brigham's proclamation. It recited that "for the last twenty-five years we have trusted officials of the government from constables and justices to judges, governors, and presidents, only to be scorned, held in derision, insulted, and betrayed. Our houses have been plundered and burned, our fields laid waste, our chief men butchered while under the pledged faith of the government for their safety; and our families driven from their homes to find that shelter in the wilderness and that protection among hostile savages which were denied them in the boasted abodes of Christianity and civilisation." It concluded by forbidding all armed forces of every description to enter the Territory under any pretence whatever, and declaring martial law to exist until further notice. The little band hurried on, eager to be at the front.

The day he reached Salt Lake City, Joel Rae was made major of militia. The following day, he attended the meeting at the tabernacle. He needed, for reasons he did not fully explain to himself, to receive fresh assurance of Brigham's infallibility, of his touch with the Holy Ghost, of his goodness as well as his might; to be caught once more by the compelling magnetism of his presence, the flash of his eye, and the inciting tones of his voice. All this he found.

"Is there," asked Brigham, "a collision between us and the United States? No, we have not collashed—that is the word that sounds nearest to what I mean. But the thread is cut between us and we will never gybe again, no, never—worlds without end. I am not going to have their troops here to protect the priests and rabble in their efforts to drive us from the land we possess. The Lord does not want us to be driven. He has said to me, 'If you will assert your rights and keep my commandments, you shall never again be brought into bondage by your enemies.' The United States says that their army is legal, but I say that such a statement is false as hell, and that those States are as rotten as an old pumpkin that has been frozen seven times over and then thawed in a harvest sun. We can't have that army here and have peace—you might as well tell me you could make hell into a powder-house. And so we shall melt those troops away. I promise you our enemies shall never 'slip the bow on old Bright's neck again.'"

Joel Rae was again under the sway of his old warlike feelings. Brigham had revived his fainting faith. He went out into the noise and hurry of war preparations in a sort of intoxication. Underneath he never ceased to be conscious of the dreadful specter that would not be gone—that stood impassive and immovable as one of the mountains about him, waiting for him to come to it and face it and live his day of reckoning,—the day of his own judgment upon himself. But he drank thirstily of the martial draught and lived the time in a fever of tumultuous drunkenness to the awful truth.

He saw to it that he was never alone by day or night. Once a new thought and a sudden hope came to him, and he had been about to pray that in the campaign he was entering he might be killed. But a second thought stayed him; he had no right to die until he had faced his own judgment.

The army of Israel was now well organised. It had taken all able-bodied males between the ages of eighteen and forty-five. There were a lieutenant-general, four generals, eleven colonels, and six majors. In addition to the Saints' own forces there were the Indians, for Brigham had told a messenger who came to ascertain his disposition toward the approaching army that he would "no longer hold the Indians by the wrist." This messenger had suggested that, while the army might be kept from entering the valley that winter, it would assuredly march in, the following spring. Brigham's reply had not lacked the point that sharpened most of his words.

"Before we shall suffer what we have in times gone by we will burn and lay waste our improvements, and you will find the desert here again. There will not be left one building, nor one foot of lumber, nor a stick or tree or particle of grass or hay that will burn. I will lay this valley utterly waste in the name of Israel's God. We have three years' provisions, which we will cache, and then take to the mountains." The messenger had returned to Fort Bridger and the measures of defense went forward in the valley.

Forces were sent into Echo Cañon, the narrow defile between the mountains through which an army would have to pass. On the east side men were put to building stone ramparts as a protection for riflemen. On the west, where the side was sloping, they dug pits for the same purpose. They also built dams to throw large bodies of water along the west side of the cañon so that an army would be forced to the east side; and here at the top of the cliff, great quantities of boulders were placed so that a slight leverage would suffice to hail them down upon the army as it marched below.

When word came that the invaders had crossed the Utah line, Brigham sent forward a copy of his proclamation and a friendly note of warning to the officer in command. In this he directed that officer to retire from the Territory by the same route he had entered it; adding, however, "should you deem this impracticable and prefer to remain until spring in the vicinity of your present position at Black's Fork or Green River, you can do so in peace and unmolested on condition that you deposit your arms and ammunition with Lewis Robinson, Quartermaster-General of the Territory, and leave as soon in the spring as the roads will permit you to march. And should you fall short of provisions they will be furnished you upon making the proper application." The officer who received this note had replied somewhat curtly that the forces he commanded were in Utah by order of the President of the United States and that their future movements would depend wholly upon orders issued by competent military authority. Thus the issue was forced.

In addition to the defense of Echo Cañon, certain aggressive moves were made. To Joel Rae was allotted command of one of these. His orders promised all he could wish of action. He read them and felt something like his old truculent enthusiasm.

"You will proceed with all possible dispatch, without injuring your animals, to the Oregon Road near the bend of Bear River, north by east of this place. When you approach the road, send scouts ahead to ascertain if the invading troops have passed that way. Should they have passed, take a concealed route and get ahead of them. On ascertaining the locality of the troops, proceed at once to annoy them in every possible way. Use every exertion to stampede their animals and set fire to their trains. Burn the whole country before them and on their flanks. Keep them from sleeping, by night surprises; blockade the road by felling trees, or destroying river fords where you can. Watch for opportunities to set fire to the grass on their windward, so as to envelope their trains if possible. Leave no grass before them that can be burned. Keep your men concealed as much as possible, and guard against surprise. God bless you and give you success.

"YOUR BROTHER IN CHRIST."

Forty-four men were placed under his command to perform this work, and all of them were soon impressed, even to alarm, by the very evident reliance of their leader upon the God of Israel rather than upon any merely human wisdom of his own.

The first capture was not difficult. After an all-night ride they came up with a supply-train of twenty-five wagons drawn by oxen. The captain of this train was ordered to "go the other way" until he reached the States. He started; but as he retraced his steps as often as they moved away, they at length burned his train and left him.

And then the recklessness of the new-fledged major became manifest. He sent one of his captains with twenty men to capture or stampede the mules of the Tenth Regiment, while he with the remainder of his force set off toward Sandy Fork in search of more wagon-trains. When his scouts late in the day reported a train of twenty-six wagons, he was advised by them that he ought not to attack it with so small a force; but to this advice he was deaf, rebuking the men for their little faith.

He allowed the train to proceed until after dark, and then drew cautiously near. Learning, however, that the drivers were drunk, he had his force lie concealed for a time, fearing that they might prove belligerent and thus compel him to shed blood, which he wished not to do.

At midnight the scouts reported that the train was drawn up in two lines for the night and that all was quiet. He mounted his command and ordered an advance. Approaching the camp, they discovered a fact that the scouts had failed to note; a second train had joined the first, and the little host of Israel was now confronted by twice the anticipated force. This discovery was made too late for them to retire unobserved. The men, however, expected their leader to make some inquiry concerning the road and then ride on. But they had not plumbed the depth of his faith.

As the force neared the camp-fire close to the wagons, the rear of the column was lost in the darkness. What the teamsters about the fire saw was an apparently endless column of men advancing upon them. Their leader halted the column, called for the captain of the train, ordered him to have his men stack their arms, collect their property, and stand by under guard. Dismounting from his horse, he fashioned a torch and directed one of the drivers to apply it to the wagons, in order that "the Gentiles might spoil the Gentiles." By the time the teamsters had secured their personal belongings and a little stock of provisions for immediate necessity the fifty wagons were ablaze. The following day, on the Big Sandy, they destroyed another train and a few straggling sutlers' wagons.

And so the campaign went forward. As the winter came on colder, the scouts brought in moving tales of the enemy's discomfiture. Colonel Alexander of the Federal forces, deciding that the cañons could be defended by the Saints, planned to approach Salt Lake City over a roundabout route to the north. He started in heavy snow, cutting a road through the greasewood and sage-brush. Often his men made but three miles a day, and his supply-train was so long that sometimes half of it would be camped for the night before the rear wagons had moved. As there was no cavalry in the force the hosts of Israel harassed them sorely on this march, on one day consecrating eight hundred head of their oxen and driving them to Salt Lake.

Albert Sidney Johnston, commanding the expedition, had also suffered greatly with his forces. The early snows deprived his stock of forage, and the unusual cold froze many oxen and mules.

Lieutenant-Colonel Cooke of the Second Dragoons, with whom travelled the newly appointed governor, was another to suffer. At Fort Laramie so many of his animals had dropped out that numbers of his men were dismounted, and the ambulances used to carry grain. Night after night they huddled at the base of cliffs in the fearful eddies of the snow, and heard above the blast the piteous cries of their famished and freezing stock. Day after day they pushed against the keen blades of the wind, toiling through frozen clouds and stinging ice blasts. The last thirty-five miles to Fort Bridger had required fifteen days, and at one camp on Black's Fork, which they called the "camp of Death," five hundred animals perished in a night.

Nor did the hardships of the troops end when they had all reached what was to be their winter quarters. Still a hundred and fifteen miles from the City of the Saints, they were poorly housed against the bitter cold, poorly fed, and insufficiently clothed, for the burning of the trains by the Lord's hosts had reduced all supplies.

Reports of this distress were duly carried to Brigham and published to the Saints. Their soldiers had made good their resolve to prevent the Federal army from passing the Wasatch Mountains. Aggressive operations ceased for the winter, and the greater part of the militia returned to their homes. A small outpost of fifty men under the command of Major Joel Rae—who had earnestly requested this assignment—was left to guard the narrows of Echo Cañon and to keep watch over the enemy during the winter. This officer was now persuaded that the Lord's hand was with them. For the enemy had been wasted away even by the elements from the time he had crossed the forbidden line.

In Salt Lake City that winter, the same opinion prevailed. They were henceforth to be the free and independent State of Deseret.

"Do you want to know," asked Brigham, in the tabernacle, "what is to be done with the enemy now on our borders? As soon as they start to come into our settlements, let sleep depart from their eyes until they sleep in death! Men shall be secreted along the route and shall waste them away in the name of the God of Battles. The United States will have to make peace with us. Never again shall we make peace with them."

And they sang with fervour:—

> "By the mountains our Zion's surrounded,
>   Her warriors are noble and brave;
> And their faith on Jehovah is founded,
>   Whose power is mighty to save.
> Opposed by a proud, boasting nation,
>   Their numbers compared may be few;
> But their Ruler is known through creation,
>   And they'll always be faithful and true."

Chapter XX
How the Lion of the Lord Roared Soft

But with the coming of spring some fever that had burned in the blood of the Saints from high to low was felt to be losing its heat. They had held the Gentile army at bay during the winter—with the winter's help. But spring was now melting the snows. Reports from Washington, moreover, indicated that a perverse generation in the States had declined to accept the decrees of Israel's God without further proofs of their authenticity.

With a view to determining this issue, Congress had voted more money for troops. Three thousand men were to march to the reinforcement of the army of Johnston on Black's Fork; forty-five hundred wagons were to transport their supplies; and fifty thousand oxen and four thousand mules were to pull these wagons. War, in short, was to be waged upon this Israel hidden in the chamber of the mountains. To Major Rae, watching on the outposts of Zion from behind the icy ramparts of Echo Cañon, the news was welcome, even enlivening. The more glory there would be in that ultimate triumph which the Lord was about to secure for them.

In Brigham and the other leaders, however, this report induced deep thought. And finally, on a day, they let it be known that there could no longer be any thought of actual war with the armies of the Gentile. Joel Rae in Echo Cañon was incredulous. There must be battle given. The Lord would make them prevail; the living God of Abraham, of Isaac, and of Jacob, would hold them up. And battle must be given for another reason, though he hardly dared let that reason be plain to himself. For only by continuing the war, only by giving actual battle to armed soldiers, by fighting to the end if need be—only so could that day in Mountain Meadows be made to appear as anything but—he shuddered and could not name it. Even if actual war were to be fought on and on for years, he believed that day could hardly be justified; but at least it could be made in years of fighting to stand less horribly high and solitary. They must fight, he thought, even if it were to lose all. But the Lord would stay them. How much more wicked and perverse, then, to reject the privilege!

When he heard that the new governor, who had been in the snow with Johnston's army all winter, was to enter Salt Lake City and take his office—a Gentile officer to sit on the throne of Brigham—he felt that the Ark of the Covenant had been thrown down. "Let us not," he implored Brigham in a letter sent him from Echo Cañon, "be again dragooned into servile obedience to any one less than the Christ of God!"

But Brigham's reply was an order to pass the new governor through Echo Cañon. According to the terms of this order he was escorted through at night, in a manner to convince him that he was passing between the lines of a mighty and far-flung host. Fires were kindled along the heights and the small force attending him was cunningly distributed and duplicated, a few of its numbers going ahead from time to time, halting the rest of the party and demanding the countersign.

Joel Rae found himself believing that he could now have been a fiercer Lion of the Lord than Brigham was; for he would have fought, while Brigham was stooping to petty strategies—as if God were needing to rely upon deceits.

He was only a little appeased when, on going to Salt Lake City, he learned Brigham's intentions more fully. The new governor had been installed; but the army of Johnston was to turn back. This was Brigham's first promise. Soon, however, this was modified. The government, it appeared, was bent upon quartering its troops in the valley; and Zion, therefore, would be again led into the wilderness. The earlier promise was repeated—and the earlier threat—to the peace commissioners now sent on from Washington.

"We are willing those troops should come into our country, but not stay in our city. They may pass through if need be, but must not be quartered within forty miles of us. And if they come here to disturb this people, before they reach here this city will be in ashes; every house and tree and shrub and blade of grass will be destroyed. Here are twenty years' gathering, but it will all burn. You will have won back the wilderness, barren again as on the day we entered it, but you will not have conquered the people. Our wives and children will go to the cañons and take shelter in the mountains, while their husbands and sons will fight you. You will be without fuel, without subsistence for yourselves or forage for your animals. You will be in a strange land, while we know every foot of it. We will haunt and harass you and pick you off by day and by night, and, as God lives, we will waste your army away."

This was hopeful. Here at least was another chance to suffer persecution, and thus, in a measure, atone for any monstrous wrong they might have done. He hoped the soldiers would come despoiling, plundering, thus compelling them to use the torch and to flee. Another forced exodus would help to drive certain memories from his mind and silence the cries that were now beginning to ring in his ears.

Obedient to priestly counsel, the Saints declined, in the language of Brigham, "to trust again in Punic faith." In April they began to move south, starting from the settlements on the north. During that and the two succeeding months thirty thousand of them left their homes. They took only their wagons, bedding, and provisions, leaving their other possessions to the mercy of the expected despoiler. Before locking the doors of their houses for the last time, they strewed shavings, straw, and other combustibles through the rooms so that the work of firing the city could be done quickly. A score of men were left behind to apply the torch the moment it became necessary,—should a gate be swung open or a latch lifted by hostile hands. Their homes and fields and orchards might be given back to the desert from which they had been won; but never to the Gentile invaders.

To the south the wagons crept, day after day, to some other unknown desert which their prophet should choose, and where, if the Lord willed, they would again charm orchards and gardens and green fields from the gray, parched barrens.

Late in June the army of Johnston descended Emigration Cañon, passed through the echoing streets of the all but deserted city and camped on the River Jordan. But, to the deep despair of one observer, these invaders committed no depredation or overt act. After resting inoffensively two days on the Jordan, they marched forty miles south to Cedar Valley, where Camp Floyd was established.

Thus, no one fully comprehending how it had come about, peace was seen suddenly to have been restored. The people, from Brigham down, had been offered a free pardon for all past treasons and seditions if they would return to their allegiance to the Federal government; the new officers of the Territory were installed, sons of perdition in the seats of the Lord's mighty; and sermons of wrath against Uncle Sam ceased for the moment to resound in the tabernacle. Early in July, Brigham ordered the people to return to their homes. They had offered these as a sacrifice, even as Abraham had offered Isaac, and the Lord had caught them a timely ram in the thicket.

In the midst of the general rejoicing, Joel Rae was overwhelmed with humiliation and despair. He was ashamed for having once wished to be another Lion of the Lord. It was a poor way to find favour with God, he thought,—this refusing battle when it had been all but forced upon them. It was plain, however, that the Lord meant to try them further,—plain, too, that in His inscrutable wisdom He had postponed the destruction of the wicked nation to the east of them.

He longed again to rise before the people and call them to repentance and to action. Once he would have done so, but now an evil shadow lay upon him. Intuitively he knew that his words would no longer come with power. Some virtue had gone out of him. And with this loss of confidence in himself came again a desire to be away from the crowded center.

Off to the south was the desert. There he could be alone; there face God and his own conscience and have his inmost soul declare the truth about himself. In his sadness he would have liked to lead the people with him, lead them away from some evil, some falsity that had crept in about them; he knew not what it was nor how it had come, but Zion had been defiled. Something was gone from the Church, something from Brigham, something from himself,—something, it almost seemed, even from the God of Israel. When the summer waned, his plan was formed to go to one of the southern settlements to live. Brigham had approved. The Church needed new blood there.

He rode out of the city one early morning in September, facing to the south over the rolling valley that lay between the hills now flaunting their first autumn colours. He was in haste to go, yet fearful of what he should meet there.

A little out of the city he passed a man from the south, huddled high on the seat under the bow of his wagon-cover, who sang as he went one of the songs that had been so popular the winter before:—

> "Old squaw-killer Harney is on the way
> The Mormon people for to slay.
> Now if he comes, the truth I'll tell,
> Our boys will drive him down to hell—   Du dah, du dah,
> day!"

He smiled grimly as the belated echo of war came back to him.

Chapter XXI
The Blood on the Page

Along the level lane between the mountain ranges he went, a lane that runs almost from Bear Creek on the north to the Colorado on the south, with a width of twenty miles or so. But for Joel Rae it became a ride down the valley of lost illusions. Some saving grace of faith was gone from the people. He passed through sturdy little settlements, bowered in gardens and orchards, and girded about by now fertile acres where once had been the bare, gray desert. Slowly, mile by mile, the Saints had pushed down the valley, battling with the Indians and the elements for every acre of land they gained. Yet it seemed to him now that they had achieved but a mere Godless prosperity. They had worked a miracle of abundance in the desert—but of what avail? For the soul of their faith was gone. He felt or heard the proof of it on every hand.

Through Battle Creek, Provo, and Springville he went; through Spanish Fork, Payson, Salt Creek, and Fillmore. He stopped to preach at each place, but he did it perfunctorily, and with shame for himself in his secret heart. Some impalpable essence of spirituality was gone from himself and from the people. He felt himself wickedly agreeing with a pessimistic elder at Fillmore, who remarked: "I tell you what, Brother Rae, it seems like when the Book of Mormon goes again' the Constitution of the United States, there's sure to be hell to pay, and the Saints allus has to pay it." He could not tell the man in words of fire, as once he would have done, that they had been punished for lack of faith.

Another told him it was madness to have thought they could "whip" the United States. "Why," said this one, "they's more soldiers back there east of the Missouri than there is fiddlers in hell!" By the orthodox teachings of the time, the good man of Israel had thus indicated an overwhelming host.

He passed sadly on. They would not understand that they had laid by and forgotten their impenetrable armour of faith.

Between Beaver and Paragonah that day, toiling intently along the dusty road in the full blaze of the August sun, he met a woman,—a tall, strong creature with a broad, kind face, burned and seamed and hardened by life in the open. Yet it was a face that appealed to him by its look of simple, trusting earnestness. Her dress was of stout, gray homespun, her shoes were coarse and heavy, and she was bareheaded, her gray, straggling hair half caught into a clumsy knot at the back of her head. She turned out to pass him without looking up, but he stopped his horse and dismounted before her. It seemed to him that here was one whose faith was still fresh, and to such a one he needed to talk. He called to her:

"You need something on your head; you are burned."

She looked up, absently at first, as if neither seeing nor hearing him. Then intelligence came into her eyes.

"You mean my Timothy needs something on his head—poor man! You see he broke out of the house last night, because the Bishop told him I was to take another husband. Cruel! Oh, so cruel!—the poor foolish man, he believed it, and he cared so for me. He thought I was bringing home a new man with me—a new wedding for time and eternity, to build myself up in the Kingdom—a new wedding night—with him sitting off, cold and neglected. But something burst in his head. It made a roar like the mill at Cedar Creek when it grinds the corn—just like that. So he went out into the cold night—it was sleeting—thinking I'd never miss him, you see, me being fondled and made over by the new man—wouldn't miss him till morning." A scowl of indignation darkened her face for an instant, and she paused, looking off toward the distant hills.

"But that was all a lie, a mean lie! I don't see how he could have believed it. I think he couldn't have been right up here—" she pointed to her head.

"But of course I followed him, and I've been following him all day. He must have got quite a start of me—poor dear—how could he think I'd break his heart? But I'll have him found by night. I must hurry, so good day, sir!" She curtsied to him with a curious awkward sort of grace. He stopped her again.

"Where will you sleep to-night?"

"In his arms, thank God!"

"But if you happen to miss him—you might not find him until to-morrow."

A puzzled look crossed her face, and then came the shadow of a disquieting memory.

"Now you speak so, I remember that it wasn't last night he left—it was the night before—no?—perhaps three or four nights. But not as much as a fortnight. I remember my little baby came the night he left. I was so mad to find him I suffered the mother-pains out in the cold rain—just a little dead baby—I could take no interest in it. And there has been a night or two since then, of course. Sleep?—oh, I'll sleep some easy place where I can hear him if he passes—sometimes by the road, in a barn, in houses—they let me sleep where I like. I must hurry now. He's waiting just over that hill ahead."

He saw her ascend the rise with a new spring in her step. When she reached the top, he saw her pause and look from side to side below her, then start hopefully down toward the next hill.

A mile beyond, back of a great cloud of dust, He found a drove of cattle, and back of these, hot and voiceful, came the good Bishop Wright. He described the woman he had just met, and inquired if the Bishop knew her.

The Wild Ram of the Mountain mopped his dusty, damp brow, took an easier seat in his saddle, and fanned himself. "Oh, yes, that's the first wife of Elder Tench. When he took his second, eight or ten years ago, something went wrong with this one in her head. She left the house the same night, and she's been on the go ever since. She don't do any harm, jest tramps back and forth between Paragonah and Parowan and Summit and Cedar City. I always *have* said that women is the contrary half of the human race and man is the sanifying half!"

The cattle were again in motion, and the Bishop after them with strong cries of correction and exhortation.

Toward evening Joel Rae entered Paragonah, a loose group of log houses amid outlying fields, now shorn and yellow. Along the street in front of him many children followed and jeered in the wake of a man who slouched some distance ahead of them. As Joel came nearer, one boy, bolder than the others, ran forward and tugged sharply at the victim's ragged gray coat. At this he turned upon his pursuers, and Joel Rae saw his face,—the face of an imbecile, with unsteady eyes and weakly drooping jaw. He raised his hand threateningly at his tormentors, and screamed at them in rage. Then, as they fell back, he chuckled to himself. As Joel passed him, he was still looking back at the group of children now jeering him from a safe distance, his eyes bright for the moment, and his face lighted with a weak, loose-lipped smile.

"Who is that fellow, Bishop?" he asked of his host for the night, a few moments later, when he dismounted in front of the cabin. The Bishop shaded his eyes with his hand and peered up the road at the shambling figure once more moving ahead of the tormenting children.

"That? Oh, that's only Tom Potwin. You heard about him, I guess. No? Well, he's a simple—been so four years now. Don't you recollect? He's the lad over at Manti who wouldn't give up the girl Bishop Warren Snow wanted. The priesthood tried every way to make him; they counselled him, and that didn't do; then they ordered him away on mission, but he wouldn't go; and then they counselled the girl, but she was stubborn too. The Bishop saw there wasn't any other way, so he had him called to a meeting at the schoolhouse one night. As soon as he got there, the lights was blowed out, and—well, it was unfortunate, but this boy's been kind of an idiot ever since."

"Unfortunate! It was awful!"

"Not so awful as refusing to obey counsel."

"What became of the girl?"

"Oh, she saw it wasn't no use trying to go against the Lord, so she married the Bishop. He said at the time that he knew she'd bring him bad luck—she being his thirteenth—and she did, she was that hifalutin. He had to put her away about a year ago, and I hear she's living in a dugout somewhere the other side of Cedar City, a-starving to death they tell me, but for what the neighbours bring her. I never did see why the Bishop was so took with her. You could see she'd never make a worker, and good looks go mighty fast."

He dreamed that night that the foundations of the great temple they were building had crumbled. And when he brought new stones to replace the old, these too fell away to dust in his hands.

The next evening he reached Cedar City. Memories of this locality began to crowd back upon him with torturing clearness; especially of the morning he had left Hamblin's ranch. As he mounted his horse two of the children saved from the wagon-train had stood near him,—a boy of seven and another a little older, the one who had fought so viciously with him when he was separated from the little girl. He remembered that the younger of the two boys had forgotten all but the first of his name. He had told them that it was John Calvin—something; he could not remember what, so great had been his fright; the people at the ranch, because of his forlorn appearance, had thereupon named him John Calvin Sorrow.

These two boys had watched him closely as he mounted his horse, and the older one had called to him, "When I get to be a man, I'm coming back with a gun and kill you till you are dead yourself," and the other, little John Calvin Sorrow, had clenched his fists and echoed the threat, "We'll come back here and kill you! Mormons is worse'n Indians!"

He had ridden quickly away, not noting that some of the men standing by had looked sharply at the boys and then significantly at one another.

One of those who had been present, whom he now met, told him of these two boys.

"You see, Elder, the orders from headquarters was to save only them that was too young to give evidence in a court. But these two was very forward and knowing. They shouldn't have been kept in the first place. So two men—no need of naming names—took both of them out one night. They got along all right with the little one, the one they called John Calvin Sorrow—only the little cuss kicked and scrambled so that we both had to see to him for a minute, and when we was ready for the other, there he was at least ten rods away, a-legging it into the scrub oak. Well, they looked and looked and hunted around till daybreak, but he'd got away all right, the moon going under a cloud. They tracked him quite a ways when it come light, till his tracks run into the trail of a big band of Navajos that had been up north trading ponies and was going back south. He was the one that talked so much about you, but you needn't ever have any fear of his talking any more. He'd be done for one way or another."

For the first time in his life that night, he was afraid to pray,—afraid even to give thanks that others were sleeping in the room with him so that he could hear their breathing and know that he was not alone.

He was up betimes to press on to the south, again afraid to pray, and dreading what was still in store for him. For sooner or later he would have to be alone in the night. Thus far since that day in the Meadows he had slept near others, whether in cabins or in camp, in some freighter's wagon or bivouacking in the snows of Echo Cañon. Each night he had been conscious, at certain terrible moments of awakening, that others were near him. He heard their breathing, or in the silence a fire's light had shown him a sleeping face, the lines of a form, or an arm tossed out. What would happen on the night he found himself alone, he knew not—death, or the loss of reason. He knew what the torture would be,—the shrieks of women in deadly terror, the shrill cries of children, the low, tense curses of men, the rattle of shots, the yells of Indians, the heavy, sickening smell of blood, the still forms fallen in strange positions of ease, the livid faces distorted to grins. He had not been able to keep the sounds from his ears, but thus far the things themselves had stayed behind him, moving always, crawling, writhing, even stepping furtively close at his back, so that he could feel their breath on his neck. When the time came that these should move around in front of him, he thought it would have to be the end. They would go before him, a wild, bleeding, raving procession, until they tore his heart from his breast. One sight he feared most of all,—a bronzed arm with a wide silver bracelet at the wrist, the hand clutching and waving before him heavy strands of long, yellow hair with a gory patch at the end,—living hair that writhed and undulated to catch the light, coiling about the arm like a golden serpent.

His way lay through the Meadows, yet he hardly realised this until he was fairly on the ground in the midst of a thousand evil signs of the day. Here, a year after, were skulls and whitening bones, some in heaps, some scattered through the sage-brush where the wolves had left them. Many of the skulls were pierced with bullet-holes, shattered as by heavy blows, or cleft as with a sharp-edged weapon. Even more terrifying than these were certain traces caught here and there on the low scrub oaks along the way,— children's sunbonnets; shreds of coarse lace, muslin, and calico; a child's shoe, the tattered sleeve of a woman's dress—all faded, dead, whipped by the wind.

He pressed through it all with set jaws, trying to keep his eyes fixed upon the ground beyond his horse's head; but his ears were at the mercy of the cries that rang from every thicket.

Once out of it, he rode hard, for it must not come yet—his first night alone. By dusk he had reached the new settlement of Amalon, a little off the main road in a valley of the Pine Mountains. Here he sought the house where he had left the child. When he had picketed his horse he went in and had her brought to him,—a fresh little flower-like woman-child, with hair and eyes that told of her mother, with reminders of her mother's ways as she stood before him, a waiting poise of the head, a lift of the chin. They looked at each other in the candle-light, the child standing by the woman who had brought her, looking up at him curiously, and he not daring to touch her or go nearer. She became uneasy and frightened at last, under his scrutiny, and when the woman would have held her from running away, began to cry, so that he gave the word to let her go. She ran quickly into the other room of the cabin, from which she called back with tears of indignation in her voice, "You're not my papa—not my *real* papa!"

When the people were asleep, he sat before the blaze in the big fireplace, on the hearth cleanly swept with its turkey-wing and buffalo-tail. There was to be one more night of his reprieve from solitude. The three women of the house and the man were sleeping around the room in bunks. The child's bed had been placed near him on the floor after she slept, as he had asked it to be. He had no thought of sleep for himself. He was too intensely awake with apprehension. On the floor beside his chair was a little bundle the woman had brought him,—the bundle he had found loosened by her side, that day, with the trinkets scattered about and the limp-backed little Bible lying open where it had fallen.

He picked the bundle up and untied it, touching the contents timidly. He took up the Bible last, and as he did so a memory flooded back upon him that sickened him and left him trembling. It was the book he had given her on her seventeenth birthday, the one she had told him she was keeping when they parted that morning at Nauvoo. He knew the truth before he opened it at the yellowed fly-leaf and read in faded ink, "From Joel to Prudence on this day when she is seventeen years old—June 2d, 1843."

In a daze of feeling he turned the pages, trying to clear his mind, glancing at the chapter headings as he turned,—"Abram is Justified by Faith," "God Instructeth Isaac," "Pharaoh's Heart Is Hardened," "The Laws of Murder," "The Curses for Disobedience." He turned rapidly and at last began to run the leaves from between his thumb and finger, and then, well over in the book something dark caught his eye. He turned the leaves back again to see what it was; but not until the book was opened flat before him and he held the page close to the light did he see what it was his eye had caught. A wash of blood was across the page.

He stared blankly at the reddish, dark stain, as if its spell had been hypnotic. Little by little he began to feel the horror of it, remembering how he picked the book up from where it had fallen before her. Slowly, but with relentless certainty, his mind cleared to what he saw.

Now for the first time he began to notice the words that showed dimly through the stain, began to read them, to puzzle them out, as if they were new to him:—

"But I say unto you which hear, Love your enemies, do
good to them which hate you,
"Bless them that curse you, and pray for them which
despitefully use you.
"And unto him that smiteth thee on the one cheek, offer
also the other; and him that taketh away thy cloke forbid
not to take thy coat also.
"Give to every man that asketh of thee; and of him that
taketh away thy goods ask them not again.
"And as ye would that men should do to you, do ye also
to them likewise."

Again and again he read them. They were illumined with a strangely terrible meaning by the blood of her he had loved and sworn to keep himself clean for.

He could no longer fight off the truth. It was facing him now in all its nakedness, monstrous to obscenity, demanding its due measure from his own soul's blood. He aroused himself, shivering, and looked out into the room where the shadows lay heavy, and from whence came the breathing of the sleepers. He picked up the now sputtering candle, set in its hole bored in a block of wood, and held it up for a last look at the little woman-child. He was full of an agony of wonder as he gazed, of piteous questioning why this should be as it was. The child stirred and flung one arm over her eyes as if to hide the light. He put out the candle and set it down. Then stooping over, he kissed the pillow beside the child's head and stepped lightly to the door. He had come to the end of his subterfuges—he could no longer delay his punishment.

Outside the moon was shining, and his horse moved about restlessly. He put on the saddle and rode off to the south, galloping rapidly after he reached the highway. Off there was a kindly desert where a man could take in peace such punishment as his body could bear and his soul decree; and where that soul could then pass on in decent privacy to be judged by its Maker.

Chapter XXII
The Picture in the Sky

If something of the peace of the night-silence came to him as he rode, he counted it only the peace of surrender and despair. He knew now that he had been cheated of all his great long-nursed hopes of some superior exaltation. Nor this only; for he had sinned unforgivably and incurred perdition. He who had fasted, prayed, and endured, waiting for his Witness, for the spreading of the heavens and the glory of the open vision, had overreached himself and was cast down.

When at last he slowed his horse to a walk, it was the spring of the day. The moon had gone, and over on his left a soft grayness began to show above the line of the hills. The light grew until it glowed with the fire of opals; through the tree-tops ran little stirs of wakefulness, and all about him were faint, furtive rustlings and whispers of the new day. Then in this glorified dusk of the dawn a squirrel loosed his bark of alarm, a crested jay screamed in answer, and he knew his hour of atonement was come.

He pressed forward again toward the desert, eager to be on with it. The page with the wash of blood across it seemed to take on a new vividness in the stronger light. Under the stain, the letters of the words were magnified before his mind,—"*And as ye would that men should do to you—*" It seemed to him that the blood through which they came heated the words so that they burned his eyes.

An hour after daybreak the trail led him down out of the hills by a little watercourse to the edge of the desert. Along the sides of this the chaparral grew thickly, and the spring by which he halted made a little spot of green at the edge of the gray. But out in front of him was the infinite stretch of death, far sweeps of wind-furrowed sand burning under a sun made sullen red by the clouds of fine dust in the air. Sparsely over the dull surface grew the few shrubs that could survive the heat and dryness,—stunted, unlovely things of burr, spine, thorn, or saw-edged leaf,—all bent one ways by the sand blown against them,—bristling cactus and crouching mesquite bushes.

In the vast open of the blue above, a vulture wheeled with sinister alertness; and far out among the dwarfed growing things a coyote skulked knowingly. The weird, phantom-like beauty of it stole upon him, torn as he was, while he looked over the dry, flat reaches. It was a good place to die in, this lifeless waste languishing under an angry sun. And he knew how it would come. Out to the south, as many miles as he should have strength to walk, away from any road or water-hole, a great thirst would come, and then delirium, perhaps bringing visions of cool running water and green trees. He would hurry toward these madly until he stumbled and fell and died. Then would come those cynical scavengers of the desert, the vulture wheeling lower, the coyote skulking nearer, pausing suspiciously to sniff and to see if he moved. Then a few poor bones, half-buried by the restless sand, would be left to whiten and crumble into particles of the same desert dust he looked upon. As for his soul, he shuddered to think its dissolution could not also be made as sure.

He stood looking out a long time, held by the weak spirit of a hope that some reprieve might come, from within or from on high. But he saw only the page wet with blood, and the words that burned through it into his eyes; heard only the cries of women in their death-agony and the stealthy movements of the bleeding shapes behind him. There was no ray of hope to his eye nor note of it to his ear—only the cries and the rustlings back of him, driving him out.

At last he gave his horse water, tied the bridle-rein to the horn of the saddle, headed him back over the trail to the valley and turned him loose. Then, after a long look toward the saving green of the hills, he started off through the yielding sand, his face white and haggard but hard-set. He was already weakened by fasting and loss of sleep, and the heat and dryness soon told upon him as the chill was warmed from the morning air.

When he had walked an hour, he felt he must stop, at least to rest. He looked back to see how far he had come. He was disappointed by the nearness of the hills; they seemed but a stone's throw away. If delirium came now he would probably wander back to the water. He lay down, determining to gather strength for many more miles. The sand was hot under him, and the heat of a furnace was above, but he lay with his head on his arm and his hat pulled over his face. Soon he was half-asleep, so that dreams would alternate with flashes of consciousness; or sometimes they merged, so that he would dream he had wandered into a desert, or that the stifling heat of a desert came to him amid the snows of Echo Cañon. He awakened finally with a cry, brushing from before his eyes a mass of yellow hair that a dark hand shook in his face.

He sat up, looked about a moment, and was on his feet again to the south, walking in the full glare of the sun, with his shadow now straight behind him. He went unsteadily at first, but soon felt new vigour from his rest.

He walked another hour, then turned, and was again disappointed—it was such a little distance; yet he knew now he must be too far out to find his way back when the madness came. So it was with a little sigh of contentment that he lay down again to rest or to take what might come.

Again he lay with his head on his arm in the scorching sands, with his hat above his face, and again his dreams alternated with consciousness of the desolation about him—alternated and mingled so that he no longer knew when he did not sleep. And again he was tortured to wakefulness, to thirst, and to heat, by the yellow hair brandished before him.

He sat up until he was quite awake, and then sank back upon the sand again, relieved to find that he felt too weak to walk further. His mind had become suddenly cleared so that he seemed to see only realities, and those in their just proportions. He knew he had passed sentence of death upon himself, knew he had been led to sin by his own arrogance of soul. It came to him in all its bare, hard simplicity, stripped of the illusions and conceits in which his pride had draped it, thrusting sharp blades of self-condemnation through his heart. In that moment he doubted all things. He knew he had sinned past his own forgiveness, even if pardon had come from on high; knew that no agony of spear and thorns upon the cross could avail to take him from the hell to which his own conscience had sent him.

He was quite broken. Not since the long-gone night on the river-flat across from Nauvoo had tears wet his eyes. But they fell now, and from sheer, helpless grief he wept. And then for the first time in two days he prayed—this time the prayer of the publican:—

"God be merciful to me, a sinner."

Over and over he said the words, chokingly, watering the hot sands with his tears. When the paroxysm had passed, it left him, weak and prone, still faintly crying his prayer into the sand, "O God, be merciful to me, a sinner."

When he had said over the words as long as his parched throat would let him, he became quiet. To his amazement, some new, strange peace had filled him. He took it for the peace of death. He was glad to think it was coming so gently—like a kind mother soothing him to his last sleep.

His head on his arm, his whole tired body relaxing in this new restfulness, he opened his eyes and looked off to the south, idly scanning the horizon, his eyes level with the sandy plain. Then something made him sit quickly up and stare intently, his bared head craning forward. To the south, lying low, was a mass of light clouds, volatile, changing with opalescent lights as he looked. A little to the left of these clouds, while his head was on the sand, he thought his eyes had detected certain squared lines.

Now he scanned the spot with a feverish eagerness. At first there was only the endless empty blue. Then, when his wonder was quite dead and he was about to lie down, there came a miracle of miracles,—a vision in the clear blue of the sky. And this time the lines were coherent. He, the dying sinner, had caught, clearly and positively for one awful second in that sky, the flashing impression of a cross. It faded as soon as it came, vanished while he gazed, leaving him in gasping, fainting wonder at the marvel.

And then, before he could think or question himself, the sky once more yielded its vision; again that image of a cross stayed for a second in his eyes, and this time he thought there were figures about it. Some picture was trying to show itself to him. Still reaching his body forward, gazing fearfully, his aroused body pulsing swiftly to the wonder of the thing, he began to pray again, striving to keep his excitement under.

"O God, have mercy on me, a sinner!"

Slowly at first, it grew before his fixed eyes, then quickly, so that at the last there was a complete picture where but an instant before had been but a meaningless mass of line and colour. Set on a hill were many low, square, flat-topped houses, brown in colour against the gray ground about them. In front of these houses was a larger structure of the same material, a church-like building such as he had once seen in a picture, with a wooden cross at the top. In an open square before this church were many moving persons strangely garbed, seeming to be Indians. They surged for a moment about the door of the church, then parted to either side as if in answer to a signal, and he saw a procession of the same people coming with bowed heads, scourging themselves with short whips and thorned branches. At their head walked a brown-cowled monk, holding aloft before him a small cross, attached by a chain to his waist. As he led the procession forward, another crowd, some of them being other brown-cowled monks, parted before the church door, and there, clearly before his wondering eyes was erected a great cross upon which he saw the crucified Saviour.

He saw those in the procession form about the cross and fling themselves upon the ground before it, while all the others round about knelt. He saw the monk, standing alone, raise the smaller cross in his hands above them, as if in blessing. High above it all, he saw the crucified one, the head lying over on the shoulder.

Then he, too, flung himself face down in the sand, weeping hysterically, calling wildly, and trying again to utter his prayer. Once more he dared to look up, in some sudden distrust of his eyes. Again he saw the prostrate figures, the kneeling ones farther back, the brown-cowled monk with arms upraised, and the face of agony on the cross.

He was down in the sand again, now with enough control of himself to cry out his prayer over and over. When he next looked, the vision was gone. Only a few light clouds ruffled the southern horizon.

He sank back on the sands in an ecstasy. His Witness had come—not as he thought it would, in a moment of spiritual uplift; but when he had been sunk by his own sin to fearful depths. Nor had it brought any message of glory for himself, of gifts or powers. Only the mission of suffering and service and suffering again at the end. But it was enough.

How long he lay in the joy of the realisation he never knew, but sleep or faintness at last overcame him.

He was revived by the sharp chill of night, and sat up to find his mind clear, alert, and active with new purposes. He had suffered greatly from thirst, so that when he tried to say a prayer of thanksgiving he could not move his swollen tongue. He was weakened, too, but the freezing cold of the desert night aroused all his latent force. He struggled to his feet, and laid a course by the light of the moon back to the spring he had left in the morning. How he reached the hills again he never knew, nor how he made his way over them and back to the settlement. But there he lay sick for many days, his mind, when he felt it at all, tossing idly upon the great sustaining consciousness of that vision in the desert.

The day which he next remembered clearly, and from which he dated his new life, was one when he was back in the Meadows. He had ridden there in the first vagueness and weakness of his recovery, without purpose, yet feeling that he must go. What he found there made him believe he had been led to the spot. Stark against the glow of the western sky as he rode up, was a huge cross. He stopped, staring in wonder, believing it to be another vision; but it stayed before him, rigid, bare, and uncompromising. He left his horse and climbed up to it. At its base was piled a cairn of stones, and against this was a slab with an inscription:—

"Here 120 Men, Women, and Children Were Massacred in Cold Blood Early in September, 1857."

On the cross itself was carved in deep letters:—

"Vengeance is mine; I will repay, saith the Lord."

He fell on his knees at the foot and prayed, not weeping nor in any fever of fear, but as one knowing his sin and the sin of his Church. The burden of his prayer was, "O God, my own sin cannot be forgiven—I know it well—but let me atone for the sins of this people and let me guide them aright. Let me die on this cross a hundred deaths for each life they put out, or as many more as shall be needed to save them."

He was strong in his faith again, conscious that he himself was lost, but burning to save others, and hopeful, too, for he believed that a miracle had been vouchsafed to him in the desert.

Nor would the good *padre*, at the head of his procession of penitents in his little mission out across the desert, have doubted less that it was a miracle than did this unhappy apostle of Joseph Smith, had he known the circumstance of its timeliness; albeit he had become familiar with such phenomena of light and air in the desert.

Chapter XXIII
The Sinner Chastens himself

How to offer the greatest sacrifice—how to do the greatest service—these had become his problems. He concerned himself no longer with his own exaltation either in this world or the world to come.

He resolved to stay south, fearing vaguely that in the North he would be in conflict with the priesthood. He knew not how; he felt that he was still sound in his faith, but he felt, too, some undefined antagonism between himself and those who preached in the tabernacle. For his home he chose the settlement of Amalon, set in a rich little valley between the shoulders of the Pine Mountains.

Late in October there was finished for him on the outer edge of the town, near the bank of a little hill-born stream, a roomy log-house, mud-chinked, with a water-tight roof of spruce shakes and a floor of whipsawed plank,—a residence fit for one of the foremost teachers in the Church, an Elder after the Order of Melchisedek, an eloquent preacher and one true to the blessed Gods. At one end of the cabin, a small room was partitioned off and a bunk built in it. A chair and a water-basin on a block comprised its furniture. This room he reserved for himself.

As to the rest of the house, his ideas were at first cloudy. He knew only that he wished to serve. Gradually, however, as his mind worked over the problem, the answer came with considerable clearness. He thought about it much on his way north, for he was obliged to make the trip to Salt Lake City to secure supplies for the winter, some needed articles of furniture for the house, and his wagons and stock.

He was helped in his thinking on a day early in the journey. Near a squalid hut on the outskirts of Cedar City he noticed a woman staggering under an armful of wood. She was bareheaded, with hair disordered, her cheeks hollowed, and her skin yellow and bloodless. He remembered the tale he had heard when he came down. He thought she must be that wife of Bishop Snow who had been put away. He rode up to the cabin as the woman threw her wood inside. She was weak and wretched-looking in the extreme.

"I am Elder Rae. I want to know if you would care to go to Amalon with me when I come back. If you do, you can have a home there as long as you like. It would be easier for you than here."

She had looked up quickly at him in much embarrassment. She smiled a little when he had finished.

"I'm not much good to work, but I think I'd get stronger if I had plenty to eat. I used to be right strong and well."

"I shall be along with my wagons in two weeks or a little more. If you will go with me then I would like to have you. Here, here is money to buy you food until I come."

"You've heard about me, have you—that I'm a divorced woman?"

"Yes, I know."

She looked down at the ground a moment, pondering, then up at him with sudden resolution.

"I can't work hard and—I'm not—pretty any longer—why do you want to marry me?"

Her question made him the more embarrassed of the two, and she saw as much, but she could not tell why it was.

"Why," he stammered, "why,—you see—but never mind. I must hurry on now. In about two weeks—" And he put the spurs so viciously to his horse that he was nearly unseated by the startled animal's leap.

Off on the open road again he thought it out. Marriage had not been in his mind when he spoke to the woman. He had meant only to give her a home. But to her the idea had come naturally from his words, and he began to see that it was, indeed, not an unnatural thing to do. He dwelt long on this new idea, picturing at intervals the woman's lack of any charm or beauty, her painful emaciation, her weakness.

Passing through another village later in the day, he saw the youth who had been so unfortunate as to love this girl in defiance of his Bishop. Unmolested for the time, the imbecile would go briskly a few steps and then pause with an important air of the deepest concern, as if he were engaged on an errand of grave moment. He was thinly clad and shivering in the chill of the late October afternoon.

Again, still later in the day, he overtook and passed the gaunt, gray woman who forever sought her husband. She was smiling as he passed her. Then his mind was made up.

As he entered Brigham's office in Salt Lake City some days later, there passed out by the same door a woman whom he seemed dimly to remember. The left half of her face was disfigured by a huge flaming scar, and he saw that she had but one hand.

"Who was that woman?" he asked Brigham, after they had chatted a little of other matters.

"That's poor Christina Lund. You ought to remember her. She was in your hand-cart party. She's having a pretty hard time of it. You see, she froze off one hand, so now she can't work much, and then she froze her face, so she ain't much for looks any longer—in fact, I wouldn't say Christina was much to start with, judging from the half of her face that's still good—and so, of course, she hasn't been able to marry. The Church helps her a little now and then, but what troubles her most is that she'll lose her glory if she ain't married. You see, she ain't a worker and she ain't handsome, so who's going to have her sealed to him?"

"I remember her now. She pushed the cart with her father in it from the Platte crossing, at Fort Laramie, clear over to Echo Cañon, when all the fingers of one hand came off on the bar of the cart one afternoon; and then her hand had to be amputated. Brother Brigham, she shouldn't be cheated of her place in the Kingdom."

"Well, she ain't capable, and she ain't a pretty person, so what can she do?"

"I believe if the Lord is willing I will have her sealed to me."

"It will be your own doings, Brother Rae. I wouldn't take it on myself to counsel that woman to anybody."

"I feel I must do it, Brother Brigham."

"Well, so be it if you say. She can be sealed to you and be a star in your crown forever. But I hope, now that you've begun to build up your kingdom, you'll do a little better, next time. There's a lot of pretty good-looking young women came in with a party yesterday—"

"All in good time, Brother Brigham! If you're willing, I'll pick up my second on the way south."

"Well, well, now that's good!" and the broad face of Brigham glowed with friendly enthusiasm. "You know I'd suspicioned more than once that you wasn't overly strong on the doctrinal point of celestial marriage. I hope your second, Brother Joel, is a little fancier than this one."

"She'll be a better worker," he replied.

"Well, they're the most satisfactory in the long run. I've found that out myself. At any rate, it's best to lay the foundations of your kingdom with workers, the plainer the better. After that, a man can afford something in the ornamental line now and then. Now, I'll send for Christina and tell her what luck she's in. She hasn't had her endowments yet, so you might as well go through those with her. Be at the endowment-house at five in the morning."

And so it befell that Joel Rae, Elder after the Order of Melchisedek, and Christina Lund, spinster, native of Denmark, were on the following day, after the endowment-rites had been administered, married for time and eternity.

At the door of the endowment-house they were separated and taken to rooms, where each was bathed and anointed with oil poured from a horn. A priest then ordained them to be king and queen in time and eternity. After this, they were conducted to a large apartment, and left in silence for some moments. Then voices were heard, the voice of Elohim in converse with Jehovah. They were heard to declare their intention of visiting the earth, and this they did, pronouncing it good, but deciding that one of a higher order was needed to govern the brutes. Michael, the Archangel, was then called and placed on earth under the name of Adam, receiving power over the beasts, and being made free to eat of the fruit of every tree but one. This tree was a small evergreen, with bunches of raisins tied to its branches.

Discovering that it was not good for man to be alone, Brigham, as God, then caused a sleep to fall upon Adam, and fashioned Eve from one of his ribs. Then the Devil entered, in black silk knee-breeches, approaching with many blandishments the woman who was enacting the rôle of Eve. The sin followed, and the expulsion from the garden.

After this impressive spectacle, Joel and the rapturous Christina were taught many signs, grips, and passwords, without which one may not pass by the gatekeepers of heaven. They were sworn also to avenge the murder of Joseph Smith upon the Gentiles who had done it, and to teach their children to do the same; to obey without questioning or murmur the commands of the priesthood; and never to reveal these secret rites under penalty of having their throats cut from ear to ear and their hearts and tongues cut out.

When this oath had been taken, they passed into a room containing a long, low altar covered with red velvet. At one end, in an armchair, sat Brigham, no longer in the rôle of God, but in his proper person of Prophet, Seer, and Revelator. They knelt on either side of this altar, and, with hands clasped above it in the secret grip last given to them, they were sealed for time and eternity.

From the altar they went to the wagons and began their journey south. Christina came out of the endowment-house, glowing, as to one side of her face. She was, also, in a state of daze that left her able to say but little. Proud and happy and silent, her sole remark, the first day of the trip, was: "Brigham—now—he make such a lovely, *bee-yoo-tiful* God in heaven!"

Nor, it soon appeared, was she ever talkative. The second day, too, she spoke but once, which was when a sudden heavy shower swept down from the hills and caught her some distance from the wagons, helping to drive the cattle. Then, although she was drenched, she only said: "It make down somet'ing, I t'ink!"

For this taciturnity her husband was devoutly thankful. He had married her to secure her place in the Kingdom and a temporal home, and not otherwise did he wish to be concerned about her. He was glad to note, however, that she seemed to be of a happy disposition; which he did at certain times when her eyes beamed upon him from a face radiant with gratitude.

But his work of service had only begun. As they went farther south he began to make inquiries for the wandering wife of Elder Tench. He came upon her at length as she was starting north from Beaver at dusk. He prevailed upon her to stop with his party.

"I don't mind to-night, sir, but I must be off betimes in the morning."

But in the morning he persuaded her to stay with them.

"Your husband is out of the country now, but he's coming back soon, and he will stop first at my house when he does come. So stay with me there and wait for him."

She was troubled by this at first, but at last agreed.

"If you're sure he will come there first—"

She refused to ride in the wagon, however, preferring to walk, and strode briskly all day in the wake of the cattle.

At Parowan he made inquiries for Tom Potwin, that other derelict, and was told that he had gone south. Him, too, they overtook on the road next day, and persuaded to go with them to a home.

When they reached Cedar City a halt was made while he went for the other woman—not without some misgiving, for he remembered that she was still young. But his second view of her reassured him—the sallow, anemic face, the skin drawn tightly over the cheek-bones, the drooping shoulders, the thin, forlorn figure. Even the certainty that her life of hardship was ended, that she was at least sure not to die of privation, had failed to call out any radiance upon her. They were married by a local Bishop, Joel's first wife placing the hand of the second in his own, as the ceremony required. Then with his wives, his charges, his wagons, and his cattle he continued on to the home he had made at the edge of Amalon.

Among the women there was no awkwardness or inharmony; they had all suffered; and the two wives tactfully humoured the whims of the insane woman. On the day they reached home, the husband took them to the door of his own little room.

"All that out there is yours," he said. "Make the best arrangements you can. This is my place; neither of you must ever come in here."

They busied themselves in unpacking the supplies that had been brought, and making the house home-like. The big gray woman had already gone down the road toward the settlement to watch for her husband, promising, however, to return at nightfall. The other derelict helped the women in their work, doing with a childish pleasure the things they told him to do. The second wife occasionally paused in her tasks to look at him from eyes that were lighted to strange depths; but he had for her only the unconcerned, unknowing look that he had for the others.

At night the master of the house, when they had assembled, instructed them briefly in the threefold character of the Godhead. Then, when he had made a short prayer, he bade them good night and went to his room. Here he permitted himself a long look at the fair young face set in the little gilt oval of the rubber case. Then, as if he had forgotten himself, he fell contritely to his knees beside the bunk and prayed that this face might never remind him of aught but his sin; that he might have cross after cross added to his burden until the weight should crush him; and that this might atone, not for his own sins, which must be punished everlastingly, but in some measure for the sins of his misguided people.

In the outer room his wives, sitting together before the big fireplace, were agreeing that he was a good man.

Chapter XXIV
The Coming of the Woman-Child

The next day he sent across the settlement for the child, waiting for her with mixed emotions, — a trembling merge of love and fear, with something, indeed, of awe for this woman-child of her mother, who had come to him so deviously and with a secret significance so mighty of portent to his own soul. When they brought her in at last, he had to brace himself to meet her.

She came and stood before him, one foot a little advanced, several dolls clutched tightly under one arm, and her bonnet swinging in the other hand. She looked up at him fearlessly, questioningly, but with no sign of friendliness. He saw and felt her mother in all her being, in her eyes and hair, in the lines of her soft little face, and indefinably in her way of standing or moving. He was seized with a sudden fear that the mother watched him secretly out of the child's eyes, and with the child's lips might call to him accusingly, with what wild cries of anguish and reproach he dared not guess. He strove to say something to her, but his lips were dry, and he made only some half-articulate sound, trying to force a smile of assurance.

Then the child spoke, her serious, questioning eyes upon him unwaveringly.

"Are you a damned Mormon?"

It broke the spell of awe that had lain upon him, so that he felt for the moment only a pious horror of her speech. He called Christina to take charge of her, and Martha, the second wife, to put away her little bundle of clothing, and Tom Potwin to fetch water for her bath. He himself went to be alone where he could think what must be done for her. From an entry in the little Bible, written in letters that seemed to shout to him the accusation of his crime, he had found that she must now be five years old. It was plainly time that he should begin to supply her very apparent need of religious instruction.

When she had become a little used to her surroundings later in the day, he sought to beguile her to this end, beginning diplomatically with other matters.

"Come, tell me your name, dear."

She allowed her attention to be diverted from her largest doll.

"My name is Prudence—" She hesitated.

"Prudence—what?"

"I—I lost my mind of it." She looked at him hopefully, to be prompted.

"Prudence Rae."

She repeated the name, doubtingly, "Prudence Rae?"

"Yes—remember now—Prudence Rae. You are my little girl—Prudence Rae."

"But you're not my really papa—he's went far off—oh, ten ninety miles far!"

"No, Prudence—God is your Father in heaven, and I am your father on earth—"

"But not my *papa!*"

"Listen, Prudence—do you know what you are?"

The puzzled look she had worn fled instantly from her face.

"I'm a generation of vipers."

She made the announcement with a palpable ring of elation in her tones, looking at him proudly, and as if waiting to hear expressions of astonishment and delight.

"Child, child, who has told you such things? You are not that!"

She retorted, indignantly now, the lines drawing about her eyes in signal of near-by tears:

"I *am* a generation of vipers—the Bishop said I was—he told that other mamma, and I *am* it!"

"Well, well, don't cry—all right—you shall be it—but I can tell you something much nicer." He assumed a knowing air, as one who withheld knowledge of overwhelming fascinations.

"Tell me—*what?*"

"BUT YOU'RE NOT MY REALLY PAPA!"

And so, little by little, hardly knowing where to begin, but feeling that any light whatsoever must profit a soul so benighted, he began to teach her. When she had been put to bed at early candle-light, he went to see if she remembered her lesson.

"What is the name of God in pure language?"

And she answered, with zest, "Ahman."

"What is the name of the Son of God?"

"Son Ahman,—the greatest of all the parts of God excepting Ahman."

"What is the name of man?"

"Sons Ahman."

"That is good—my little girl shall be chosen of the Lord."

He waited by her until sleep should come, but her mind had been stirred, and long after he thought she slept she startled him by asking, in a voice of entire wakefulness: "If I am a good little girl, and learn all the *right* things— *then* can I be a generation of vipers?" She lingered with relish on the phrase, giving each syllable with distinctness and gusto. When he was sure that she slept, he leaned over very carefully and kissed the pillow beside her head.

In the days that followed he wooed her patiently, seeking constantly to find some favour with her, and grateful beyond words when he succeeded ever so little. At first, he could win but slight notice of any sort from her, and that only at rare and uncertain intervals. But gradually his unobtrusive efforts told, and, little by little, she began to take him into her confidence. The first day she invited him to play with her in one of her games was a day of rejoicing for him. She showed him the dolls.

"Now, this is the mother and this is the little baby of it, and we will have a tea-party."

She drew up a chair, placed the two dolls under it, and pointed to the opening between the rungs.

"Here is the house, and here is a little door where to go in at. You must be very, very particulyar when you go in. Now what shall we cook?" And she clasped her hands, looking up at him with waiting eagerness.

He suggested cake and tea. But this answer proved to be wrong.

"Oh, no!"—there was scorn in her tones—"Buffalo-hump and marrowbones and vebshtulls and lemon-coffee."

He received the suggestion cordially, and tried to fall in with it, but she soon detected that his mind was not pliable enough for the game. She was compelled at last to dismiss him, though she accomplished the ungracious thing tactfully.

"Perhaps you have some farming to do out at the barn, because my dollies can't be very well with you at a tea-party, because you are too much."

But she had shown a purpose of friendliness, and this sufficed him. And that night, before her bed-time, when he sat in front of the fire, she came with a most matter-of-fact unconsciousness to climb into his lap. He held her a long time, trying to breathe gently and not daring to move lest he make her uncomfortable. Her head pillowed on his arm, she was soon asleep, and he refused to give her up when Martha came to put her to bed.

Though their intimacy grew during the winter, so that she called him her father and came confidingly to him at all times, in tears or in laughter, yet he never ceased to feel an aloofness from her, an awkwardness in her presence, a fear that the mother who looked from her eyes might at any moment call to him.

That winter was also a time for the other members of the household to adapt themselves to their new life. The two wives attended capably to the house. The imbecile boy, who had once loved one of them to his own undoing, but who no longer knew her, helped them a little with the work, though for the most part he busied himself by darting off upon mysterious and important errands which he would appear to recall suddenly, but which, to his bewilderment, he seemed never able to finish. The other member of the household, Delight Tench, the gaunt, gray woman, still made sallies out to the main road to search for her deceived husband; but they taught her after a little never to go far from the settlement, and to come back to her home each night.

During the winter evenings, when they sat about the big fireplace, the master of the house taught them the mysteries of the Kingdom as revealed by God to Joseph, and then to Brigham, who had been chosen by Joseph as was Joshua by Moses to be a prophet and leader.

In time Brigham would be gathered to his Father, and in the celestial Kingdom, his wives having been sealed to him for eternity, he would beget millions and myriads of spirits. During this period of increase he would grow in the knowledge of the Gods, learning how to make matter take the form he desired. Noting the vast increase in his family, he would then say: "Let us go and make a world upon which my family of spirits may live in bodies of grosser matter, and so gain valuable experience."

At the word of command, thereupon spoken by Brigham, the elements would come together in a new world. This he would beautify, planting seeds upon it, telling the waters where to flow, placing fishes in them, putting fowls in the air and beasts in the field. Then, calling it all good, he would say to his favourite wife: "Let us go down and inhabit this new home." And they would go down, to be called Adam and Eve by some future Moses.

Eve would presently be tempted by Satan to eat fruit from the one tree they had been forbidden to touch, and Brigham as Adam would then partake of it, too, so she should not have to suffer alone. In a thousand years they would die, after raising many tabernacles of flesh into which their spirit children from the celestial world would have come to find abode.

Brigham, going back to the celestial world, would keep watch over these earthly children of his. Yet in their fallen nature they would in time forget their father Brigham, the world whence they came, and the world whither they were going. Sometimes he would send messages to the purest of them, and at all times he would keep as near to them as they would let him. At last he would lay a plan to bring them all again into his presence. For he would now have become the God they should worship. He would send to these children of earth his oldest son, entrusted with the mission of redeeming them, and only faith in the name of this son would secure the favour of the father.

Joel Rae instructed his wondering household, further, that such glory as this would be reserved, not for Brigham alone, but for the least of the Saints. Each Saint would progress to Godhead, and go down with his Eve to make and people worlds without end. This, he explained, was why God had made space to be infinite, since nothing less could have room for the numberless seed of man. In conclusion, he gave them the words of the Heaven-gifted Brigham: "Let all who hear these doctrines pause before they make light of them or treat them with indifference, for they will prove your salvation or your damnation."

Yet often during that winter while he talked these doctrines he would find his mind wandering, and there would come before his eyes a little printed page with a wash of blood across it, and he would be forced to read in spite of himself the verses that were magnified before his eyes. The priesthood of which he was a product dealt but little with the New Testament. They taught from the Old almost wholly, when they went outside the Book of Mormon and the revelations to Joseph Smith—of the God of Israel who was a God of Battle, loving the reek of blood and the smell of burnt flesh on an altar—rather than of the God of the Nazarene.

He found himself turning to this New Testament, therefore, with a curious feeling of interest and surprise, dwelling long at a time upon its few, simple, forthright teachings, being moved by them in ways he did not comprehend, and finding certain of the dogmas of his Church sounding strangely in his ears even when his own lips were teaching them.

One of the verses he especially dreaded to see come before him: "But whoso shall offend one of these little ones which believe in me, it were better for him that a millstone were hanged about his neck, and that he were drowned in the depth of the sea." He taught the child to pray, "O God, let my father have due punishment for all his sins, but teach him never to offend any little child from this day forth."

He used to listen for this and to be soothed when he heard it. Sometimes the words would come to him when he was shut in his room; for if neither of the women was by her when she prayed, it was her custom to raise her voice as high as she could, in the belief that otherwise her prayer would not be heard by the Power she addressed. In high, piping tones this petition for himself would come through his door, following always after the request that the Lord would bless Brigham Young in his basket and in his store, multiplying and increasing him in wives, children, flocks and herds, houses and lands.

Chapter XXV
The Entablature of Truth Makes
a Discovery at Amalon

The house of Rae became a house of importance in the little settlement in the Pine Valley. It was not only the home of the highest Church official in the community, but it was the largest and best-furnished house, so that visiting dignitaries stayed there. It stood a little way from the loose-edged group of cabins that formed the nucleus of the settlement, on ground a little higher, and closer to the wooded cañon that gashed the hills on the east.

The style of house most common in the village was long, low-roofed, of hewn logs, its front pierced by alternating doors and windows. From the number of these might usually be inferred the owner's current prospects for glory in the Kingdom; for behind each door would be a wife to exalt him, and to be exalted herself thereby in the sole way open to her, to thrones, dominion, and power in the celestial world. There were many of these long, profusely doored houses; but many, too, of less external promise; of two doors or even one. Yet in a hut of one door a well-wived Saint might be building up the Kingdom temporarily, until he could provide a more spacious setting for the several stars in his crown.

Then there was the capable Bishop Wright, whose long domestic barracks were the first toward the main road beyond Bishop Coltrin's modest two-doored hut. The Wild Ram of the Mountains, having lately been sealed to his twelfth wife, and having no suitable apartment for her, had ingeniously contrived a sleeping-place in a covered wagon-box at the end of the house, — an apartment which was now being occupied, not without some ungraceful remonstrance, by his first wife, a lady somewhat far down in the vale of years and long past the first glamour of her enthusiasm for the Kingdom. It had been her mischance to occupy previously in the community-house that apartment which the good man saw to be most suitable for his young and somewhat fastidious bride. Not without makeshifts, indeed, many of which partook of this infelicity, was the celestial order of marriage to be obeyed and the world brought back to its primitive purity and innocence.

And of all persons in any degree distressed about these or other matters of faith, Joel Rae was made the first confidant and chief comforter. In the case just cited, for example, Bishop Wright had confessed to him that, if anything could make him break asunder the cable of the Church of Christ, it would be the perplexity inevitable to a maintenance of domestic harmony under the celestial order. The first wife also distressed this adviser with a moving tale of her expulsion from a comfortable room into the incommodious wagon-box.

Many of these confidences, as the days went by, he found spirit-grieving in the extreme, so that he was often weary and longed for refuge in a wilderness. Yet he never failed to let fall some word that might be monitory or profitable to those who took him their troubles; nor did he forget to exult in these burdens that were put upon him, for he had resolved that his cross should be made as heavy as he could bear.

In addition to his duties as spiritual adviser to the community, it was his office to preach; also to hold himself at the call of the afflicted, to anoint their heads with oil and rebuke their fevers. He took an especial pleasure in this work of healing, being glad to leave his fields by day or his bed by night for the sickroom. By couches of suffering he watched and prayed, and when they began to say in Amalon that his word of rebuke to fevers came with strange power, that his touch was marvellously healing, and his prayers strangely potent, he prayed not to be set up thereby, nor to forget that the power came, not by him but through him, because of his knowing his own unworthiness. He fasted and prayed to be trusted still more until he should be worthy of that complete power which the Master had said came only by prayer and fasting.

The conscientious manner in which he performed his offices was favourably commented upon by Bishop Wright. This good man believed there had been a decline of late in the ardour of the priesthood.

"I tell you, Elder, I wish they was all as careful as you be, but they're falling into shiftless ways. If I'm sick and have to depend on myself, all right. I'll dose up with lobelia or gamboge, or put a blister-plaster on the back of my neck or take a drink of catnip tea or composition, and then the cure of my misery is with the Lord God of Hosts. But if I send for an administrator, it's different. He takes the responsibility and I want him to fulfil every will of the Lord. When an Elder comes to administer to me and is afraid of greasing his fingers or of dropping a little oil on his vest, and says, 'Oh, never mind the oil! there ain't any virtue in the olive-oil; besides, I might grease my gloves,' why I feel like telling such a Godless critter to walk off. When God says anoint with oil, *anoint*, I don't care if it runs down his beard as it ran down Aaron's. And I don't want to talk anybody down or mention any names; but, well, next time when I got a cold and Elder Beil Wardle is the only administrator free, why, I'll just stand or fall by myself. A basin of water-gruel, hot, with half a quart of old rum in it and lots of brown sugar, is better than all *his* anointing."

To make his days busier there were the affairs of the Church to oversee, for he was now President of the local Stake of Zion; reports of the teachers to consider in council meeting, of their weekly visits to each family, and of the fidelity of each of its members to the Kingdom. And there were the Deacons and Priests of the Aaronic Order and other Elders and Bishops of the Order of Melchisedek to advise with upon the temporal and spiritual affairs of Israel; to labour and pray with Peregrine Noble, who had declared that he would no longer be as limber as a tallowed rag in the hands of the priesthood, and to deliver him over to the buffetings of Satan in the flesh if he persisted in his blasphemy; to rebuke Ozro Cutler for having brazenly sought to pay on his tithing some ten pounds of butter so redolent of garlic that the store had refused to take it from him in trade; to counsel Mary Townsley that Pye Townsley would come short of his glory before God if she remained rebellious in the matter of his sealing other jewels to his crown; to teach certain unillumined Saints something of the ethics of unbranded cattle; and to warn settlers against isolating themselves in the outlying valleys where they would be a temptation to the red sons of Laman.

Again there was the rite of baptism to be administered,—not an onerous office in the matter of the living, but apt to become so in the case of the dead; for the whole world had been in darkness and sin since the apostolic gifts were lost, ages ago, and the number of dead whose souls now waited for baptism was incalculable; and not until the living had been baptised for them could they enter the celestial Kingdom. In consequence, all earnest souls were baptised tirelessly for their loved ones who had gone behind the veil before Peter, James, and John ordained Joseph Smith.

But the unselfish did not confine their efforts to friends and relatives. In the village of Amalon that winter and spring, Amarintha, third wife of Sarshell Sweezy, bethought her to be baptised for Queen Anne; whereupon Ezra Colver at once underwent the same rite for this lamented queen's husband, Prince George of Denmark; thereby securing the prompt admission of the royal couple to the full joys of the Kingdom.

Attention being thus turned to royalty, the first Napoleon and his first consort were baptised into heaven by thoughtful proxies; then Queen Elizabeth and Henry the Eighth. Eric Glines, being a liberal-minded man, was baptised for George Washington, thus adding the first President of the Gentile nation to the galaxy of Mormon Saints reigning in heaven. Gilbroid Sumner thereupon won the fervent commendation of his Elder by submitting twice to burial in the waters of baptism for the two thieves on the cross.

From time to time the little settlement was visited by officials of the Church who journeyed south from Salt Lake City; perhaps one of the powerful Twelve Apostles, those who bind on earth that which is bound in heaven; or High Priests, Counsellors, or even Brigham himself with his favourite wife and a retinue of followers in stately procession.

Late in the spring, also, came the Patriarch in the Church, Uncle John Young, eldest brother of Brigham. It was the office of this good man to dispense blessings to the faithful; blessings written and preserved reverently in the family archives as charms to ward off misfortune. Through all the valleys Uncle John was accustomed to go on his mission of light. When he reached a settlement announcement was made of his headquarters, and the unblessed were invited to wait upon him.

The cynical had been known to complain that Uncle John was a hard man to deal with, especially before money was current in the Territory, when blessings had to be paid for in produce. Many a Saint, these said, had long gone unblessed because the only produce he had to give chanced to meet no need of Uncle John. Further, they gossiped, if paid in butter or fine flour or fat turkeys when these were scarce, Uncle John was certain to give an unusually strong blessing, perhaps insuring, on top of freedom from poverty and disease, the prolongation of life until the coming of the Messiah. Yet it is not improbable that all these tales were insecurely based upon a single instance wherein one Starling Driggs, believing himself to stand in urgent need of a blessing, had offered to pay Uncle John for the service in vinegar. It had been unexceptionable vinegar, as Uncle John himself admitted, but being a hundred miles from home, and having no way to carry it, the Patriarch had been obliged to refuse; which had seemed to most people not to have been more than fell within the lines of reason.

As for the other stories, it is enough to say that Uncle John was himself abundantly blessed with wives and children needing to be fed, that the labourer is worthy of his hire, and that it was sometimes vexatious to follow rapid fluctuations in the market value of butter, eggs, beef, potatoes, beet-molasses, and the like. Certain it is that after money came to circulate it was a much more satisfactory business all around; two dollars a blessing—flat, and no grievances on either side, with a slight reduction if several were blessed in one family. When Uncle John laid his hands upon a head after that, every one knew the exact pecuniary significance of the act.

When the Patriarch stopped at Amalon that spring, at the house of Joel Rae, there were many blessings to be made, and from morning until night for several days he was busy with the writing of them. Two members of the household he interested to an uncommon degree,—the child, Prudence, who forthwith began daily to promise her dolls that they should not taste of death till Christ came, and Tom Potwin, the imbecile, who became for some unknown reason covetous of a blessing for himself. He stayed about the Patriarch most of the time, bothering him with appeals for one of his blessings. But Uncle John, though a good man, had been gifted by Heaven with slight imagination, and Tom Potwin would doubtless have had to go without this luxury but for a chance visitor to the house one day.

This was no less a person than Bishop Snow, he who had once been Tom Potwin's rival for the hand of her who was now the second Mrs. Rae. With his portly figure, his full, florid face with its massive jaw, and his heavy locks of curling white hair, the good Bishop seemed indeed to have deserved the title put upon him years ago by the Church Poet,—The Entablature of Truth.

He alighted from his wagon and greeted Uncle John, busy with the writing of his blessings in the cool shade just outside the door.

"Good for you, Uncle John! Be a fountain of living waters to the thirsty in Zion. Say, who's that?" and he pointed to Tom Potwin who had been wistfully watching the pen of the Patriarch as it ran over his paper. Uncle John regarded the Bishop shrewdly.

"You ought to know, Brother Snow. 'Tain't so long since you and him were together."

The Bishop looked closely again, and the boy now returned his gaze with his own weakly foolish look.

"Well! If it ain't that Tom Potwin. The Lord certainly hardened *his* heart against counsel to his own undoing. I tried every way in the world—say, what's he doing here?"

"Oh, Brother Rae has given him a home here along with that first woman of Brother Tench's. The crazy loon has been bothering me all week to give him a blessing."

The Entablature of Truth chuckled, being not without a sense of humour.

"Well, say, give him one if he wants it. Here—here's your two dollars—write him a good one now."

Uncle John took the money, and at once began writing upon a clean sheet of paper. The boy stood by watching him eagerly, and when the

Patriarch had finished the document took it from him with trembling hands. The Bishop spoke to him.

"Here, boy, let's see what Uncle John gives us for our money."

With some misgiving the owner of the blessing relinquished it into the Bishop's hand, watching it jealously, though listening with delight while his benefactor read it.

"Patriarchal blessing of Tom Potwin by John Young, Patriarch, given at Amalon June 1st, 1859. Brother Tom Potwin, in the name of Jesus of Nazareth and by authority of the Holy Priesthood in me vested, I confer upon thee a Patriarch's blessing. Thou art of Ephraim through the loins of Joseph that was sold into Egypt. And inasmuch as thou hast obeyed the requirements of the Gospel thy sins are forgiven thee. Thy name is written in the Lamb's book of life never more to be blotted out. Thou art a lawful heir to all the blessings of Abraham, Isaac, and Jacob in the new and everlasting covenant. Thou shalt have a numerous posterity who shall rise up to call thee blessed. Thou shalt have power over thine enemies. They that oppose thee shall yet come bending unto thee. Thou shalt come forth in the morning of the first resurrection, and no power shall hinder except the shedding of innocent blood or the consenting thereto. I seal thee up to eternal life in the name of the Father and of the Son and of the Holy Ghost. Amen and amen!"

The worthy Bishop handed the paper back to the enraptured boy, and turned to Joel Rae, who now came up.

"Hello, Brother Rae. I hear you took on that thirteenth woman of mine. Much good it'll do you! She was unlucky for me, sure enough—rambunctious when she was healthy, and lazy when she was sick!"

When they came out of the house half an hour later, he added in tones of confidential warning:

"Say, you want to look out for her—I see she's getting the red back in her blood!"

Chapter XXVI
How the Red Came Back to
the Blood to be a Snare

The watchful eyes of the Bishop had seen truly. Not only was the red coming back to the blood of Martha, but the fair flesh to her meagre frame, the spring of youth to her step and living fire to her voice and the glance of her eyes. Her husband was pleased. He had made a new creature of the poor, worn wreck found by the wayside, weak, emaciated, reeling under her burden. He rejoiced to know he had done a true service. He was glad, moreover, to know that she made an admirable mother to the little woman-child. Prudence, indeed, had brought them closer to each other, slowly, subtly, in little ways to disarm the most timid caution.

And this mothering and fathering of little Prudence was a work by no means colourless or uneventful. The child had displayed a grievous capacity for remaining unimpressed by even the best-weighed opinions of her protector. She was also appallingly fluent in and partial to the idioms and metaphors of revealed religion,—a circumstance that would not infrequently cause the sensitive to shudder.

Thus, when she chose to call her largest and least sightly doll the Holy Ghost, the ingenuity of those about her was taxed to rebuke her in ways that would be effective without being harsh. It was felt, too, that her offence had been but slightly mitigated when she called the same doll, thereafter, "Thou son of perdition and shedder of innocent blood." Not until this disfigured effigy became Bishop Wright, and the remaining dolls his more or less disobedient wives, was it felt that she had approached even remotely the plausible and the decorous.

A glance at some of the verses she was from time to time constrained to learn will perhaps indicate the line of her transgressions, and yet avert a disclosure of details that were often tragic. She was taught these verses from a little old book bound in the gaudiest of Dutch gilt paper, as if to relieve the ever-present severity of the text and the distressing scenes portrayed in the illustrating copperplates. For example, on a morning when there had been hasty words at breakfast, arising from circumstances immaterial to this narrative, she might be made to learn:—

"That I did not see Frances just now I am glad,
For Winifred says she looked sullen and sad.
When I ask her the reason, I know very well
That Frances will blush the true reason to tell.

"And I never again shall expect to hear said
That she pouts at her milk with a toast of white bread,
When both are as good as can possibly be—
Though Betsey, for breakfast, perhaps may have tea."

With no sort of propriety could be set down in printed words the occurrence that led to her reciting twenty times, somewhat defiantly in the beginning, but at last with the accents and expression of countenance proper to remorse, the following verses:—

"Who was it that I lately heard
Repeating an improper word?
I do not like to tell her name
Because she is so much to blame."

Indeed, she came to thunder the final verse with excellent gestures of condemnatory rage:—

"Go, naughty child! and hide your face,
I grieve to see you in disgrace;
Go! you have forfeited to-day
All right at trap and ball to play."

Nor is it necessary to go back of the very significant lines themselves to explain the circumstance of her having the following for a half-day's burden:—

"Jack Parker was a cruel boy,
For mischief was his sole employ;
And much it grieved his friends to find
His thoughts so wickedly inclined.

"But all such boys unless they mend
May come to an unhappy end,
Like Jack, who got a fractured skull
Whilst bellowing at a furious bull."

Nor is there sufficient reason to say why she was often counselled to regard as her model:—

"Miss Lydia Banks, though very young,
Will never do what's rude or wrong;

When spoken to she always tries
To give the most polite replies."

And painful, indeed, would it be to relate the events of one sad day
which culminated in her declaiming at night, with far more than perfunctory
warmth, and in a voice scarce dry of tears:—

"Miss Lucy Wright, though not so tall,
Was just the age of Sophy Ball;
But I have always understood
Miss Sophy was not half so good;
For as they both had faded teeth,
Their teacher sent for Doctor Heath.

"But Sophy made a dreadful rout
And would not have hers taken out;
While Lucy Wright endured the pain,
Nor did she ever once complain.
Her teeth returned quite sound and white,
While Sophy's ached both day and night."

Yet her days were by no means all of reproof nor was her reproof ever
harsher than the more or less pointed selections from the moral verses
could inflict. Under the watchful care of Martha she flourished and was
happy, her mother in little, a laughing whirlwind of tender flesh, tireless
feet, dancing eyes, hair of sunlight that was darkening as she grew older,
and a mind that seemed to him she called father a miracle of unfoldment. It
was a mind not so quickly receptive as he could have wished to the learning
he tried patiently to impart; he wondered, indeed, if she were not unduly
frivolous even for a child of six; for she would refuse to study unless she
could have the doll she called Bishop Wright with her and pretend that
she taught the lesson to him, finding him always stupid and loth to learn.
He hoped for better things from her mind as she aged, watching anxiously
for the buddings of reason and religion, praying daily that she should be
increased in wisdom as in stature. He had become so used to the look of her
mother in her face that it now and then gave him an instant of unspeakable
joy. But the sound of his own voice calling her "Prudence" would shock him
from this as with an icy blast of truth.

When the children of Amalon came to play with her, the little Nephis,
Moronis, Lehis, and Juabs, he saw she was a creature apart from them,
of another fashion of mind and body. He saw, too, that with some native
intuition she seemed to divine this, and to assume command even of those
older than herself. Thus Wish Wright and his brother, Welcome, both
her seniors by several years, were her awe-bound slaves; and the twin
daughters of Zebedee Bloom obeyed her least whim without question, even

when it involved them in situations more or less delicate. With her quick ear for rhythm she had been at once impressed by their names—impressed to a degree that savoured of fascination. She would seat the two before her, range the other children beside them, and then lead the chorus in a spirited chant of these names:—

"Isa Vinda Exene Bloom!
Ella Minda Almarine Bloom!"

repeating this a long time until they were all breathless, and the solemn twins themselves were looking embarrassed and rather foolishly pleased.

As he observed her day by day in her joyous growth, it was inevitable that he came more and more to observe the woman who was caring for her, and it was thus on one night in late summer that he awoke to an awful truth,—a truth that brought back the words of the woman's former husband with a new meaning.

He had heard Prudence say to her, "You are a pretty mamma," and suddenly there came rushing upon him the sum of all the impressions his eyes had taken of her since that day when the Bishop had spoken. He trembled and became weak under the assault, feeling that in some insidious way his strength had been undermined. He went out into the early evening to be alone, but she, presently, having put the child to bed, came and stood near, silently in the doorway.

He looked and saw she was indeed made new, restored to the lustre and fulness of her young womanhood. He remembered then that she had long been silent when he came near her, plainly conscious of his presence but with an apparent constraint, with something almost tentative in her manner. With her return to health and comeliness there had come back to her a thousand little graces of dress and manner and speech. She drew him, with his starved love of beauty and his need of companionship; drew him with a mighty power, and he knew it at last. He remembered how he had felt and faintly thrilled under a certain soft suppression in her tones when she had spoken to him of late; this had drawn him, and the new light in her eyes and her whole freshened womanhood, even before he knew it. Now that he did know it he felt himself shaken and all but lost; clutching weakly at some support that threatened every moment to give way.

And she was his wife, his who had starved year after year for the light touch of a woman's hand and the tones of her voice that should be for him alone. He knew now that he had ached and sickened in his yearning for this, and she stood there for him in the soft night. He knew she was waiting, and he knew he desired above all things else to go to her; that the comfort of her, his to take, would give him new life, new desires, new powers; that with her he would revive as she had done. He waited long, indulging freely in hesitation, bathing his wearied soul in her nearness—yielding in fancy.

Then he walked off into the night, down through the village, past the light of open doors, and through the voices that sounded from them, out on to the bare bench of the mountain—his old refuge in temptation—where he could be safe from submitting to what his soul had forbidden. He had meant to take up a cross, but before his very eyes it had changed to be a snare set for him by the Devil.

He stayed late on the ground in the darkness, winning the battle for himself over and over, decisively, he thought, at the last. But when he went home she was there in the doorway to meet him, still silent, but with eyes that told more than he dared to hear. He thought she had in some way divined his struggle, and was waiting to strengthen the odds against him, with her face in the light of a candle she held above her head.

He went by her without speaking, afraid of his weakness, and rushed to his little cell-like room to fight the battle over. As a last source of strength he took from its hiding-place the little Bible. And as it fell open naturally at the blood-washed page a new thing came, a new torture. No sooner had his eyes fallen on the stain than it seemed to him to cry out of itself, so that he started back from it. He shut the book and the cries were stilled; he opened it and again he heard them—far, loud cries and low groans close to his ear; then long piercing screams stifled suddenly too low, horrible gurglings. And before him came the inscrutable face with the deep gray eyes and the shining lips, lifting, with love in the eyes, above a gashed throat.

He closed the book and fell weakly to his knees to pray brokenly, and almost despairingly: "Help me to keep down this self within me; let it ask for nothing; fan the fires until they consume it! *Bow me, bend me, break me, burn me out—burn me out!*"

In the morning, when he said, "Martha, the harvest is over now, and I want you to go north with me," she prepared to obey without question.

He talked freely to her on the way, though it is probable that he left in her mind little more than dark confusion, beyond the one clear fact of his wish. As to this, she knew she must have no desire but to comply. Reaching Salt Lake City, they went at once to Brigham's office. When they came out they came possessed of a document in duplicate, reciting that they both did "covenant, promise, and agree to dissolve all the relations which have hitherto existed between us as husband and wife, and to keep ourselves separate and apart from each other from this time forth."

This was the simple divorce which Brigham was good enough to grant to such of the Saints as found themselves unhappily married, and wished it. As Joel Rae handed the Prophet the fee of ten dollars, which it was his custom to charge for the service, Brigham made some timely remarks. He said he feared that Martha had been perverse and rebellious; that her first husband had found her so; and that it was doubtless for the good of all that her second had taken the resolution to divorce her. He was afraid that Brother Joel was an inferior judge of women; but he had surely shown himself to be generous in the provision he was making for the support of this contumacious wife.

They parted outside the door of the little office, and he kissed her for the first time since they had been married—on the forehead.

Chapter XXVII
A New Cross Taken up and an
Old Enemy Forgiven

Christina would now be left alone with the cares of the house, and he knew he ought to have some one to help her. The fever of sacrifice was also upon him. And so he found another derelict, to whom he was sealed forever.

At a time of more calmness he might have balked at this one. She was a cross, to be sure, and it was now his part in life to bear crosses. But there were plenty of these, and even one vowed to a life of sacrifice, he suspected, need not grossly abuse the powers of discrimination with which Heaven had seen fit to endow him. But he had lately been on the verge of a seething maelstrom, balancing there with unholy desire and wickedly looking far down, and the need to atone for this sin excited him to indiscretions.

It was not that this star in his crown was in her late thirties and less than lovely. He had learned, indeed, that in the game which, for the chastening of his soul, he now played with the Devil, it were best to choose stars whose charms could excite to little but conduct of a saintlike seemliness. The fat, dumpy figure of this woman, therefore, and her round, flat, moonlike face, her mouse-coloured wisps of hair cut squarely off at the back of her neck, were points of a merit that was in its whole effect nothing less than distinguished.

But she talked. Her tones played with the constancy of an ever-living fountain. Artlessly she lost herself in the sound of their music, until she also lost her sense of proportion, of light and shade, of simple, Christian charity. Her name was Lorena Sears, and she had come in with one of the late trains of converts, without friends, relatives, or means, with nothing but her natural gifts and an abiding faith in the saving powers of the new dispensation. And though she was so alive in her faith, rarely informed in the Scriptures, bubbling with enthusiasm for the new covenant, the new Zion, and the second coming of the Messiah, there had seemed to be no place for her. She had not been asked in marriage, nor had she found it easy to secure work to support herself.

"She's strong," said Brigham, to his inquiring Elder, "and a good worker, but even Brother Heber Kimball wouldn't marry her; and between you and me, Brother Joel, I never knew Heber to shy before at anything that would work. You can see that, yourself, by looking over his household."

But, after the needful preliminaries, and a very little coy hesitation on the part of the lady, Lorena Sears, spinster, native of Elyria, Ohio, was duly sealed to, for time and eternity, and became a star forever in the crown of, Joel Rae, Elder after the Order of Melchisedek in the Church of Jesus Christ of Latter-day Saints and President of the Amalon Stake of Zion.

In the bustle of the start south there were, of necessity, moments in which the crown's new star could not talk; but these blessed respites were at an end when at last they came to the open road.

At first, as her speech flowed on, he looked sidelong at her, in a trouble of fear and wonder; then, at length, absently, trying to put his mind elsewhere and to leave her voice as the muted murmur of a distant torrent. He succeeded fairly well in this, for Lorena combined admirably in herself the parts of speaker and listener, and was not, he thankfully noted, watchful of his attention.

But in spite of all he could do, sentences would come to seize upon his ears: "... No chance at all back there for a good girl with any heart in her unless she's one of the doll-baby kind, and, thank fortune, I never was *that*! Now there was Wilbur Watkins—his father was president of the board of chosen freeholders—Wilbur had a way of saying, 'Lorena's all right—she weighs a hundred and seventy-eight pounds on the big scales down to the city meatmarket, and it's most of it heart—a hundred and seventy-eight pounds and most all heart—and she'd be a prize to anybody,' but then, that was his way,—Wilbur was a good deal of a take-on,—and there was never anything between him and me. And when the Elder come along and begun to preach about the new Zion and tell about the strange ways that the Lord had ordered people to act out here, something kind of went all through me, and I says, 'That's the place for *me*!' Of course, the saying is, 'There ain't any Gawd west of the Missouri,' but them that says it ain't of the house of Israel—lots of folks purtends to be great Bible readers, but pin 'em right down and what do you find?—you find they ain't really studied it—not what you could call *pored* over it. They fuss through a chapter here and there, and rush lickety-brindle through another, and ain't got the blessed truth out of any of 'em—little fine points, like where the Lord hardened Pharaoh's heart every time, for why?—because if He hadn't 'a' done it Pharaoh would 'a' give in the very first time and spoiled the whole thing. And then the Lord would visit so plumb natural and commonlike with Moses—like tellin' him, 'I appeared unto Abraham, unto Isaac, and unto Jacob by the name of God Almighty, for by my name Jehovah was I not known unto them.' I thought that was awful cute and friendly, stoppin' to talk about His name that way. Oh, I've spent hours and hours over the blessed Book. I bet I know something you don't, now—what verse in the Bible has every letter in the alphabet in it except 'J'? Of course you wouldn't know. Plenty of preachers don't. It's the twenty-first verse of the seventh chapter of the book of Ezra. And the Book of Mormon—I do love to git set down in a rocker with my shoes off—I'm kind of a heavy-footed person to be on my feet all day— and that blessed Book in my hands—such beautiful language it uses—that verse I love so, 'He went forth among the people waving the rent of his garment in the air that all might see the writing which he had wrote upon the rent,'—that's sure enough Bible language, ain't it? And yet some folks say the Book of Mormon ain't inspired. And that lovely verse in Second Niphi, first chapter, fourteenth verse: 'Hear the words of a trembling parent whose limbs you must soon lay down in the cold and silent grave from whence no traveller can return.' Back home the school-teacher got hold of that—he's an awful smarty—and he says, 'Oh, that's from Shakespeare,' or some such book, just like that—and I just give him one look, and I says, 'Mr. Lyman Hickenlooper, if you'll take notice,' I says, 'you'll see those words was composed by the angel Moroni over two thousand years ago and revealed to Joseph Smith in the sacred light of the Urim and Thummim,' I says, and the plague-oned smarty snickered right in my face—and say, now, what did you and your second git a separation for?"

He was called back by the stopping of her voice, but she had to repeat her question before he understood it. The Devil tempted him in that moment. He was on the point of answering, "Because she talked too much," but instead he climbed out of the wagon to walk. He walked most of the three hundred miles in the next ten days. Nights and mornings he falsely pretended to be deaf.

He found himself in this long walk full of a pained discouragement; not questioning or doubting, for he had been too well trained ever to do either. But he was disturbed by a feeling of bafflement, as might be a ground-mole whose burrow was continually destroyed by an enemy it could not see. This feeling had begun in Salt Lake City, for there he had seen that the house of Israel was no longer unspotted of the world. Since the army with its camp-followers had come there was drunkenness and vice, the streets resounded with strange oaths, and the midnight murder was common. Even Brigham seemed to have become a gainsayer in behalf of Mammon, and the people, quick to follow his lead, were indulging in ungodly trade with Gentiles; even with the army that had come to invade them. And more and more the

Gentiles were coming in. He heard strange tales of the new facilities afforded them. There was actually a system of wagon-trains regularly hauling freight from the Missouri to the Pacific; there was a stage-route bringing passengers and mail from Babylon; even Horace Greeley had been publicly entertained in Zion,—accorded honour in the Lord's stronghold. There was talk, too, of a pony-express, to bring them mail from the Missouri in six days; and a few visionaries were prophesying that a railroad would one day come by them. The desert was being peopled all about them, and neighbours were forcing a way up to their mountain retreat.

It seemed they were never to weld into one vast chain the broken links of the fated house of Abraham; never to be free from Gentile contamination. He groaned in spirit as he went—walking well ahead of his wagon.

But he had taken up a new cross and he had his reward. The first night after they reached home he took the little Bible from its hiding-place and opened it with trembling hands. The stain was there, red in the candle-light. But the cries no longer rang in his ears as on that other night when he had been sinful before the page. And he was glad, knowing that the self within him had again been put down.

Then came strange news from the East—news of a great civil war. The troops of the enemy at Camp Floyd hurried east to battle, and even the name of that camp was changed, for the Gentile Secretary of War, said gossip from Salt Lake City, after doing his utmost to cripple his country by sending to far-off Utah the flower of its army, had now himself become not only a rebel but a traitor.

Even Johnston, who had commanded the invading army, denouncing the Saints as rebels, had put off his blue uniform for a gray and was himself a rebel.

When the news came that South Carolina had actually flung the palmetto flag to the breeze and fired the first gun, he was inclined to exult. For plainly it was the Lord's work. There was His revelation given to Joseph Smith almost thirty years before: "Verily, thus saith the Lord concerning the wars that will come to pass, beginning at the rebellion of South Carolina." And ten years later the Lord had revealed to Joseph further concerning this prophecy that this war would be "previous to the coming of the Son of Man." Assuredly, they were now near the time when other Prophets of the Church had said He would come—the year 1870. He thrilled to be so near the actual moving of the hand of God, and something of the old spirit revived within him.

From Salt Lake City came news of the early fighting and of meetings for public rejoicing held in the tabernacle, with prophecies that the Gentile nation would now be rent asunder in punishment for its rejection of the divine message of the Book of Mormon and its persecution of the prophets of God. In one of these meetings of public thanksgiving Brigham had said from the tabernacle pulpit: "What is the strength of this man Lincoln? It is like a rope of sand. He is as weak as water,—an ignorant, Godless shyster from the backwoods of Illinois. I feel disgraced in having been born under a government that has so little power for truth and right. And now it will be broken in pieces like a potter's vessel."

These public rejoicings, however, brought a further trial upon the Saints. The Third California Infantry and a part of the Second Cavalry were now ordered to Utah. The commander of this force was one Connor, an officer of whom extraordinary reports were brought south. It was said that he had issued an order directing commanders of posts, camps, and detachments to arrest and imprison "until they took the oath of allegiance, all persons who from this date shall be guilty of uttering treasonable sentiments against the government of the United States." Even liberty of opinion, it appeared, was thus to be strangled in these last days before the Lord came.

Further, this ill-tempered Gentile, instead of keeping decently remote from Salt Lake City, as General Johnston had done, had marched his troops into the very stronghold of Zion, despite all threats of armed opposition, and in the face of a specific offer from one Prophet, Seer, and Revelator to wager him a large sum of money that his forces would never cross the River Jordan. To this fair offer, so reports ran, the Gentile officer had replied that he would cross the Jordan if hell yawned below it; that he had thereupon viciously pulled the ends of a grizzled, gray moustache and proceeded to behave very much as an officer would be expected to behave who was commonly known as "old Pat Connor."

Knowing that the forces of the Saints outnumbered his own, and that he was, in his own phrase, "six hundred miles of sand from reinforcements," he had halted his command two miles from the city, formed his column with an advance-guard of cavalry and a light battery, the infantry and the commissary-wagons coming next, and in this order, with bayonets fixed, cannon shotted, and two bands playing, had marched brazenly in the face of the Mormon authorities and through the silent crowds of Saints to Emigrant Square. Here, in front of the governor's residence, where flew the only American flag to be seen in the whole great city, he had, with entire lack of dignity, led his men in three cheers for the country, the flag, and the Gentile governor.

After this offensive demonstration, he had perpetrated the supreme indignity by going into camp on a bench at the base of Wasatch Mountain, in plain sight of the city, there in the light of day training his guns upon it, and leaving a certain twelve-pound howitzer ranged precisely upon the residence of the Lion of the Lord.

Little by little these galling reports revived the military spirit in an Elder far to the south, who had thought that all passion was burned out of him. But this man chanced to open a certain Bible one night to a page with a wash of blood across it. From this page there seemed to come such cries and screams of fear in the high voices of women and children, such sounds of blows on flesh, and the warm, salt smell of blood, that he shut the book and hastily began to pray. He actually prayed for the preservation of that ancient first enemy of his Church, the government of the United States. Individually and collectively, as a nation, as States, and as people, he forgave them and prayed the Lord to hold them undivided.

Then he knew that an astounding miracle of grace had been wrought within him. For this prayer for the hostile government was thus far his greatest spiritual triumph.

--

Chapter XXVIII
Just Before the End of the World

The years of the Civil War passed by, and the prayer of Joel Rae was answered. But the time was now rapidly approaching when the Son of Man was to come in person to judge Israel and begin his reign of a thousand years on the purified earth. The Twelve, confirmed by Brigham, had long held that this day of wrath would not be deferred past 1870. In the mind of Joel Rae the time had thus been authoritatively fixed. The date had been further confirmed by the fulfilment of Joseph's prophecy of war. The great event was now to be prepared for and met in all readiness.

It was at this time that he betrayed in the pulpit a leaning toward views that many believed to be heterodox. "A likely man is a likely man," he preached, "and a good man is a good man—whether in this Church or out of it." He also went so far as to intimate that being in the Church would not of itself suffice to the attainment of glory; that there were, to put it bluntly, all kinds of fish in the gospel net; sinners not a few in Zion who would have to be forgiven their misdeeds seventy times seven on that fateful day drawing near.

Bishop Wright, who followed him on this Sabbath, was bold to speak to another effect.

"Me and my brethren," he insisted, "have received our endowments, keys, and blessings—all the tokens and signs that can be given to man for his entrance through the celestial gate. If you have had these in the house of the Lord, when you depart this life you will be able to walk back to the presence of the Father, passing the angels that stand as sentinels; because why?—because you can give them the tokens, signs, and grips pertaining to the holy priesthood and gain your eternal exaltation in spite of earth and hell. But how about the likely and good man outside this Church who has rejected the message of the Book of Mormon and ain't got these signs and passwords? If he's going to be let in, too, why have doorkeepers, and what's the use of the whole business? Why in time did the Lord go to all this trouble, any way, if Brother Rae is right? Why was Joseph Smith visited by an angel clad in robes of light, who told him where the golden plates had been hid up by the Lord, and the Urim and Thummim, and who laid hands on him and give him the Holy Ghost? And after all that trouble He's took, do you think He's going to let everybody in? Not much, Mary Ann! The likely men may come the roots on some of our soft-hearted Elders, but they won't fool the Lord's Christ and His angel gatekeepers."

Elder Beil Wardle, on the other hand, showed a tendency to side with the liberalism of Brother Rae. He cited the fact that not all revelations were from God. Some were from perverse human spirits and some from the very Devil himself. There was Elder Sidney Roberts, who had once suffered a revelation that a certain brother must give him a suit of finest broadcloth and a gold watch, the best to be had; and another revelation directing him to salute all the younger sisters, married or single, with a kiss of holiness. Urged to confess that these revelations were from the Devil, he had refused, and so had been cut off and delivered over to the buffetings of Satan in the flesh.

"And you can't always be sure of the Holy Ghost, either," he continued. "When the Lord pours out the Holy Ghost on an individual, he will have spasms, and you would think he was going to have fits; but it don't make him get up and go pay his debts—not by a long shot. Of course I don't feel to mention any names, but what can you expect, anyway? A flock of a thousand sheep has got to be mighty clean if some of them ain't smutty. This is a large flock of sheep that has come up into this valley of the mountains, and some of them have got tag-locks hanging about them. But it don't seem to pester the Lord any. He sifted us good in Missouri, and He put us into another sieve at Nauvoo, and I reckon His sieve will be brought along with Him on the day of judgment. And if there are some lost sheep in the fold of Zion, maybe, on the other hand, there's some outside the fold that will be worth saving; that will be broke off from the wild olive-tree and grafted on to the tame olive-tree to partake of its sap and fatness."

Joel Rae would have taken more comfort in this championship of his views if it were not for his suspicion that Elder Wardle sometimes spoke in a tone of levity, and had indeed more than once been reckoned as a doubter. It was even related of him that a perverted sense of humour had once inspired him to deliver an irreverent and wholly immaterial address in pure Choctaw at a service where many others of the faithful had been moved to speak in tongues; and that an earnest sister, believing the Holy Ghost to be strong upon her, had thereupon arisen and interpreted his speech to be the Lord's description of the glories of their new temple, which it had not been at all. Such a man might have a good heart, as he knew Elder Wardle to have; but he must be an inferior guide to the Father's presence. He was even less inclined to trust him when Wardle announced confidentially at the close of the meeting that day, "Brother Wright talks a good deal jest to hear his head roar. You'd think he'd been the midwife at the borning of the world, and helped to nurse it and bring it up—he's that knowing about it. My opinion is he don't know twice across or straight up about the Lord's secret doings!"

Yet if he had sought to render a little elastic the rigid teachings of the priesthood, he had done so innocently. The foundations of his faith were unshaken; for him the rock upon which his Church was built had never been more stable. As to doubting its firmness, he would as soon have blasphemed the Holy Ghost or disputed the authority of Brigham, with whom was the sacred deposit of doctrine and all temporal and spiritual power.

So he sighed often for those Gentile sheep on whom the wrath of God was so soon to fall. Even with the utmost stretching of the divine mercy, the greater part of them must perish; and for the lost souls of these he grieved much and prayed each day.

It was more than ten years since that day in the Meadows, and the blight there put upon his person had waxed with each year. His hair showed now but the faintest sprinkle of black, his shoulders were bent and rounded as if bearing invisible burdens, and his face had the look of drooping in grief and despair, as one who was made constantly to look upon all the suffering of all the world. Yet he wore always, except when alone, a not unpleasant little effort of a smile, as if he would conceal his pain. But this deceived few. The women of the settlement had come to call him "the little man of sorrows." Even his wife, Lorena, had divined that his mind was not one with hers; that, somehow, there was a gulf between them which her best-meant cheerfulness could not span. In a measure she had ceased to try, doing little more than to sing, when he was near, some hymn which she considered suitable to his condition. One favourite at such times began:—

"Lord, we are vile, conceived in sin,
And born unholy and unclean;
Sprung from the man whose guilty fall
Corrupts his race and taints us all.

"Soon as we draw our infant breath,
The seeds of sin grow up for death;
The law demands a perfect heart,
But we're defiled in every part."

She would sing many verses of this with appealing unction, so long as he was near; yet when he came upon her unawares he might hear her voicing some cheerful, secular ballad, like—

"As I went down to Coffey's mills
 Some pleasure for to see,
I fell in love with a railroad-er,
 He fell in love with me."

The stolid Christina listened entranced to all of Lorena's songs, charmed by the melody not less than she was awed by her sister-wife's superior gifts of language. The husband, too, listened not without resignation, reflecting that, when Lorena did not sing, she talked. For the unspeaking Christina he had learned to feel an admiration that bordered upon reverence, finding in her silence something spiritually great. Yet of the many-worded Lorena he was never heard to complain through all the years. The nearest he approached to it was on a day when Elder Beil Wardle had sought to condole with him on the affliction of her ready speech.

"That woman of yours," said this observant friend, "sure takes large pie-bites out of any little talk that happens to get going."

"She *does* have the gift of continuance," her husband had admitted. But he had added, hastily, "Though her heart is perfect with the Lord."

The fact that she was sealed to him for eternity, and that she believed she would constitute one of his claims to exaltation in the celestial world, were often matters of pious speculation with him. He wondered if he had done right by her. She deserved a husband who would be saved into the kingdom, while he who had married her was irrevocably lost.

There had been a time when he read with freshened hope the promises of forgiveness in that strange New Testament. Once he had even believed that these might save him; that he was again numbered with the elect. But when this belief had grown firm, so that he could seem to rest his weight upon it, he felt it fall away to nothing under him, and the truth he had divined that day in the desert was again bared before him. He saw that how many times soever God might forgive the sins of a man, it would avail that man nothing unless he could forgive himself. He knew at last that in his own soul was fixed a gauge of right, unbending and implacable when wrong had been done, waiting to be reckoned with at the very last even though the great God should condone his sin. It seemed to him that, however surely his endowments took him through the gates of the Kingdom, with whatsoever power they raised him to dominion; even though he came into the Father's presence and sat a throne of his own by the side of Joseph and Brigham, that there would still ring in his ears the cries of those who had been murdered at the priesthood's command; that there would leap before his eyes fountains of blood from the breasts of living women who knelt and clung to the knees of their slayers—to the knees of the Church of Jesus Christ of Latter-day Saints; that he would see two spots of white in the dim light of a morning where the two little girls lay who had been sent for water; that he would see the two boys taken out to the desert, one to die at once, the other to wander to a slower death; that before his sinful eyes would come the dying face of the woman who had loved him and lost her soul rather than betray him. He knew that, even in celestial realms exalted beyond the highest visions of their priesthood, his soul would still burn in this fire that he could not extinguish within his own breast. He knew that he carried hell as an inseparable part of himself, and that the forgiveness of no other power could avail him. He no longer feared God, but himself alone.

From this fire of his own building it seemed to him that he could obtain surcease only by reducing the self within him. As surely as he let it feel a want, all the torture came back upon him. When his pride lifted up its head, when he desired any satisfaction for himself, when he was tempted for a moment to lay down his cross, the cries came back, the sea of blood surged before him, and close behind came the shapes that crawled or moved furtively, ever about to spring in front and turn upon him. Small wonder, then, that his shoulders bent beneath unseen burdens, that his air was of one who suffered for all the world, and that they called him "the little man of sorrows."

With this knowledge he learned to permit himself only one great love, a love for the child Prudence. He was sure that no punishment could come through that. It was his day-star and his life, the one pleasure that brought no suffering with it. She was a child of fourteen now, a half-wild, firm-fleshed, glowing creature of the out-of-doors, who had lost with her baby softness all her resemblance to her mother. Her hair and eyes had darkened as she grew, and she was to be a larger woman, graver, deeper, more reserved; perhaps better calculated for the Kingdom by reason of a more reflective mind. He adored her, and was awed by her even when he taught her the truths of revealed religion. He closed his eyes at night upon a never-ending prayer for her soul; and opened them each day to a love of her that grew insidiously to enthrall him while he was all unconscious of its power—even while he knew with an awful certainty that he must have no treasure of his own which he could not willingly relinquish at the first call. She, in turn, loved and confided in her father, the shy, bent, shrunken little man with the smile.

"He always smiles as if he'd hurt himself and didn't want to show it before company," were the words in which she announced one of her early discoveries about him. But she liked and ruled him, and came to him for comfort when she was hurt or when Lorena scolded. For the third wife did not hesitate to characterise the child as "ready-made sin," and to declare that it took all her spare time, "and a lot that ain't spare," to neat up the house after her. "And her paw—though Lord knows who her maw was—a-dressing her to beat the cars; while he ain't never made over me since the blessed day I married him—not that *much*! But, thank heavens, it can't last very long, with the Son of Man already started, like you might say."

Chapter XXIX
The Wild Ram of the Mountains Offers to Become a Saviour on Mount Zion

In the valley of which Amalon was the centre, they made ready for the end of the world. It is true that in the north, as the appointed year drew nigh, an opinion had begun to prevail that the Son of Man might defer his coming; and presently it became known that Brigham himself was doubtful about the year 1870, and was inspiring others to doubt. But in Amalon they were untainted by this heresy, choosing to rely upon what Brigham had said in moments more inspired.

He had taught that Joseph was to be the first person resurrected; that after his frame had been knit together and clothed with immortal flesh he would resurrect those who had died in the faith, according to their rank in the priesthood; then all his wives and children. Resurrected Elders, having had the keys of the resurrection conferred upon them by Joseph, would in turn call from the grave their own households; and when the last of the faithful had come forth, another great work would be performed; the Gentiles would then be resurrected to act as servants and slaves to the Saints. In his lighter moments Brigham had been wont to name a couple of Presidents of the United States who would then act as his valets.

Some doubt had been expressed that the earth's surface could contain the resurrected host, but Apostle Orson Pratt had removed this. He cited the prophet who had foretold that the hills should be laid low, the valleys exalted, and the crooked places made straight. With the earth thus free of mountains and waste places, he had demonstrated that there would be an acre and a quarter of ground for each Saint that had ever lived from the morning of creation to the day of doom. And, lest some carping mathematician should dispute his figures, he had declared that if, by any miscalculation, the earth's surface should not suffice for the Saints and their Gentile slaves, the Lord "would build a gallery around the earth." Thus had confusion been brought to the last quibbler in Zion.

It was this earlier teaching that the faithful of Amalon clung to, perhaps not a little by reason that immediately over them was a spiritual guide who had been trained from infancy to know that salvation lay in belief,—never in doubt. For a sign of the end they believed that on the night before the day of it there would be no darkness. This would be as it had been before the birth of the Saviour, as told in the Book of Mormon: "At the going down of the sun there was no darkness, and the people began to be astonished because there was no darkness when the night came; and there was no darkness in all that night, but it was as light as if it were midday."

They talked of little but this matter in that small pocket of the intermountain commonwealth, in Sabbath meetings and around the hearths at night. The Wild Ram of the Mountains thought all proselyting should cease in view of the approaching end; that the Elders on mission should withdraw from the vineyard, shake the dust from their feet, and seal up the rebellious Gentiles to damnation. To this Elder Beil Wardle had replied, somewhat testily:

"Well, now, since these valleys of Ephraim have got a little fattened a whole lot of us have got the sweeny, and our skins are growing too tight on our flesh." He had been unable to comprehend that the Gentiles were a rejected lot, the lost sheep of the house of Israel. On this occasion it had required all the tact of Elder Rae to soothe the two good men into an amiable discussion of the time when Sidney Rigdon went to the third heaven and talked face to face with God. They had agreed in the end, however, that they were both of the royal seed of Abraham, and were on the grand turnpike to exaltation.

To these discussions and sermons the child, Prudence, listened with intense interest, looking forward to the last day as an occasion productive of excitement even superior to that of her trips to Salt Lake City, where her father went to attend the October conference, and where she was taken to the theatre.

Of any world outside the valley she knew but little. Somewhere, far over to the east, was a handful of lost souls for whom she sometimes indulged in a sort of luxurious pity. But their loss, after all, was a part of the divine plan, and they would have the privilege of serving the glorified Saints, even though they were denied Godhood. She half-believed that even this mission of service was almost more of glory than they merited; for, in the phrasing of Bishop Wright, they "made a hell all the time and raised devils to keep it going." They had slain the Prophets of the Lord and hunted his people, and the best of them were lucky, indeed, to escape the fire that burns unceasingly; a fire hotter than any made by beech or hickory. Still she sometimes wondered if there were girls among them like her; and she had visions of herself as an angel of light, going down to them with the precious message of the Book of Mormon, and bringing them into the fold.

One day in this spring when she was fourteen, the good Bishop Wright, on his way down from Box Cañon with a load of wood, saw her striding up the road ahead of him. Something caught his eye, either in her step which had a child's careless freedom, or in the lines of her swinging figure that told of coming womanhood, or in the flashing, laughing appeal of her dark eyes where for the moment both woman and child looked out. He set the brake on his wagon and waited for her to pass. She came by with a smile and a word of greeting, to which his rapt attention prevented any reply except a slight nod. When she had passed, he turned and looked after her until she had gone around the little hill on the road that entered the cañon.

After the early evening meal that day, along the many-roomed house of this good man, from door to door there ran the words, starting from her who had last been sealed to him:

"He's making himself all proud!"

They knew what it meant, and wondered whom.

A little later the Bishop set out, his face clean-shaven to the ruffle of white whisker that ran under his chin from ear to ear, his scant hair smooth and shining with grease from the largest bear ever trapped in the Pine Mountains, and his tall form arrayed in his best suit of homespun. As he went he trolled an ancient lay of love, and youth was in his step. For there had come all day upon this Prince of Israel those subtle essences distilled by spring to provoke the mating urge. At the Rae house he found only Christina.

"Where's Brother Joel, Sister Rae?"

"Himself has gone out there," Christina had answered with a wave of her hand, and using the term of respect which she always applied to her husband.

He went around the house, out past the stable and corrals and across the irrigating ditch to where he saw Joel Rae leaning on the rail fence about the peach orchard. Far down between two rows of the blossoming trees he could see the girl reaching up to break off a pink-sprayed bough. He quickened his pace and was soon at the fence.

"Brother Joel, —I—the—"

The good man had been full of his message a moment before, but now he stammered and hesitated because of something cold in the other's eye as it seemed to note the unwonted elegance of his attire. He took a quick breath and went on.

"You see the Lord has moved me to add another star to my crown."

"I see; and you have come to get me to seal you?"

"Well, of course I hadn't thought of it so soon, but if you want to do it to-night—"

"As soon as you like, Bishop,—the sooner the better if you are to save the soul of another woman against the day of desolation. Where is she?" and he turned to go back to the house. But the Bishop still paused, looking toward the orchard.

"Well, the fact is, Brother Joel, you see the Lord has made me feel to have Prudence for another star in my crown of glory—your daughter Prudence," he repeated as the other gazed at him with a sudden change of manner.

"My daughter Prudence—little Prue—that child—that *baby*?"

"*Baby*?—she's fourteen; she was telling my daughter Mattie so jest the other day, and the Legislatur has made the marrying age twelve for girls and fifteen for boys, so she's two years overtime already. Of course, I ain't fifteen, but I'm safer for her than some young cub."

"But Bishop—you don't consider—"

"Oh, of course, I know there's been private talk about her; nobody knows who her mother was, and they say whoever she was you was never married to her, so she couldn't have been born right, but I ain't bigoted like some I could name, and I stand ready to be her Saviour on Mount Zion."

He waited with something of noble concession in his mien.

The other seemed only now to have fully sensed the proposal, and, with real terror in his face, he began to urge the Bishop toward the house, after looking anxiously back to where the child still lingered with the mist of pink blossoms against the leafless boughs above her.

"Come, Brother Seth—come, I beg of you—we'll talk of it—but it can't be, indeed it can't!"

"Let's ask *her*," suggested the Bishop, disinclined to move.

"Don't, *don't* ask her!" He seized the other by the arm.

"Come, I'll explain; don't ask her now, at any rate—I beg of you as a gentleman—as a gentleman, for you are a gentleman."

The Bishop turned somewhat impatiently, then remarked with a dignified severity:

"Oh, I can be a gentleman whenever it's *necessary*!"

They went across the fields toward the house, and the Bishop spoke further.

"There ain't any need to get into your high-heeled boots, Brother Rae, jest because I was aiming to save her to a crown of glory,—a girl that's thought to have been born on the wrong side of the blanket!"

They stopped by the first corral, and Joel Rae talked. He talked rapidly and with power, saying many things to make it plain that he was determined not to look upon the Wild Ram of the Mountains as an acceptable son-in-law. His manner was excited and distraught, terrified and indignant,—a manner hardly justified by the circumstances, about which there was nothing extraordinary, nothing not pleasing to God and in conformity to His revealed word. Bishop Wright indeed was puzzled to account for the heat of his manner, and in recounting the interview later to Elder Wardle, he threw out an intimation about strong drink. "To tell you the truth," he said, "I suspicion he'd jest been putting a new faucet in the cider barrel."

When Prudence came in from the blossoming peach-trees that night her father called her to him to sit on his lap in the dusk while the crickets sang, and grow sleepy as had been her baby habit.

"What did Bishop Wright want?" she asked, after her head was pillowed on his arm. Relieved that it was over, now even a little amused, he told her:

"He wanted to take my little girl away, to marry her."

She was silent for a moment, and then:

"Wouldn't that be fine, and we could build each other up in the Kingdom."

He held her tighter.

"Surely, child, you couldn't marry him?"

"But of course I could! Isn't he tried in the Kingdom, so he is sure to have all those thrones and dominions and power?"

"But child, child! That old man with all his wives—"

"But they say old men are safer than young men. Young men are not tried in the Kingdom. I shouldn't like a young husband anyway—they always want to play rough games, and pull your hair, and take things away from you, and get in the way."

"But, baby,—don't, *don't*—"

"Why, you silly father, your voice sounds as if you were almost crying—please don't hold me so tight—and some one must save me before the Son of Man comes to judge the quick and the dead; you know a woman can't be saved alone. I think Bishop Wright would make a fine husband, and I should have Mattie Wright to play with every day."

"And you would leave me?"

"Why, that's so, Daddy! I never thought—of course I can't leave my little sorry father—not yet. I forgot that. I couldn't leave you. Now tell me about my mother again."

He told her the story she already knew so well—how beautiful her mother was, the look of her hair and eyes, her slenderness, the music of her voice, and the gladness of her laugh.

"And won't she be glad to see us again. And she will come before Christina and Lorena, because she was your first wife, wasn't she?"

He was awake all night in a fever of doubt and rebellion. By the light of the candle, he read in the book of Mormon passages that had often puzzled but never troubled him until now when they were brought home to him; such as, "And now it came to pass that the people Nephi under the reign of the second king began to grow hard in their hearts, and indulged themselves somewhat in wicked practises, like unto David of old, desiring many wives—"

Again he read, "Behold, David and Solomon truly had many wives, which thing was abominable before me, saith the Lord."

Still again, "For there shall not be any man among you have save it shall be one wife."

Then he turned to the revelation on celestial marriage given years after these words were written, and in the first paragraph read:

"Verily, thus saith the Lord unto you my servant Joseph, that inasmuch as you have inquired of my hand to know and understand wherein I, the Lord, justified my servants Abraham, Isaac, and Jacob, as also Moses, David, and Solomon, my servants, as touching the principle and doctrine of their having many wives—"

He turned from one to the other; from the many explicit admonitions and commands against polygamy, the denunciations of the patriarchs for their indulgence in the practise, to this last passage contradicting the others, and vexed himself with wonder. In the Book of Mormon, David was said to be wicked for doing this thing. Now in the revelation to Joseph he read,

"David's wives were given unto him of me, by the hand of Nathan, my servant."

He recalled old tales that were told in Nauvoo by wicked apostates and the basest of Gentile scandalmongers; how that Joseph in the day of his great power had suffered the purity of his first faith to become tainted; how his wife, Emma, had upbraided him so harshly for his sins that he, fearing disgrace, had put out this revelation as the word of God to silence her. He remembered that these gossips had said the revelation itself proved that Joseph had already done, before he received it, that which it commanded him to do, citing the clause, "And let my handmaid, Emma Smith, receive all those that have been given unto my servant Joseph, and who are virtuous and pure before me."

They had gossiped further, that still fearing her rebellion, he had worded a threat for her in the next clause, "And I command my handmaid, Emma Smith, to abide and cleave unto my servant Joseph and to none else. But if she will not abide this commandment she shall be destroyed, saith the Lord; for I am the Lord thy God, and will destroy her if she abide not in my law ... and again verily I say, let mine handmaid forgive my servant Joseph his trespasses and then shall she be forgiven her trespasses."

This was the calumny the Gentile gossips back in Nauvoo would have had the world believe,—that this great doctrine of the Church had been given to silence the enraged wife of a man detected in sin.

But in the midst of his questionings he seemed to see a truth,—that another snare had been set for him by the Devil, and that this time it had caught his feet. He, who knew that he must have nothing for himself, had all unconsciously so set his heart upon this child of her mother that he could not give her up. And now so fixed and so great was his love that he could not turn back. He knew he was lost. To cling to her would be to question, doubt, and to lose his faith. To give her up would kill him.

But at least for a little while he could put it off.

Chapter XXX
How the World Did not Come to an End

In doubt and fear, the phantom of a dreadful certainty creeping always closer, the final years went by. When the world came to be in its very last days, when the little bent man was drooping lower than ever, and Prudence was seventeen, there came another Prince of Israel to save her into the Kingdom while there was yet a time of grace. On this occasion the suitor was no less a personage than Bishop Warren Snow, a holy man and puissant, upon whom the blessed Gods had abundantly manifested their favour. In wives and children, in flocks and herds, he was rich; while, as to spiritual worth, had not that early church poet styled him the Entablature of Truth?

But Prudence Rae, once so willing to be saved by the excellent Wild Ram of the Mountains, had fled in laughing confusion from this later benefactor, when he had made plain one day the service he sought to do her soul. A moment later he had stood before her father in all his years of patriarchal dignity, hale, ruddy, and vast of girth.

"She's a woman now, Brother Snow,—free to choose for herself," the father had replied to his first expostulations.

"Counsel her, Brother Rae." In the mind of the Bishop, "counsel," properly applied, was a thing not long to be resisted.

"She would treat my counsel as shortly as she treated your proposal, Brother Snow."

The Entablature of Truth glanced out of the open door to where Tom Potwin could be seen, hastening importantly upon his endless and mysterious errands, starting off abruptly a little way, stopping suddenly, with one hand raised to his head, as if at that instant remembering a forgotten detail, and then turning with new impetus to walk swiftly in the opposite direction.

"There ain't any one else after her, is there, Brother Rae,—any of these young boys?"

"No, Bishop—no one."

"Well, if there is, you let me know. I'll be back again, Brother Rae. Meantime, counsel her—counsel her with authority."

The Entablature of Truth had departed with certain little sidewise noddings of his head that seemed to indicate an unalterable purpose.

The girl came to her father, blushing and still laughing confusedly, when the rejected one had mounted his horse and ridden away.

"Oh, Daddy, how funny!—to think of marrying him!"

He looked at her anxiously. "But you wanted to marry Bishop Wright—at least, you—"

She laughed again. "How long ago—years ago—I must have been a baby."

"You were old enough to point out that he would save you in the after-time."

"I remember; I could see myself sitting by him on a throne, with the Saints all around us on other thrones, and the Gentiles kneeling to serve us. We were in a big palace that had a hundred closets in it, and in every closet there hung a silk dress for me—a hundred silk dresses, each a different colour, waiting for me to wear them."

"But have you thought sufficiently—now? The time is short. Bishop Snow could save you."

"Yes—but he would kiss me—he wanted to just now." She put both hands over her mouth, with a mocking little grimace that the Entablature of Truth would not have liked to see.

"He would be certain to exalt you."

She took the hands away long enough to say, "He would be certain to kiss me."

"You may be lost."

"I'd *rather!*"

And so it had ended between them. Ever since a memorable visit to Salt Lake City, where she had gone to the theatre, she had cherished some entirely novel ideas concerning matrimony. In that fairyland of delights she had beheld the lover strangely wooing but one mistress, the husband strangely cherishing but one wife. There had been no talk of "the Kingdom," and no home portrayed where there were many wives. That lover, swearing to cherish but one woman for ever, had thrilled her to new conceptions of her own womanhood, had seemed to meet some need of her own heart that she had not until then been conscious of. Ever after, she had cherished this ideal of the stage, and refused to consider the other. Yet she had told her father nothing of this, for with her womanhood had come a new reserve—truths half-divined and others clearly perceived—which she could not tell any one.

He, in turn, now kept secret from her the delight he felt at her refusal. He had tried conscientiously to persuade her into the path of salvation, when his every word was a blade to cut at his heart. Nor was he happy when she refused so definitely the saving hand extended to her. To know she was to come short of her glory in the after-time was anguish to him; and mingling with that anguish, inflaming and aggravating it, were his own heretical doubts that would not be gone.

In a sheer desperation of bewilderment he longed for the end, longed to know certainly his own fate and hers—to have them irrevocably fixed—so that he might no more be torn among many minds, but could begin to pay his own penalties in plain suffering, uncomplicated by this torturing necessity to choose between two courses of action.

And the time was, happily, to be short. With the first day of 1870 he began to wait. With prayer and fasting and vigils he waited. Now was the day when the earth should be purified by fire, the wicked swept from the land, and the lost tribes of Israel restored to their own. Now was to come the Son of Man who should dwell in righteousness with men, reigning over them on the purified earth for a thousand years.

He watched the mild winter go, with easy faith; and the early spring come and go, with a dawning uneasiness. For the time was passing with never the blast of a trumpet from the heavens. He began to see then that he alone, of all Amalon, had kept his faith pure. For the others had foolishly sown their fields, as if another crop were to be harvested,—as if they must continue to eat bread that was earth-grown. Even Prudence had strangely ceased to believe as he did. Something from the outside had come, he knew not what nor how, to tarnish the fair gold of her certainty. She had not said so, but he divined it when he shrewdly observed that she was seeking to comfort him, to support his own faith when day after day the Son of Man came not.

"It will surely be in another month, Daddy—perhaps next week—perhaps to-morrow," she would say cheerfully. "And you did right not to put in any crops. It would have been wicked to doubt."

He quickly detected her insincerity, seeing that she did not at all believe. As the summer came and went without a sign from the heavens, she became more positive and more constant in these assurances. As the evening drew on, they would walk out along the unsown fields, now grown rankly to weeds, to where the valley fell away from their feet to the west. There they could look over line after line of hills, each a little dimmer as it lay farther into the blue through which they saw it, from the bold rim of the nearest shaggy-sided hill to the farthest feathery profile all but lost in the haze. Day after day they sat together here and waited for the sign,—for the going down of the sun upon a night when there should be no darkness; when the light should stay until the sun came back over the eastern verge; when the trumpet should wind through the hills, and when the little man's perplexities, if not his punishment, should be at an end.

And always when the dusk came she would try to cheer him to new hope for the next night, counting the months that remained in the year, the little time within which the great white day *must* be. Then they would go back through the soft light of the afterglow, he with his bent shoulders and fallen face, shrunk and burned out, except for the eyes, and she in the first buoyant flush of her womanhood, free and strong and vital, a thing of warmth and colour and luring curve, restraining her quick young step to his, as she suppressed now a world of strange new fancies to his soberer way of thought. When they reached home again, her words always were: "Never mind, Daddy—it must come soon—there's only a little time left in the year."

It was on these occasions that he knew she was now the stronger, that he was leaning on her, had, in fact, long made her his support—fearfully, lest she be snatched away. And he knew at last that another change had come with her years; that she no longer confided in him unreservedly, as the little child had. He knew there were things now she could not give him. She communed with herself, and her silences had come between them. She looked past him at unseen forms, and listened as if for echoes that she alone could hear, waiting and wanting, knowing not her wants—yet driven to aloofness by them from the little bent man of sorrows, whose whole life she had now become.

His hope lasted hardly until the year ended. Before the time was over, there had crept into his mind a conviction that the Son of Man would not come; that the Lord's favour had been withdrawn from Israel. He knew the cause,—the shedding of innocent blood. They might have made war; indeed, many of the revelations to Joseph discriminated even between murder and that murder in which innocent blood should be shed; but the truth was plain. They had shed innocent blood that day in the Meadows. Now the Lord's favour was withdrawn and His coming deferred, perhaps another thousand years. The torture of the thing came back to him with all its early colouring, so that his days and nights were full of anguish. He no longer dared open the Bible to that reddened page. The cries already rang in his ears, and he knew not what worse torture might come if he looked again upon the stain; nor could he free himself from these by the old expedient of prayer, for he could no longer pray with an honest heart; he was no longer unselfish, could no longer kneel in perfect submission; he was wholly bound to this child of her mother, and the peace of absolute and utter sacrifice could not come back to him. Full of unrest, feeling that somehow the end, at least for him, could not be far off, he went north to the April Conference. He took Prudence with him, not daring to leave her behind.

She went with high hopes, alive with new sensations. Another world lay outside her valley of the mountains, and she was going to peep over the edge at its manifold fascinations. She had been there before as a child; now she was going as a woman. She remembered the city, bigger and grander than fifty Amalons, with magnificent stores filled with exotic novelties and fearsome luxuries from the land of the wicked Gentile. She recalled even the strange advertisements and signs, from John and Enoch Reese, with "All necessary articles of comfort for the wayfarer, such as flour, hard bread, butter, eggs and vinegar, buckskin pants and whip-lashes," to the "Surgeon Dentist from Berlin and Liverpool," who would "Examine and Extract Teeth, besides keeping constantly on hand a supply of the Best Matches, made by himself." From William Hennefer, announcing that, "In Connection with my Barber Shop, I have just opened an Eating House, where Patrons will be Accommodated with every Edible Luxury the Valley Affords," to William Nixon, who sold goods for cash, flour, or wheat "at Jacob Hautz's house on the southeast corner of Council-House Street and Emigration Square, opposite to Mr. Orson Spencer's."

She remembered the hunters and trappers in bedraggled buckskin, the plainsmen with revolvers in their belts, wearing the blue army cloak, the teamsters in leathern suits, and horsemen in fur coats and caps, buffalo-hide boots with the hair outside, and rolls of blankets behind their high Mexican saddles.

More fondly did she recall two wonderful evenings at the theatre. First had been the thrilling "Robert Macaire," then the romantic "Pizarro," in which Rolla had been a being of such overwhelming beauty that she had felt he could not be of earth.

This time her visit was an endless fever of discovery in a realm of magic and mystery, of joys she had supposed were held in reserve for those who went behind the veil. It was a new and greater city she came to now, where were buildings of undreamed splendour, many of them reaching dizzily three stories above the earth. And the shops were more fascinating than ever. She still shuddered at the wickedness of the Gentiles, but with a certain secret respect for their habits of luxury and their profusion of devices for adornment.

And there were strange new faces to be seen, people surely of a different world, of a different manner from those she had known, wearing, with apparent carelessness, garments even more strangely elegant than those in the shop windows, and speaking in strange, soft accents. She was told that these were Gentiles, tourists across the continent, who had ventured from Ogden to observe the wonders of the new Zion. The thought of the railroad was in itself thrilling. To be so near that wonderful highway to the land of the evil-doers and to a land, alas! of so many strange delights. She shuddered at her own wickedness, but fell again and again, and was held in bondage by the allurements about her. So thrilled to her soul's center was she that the pleasure of it hurt her, and the tears would come to her eyes until she felt she must be alone to cry for the awful joy of it.

The evening brought still more to endure, for they went to the play. It was a play that took her out of herself, so that the crowd was lost to her from the moment the curtain went up in obedience to a little bell that tinkled mysteriously,—either back on the stage or in her own heart, she was not sure which.

It was a love story; again that strangely moving love of one man for one woman, that seemed as sweet as it was novel to her. But there was war between the houses in the play, and the young lover had to make a way to see his beloved, climbing a high wall into her garden, climbing to her very balcony by a scarf she flung down to him. To the young woman from Amalon, these lovers' voices came with a strange compulsion, so that they played with her heart between them. She was in turn the youth, pleading in a voice that touched every heart string from low to high; then she was the woman, soft and timid, hesitating in moments of delicious doubt, yet almost fearful of her power to resist,—half-wishing to be persuaded, half-frightened lest she yield.

When the moment of surrender came, she became both of them; and, when they parted, it was as if her heart went in twain, a half with each, both to ache until they were reunited. Between the acts she awoke to reality, only to say to herself: "So much I shall have to think about—so much—I shall never be able to think about it enough."

Feverishly she followed the heart-breaking tragedy to its close, suffering poignantly the grief of each lover, suffering death for each, and feeling her life desolated when the end came.

But then the dull curtain shut her back into her own little world, where there was no love like that, and beside the little bent man she went out into the night.

The next morning had come a further delight, an invitation to a ball from Brigham. Most of the day was spent in one of the shops, choosing a gown of wondrous beauty, and having it fitted to her.

FULL OF ZEST FOR THE
MEASURE AS ANY YOUTH

When she looked into the little cracked mirror that night, she saw a strange new face and figure; and, when she entered the ballroom, she felt that others noted the same strangeness, for many looked at her until she felt her cheeks burn. Then Brigham arose from a sofa, where he had been sitting with his first wife and his last. He came gallantly toward her; Brigham, whom she knew to be the most favoured of God on earth and the absolute ruler of all the realm about her—an affable, unpretentious yet dignified gentleman of seventy, who took her hand warmly in both his own, looked her over with his kindly blue eyes, and welcomed her to Zion in words of a fatherly gentleness. Later, when he had danced with some of his wives, Brigham came to dance with her, light of foot and full of zest for the measure as any youth.

Others danced with her, but during it all she kept finding herself back before the magic square that framed the land where a man loved but one woman. She remembered that Brigham sat with four of his wives in one of the boxes, enthusiastically applauding that portrayal of a single love. As the picture came back to her now, there seemed to have been something incongruous in this spectacle. She observed the seamed and hardened features of his earliest wife, who kept to the sofa during the evening, beside the better favoured Amelia, whom the good man had last married, and she thought of his score or so of wives between them.

Then she knew that what she had seen the night before had been the truth; that she could love no man who did not love her alone. She tried to imagine the lover in the play going from balcony to balcony, sighing the same impassioned love-tale to woman after woman; or to imagine him with many wives at home, to whom would be taken the news of his death in the tomb of his last. So she thought of the play and not of the ball, stepping the dances absently, and, when it was all over, she fell asleep, rejoicing that, before their death, the two dear lovers had been sealed for time and eternity, so that they could awaken together in the Kingdom.

They went home the next day, driving down the valley that rolled in billows of green between the broken ranges of the Wasatch and the Oquirrh. It was no longer of the Kingdom she thought, nor of Brigham and his wives; only of a clean-limbed youth in doublet and hose, a plumed cap, and a silken cloak, who, in a voice that brought the tears back of her eyes, told of his undying love for one woman—and of the soft, tender woman in the moonlight, who had trusted him and let herself go to him in life and in death.

The world had not ended. She thought that, in truth, it could not have ended yet; for had she not a life to live?

Chapter XXXI
The Lion of the Lord Sends an Order

They reached home in very different states of mind. The girl was eager for the solitude of her favourite nook in the cañon, where she could dream in peace of the wonderland she had glimpsed; but the little bent man was stirred by dread and chilled with forebodings. To him, as well as to the girl, the change in the first city of Zion had been a thing to wonder at. But what had thrilled her with amazed delight brought pain to him. Zion was no longer held inviolate.

And now the truth was much clearer to him. Not only had the Lord deferred His coming, but He had set His hand again to scatter Israel for its sin. Instead of letting them stay alone in their mountain retreat until the beginning of His reign on earth, He had brought the Gentiles upon them in overwhelming numbers. Where once a thousand miles of wilderness lay between them and Gentile wickedness, they were now hemmed about with it, and even it polluted the streets of the holy city itself.

Far on the east the adventurous Gentile had first pushed out of the timber to the richly grassed prairies; then, later, on to the plains, scorched brown with their sparse grass, driving herds of cattle ahead, and stopping to make farms by the way. And now on the west, on the east, and on the north, the Lord had let them pitch their tents and build their cabins, where they would barter their lives for gold and flocks and furs and timber, for orchard fruits and the grains of the field. Little by little they had ventured toward the outer ramparts of Israel, their numbers increasing year by year, and the daring of their onslaughts against the desert and mountain wastes. With the rifle and the axe they had made Zion but a station on the great highway between the seas; a place where curious and irreverent Gentiles stopped to gaze in wonder at and perhaps to mock the Lord's chosen; a place that would become but one link in a chain of Gentile cities, that would be forced to conform to the meretricious customs of Gentile benightedness.

It had been a fine vengeance upon them for their sin; one not unworthy of Him who wrought it. It had come so insidiously, with such apparent naturalness, little by little—a settler here, a settler there; here an acre of gray desert charmed to yellow wheat; there a pouch of shining gold washed from the burning sands; another wagon-train with hopeful men and faithful women; a cabin, two cabins, a settlement, a schoolhouse, a land of unwalled villages,—and democracy; a wicked government of men set up in the very face and front of God-governed Israel.

At first they had come with ox-teams, but this was slow, and the big Kentucky mules brought them faster; then had come the great rolling Concord stages with their six horses; then the folly of an electric telegraph, so that instant communication might be had with far-off Babylon; and now the capstone in the arch of the Lord's vengeance,—a railway,—flashing its crowded coaches over the Saints' old trail in sixty easy hours,—a trail they had covered with their oxen in ninety days of hardship. The rock of their faith would now be riven, the veil of their temple rent, and their leaders corrupted.

Even of Brigham, the daring already told tales that promised this last thing should come to pass; how he was become fat-souled, grasping, and tricky, using his sacred office to enlarge his wealth, seizing the cañons with their precious growths of wood, the life-giving waterways, and the herding-grounds; taking even from the tithing, of which he rendered no stewardship, and hiding away millions of the dollars for which the faithful had toiled themselves into desert graves. Truly, thought Joel Rae, that bloody day in the Meadows had been cunningly avenged.

One morning, a few weeks after he had reached home from the north, he received a call from Seth Wright.

"Here's a letter Brother Brigham wanted me to be sure and give you," said this good man. "He said he didn't know you was allowing to start back so soon, or he'd have seen you in person."

He took the letter and glanced at the superscription, written in Brigham's rather unformed but plain and very decided-looking hand.

"So you've been north, Brother Seth? What do you think of Israel there?"

The views of the Wild Ram of the Mountains partook in certain ways of his own discouragement.

"Zion has run to seed, Brother Rae; the rank weeds of Babylon is a-goin' to choke it out, root and branch! We ain't got no chance to live a pure and Godly life any longer, with railroads coming in, and Gentiles with their fancy contraptions. It weakens the spirit, and it plays the very hob with the women. Soon as they git up there now, and see them new styles from St. Looey or Chicago, they git downright daft. No more homespun for 'em, no more valley tan, no more parched corn for coffee, nor beet molasses nor unbolted flour. Oh, I know what I'm talkin' about."

The tone of the good man became as of one who remembers hurts put upon his own soul. He continued:

"You no sooner let a woman git out of the wagon there now than she's crazy for a pink nubia, and a shell breastpin, and a dress-pattern, and a whole bolt of factory and a set of chiny cups and saucers and some of this here perfumery soap. And *that* don't do 'em. Then they let out a yell for varnished rockin'-cheers with flowers painted all over 'em in different colours, and they tell you they got to have bristles carpet—bristles on it that long, prob'ly!" The injured man indicated a length of some eighteen or twenty inches.

"Of course all them grand things would please our feelings, but they take a woman's mind off of the Lord, and she neglects her work in the field, and then pretty soon the Lord gets mad and sics the Gentiles on to us again. But I made my women toe the mark mighty quick, I told 'em they could all have one day a week to work out, and make a little pin-money, hoein' potatoes or plantin' corn or some such business, and every cent they earned that way they could squander on this here pink-and-blue soap, if they was a mind to; but not a York shilling of my money could they have for such persuasions of Satan—not while we got plenty of soap-grease and wood-ashes to make lye of and a soap-kittle that cost four eighty-five, in the very Lord's stronghold. I dress my women comfortable and feed 'em well—not much variety but plenty *of*, and I've done right by 'em as a husband, and I tell 'em if they want to be led away now into the sinful path of worldliness, why, I ain't goin' to have any ruthers about it at all! But you be careful, Brother Rae, about turning your women loose in one of them ungodly stores up there. That reminds me, you had Prudence up to Conference, and I guess you don't know what that letter's about."

"Why, no; do you?"

"Well, Brother Brigham only let a word or two drop, but plain enough; he don't have to use many. He was a little mite afraid some one down here would cut in ahead of him."

Joel Rae had torn open the big blue envelope in a sudden fear, and now he read in Brigham's well-known script:—

"DEAR BROT. JOEL:—

"I was ancus to see more of your daughter, and would of kept her hear at my house if you had not hurried off. I will let you seal her to me when I come to Pine valle next, late this summer or after Oct. conference.

If anything happens and I am to bisy will have you bring her hear. Tell her of this and what it will mean to her in the Lord's kingdom and do not let her company with gentiles or with any of the young brethren around there that might put Notions into her head. Try to due right and never faint in well duing, keep the faith of the gospel and I pray the Lord to bless you. BRIGHAM YOUNG."

The shrewd old face of the Bishop had wrinkled into a smile of quiet observation as the other read the letter. In relating the incident to the Entablature of Truth subsequently, he said of Joel Rae at the moment he looked up from this letter: "He'll never be whiter when he's dead! I see in a minute that the old man had him on the bark."

"You know what's in this, Brother Seth—you know that Brigham wants Prudence?" Joel Rae had asked, looking up from the letter, upon which both his hands had closed tightly.

"Well, I told you he dropped a word or two, jest by way of keeping off the Princes of Israel down here."

"I must go to Salt Lake at once and talk to him."

"Take her along; likely he'll marry her right off."

"But I can't—I couldn't—Brother Seth, I wish her not to marry him."

The Bishop stared blankly at him, his amazement freezing upon his lips, almost, the words he uttered.

"Not—want—her—to marry—Brother Brigham Young, Prophet, Seer, and Revelator, President of the Church of Jesus Christ of Latter-day Saints in all the world!"

"I must go up and talk to him at once."

"You won't talk him out of it. Brother Brigham has the habit of prevailing. Of course, he's closer than Dick's hat-band, but she'll have the best there is until he takes another."

"He may listen to reason—"

"Reason?—why, man, what more reason could he want,—with that splendid young critter before him, throwing back her head, and flashing her big, shiny eyes, and lifting her red lips over them little white teeth—reason enough for Brother Brigham—or for other people I could name!"

"But he wouldn't be so hard—taking her away from me—"

Something in the tones of this appeal seemed to touch even the heart of the Wild Ram of the Mountains, though it told of a suffering he could not understand.

"Brigham is very sot in his ways," he said, after a little, with a curious soft kindness in his voice, — "in fact, a *sotter* man I never knew!"

He drove off, leaving the other staring at the letter now crumpled in his hand. He also said, in his subsequent narrative to the Entablature of Truth: "You know I've always took Brother Rae for jest a natural born *not*, a shy little cuss that could be whiffed around by anything and everything, but when I drove off he had a plumb ornery fighting look in them deep-set eyes of his, and blame me if I didn't someway feel sorry for him, — he's that warped up, like an old water-soaked sycamore plank that gits laid out in the sun."

But this look of belligerence had quickly passed from the face of Joel Rae when the first heat of his resentment had cooled.

After that he merely suffered, torn by his reverence for Brigham, who represented on earth no less a power than the first person of the Trinity, and by the love for this child who held him to a past made beautiful by his love for her mother, — by a thousand youthful dreams and fancies and wayward hopes that he had kept fresh through all the years; torn between Brigham, whose word was as the word of God, and Prudence who was the living flower of her dead mother and all his dead hopes.

Could he persuade Brigham to leave her? The idea of refusing him, if he should persist, was not seriously to be thought of. For twenty-five years he, in common with the other Saints, had held Brigham's lightest command to be above all earthly law; to be indeed the revealed will of God. His kingship in things material no less than in things spiritual had been absolute, undisputed, undoubted — indeed, gloried in by the people as much as Brigham himself gloried when he declared it in and out of the tabernacle. Their blind obedience had been his by divine right, by virtue of his iron will, his matchless courage, his tireless spirit, and his understanding of their hearts and their needs, born of his common suffering with them. Nothing could be done without his sanction. No man could enter a business, or change his home from north to south, without first securing his approval; even the merchants who went east or west for goods must first report to him their wishes, to see if he had contrary orders for them! From the invitation list of a ball to the financing of a corporation, his word was law; in matters of marriage as well — no man daring even to seek a wife until the Prophet had approved his choice. The whole valley for five hundred miles was filled with his power as with another air that the Saints must breathe. In his oft-repeated own phrase, it was his God-given right to dictate all matters, "even to the ribbons a woman should wear, or the setting up of a stocking." And his people had not only submitted blindly to his rule, but had reverenced and even loved him for it.

Twenty-five years of such allegiance, preceded by a youth in which the same gospel of obedience was bred into his marrow—this was not to be thrown off by a mere heartache; not to be more than striven against, half-heartedly, in the first moment of anguish.

He thought of Brigham's home in the Lion House, the score or so of plain, elderly women, hard-working, simple-minded; the few favourites of his later years, women of sightlier exteriors; and he pictured the long dining-room, where, at three o'clock each afternoon, to the sound of a bell, these wives and half a hundred children marched in, while the Prophet sat benignantly at the head of the table and blessed the meal. He tried to fix Prudence in this picture, but at every effort he saw, not her, the shy, sweet woman, full of surprised tenderness, but a creature hardened, debased, devoid of charm, dehumanised, a brood-beast of the field.

And yet this was not rebellion. His mind was clear as to that. He could not refuse, even had refusal not been to incur the severest penalties both in this world and in the world to come. The habit of obedience was all-powerful.

Presently he saw Prudence coming across the fields in the late afternoon from the road that led to the cañon. He watched her jealously until she drew near, then called her to him. In a few words he told her very gravely the honour that was to be done her.

When she fully understood, he noted that her mind seemed to attain an unusual clearness, her speech a new conciseness; that she was displaying a force of will he had never before suspected.

Her reply, in effect, was that she would not marry Brigham Young if all the angels in heaven came to entreat her; that the thought was not a pretty one; and that the matter might be considered settled at that very moment. "It's too silly to talk about," she concluded.

Almost fearfully he looked at her, yielding a little to her spirit of rebellion, yet trying not to yield; trying not to rejoice in the amused flash of her dark eyes and the decision of her tones. But then, as he looked, and as she still faced him, radiant in her confidence, he felt himself going with her—plunging into the tempting wave of apostasy.

Chapter XXXII
A New Face in the Dream

In a settled despair the little bent man waited for the end. Already he felt himself an outcast from Israel. In spirit he had disobeyed the voice of Brigham, which was the voice of God; exulting sinfully in spite of himself in this rebellion. Praying to be bowed and bent and broken, to have all trace of the evil self within him burned out, he had now let that self rise up again to cry out a want. Praying that crosses might daily be added to his burden, he had now refused to take up one the bearing of which might have proved to Heaven the extinction of his last selfish desire. He had been put to the test, as he prayed to be, and he had failed miserably to meet it. And now he knew that even his life was waning with his faith.

During the year when he waited for the end of the world, he had been nerved to an unwonted vigour. Now he was weak and fit for no further combat. He waited, with an indifference that amazed him, for the day when he should openly defy Brigham, and have penalties heaped upon him.

First he would be ordered on a mission to some far corner of the world. It would mean that he must go alone, "without purse or scrip," leaving Prudence. He would refuse to go. Thereupon he would be sternly disfellowshiped. Then, having become an apostate, he would be a fair mark for many things, perhaps for simple persecution—perhaps for blood atonement. He had heard Brigham himself say in the tabernacle that he was ready to "unsheathe his bowie knife" and send apostates "to hell across lots."

He was ready to welcome that. It were easier to die now than to live; and, as for being cut off from his glory in the after-time, he had already forfeited that; would miss it even if he died in fellowship with Brigham and full of churchly honours; would miss it even if the power on high should forgive him,—for he himself, he knew, could not forgive his own sin. So it was little matter about his apostasy, and Prudence should be saved from a wifehood that, ever since he had pictured her in it, had seemed to him for the first time unspeakably bad.

They talked but little about it that day, after her first abrupt refusal. There was too much for each of them to think of. He was obliged to dwell upon the amazing fact that he must lie in hell until he could win his own forgiveness, regardless of what gentle pardoning might be his from God. This, to him, simple and obvious truth, was now his daily torture.

As for Prudence, she had to be alone to dream her dreams of a love that should be always single. Brigham's letter, far from disturbing these, had brought them a zest hitherto lacking. Neither the sacrilege of refusing him, its worldly unwisdom, nor its possible harm to the little bent man of sorrows, had as yet become apparent to her. Each day, when such duties as were hers in the house had been performed, she walked out to be alone,—always to Box Cañon, that green-sided cleft in the mountain, with the brook lashing itself to a white fury over the boulders at the bottom. She would go up out of the hot valley into its cool freshness and its pleasant wood smells, and there, in the softened blue light of a pine-hung glade, she would rest, and let her fancy build what heaven-reaching towers it would. On some brown bed of pine-needles, or on a friendly gray boulder close by the water-side, where she could give her eyes to its flow and foam, and her ears to its music,—music like the muffled tinkling of little silver bells in the distance,—she would let herself go out to her dream with the joyous, reckless abandon of falling water.

It was commonly a dream of a youth in doublet and hose, a plumed cap, and a cloak of purple satin, who came in the moonlight to the balcony of his love, and sighed his passion in tones so moving that she thought an angel must have yielded—as did the girl in the balcony who had let down the scarf to him. She already knew how that girl's heart must have fluttered at the moment,—how she must have felt that the hands were mad, wicked, uncontrollable hands, no longer her own.

There was one place in the dream that she managed not without some ingenuity. It had to be made plain that the lover under the window did not come from a long, six-doored house, with a wife behind each door; that this girl, pale in the moonlight, with quickening heart and rebellious hands on the scarf, and arms that should open to him, was to be not only his first wife but his last; that he was never even to consider so much as the possibility of another, but was to cleave unto her, and to love her with a single heart for all the days of her life and his own.

There were various ways of bringing this circumstance forward. Usually she had Brigham march on at the head of his great family and counsel the youth to take more wives, in order that he should be exalted in the Kingdom. Whereupon the young man would fold his love in his arms and speak words of scorn, in the same thrilling manner that he spoke his other words, for any exaltation which they two could not share alone. Brigham, at the head of his wives, would then slink off, much abashed.

She had come naturally to see her own face as the face of this happily loved girl in the dream. She knew no face for the youth. There was none in Amalon; not Jarom Tanner, six feet three, who became a helpless, grinning child in her presence; nor Moroni Peterson, who became a solemn and ghastly imbecile; nor Ammaron Wright, son of the Bishop, who had opened the dance of the Young People's Auxiliary with prayer, and later tried to kiss her in a dark corner of the room. So the face of the other person in her dream remained of an unknown heavenly beauty.

And then one afternoon in early May a strange youth came singing down the cañon; came while she mused by the brook-side in her best-loved dream. Long before she saw him, she heard his music, a young, clear, care-free voice ringing down from the trail that went over the mountains to Kanab and into Kimball Valley; one of the ways that led out to the world that she wondered about so much. It was a voice new to her, and the words of his ballad were also new. At first she heard them from afar: —

> "There was a young lady came a-tripping along,
>   And at each side a servant-O,
> And in each hand a glass of wine
>   To drink with the Gypsy Davy-O.
>
> "And will you fancy me, my dear,
>   And will you be my Honey-O?
> I swear by the sword that hangs by my side
>   You shall never want for money-O.
>
> "Oh, yes, I will fancy you, kind sir,
>   And I will be your Honey-O,
> If you swear by the sword that hangs by your side
>   I shall never want for money-O."

The singer seemed to be making his way slowly. Far up the trail, she had one fleeting glimpse of a man on a horse, and then he was hid again in the twilight of the pines. But the music came nearer: —

> "Then she put on her high-heeled shoes,
>   All made of Spanish leather-O,
> And she put on her bonnie, bonnie brown,
>
>   And they rode off together-O.
> "Soon after that, her lord came home
>   Inquiring for his lady-O,

When some of the servants made this reply,
  She's a-gone with the Gypsy Davy-O.
"Then saddle me my milk-white steed,
  For the black is not so speedy-O,
And I'll ride all night and I'll ride all day
  Till I overtake my lady-O."

She stood transfixed, something within her responding to the hidden singer, as she had once heard a closed piano sound to a voice that sang near it. Soon she could get broken glimpses of him as he wound down the trail, now turning around the end of a fallen tree, then passing behind a giant spruce, now leaning far back while the horse felt a way cautiously down some sharp little declivity. The impression was confused,—a glint of red, of blue, of the brown of the horse, a figure swaying loosely to the horse's movements, and then he was out of sight again around the big rock that had once fallen from high up on the side of the cañon; but now, when he came from behind that, he would be squarely in front of her. This recalled and alarmed her. She began to pick a way over the boulders and across the trail that lay between her and the edge of the pines, hearing another verse of the song, almost at her ear:—

"He rode all night and he rode all day,
  Till he came to the far deep water-O,
Then he stopped and a tear came a-trickling down his cheek,
  For there he saw his lady-O."

Before she could reach a shelter in the pines, while she was poised for the last step that would take her out of the trail, he was out from behind the rock, before her, almost upon her, reining his horse back upon its haunches,—then in another instant lifting off his broad-brimmed hat to her in a gracious sweep. It was the first time she had seen this simple office performed outside of the theatre.

She looked up at him, embarrassed, and stepped back across the narrow trail, her head down again, so that he was free to pass. But instead of passing, she became aware that he had dismounted.

When she looked up, he was busily engaged in adjusting something about his saddle, with an expression of deepest concern in his blue eyes. His hat was on the ground and his yellow hair glistened where the band had pressed it about his head.

"It's that latigo strap," he remarked, in a tone of some annoyance. "I've had to fix it every five miles since I left Kanab!" Then looking up at her with a friendly smile: "Dandy most stepped on you, I reckon."

The amazement of it was that, after her first flurry at the sound of his voice and his half-seen movements up the trail, it should now seem all so commonplace.

"Oh, no, I was well out of his way."

She started again to cross the trail, stepping quickly, with her eyes down, but again his voice came, less deliberate this time, and with words in something less than intelligible sequence.

"Excuse me, Miss—but—now how many miles to—what's the name of the nearest settlement—I suppose you live hereabouts?"

"What did you say?"

"I say is there any place where I could get to stop a day or so in Amalon?"

"Oh—I didn't understand—I think so; at least, my father sometimes— but there's Elder Wardle, he often takes in travellers."

"You say your father—"

"Not always—I don't know, I'm sure—" she looked doubtful.

"Oh, all right! I'll ask him,—if you'll show me his place."

"It's the first place on the left after you leave the cañon—with the big peach orchard—I'm not going home just yet."

He stroked the muzzle of the horse.

"Oh, I'm in no hurry, I'm just looking over the country a little. Your father's name is—"

"Ask for Elder Rae—or one of his wives will say if they can keep you over night."

She caught something new in his glance, and felt the blood in her face.

"I must go now—you can find your way—I must go."

"Well, if you *must* go,"—he picked up his hat,—"but I'll see you again. You'll be coming home this evening, I reckon?"

"The first house on the left," she answered, and stepped once more across the trail and into the edge of the pines. She went with the same mien of importance that Tom Potwin wore on his endless errands; and with quite as little reason, too; for the direction in which she had started so earnestly would have led her, after a few steps, straight up a granite cliff a thousand feet high. As she entered the pines she heard him mount his horse and ride down the trail, and then the rest of his song came back to her:—

"Will you forsake your houses and lands,
   Will you forsake your baby-O?
Will you forsake your own wedded lord
   To foller a Gypsy Davy-O?

"Yes, I'll forsake my houses and lands,
   Yes, I'll forsake my baby-O,
For I am bewitched, and I know the reason why;
   It's a follering a Gypsy Davy-O.

"Last night I lay on a velvet couch
   Beside my lord and baby-O;
To-night I shall lie on the cold, cold ground,
   In the arms of a Gypsy Davy-O.

"To-night I shall lie on the cold, cold ground,
   In the arms of a Gypsy Davy-O!"

When his voice died away and she knew he must be gone, she came out again to her nook beside the stream where, a moment before, her dream had filled her. But now, though nothing had happened beyond the riding by of a strange youth, the dream no longer sufficed. In place of the moonlit balcony was the figure of this young stranger swaying with his horse down between the hollowed shoulders of the Pine Mountains and reining up suddenly to sweep his broad hat low in front of her. She was surprised by the clearness with which she could recall the details of his appearance,—a boyish-looking fellow, with wide-open blue eyes and a sunbrowned face under his yellow hair, the smallest of moustaches, and a smile of such winning good-humour that it had seemed to force her own lips apart in answer.

Around the broad, gray hat had been a band of braided silver; when he stepped, the spurs on his high-heeled boots had jingled and clanked of silver; around his neck with a knot at the back and the corners flapping down on the front of his blue woollen shirt, had been a white-dotted handkerchief of scarlet silk; and about his waist was knotted a long scarf of the same colour; dogskin "chapps" he had worn, fronted with the thick yellowish hair outside; his saddle-bags, back of the saddle, showing the same fur; his saddle had been of stamped Spanish leather with a silver capping on the horn and on the circle of the cantle; and on the right of the saddle she had seen the coils of a lariat of plaited horsehair.

The picture of him stayed in her mind, the sturdy young figure,—rather loose-jointed but with an easy grace of movement,—and the engaging naturalness of his manner. But after all nothing had happened save the passing of a stranger, and she must go alone back to her dream. Yet now the dream might change; a strange youth might come riding out of the east, sitting a sorrel horse with a star and a white hind ankle, a long rangy neck and strong quarters; and he—the youth—would wear a broad, gray hat, with a band of silver filigree, a scarlet kerchief at his throat, a scarlet sash at his waist, and yellow dogskin "chapps."

Still, she thought, he could hardly have a place in the dream. The real youth of the dream had been of an unearthly beauty, with a rose-leaf complexion and lustrous curls massed above a brow of marble. The stranger had not been of an unearthly beauty. To be sure, he was very good to look at, with his wide-open blue eyes and his yellow hair, and he had appeared uncommonly fresh and clean about the mouth when he smiled at her. But she could not picture him sighing the right words of love under a balcony in the moonlight. He had looked to be too intensely business-like.

Chapter XXXIII
The Gentile Invasion

When she came across the fields late in the afternoon, the strange youth's horse was picketed where the bunch-grass grew high, and the young man himself talked with her father by the corral bars. She had never realised how old her father was, how weak, and small, and bent, until she saw him beside this erect young fellow. Her heart went out to the older man with a new sympathy as she saw his feebleness so sharply in relief against the well-blooded, hard-muscled vigour of the younger. When she would have passed them, her father called to her.

"Prudence, this is Mr. Ruel Follett. He will stay with us to-night."

The sombrero was off again and she felt the blue eyes seeking hers, though she could not look up from the ground when she had given her little bow. She heard him say:

"I already met your daughter, sir, at the mouth of the cañon."

She went on toward the house, hearing them resume their talk, the stranger saying, "That horse can sure carry all the weight you want to put on him and step away good; he'll do it right at both ends, too—Dandy will—and he's got a mighty tasty lope."

Later she brought him a towel when he had washed himself in the tin basin on the bench outside the house. He had doffed the "chapps" and hung them on a peg, the scarlet kerchief was also off, his shirt was open at the neck, and soap and water had played freely over his head. He took the towel from her with a sputtering, "Thank you," and with a pair of muscular, brown hands proceeded to scour himself dry until the yellow hair stood about him as a halo—without, however, in the least suggesting the angelic or even saintly: for his face, from the friction inflamed to a high degree, was now a mass of red with two inquiring spots of blue near the upper edge. But then the clean mouth opened in its frank smile, and her own dark lashes had to fall upon her cheeks until she turned away.

At supper and afterwards Mr. Follett talked freely of himself, or seemed to. He was from the high plains and the short-grass country, wherever that might be—to the east and south she gathered. He had grown up in that country, working for his father, who had been an overland freighter, until the day the railroad tracks were joined at Promontory. He, himself, had watched the gold and silver spikes driven into the tie of California mahogany two years before; and then, though they still kept a few wagon trains moving to the mining camps north and south of the railroad, they had looked for other occupations.

Now their attention was chiefly devoted to mines and cattle. There were great times ahead in the cattle business. His father remembered when they had killed cattle for their hides and tallow, leaving the meat to the coyotes. But now, each spring, a dozen men, like himself, under a herd boss, would drive five thousand head to Leavenworth, putting them through ten or twelve miles a day over the Abiline trail, keeping them fat and getting good prices for them. There was plenty of room for the business. "Over yonder across the hills," as Mr. Follett put it. There was a herding ground four hundred miles wide, east and west, and a thousand miles north and south, covered with buffalo grass, especially toward the north, that made good stock feed the year around. He himself had, in winter, followed a herd that drifted from Montana to Texas; and in summer he had twice ranged from Corpus Christi to Deadwood.

Down in the Panhandle they were getting control of a ranch that would cover five thousand square miles. Some day they would have every one of its three million acres enclosed with a stout wire fence. It would be a big ranch, bigger than the whole state of Connecticut—bigger than Delaware and Rhode Island "lumped together", he had been told. Here they would have the "C lazy C" brand on probably a hundred and fifty thousand head of cattle. He thought the business would settle down to this conservative basis with the loose ends of it pulled together; with closer attention paid to branding, for one thing; branding the calves, so they would no longer have to rope a full-grown steer, and tie it with a scarf such as he wore about his waist.

But they were also working some placer claims up around Helena, and developing a quartz prospect over at Carson City. And the freighting was by no means "played out." He, himself, had driven a six-mule team with one line over the Santa Fé trail, and might have to do it again. The resources of the West were not exhausted, whatever they might say. A man with a head on him would be able to make a good living there for some years to come.

Both father and daughter found him an agreeable young man in spite of his being an alien from the Commonwealth of Israel. He remained with them three days looking over the country about Amalon, talking with its people and making himself at least not an object of suspicion and aversion, as the casual Gentile was apt to be. Prudence found herself usually at ease with him; he was so wholly likable and unassuming. Yet at times he seemed strangely mature and reserved to her, so that she was just a little awed.

He told her in their evenings many wonder-tales of that outside world where the wicked Gentiles lived; of populous cities on the western edge of it, and of vast throngs that crowded the interior clear over to the Atlantic Ocean. She had never realised before what a small handful of people the Lord had set His hand to save, and what vast numbers He had made with hearts that should be hardened to the glorious articles of the new covenant.

The wastefulness of it rather appalled her. Out of the world with its myriad millions, only the few thousand in this valley of the mountains had proved worthy of exaltation. And this young man was doubtless a fair sample of them,—happy, unthinking, earning perdition by mere carelessness. If only there were a way to save them—if only there were a way to save even this one—but she hardly dared speak to him of her religion.

When he left he told them he was making a little trip through the settlements to the north, possibly as far as Cedar City. He did not know how long he would be gone, but if nothing prevented he might be back that way. He shook hands with them both at parting, and though he spoke so vaguely about a return, his eyes seemed to tell Prudence that he would like very much to come. He had talked freely about everything but the precise nature of his errand in the valley.

In her walks to the cañon she thought much of him when he had gone. She could not put his face into the dream because he was too real and immanent. He and the dream would not blend, even though she had decided that his fresh-cheeked, clear-eyed face, with its clean smile and the yellow hair above it was almost better to look at than the face of the youth in the play. It was not so impalpable; it satisfied. So she mused about them alternately, the dream and the Gentile,—taking perhaps a warmer interest in the latter for his aliveness, for the grasp of his hand at parting, which she, with astonishment, had felt her own hand cordially returning.

Her father talked much of the young man. In his prophetic eye this fearless, vigorous young stranger was the incarnate spirit of that Gentile invasion to which the Lord had condemned them for their sins. He had come, resourceful, determined, talking of mighty enterprises, of cattle, and gold, and wheat, of wagon-trains, and railroad,—an eloquent forerunner of the Gentile hordes that should come west upon the shoulders of Israel, and surround, assimilate, and reduce them, until they should lose all their powers and gifts and become a mere sect among sects, their name, perhaps, a hissing and a scorn. He foresaw the invasion of which this self-poised, vital youth of three or four and twenty was a sapper; and he knew it was a just punishment from on high for the innocent blood they had shed. Yet now he viewed it rather impersonally, for he felt curiously disconnected from the affairs of the Church and the world.

He no longer preached on the Sabbath, giving his ill-health as an excuse. In truth he felt it would not be honest since, in his secret heart, he was now an apostate. But with his works of healing he busied himself more than ever, and in this he seemed to have gained new power. Weak as he was physically, gray-haired, bloodless, fragile, with what seemed to be all of his remaining life burning in his deep-set eyes, he yet laid his hands upon the sick with a success so marked that his fame spread and he was sent for to rebuke plagues and fevers from as far away as Beaver.

For two weeks they heard nothing of the wandering Gentile, and Prudence had begun to wonder if she would ever see him again; also to wonder why an uncertainty in the matter should seem to be of importance.

But one evening early in June they saw him walking up in the dusk, the light sombrero, the scarlet kerchief against the blue woollen shirt, the holster with its heavy Colt's revolver at either hip, the easy moving figure, and the strong, yet boyish face.

He greeted them pleasantly, though, the girl thought, with some restraint. She could not hear it in his words, but she felt it in his manner, something suppressed and deeply hidden. They asked where his horse was and he replied with a curious air of embarrassment:—

"Well, you see, I may be obliged to stop around here a quite some while, so I put up with this man Wardle—not wanting to impose upon you all— and thanking you very kindly, and not wishing to intrude—so I just came to say 'howdy' to you."

They expressed regret that he had not returned to them, Joel Rae urging him to reconsider; but he declined politely, showing a desire to talk of other things.

They sat outside in the warm early evening, the young man and Prudence near each other at one side of the door, while Joel Rae resumed his chair a dozen feet the other side and lapsed into silence. The two young people fell easily into talk as on the other evenings they had spent there. Yet presently she was again aware, as in the moment of his greeting, that he laboured under some constraint. He was uneasy and shifted his chair several times until at length it was so placed that he could look beyond her to where her father had tilted his own chair against the house and sat huddled with his chin on his breast. He talked absently, too, at first, of many things and without sequence; and when he looked at her, there was something back of his eyes, plain even in the dusk, that she had not seen there before. He was no longer the ingenuous youth who had come to them from off the Kanab trail.

In a little while, however, this uneasiness seemed to vanish and he was speaking naturally again, telling of his life on the plains with a boyish enthusiasm; first of the cattle drives, of the stampede of a herd by night, when the Indians would ride rapidly by in the dark, dragging a buffalo-robe over the ground at the end of a lariat, sending the frightened steers off in a mad gallop that made the earth tremble. They would have to ride out at full speed in the black night, over ground treacherous with prairie-dog holes, to head and turn the herd of frenzied cattle, and by riding around and around them many times get them at last into a circle and so hold them until they became quiet again. Often this was not until sunrise, even with the lullabys they sang "to put them to sleep."

Then he spoke of adventures with the Indians while freighting over the Santa Fé trail, and of what a fine man his father, Ezra Calkins, was. It was the first time he had mentioned the name and her ear caught it at once.

"Your father's name is Calkins?"

"Yes—I'm only an adopted son."

Unconsciously she had been letting her voice fall low, making their chat more confidential. She awoke to this now and to the fact that he had done the same, by noting that he raised his voice at this time with a casual glance past her to where her father sat.

"Yes—you see my own father and mother were killed when I was eight years old, and the people that murdered them tried to kill me too, but I was a spry little tike and give them the slip. It was a bad country, and I like to have died, only there was a band of Navajos out trading ponies, and one morning, after I'd been alone all night, they picked me up and took care of me. I was pretty near gone, what with being scared and everything, but they nursed me careful. They took me away off to the south and kept me about a year, and then one time they took me with them when they worked up north on a buffalo hunt. It was at Walnut Creek on the big bend of the Arkansas that they met Ezra Calkins coming along with one of his trains and he bought me of those Navajos. I remember he gave fifty silver dollars for me to the chief. Well, when I told him all that I could remember about myself—of course the people that did the killing scared a good deal of it out of me—he took me to Kansas City where he lived, and went to law and made me his son, because he'd lost a boy about my age. And so that's how we have different names, he telling me I'd ought to keep mine instead of taking his."

She was excited by the tale, which he had told almost in one breath, and now she was eager to question, looking over to see if her father would not also be interested; but the latter gave no sign.

"You poor little boy, among those wretched Indians! But why were your father and mother killed? Did the Indians do it?"

"No, not Indians that did it—and I never did know why they killed them—they that *did* do it."

"But how queer! Don't you know who it was?"

Before answering, he paused to take one of the long revolvers from its holster, laying it across his lap, his right hand still grasping it.

"It was tiring my leg where it was," he explained. "I'll just rest myself by holding it here. I've practised a good smart bit with these pistols against the time when I'd meet some of them that did it—that killed my father and mother and lots of others, and little children, too."

"How terrible! And it wasn't Indians?"

"No—I *told* you that already—it wasn't Indians."

"Don't you know who it was?"

"Oh, yes, I know all of them I want to know. The fact is, up there at Cedar City I met some people that got confidential with me one day, and told me a lot of their names. There was Mr. Barney Carter and Mr. Sam Woods, and they talked right freely about some folks. I found out what I was wanting to know, being that they were drinking men."

He had moved slightly as he spoke and she glanced at the revolver still held along his knee.

"Isn't that dangerous—seems to me it's pointed almost toward father."

"Oh, not a bit dangerous, and it rests me to hold it there. You see it was hereabouts this thing happened. In fact, I came down here looking for a big man, and a little girl that I remembered, whose father and mother were killed at the same time mine was. This little girl was about three or four, I reckon, and she was taken by one of the murderers. He seemed like an awful big man to me. By the way, that's mean whiskey your Bishop sells on the sly up at Cedar City. Why, it's worse than Taos lightning. Well, this Barney Carter and Mr. Sam Woods, they would drink it all right, but they said one drink made a man ugly and two made him so downright bad that he'd just as lief tear his wife's best bonnet to pieces as not. But they seemed to like me pretty well, and they drank a lot of this whiskey that the Bishop sold me, and then they got talking pretty freely about old times. I gathered that this man that took the little girl is a pretty big man around here. Of course I wasn't expecting anything like that; I thought naturally he'd be a low-down sort to have been mixed up in a thing like that."

He spoke his next words very slowly, with little pauses.

"But I found out what his name was—it was—"

He stopped, for there had been an indistinct sound from where her father sat, now in the gloom of the evening. She called to him:

"Did you speak, father?"

There was no reply or movement from the figure in the chair, and Follett resumed:

"I guess he was just asleep and dreaming about something. Well, anyway—I—I found out afterwards by telling it before him, that Mr. Barney Carter and his drunken friend had given me his name right, though I could hardly believe it before."

"What an awful, awful thing! What wickedness there is in the world!"

"Oh, a tolerable lot," he assented.

He had been all animation and eagerness in the telling of the story, but had now become curiously silent and listless; so that, although she was eager with many questions about what he had said, she did not ask them, waiting to see if he would not talk again. But instead of talking, he stayed silent and presently began to fidget in his chair. At last he said, "If you'll excuse us, Miss Prudence, your pa and I have got a little business matter to talk over—to-night. I guess we can go down here by the corral and do it."

But she arose quickly and bade him good night. "I hope I shall see you to-morrow," she said.

She bent over to kiss her father as she went in, and when she had done so, warned him that he must not sit in the night air.

"Why your face is actually wet with a cold sweat. You ought to come in at once."

"After a very little, dear. Go to bed now—and always be a good girl!"

"And you've grown so hoarse sitting here."

"In a little while,—always be a good girl!"

She went in with a parting admonition: "Remember your cough—good night!"

When she had gone neither man stirred for the space of a minute. The little man, huddled in his seat, had not changed his position; he still sat with his chair tilted back against the house, his chin on his breast.

The other had remained standing where the girl left him, the revolver in his hand. After the minute of silence he crossed over and stood in front of the seated man.

"Come," he said, gruffly, "where do you want to go?"

Chapter XXXIV
How the Avenger Bungled His Vengeance

At last he stood up, slowly, unsteadily, grasping Follett by the arm for support. He spoke almost in a whisper.

"Come back here first—to talk—then I'll go with you."

He entered the house, the young man following close, suspicious, narrowly watchful.

"No fooling now,—feel the end of that gun in your back?" The other made no reply. Inside the door he took a candle from the box against the wall and lighted it.

"Don't think I'm trying anything—come here."

They went on, the little bent man ahead, holding the candle well up. His room was at the far end of the long house. When they reached it, he closed the door and fixed the candle on the table in some of its own grease. Then he pointed Follett to the one stool in the little cell-like room, and threw himself face down on the bed.

Follett, still standing, waited for him to speak. After a moment's silence he grew impatient.

"Come, come! What would you be saying if you were talking? I can't wait here all night."

But the little man on the bed was still silent, nor did he stir, and after another wait Follett broke out again.

"If you want to talk, *talk*, I tell you. If you don't want to, I can say all I have to say, *quick*."

Then the other turned himself over on the bed and half sat up, leaning on his elbow.

"I'm sorry to keep you waiting, but you see I'm so weak"—the strained little smile came to his face—"and tremble so, there's so much to think of—do *you* hear those women scream—*there*! did you hear that?—but of course not. Now—wait just a moment—have you come to kill me?"

"You and those two other hellions—the two that took me and that boy out that night to bury us."

"Did you think of the consequences?"

"I reckoned you'd be called paid for, any time any one come gunning for you. I didn't think there'd *be* any consequences."

"Hereafter, I mean; to your soul. What a pity you didn't wait a little longer! Those other two are already punished."

"Don't lie to me now?"

The little smile lighted his face again.

"I have a load of sin on me—but I don't think I ever did lie to any one—I guess I never was tempted—"

"Oh, you've *acted* lies enough."

"OH, MAN ... HOW I'VE LONGED FOR THAT BULLET OF YOURS!"

"You're right—that's so. But I'm telling you truth now—those two men had both been in the Meadows that day and it killed them. One went crazy and ran off into the desert. They found his bones. The other shot himself a few years ago. Those of us that live are already in hell—"

He sat up, now, animated for the moment.

"—in hell right here, I tell you. I'd have welcomed you, or any other man that would kill me, any time this fifteen years. I'd have gone out to meet you. Do you think I like to hear the women scream? Do you think

I'm not crazed myself by this thing—right back of me here, *now*—crawling, bleeding, breathing on me—trying to come here in front where I must *see* it? Don't you see God has known how to punish me worse than you could, just by keeping me alive and sane? Oh, man! you don't know how I've longed for that bullet of yours, right here through the temples where the cries sound worst. I didn't dare to do it myself—I was afraid I'd make my punishment worse if I tried to shirk; but I used to hope you would come as you said you would. I wonder I didn't know you at once."

He put his hands to his head and fell back again on the pillow, with a little moan.

"Well, it ain't strange I didn't know *you*. I was looking for a big man. You seemed as big as a house to me that day. I forgot that I'd grown up and you might be small. When those fellows got tight up there and let on like it was you that some folks hinted had took a child and kept it out of that muss, I couldn't hardly believe it; and everybody seeming to regard you so highly. And I couldn't believe this big girl was little Prue Girnway that I remembered. It seemed like you two would have to be a great big man and a little bit of a baby girl with yellow hair; and now I find you're—say, Mister, *honestly*, you're such a poor, broke-down, little coot it seems a'most like a shame to put a bullet through you, in spite of all your doings!"

The little man sat up again, with new animation in his eyes,—the same eager boyishness that he had somehow kept through all his years.

"*Don't!*" he exclaimed, earnestly. "Let me beg you, don't kill me! For your own sake—not for mine. I'm a poor, meatless husk. I'll die soon at best, and I'm already in a hell you can't make any hotter. Let me do you this service; let me persuade you not to kill me. Have you ever killed a man?"

"No, not yet; I've allowed to a couple of times, but it's never come just that way."

"You ought to thank God. Don't ever. You'll be in hell as sure as you do,—a hell right here that you must carry inside of you forever—that even God can't take out of you. Listen—it's a great secret, worth millions. If you're so bad you can't forgive yourself, you have to suffer hell-fire no matter how much the Lord forgives you. It sounds queer, but there's the limit to His power. He's made us so nearly in His image that we have to win our own forgiveness; why, you can see yourself, it *had* to be that way; there would have been no dignity to a soul that could swallow all its own wickedness so long as the Lord could. God has given us to know good and evil for ourselves—and we have to take the consequences. Look at me. I suffer day and night, and always must. God has forgiven me, but I can't forgive myself, for my own sin and my people's sin,—for my preaching was one of the things that led them into that meadow. I know that Christ died for us, but that can't put out this fire that I *have* to build in my own soul. I tell you a man is like an angel, he can be good or bad; he has a power for heaven but the same power for hell—"

"See here, I don't know anything about all this hell-talk, but I do know—"

"I tell you death is the very last thing I have left to look forward to, but if you kill me it will be your own undoing. You will never get me out of your eyes or your ears, poor wreck as I am—so feeble. You can see what my punishment has been. A little while ago I was young, and strong, and proud like you, fearing nothing and wanting everything, but something was wrong. I was climbing up as I thought, and then all at once I saw I had been climbing down—down into a pit I never could get out of. You will be there if you kill me." He sank back on the bed again.

Follett slowly put the revolver into its holster and sat down on the low stool.

"I don't know anything about all this hell-talk, but I see I can't kill you—you're such a poor, miserable cuss. And I thought you were a big strong man, handy with a gun and all that, and like as not I'd have to make a quick draw on you when the time come. And now look at you! Why, Mister, I'm doggoned if I ain't almost *sorry* for you! You sure have been getting your deservance good and plenty. Say, what in God's name did you all do such a hellish thing for, anyway?"

"We had been persecuted, hunted, and driven, our Prophet murdered, our women and children butchered, and another army was on the way."

"Well, that was because you were such an ornery lot, always setting yourself up against the government wherever you went, and acting scandalous—"

"We did as the Lord directed us—"

"Oh, shucks!"

"And then we thought the time had come to stand up for our rights; that the Lord meant us to be free and independent."

"Secesh, eh?" Follett was amused. "You handful of Mormons—Uncle Sam could have licked you with both hands tied behind him. Why, you crazy fool, he'd have spit on you and drowned every last one of you, old Brigham Young and all. Fighting the United States! A few dozen women-butchers going to do what the whole South couldn't! Well, I *am* danged."

He mused over it, and for awhile neither spoke.

"And the nearest you ever got to it was cutting up a lot of women and children after you'd cheated the men into giving up their guns!"

The other groaned.

"There now, that's right—don't you see that hurts worse than killing?"

"But I certainly wish I could have got those other two that took us off into the sage-brush that night. I didn't guess what for, but the first thing I knew the other boy was scratching, and kicking, and hollering, and like to have wriggled away, so the cuss that was with me ran up to help. Then I heard little John making kind of a squeally noise in his throat like he was being choked, and that was all I wanted. I legged it into the sage-brush. I heard them swearing and coming after me, and ran harder, and, what saved me, I tripped and fell down and hurt myself, so I lay still and they lost track of me. I was scared, I promise you that; but after they got off a ways I worked in the other direction by spells till I got to a little wady, and by sunup they weren't in sight any longer. When I saw the Indians coming along I wasn't a bit scared. I knew *they* weren't Mormons."

"I used to pray that you might come back and kill me."

"I used to wish I would grow faster so I could. I was always laying out to do it."

"But see how I've been punished. Look at me—I'm fifty. I ought to be in my prime. See how I've been burnt out."

"But look here, Mister, what about this girl? Do you think you've been doing right by keeping her here?"

"No, no! it was a wrong as great as the other."

"Why, they're even passing remarks about her mother, those that don't know where you got her,—saying it was some one you never married, because the book shows your first wife was this one-handed woman here."

"I know, I know it. I meant to let her go back at first, but she took hold of me, and her father and mother were both dead."

"She's got a grandfather and grandmother, alive and hearty, back at Springfield."

"She is all that has kept me alive these last years."

"She's got to go back to her people now. She'll want to bad enough when she knows about this."

"About this? Surely you won't tell her—"

"Look here now, why not? What do you expect?"

"But she loves me—she *does*—and she's all I've got. Man, man! don't pile it all on me just at the last."

He was off the bed and on his knees before Follett.

"Don't put it all on me. I've rounded up my back to the rest of it, but keep this off; please, please don't. Let her always think I'm not bad. Give me that one thing out of all the world."

He tried to reach the young man's hand, but was pushed roughly away.

"Don't do that—get up—stop, I tell you. That ain't any way to do. There now! Lie down again. What do you *want*? I'm not going to leave that ain't any way to do. There now! Lie down again. What do you want? I'm not going to leave that girl with you nor with your infernal Church. You understand that."

"Yes, yes, I know it. It was right that you should be the one to come and take her away. The Lord's vengeance was well thought out. Oh, how much more he can make us suffer than you could with your clumsy killings! She must go, but wait—not yet—not yet. Oh, my God! I couldn't stand it to see her go. It would cut into my heart and leave me to bleed to death. No, no, no—don't! Please don't! Don't pile it all on me at the last. The end has come anyway. Don't do that—don't, don't!"

"There, there, be still now." There was a rough sort of soothing in Follett's voice, and they were both silent a moment. Then the young man went on:

"But what do you expect? Suppose everything was left to you, Mister. Come now, you're *trying* to talk fair. Suppose I leave it to you—only you know you can't keep her."

"Yes, it can't be, but let her stay a little while; let me see her a few times more; let me know she doesn't think I'm bad; and promise never to tell her all of it. Let her always think I was a good man. Do promise me that. I'd do it for you, Follett. It won't hurt you. Let her think I was a good man."

"How long do you want her to stay here?—a week, ten days?"

"It will kill me when she goes!"

"Oh, well, two weeks?"

"That's good of you; you're kinder at your age than I was—I shall die when she goes."

"Well, I wouldn't want to live if I were you."

"Just a little longer, knowing that she cares for me. I've never been free to have the love of a woman the way you will some day, though I've hungered and sickened for it—for a woman who would understand and be close. But this girl has been the soul of it some way. See here, Follett, let her stay this summer, or until I'm dead. That can't be a long time. I've felt the end coming for a year now. Let her stay, believing in me. Let me know to the last that I'm the only man who has been in her heart, who has won her confidence and her love. Oh, I mean fair. You stay with us yourself and watch. Come—but look there, *look*, man!"

"Well,—what?"

"That candle is going out,—we'll be in the dark"—he grasped the other's arm—"in the dark, and now I'm afraid again. Don't leave me here! It would be an awful death to die. Here's that thing now on the bed behind me. It's trying to get around in front where I'll have to see it—get another candle. No—don't leave me,—this one will go out while you're gone." All his strength went into the grip on Follett's arm. The candle was sputtering in its pool of grease.

"There, it's gone—now don't, don't leave me. It's trying to crawl over me—I smell the blood—"

"Well—lie down there—it serves you right. There—stop it—I'll stay with you."

Until dawn Follett sat by the bunk, submitting his arm to the other's frenzied grip. From time to time he somewhat awkwardly uttered little words that were meant to be soothing, as he would have done to a frightened child.

When morning brought the gray light into the little room, the haunted man fell into a doze, and Follett, gently unclasping the hands from his arm, arose and went softly out. He was cramped from sitting still so long, and chilled, and his arm hurt where the other had gripped it. He pulled back the blue woollen sleeve and saw above his wrist livid marks where the nails had sunk into his flesh.

Then out of the room back of him came a sharp cry, as from one who had awakened from a dream of terror. He stepped to the door again and looked in.

"There now—don't be scared any more. The daylight has come; it's all right—all right—go to sleep now—"

He stood listening until the man he had come to kill was again quiet. Then he went outside and over to the creek back of the willows to bathe in the fresh running water.

Chapter XXXV
Ruel Follett's Way of Business

By the time the women were stirring that morning, Follett galloped up on his horse. Prudence saw him from the doorway as he turned in from the main road, sitting his saddle with apparent carelessness, his arms loose from the shoulders, shifting lightly with the horse's motion, as one who had made the center of gravity his slave. It was a style of riding that would have made a scandal in any riding-school; but it seemed to be well calculated for the quick halts, sudden swerves, and acute angles affected by the yearling steer in his moments of excitement.

He dismounted, glowing from his bath in the icy water of the creek and from the headlong gallop up from Beil Wardle's corral.

"Good morning, Miss Prudence."

"Good morning, Mr. Follett. Will you take breakfast with us directly?"

"Yes, and it can't be too directly for me. I'm wolfish. Miss Prudence, your pa and me had some talk last night, and I'm going to bunk in with you all for awhile, till I get some business fixed up."

She smiled with unaffected gladness, and he noticed that her fresh morning colour was like that of the little wild roses he had lately brushed the dew from along the creek.

"We shall be glad to have you."

"It's right kind of you; I'm proud to hear you say so." He had taken off the saddle with its gay coloured Navajo blanket, and the bridle of plaited rawhide with its conchos and its silver bit. Now he rubbed the back of his horse where the saddle had been, ending with a slap that sent the beast off with head down and glad heels in the air.

"There now, Dandy! don't bury your ribs too deep under that new grass."

"My father will be glad to have you and Dandy stay a long time."

He looked at her quickly, and then away before he spoke. It was a look that she thought seemed to say more than the words that followed it.

"Well, the fact is, Miss Prudence, I don't just know how long I'll have to be in these parts. I got some particular kind of business that's lasting longer than I thought it would. I reckon it's one of those jobs where you have to let it work itself out while you sit still and watch. Sometimes you get business on hand that seems to know more about itself than you do."

"That's funny."

"Yes, it's like when they first sent me out on the range. They were cutting out steers from a big bunch, and they put me on a little blue roan to hold the cut. Well, cattle hate to leave the bunch, so those they cut out would start to run back, and I had to head and turn them. I did it so well I was surprised at myself. No sooner did a steer head back than I had the spurs in and was after it, and I'd always get it stopped. I certainly did think I was doing it high, wide, and handsome, like you might say; only once or twice I noticed that the pony stopped short when the steer did without my pulling him up, as if he'd seen the stop before I did. And then pretty soon after, a yearling that was just the—excuse me—that was awful spry at dodging, led me a chase, the pony stopped stiff-legged when the steer did, and while I was leaning one way he was off after the steer the other way so quick that I just naturally slid off. I watched him head and turn that steer all by himself, and then I learned something. It seemed like he went to sleep when I got on him. But after that I didn't pay any attention to the cattle. I let him keep the whole lookout, and all I did was to set in the saddle. He was a wise old cow-pony. He taught me a lot about chasing steers. He was always after one the minute it left the cut, and he'd know just the second it was going to stop and turn; he'd never go a foot farther than the steer did, and he'd turn back just as quick. I knew he knew I was green, but I thought the other men didn't, so I just set quiet and played off like I was doing it all, when I wasn't really doing a thing but holding on. He was old, and they didn't use him much except when they wanted a rope-horse around the corral. And he'd made a lifelong study of steers. He knew them from horns to tail, and by saying nothing and looking wise I thought I'd get the credit of being smart myself. It's kind of that way now. I'm holding tight and looking wise about some business that I ain't what you could call up in."

He carried the saddle and bridle into the house, and she followed him. They found Lorena annoyed by the indisposition of her husband.

"Dear me suz! Here's your pa bed-fast again. He's had a bad night and won't open the door to let me tell him if he needs anything. He says he won't even take spoon victuals, and he won't get up, and his chest don't hurt him so that ain't it, and I never was any hand to be nattering around a body, but he hadn't ought to go without his food like he does, when the Father himself has a tabernacle of flesh like you or me—though the Holy Ghost has not—and it's probably mountain fever again, so I'll make some composition tea and he's just *got* to take it. Of course I never had no revelations from the Lord and never did I claim to have, but you don't need the Holy Ghost coming upon you to tell you the plain doings of common sense."

Whatever the nature of Mr. Follett's business, his confidence in the soundness of his attitude toward it was perfect. He showed no sign of abstraction or anxiety; no sign of aught but a desire to live agreeably in the present,—a present that included Prudence. When the early breakfast was over they went out about the place, through the peach-orchard and the vineyard still dewy, lingering in the shade of a plum-tree, finding all matters to be of interest. For a time they watched and laughed at the two calves through the bars of the corral, cavorting feebly on stiffened legs while the bereaved mothers cast languishing glances at them from outside, conscious that their milk was being basely diverted from the rightful heirs. They picked many blossoms and talked of many things. There was no idle moment from early morning until high noon; and yet, though they were very busy, they achieved absolutely nothing.

In the afternoon Prudence donned her own sombrero, and they went to the cañon to fish. From a clump of the yellowish green willows that fringed the stream, Follett cut a slender wand. To this he fixed a line and a tiny hook that he had carried in his hat, and for the rest of the distance to the cañon's mouth he collected such grasshoppers as lingered too long in his shadow. Entering the cañon, they followed up the stream, clambering over broken rocks, skirting huge boulders, and turning aside to go around a gorge that narrowed the torrent and flung it down in a little cascade.

Here and there Follett would flicker his hook over the surface of a shaded pool, poise it at the foot of a ripple, skim it across an eddy, cast it under a shelf of rock or dangle it in some promising nook by the willow roots, shielding himself meanwhile as best he could; here behind a boulder, there bending a willow in front of him, again lying flat on the bank, taking care to keep even his shadow off the stream and to go silently.

From where she followed, Prudence would see the surface of the water break with a curling gleam of gold, which would give way to a bubbling splash; then she would see the willow rod bend, see it vibrate and thrill and tremble, the point working slowly over the bank. Then perhaps the rod would suddenly straighten out for a few seconds only to bend again, slowly, gently, but mercilessly. Or perhaps the point continued to come in until it was well over the bank and the end of the line close by. Then after a frantic splashing on the margin of the stream the conquered trout would be gasping on the bank, a thing of shivering gleams of blended brown and gold and pink. At first she pitied the fish and regretted the cruelty of man, but Follett had other views.

"Why," he said, "a trout is the crudest beast there is. Look at it trying to swallow this poor little hopper that it thought tumbled into the water by accident. It just loves to eat its stuff alive. And it isn't particular. It would just as lief eat its own children. Now you take that one there, and say he was ten thousand times as big as he is, and you were coming along here and your foot slipped and Mr. Trout was lying behind this rock here—*hungry*. Say! What a mouthful you'd make, pink dress and all—he'd have you swallowed in a second, and then he'd sneak back behind the rock there, wiping his mouth, and hoping your little sister or somebody would be along in a minute and fall in too."

"Ugh!—Why, what horrible little monsters! Let me catch one."

And so she fished under his direction. They lurked together in the shadows of rocks, while he showed her how to flicker the bait in the current, here holding her hand on the rod, again supporting her while she leaned out to cast around a boulder, each feeling the other's breathless caution and looking deep into each other's eyes through seconds of tense silence.

Such as they were, these were the only results of the lesson; results that left them in easy friendliness toward each other. For the fish were not deceived by her. He would point out some pool where very probably a hungry trout was lying in wait with his head to the current, and she would try to skim the lure over it. More than once she saw the fish dart toward it, but never did she quite convince them. Oftener she saw them flit up-stream in fright, like flashes of gray lightning. Yet at length she felt she had learned all that could be taught of the art, and that further failure would mean merely a lack of appetite or spirit in the fish. So she went on alone, while Follett stopped to clean the dozen trout he had caught.

While she was in sight he watched her, the figure bending lithe as the rod she held, moving lightly, now a long, now a short step, half kneeling to throw the bait into an eddy; then off again with determined strides to the next likely pool. When he could no longer see her, he fell to work on his fish, scouring their slime off in the dry sand.

When she returned, she found him on his back, his hat off, his arms flung out above his head, fast asleep. She sat near by on a smooth rock at the water's edge and waited—without impatience, for this was the first time she had been free to look at him quite as she wished to. She studied him closely now. He seemed to her like some young power of that far strange eastern land. She thought of something she had heard him say about Dandy: "He's game and fearless and almighty prompt,—but he's kind and gentle too." She was pleased to think it described the master as well as the horse. And she was glad they had been such fine playmates the whole day long. When the shadow moved off his face and left it in the slanting rays of the sun, she broke off a spruce bough and propped it against the rock to shield him.

And then she sighed, for they could be playmates only in forgetfulness. He was a Gentile, and by that token wicked and lost; unless—and in that moment she flushed, feeling the warmth of a high purpose.

She would save him. He was worth saving, from his crown of yellow hair to the high heels of his Mexican boots. Strong, clean, gentle, and—she hesitated for a word—interesting—he must be brought into the Kingdom, and she would do it. She looked up again and met his wide-open eyes.

They both laughed. "I sat up with your pa last night," he said, ashamed of having slept. "We had some business to palaver about."

He had tied the fish into a bundle with aspen leaves and damp moss around them, and now they went back down the stream. In the flush of her new rôle as missionary she allowed herself to feel a secret motherly tenderness for his immortal soul, letting him help her by hand or arm over places where she knew she could have gone much better alone.

Back at the house they were met by the little bent man, who had tossed upon his bed all day in the fires of his hell. He looked searchingly at them to be sure that Follett had kept his secret. Then, relieved by the frank glance of Prudence, he fell to musing on the two, so young, so fresh, so joyous in the world and in each other, seeing them side by side with those little half-felt, timidly implied, or unconsciously expressed confidences of boy and girl; sensing the memory of his own lost youth's aroma, his youth that had slipped off unrecked in the haze of his dreams of glory. For this he felt very tenderly toward them, wishing that they were brother and sister and his own.

That evening, while they sat out of doors, she said, very resolutely:

"I'm going to teach Mr. Follett some truth tomorrow from the Book of Mormon. He says he has never been baptised in any church."

Follett looked interested and cordial, but her father failed to display the enthusiasm she had expected, and seemed even a little embarrassed.

"You mean well, daughter, but don't be discouraged if he is slow to take our truth. Perhaps he has a kind of his own as good as ours. A woman I knew once said to me,' Going to heaven is like going to mill; if your wheat is good the miller will never ask how you came.'"

"But, Father, suppose you get to mill and have only chaff?"

"That is the same answer I made, dear. I wish I hadn't."

Later, when Prudence had gone, the two men made their beds by the fire in the big room. Follett was awakened twice by the other putting wood on the fire; and twice more by his pitiful pleading with something at his back not to come in front of him.

Chapter XXXVI
The Mission to a Deserving Gentile

Not daunted by her father's strange lack of enthusiasm, Prudence arose with the thought of her self-imposed mission strong upon her. Nor was she in any degree cooled from it by a sight of the lost sheep striding up from the creek, the first level sunrays touching his tousled yellow hair, his face glowing, breathing his full of the wine-like air, and joyously showing in every move his faultless attunement with all outside himself. The frank simplicity of his greeting, his careless unenlightenment of his own wretched spiritual state, thrilled her like an electric shock with a strange new pity for him. She prayed on the spot for power to send him into the waters of baptism. When the day had begun, she lost no time in opening up the truth to him.

If the young man was at all amazed by the utter wholeness of her conviction that she was stooping from an immense height to pluck him from the burning, he succeeded in hiding it. He assumed with her at once that she was saved, that he was in the way of being lost, and that his behooving was to listen to her meekly. Her very evident alarm for his lost condition, her earnest desire to save him, were what he felt moved to dwell upon, rather than a certain spiritual condescension which he could not wholly ignore.

After some general counsel, in the morning, she took out her old, dog-eared "Book of Mormon," a first edition, printed at Palmyra, New York, in 1830, "By Joseph Smith, Jr., Author and Proprietor," and led the not unworthy Gentile again to the cañon. There in her favourite nook of pines beside the stream, she would share with him as much of the Lord's truth as his darkened mind could be made conscious of.

When at last she was seated on the brown carpet under the pines, her back to a mighty boulder, the sacred record in her lap, and the Gentile prone at her feet, she found it no easy task to begin. First he must be brought to repent of his sins. She began to wonder what his sins could be, and from that drifted into an idle survey of his profile, the line of his throat as his head lay back on the ground, and the strong brown hand, veined and corded, that curled in repose on his breast. She checked herself in this; for it could be profitable neither to her soul nor to his.

"I'll teach you about the Book of Mormon first," she ventured.

"I'd like to hear it," said Follett, cheerfully.

"Of course you don't know anything about it."

"It isn't my fault, though. I've been unfortunate in my bringing up, that's all." He turned on his side and leaned upon his elbow so he could look at her.

"You see, I've been brought up to believe that Mormons were about as bad as Mexicans. And Mexicans are so mean that even coyotes won't touch them. Down at the big bend on the Santa Fé Trail they shot a Mexican, old Jesus Bavispee, for running off cattle. He was pretty well dried out to begin with, but the coyotes wouldn't have a thing to do with him, and so he just dried up into a mummy. They propped him up by the ford there, and when the cowboys went by they would roll a cigarette and light it and fix it in his mouth. Then they'd pat him on the head and tell him what a good old boy he was—*star bueno*—the only good Mexican above ground—and his face would be grinning all the time, as if it tickled him. When they find a Mexican rustling cattle they always leave him there, and they used to tell me that the Mormons were just as bad and ought to be fixed that way too."

"I think that was horrible!"

"Of course it was. They were bigoted. But I'm not. I know right well there must be good Mexicans alive, though I never saw one, and I suppose of course there must be—"

"Oh, you're worse than I thought!" she cried. "Come now, do try. I want you to be made better, for my sake." She looked at him with real pleading in her eyes. He dropped back to the ground with a thrill of searching religious fervour.

"Go on," he said, feelingly. "I'm ready for anything. I have kind of a good feeling running through me already. I do believe you'll be a powerful lot of benefit to me."

"You must have faith," she answered, intent on the book. "Now I'll tell you some things first."

Had the Gentile been attentive he might have learned that the Book of Mormon is an inspired record of equal authority with the Jewish Scriptures, containing the revelations of Jehovah to his Israel of the western world as the Bible his revelations to Israel in the Orient,—the veritable "stick of Joseph," that was to be one with "the stick of Judah;" that the angel Moroni, a messenger from the presence of God, appeared to Joseph Smith, clad in robes of light, and told him where were hid the plates of gold on which were graven this fulness of the everlasting gospel; how that Joseph, after a few years of preparation, was let to take these sacred plates from the hill of Cumorah; also an instrument called the Urim and Thummim, consisting of two stones set in a silver bow and made fast to a breast-plate, this having been prepared by the hands of God for use in translating the record on the plates; how Joseph, seated behind a curtain and looking through the Urim and Thummim at the characters on the plates, had seen their English equivalents over them, and dictated these to his amanuensis on the other side of the curtain.

He might have learned that when the book was thus translated, the angel Moroni had reclaimed the golden plates and the Urim and Thummim, leaving the sacred deposit of doctrine to be given to the world by Joseph Smith; that the Saviour had subsequently appeared to Joseph; also Peter, James, and John, who laid hands upon him, ordained him, gave him the Holy Ghost, authorised him to baptise for the remission of sins, and to organise the Kingdom of God on earth.

"Do you understand so far?" she asked.

"It's fine!" he answered, fervently. "I feel kind of a glow coming over me already."

She looked at him closely, with a quick suspicion, but found his profile uninforming; at least of anything needful at the moment.

"Remember you must have faith," she admonished him, "if you are to win your inheritance; and not question or doubt or find fault, or—or make fun of anything. It says right here on the title-page, 'And now if there be faults, it be the mistake of men; wherefore condemn not the things of God that ye may be found spotless at the judgment seat of Christ.' There now, remember!"

"Who's finding fault or making fun?" he asked, in tones that seemed to be pained.

"Now I think I'd better read you some verses. I don't know just where to begin."

"Something about that Urim and Thingamajig," he suggested.

"Urim and Thummim," she corrected—"now listen."

Again, had the Gentile remained attentive, he might have learned how the Western Hemisphere was first peopled by the family of one Jared, who, after the confusion of tongues at Babel, set out for the new land; how they grew and multiplied, but waxed sinful, and finally exterminated one another in fierce battles, in one of which two million men were slain.

At this the fallen one sat up.

"'And it came to pass that when they had all fallen by the sword, save it were Coriantumr and Shiz, behold Shiz had fainted with loss of blood. And it came to pass when Coriantumr had leaned upon his sword and rested a little, he smote off the head of Shiz. And it came to pass, after he had smote off the head of Shiz, that Shiz raised up on his hands and fell; and after he had struggled for breath he died.'"

The Gentile was animated now.

"Say, that Shiz was all right,—raised up on his hands and struggled for breath after his head was cut off!"

Hereupon she perceived that his interest was become purely carnal. So she refused to read of any more battles, though he urged her warmly to do it. She returned to the expedition of Jared, while the lost sheep fell resignedly on his back again.

"'And the Lord said, Go to work and build after the manner of barges which ye have hitherto built. And it came to pass that the brother of Jared did go to work, and also his brethren, and built barges after the manner which they had built, after the instructions of the Lord. And they were small, and they were light upon the water, like unto the lightness of a fowl upon the water; and they were built like unto a manner that they were exceeding tight, even that they would hold water like unto a dish; and the bottom thereof was tight like unto a dish, and the ends thereof were peaked; and the top thereof was tight like unto a dish; and the length thereof was the length of a tree; and the door thereof when it was shut was tight like unto a dish. And it came to pass that the brother of Jared cried unto the Lord, saying—'"

She forgot him a little time, in the reading, until it occurred to her that he was singularly quiet. She glanced up, and was horrified to see that he slept. The trials of Jared's brother in building the boats that were about the length of a tree, combined with his broken rest of the night before, had lured him into the dark valley of slumber where his soul could not lave in the waters of truth. But something in the sleeping face softened her, and she smiled, waiting for him to awaken. He was still only a waymark to the kingdom of folly, but she had made a beginning, and she would persevere. He must be saved into the household of faith. And indeed it was shameful that such as he should depend for their salvation upon a chance meeting with an unskilled girl like herself. She wondered somewhat indignantly how any able-bodied Saint could rest in the valley while this man's like were dying in sin for want of the word. As her eye swept the sleeping figure, she was even conscious of a little wicked resentment against the great plan itself, which could under any circumstances decree such as he to perdition.

He opened his eyes after awhile to ask her why she had stopped reading, and when she told him, he declared brazenly that he had merely closed his eyes to shut out everything but her words.

"I heard everything," he insisted, again raised upon his elbows. "'It was built like unto a dish, and the length was about as long as a tree—'"

"What was?"

"The Urim and Thummim."

When he saw that she was really distressed, he tried to cheer her.

"Now don't be discouraged," he said, as they started home in the late afternoon. "You can't expect to get me roped and hog-tied the very first day. There's lots of time, and you'll have to keep at it. When I was a kid learning to throw a rope, I used to practise on the skull of a steer that was nailed to a post. At first it didn't look like I could ever do it. I'd forget to let the rope loose from my left hand, or I wouldn't make the loop line out flat around my head, or she'd switch off to one side, or something. But at last I'd get over the horns every time. Then I learned to do it running past the post; and after that I'd go down around the corral and practise on some quiet old heifer, and so on. The only thing is—never give up."

"But what good does it do if you won't pay attention?"

"Oh, well, I can't learn a new religion all at once. It's like riding a new saddle. You put one on and 'drag the cinches up and lash them, and you think it's going to be fine, and you don't see why it isn't. But you find out that you have to ride it a little at a time and break it in. Now, you take a fresh start with me to-morrow."

"Of course I'm going to try."

"And it isn't as if I was regular out-and-out sinful. My adopted father, Ezra Calkins, he's a good man. But, now I think of it, I don't know what church he ever did belong to. He'll go to any of 'em,—don't make any difference which,—Baptist, Methodist, Lutheran, Catholic; he says he can get all he's looking for out of any of 'em, and he kind of likes to change off now and then. But he's a good man. He won't hire any one that cusses too bad or is hard on animals, and he won't even let the freighters work on Sunday. He brought me up not to drink or gamble, or go round with low folks and all like that, and not to swear except when you're driving cattle and have to. 'Keep clean inside and out,' he says, 'and then you're safe,' he says. 'Then tie up to some good church for company, if you want to, not thinking bad of the others, just because you didn't happen to join them. Or it don't hurt any to graze a little on all the ranges,' he says. And he sent me to public school and brought me up pretty well, so you can see I'm not plumb wicked. Now after you get me coming, I may be easier than you think."

She resolved to pray for some special gift to meet his needs. If he were not really sinful, there was all the more reason why he should be saved into the Kingdom. The sun went below the western rim of the valley as they walked, and the cooling air was full of the fresh summer scents from field and garden and orchard.

Down the road behind them, a half-hour later, swung the tall, loose-jointed figure of Seth Wright, his homespun coat across his arm, his bearskin cap in his hand, his heated brow raised to the cooling breeze. His ruffle of neck whiskers, virtuously white, looked in the dying sunlight quite as if a halo he had worn was dropped under his chin. A little past the Rae place he met Joel returning from the village.

"Evening, Brother Rae! You ain't looking right tol'lable."

"It's true, Brother Seth. I've thought lately that I'm standing in the end of my days."

"Peart up, peart up, man! Look at me,—sixty-eight years come December, never an ache nor a pain, and got all my own teeth. Take another wife. That keeps a man young if he's got jedgment." He glanced back toward the Rae house.

"And I want to speak to you special about something—this young dandy Gentile you're harbouring. Course it's none of my business, but I wouldn't want one of my girls companying with a Gentile—off up in that cañon with him, at that—fishing one day, reading a book the next, walking clost together,—and specially not when Brigham had spoke for her. Oh, I know what I'm talking about! I had my mallet and frow up there two days now, just beyond the lower dry-fork, splitting out shakes for my new addition, and I seen 'em with my own eyes. You know what young folks is, Elder. That reminds me—I'm going to seal up that sandy-haired daughter of Bishop Tanner's next week some time; soon as we get the roof on the new part. But I thought I'd speak to you about this—a word to the wise!"

The Wild Ram of the Mountains passed on, whistling a lively air. The little bent man went with slow, troubled steps to his own home. He did know the way of young people, and he felt that he was beginning to know the way of God. Each day one wall or another of his prison house moved a little in upon him. In the end it would crush. He had given up everything but Prudence; and now, for his wicked clinging to her, she was to be taken from him; if not by Brigham, then by this Gentile, who would of course love her, and who, if he could not make her love him, would be tempted to alienate her by exposing the crime of the man she believed to be her father. The walls were closing about him. When he reached the house, they were sitting on the bench outside.

"Sometimes," Follett was saying, "you can't tell at first whether a thing is right or wrong. You have to take a long squint, like when you're in the woods on a path that ain't been used much lately and has got blind. Put your face right close down to it and you can't see a sign of a trail; it's the same as the ground both sides, covered with leaves the same way and not a footprint or anything. But you stand up and look along it for fifty feet, and there she is so plain you couldn't miss it. Isn't that so, Mr. Rae?"

Prudence went in, and her father beckoned him a little way from the door.

"You're sure you will never tell her anything about—anything, until I'm gone?—You promised me, you know."

"Well, didn't I promise you?"

"Not under any circumstances?"

"You don't keep back anything about 'circumstances' when you make a promise," retorted Mr. Follett.

Chapter XXXVII
The Gentile Issues an Ultimatum

June went; July came and went. It was a hot summer below, where the valley widens to let in Amalon; but up in the little-sunned aisle of Box Cañon it was always cool. There the pines are straight and reach their heads far into the sky, each a many-wired harp to the winds that come down from the high divide. Their music is never still; now a low, ominous rush, soft but mighty, swelling as it nears, the rush of a winged host, rising swiftly to one fearsome crescendo until the listener cowers instinctively as if under the tread of many feet; then dying away to mutter threats in the distance, and to come again more fiercely; or, it may be, to come with a gentler sweep, as if pacified, even yearning, for the moment. Or, again, the same wind will play quieter airs through the green boughs, a chamber-music of silken rustlings, of feathered fans just stirring, of whisperings, and the sighs of a woman.

It is cool beneath these pines, and pleasant on the couches of brown needles that have fallen through all the years. Here, in the softened light, amid the resinous pungence of the cones and the green boughs, where the wind above played an endless, solemn accompaniment to the careless song of the stream below, the maiden Saint tried to save into the Kingdom a youthful Gentile of whom she discovered almost daily some fresh reason why he should not be lost. The reasons had become so many that they were now heavy upon her. And yet, while the youth submitted meekly to her ministry, appearing even to crave it, he was undeniably either dense or stubborn—in either case of defective spirituality.

She was grieved by the number of times he fell asleep when she read from the Book of Mormon. The times were many because, though she knew it not, he had come to be, in effect, a night-nurse to the little bent man below, who was now living out his days in quiet desperation, and his nights in a fear of something behind him. Some nights Follett would have unbroken rest; but oftener he was awakened by the other's grip on his arm. Then he would get up, put fresh logs on the fire or light a candle and talk with the haunted man until he became quiet again.

After a night like this it was not improbable that he would fall asleep in very sound of the trumpet of truth as blown, by the grace of God, through the seership of Joseph Smith. Still he had learned much in the course of the two months. She had taught him between naps that, for fourteen hundred years, to the time of Joseph Smith, there had been a general and awful apostasy from the true faith, so that the world had been without an authorised priesthood. She had also taught him to be ill at ease away from her,—to be content when with her, whether they talked of religion or tried for the big, sulky three-pounder that had his lair at the foot of the upper Cascade.

Again she had taught him that other churches had wickedly done away with immersion for the remission of sins and the laying on of hands for the gift of the Holy Ghost; also that there was a peculiar quality in the satisfaction of being near her that he had never known before,—an astonishing truth that it was fine to think about when he lay where he could look up at her pretty, serious face.

He fell asleep at night usually with a mind full of confusion,—infant baptism—a slender figure in a pink dress or a blue—the Trinity—a firm little brown hand pointing the finger of admonition at him—the regeneration of man—hair, dark and lustrous, that fell often half away from what he called its "lashings"—eternal punishment—earnest eyes—the Urim and Thummim,—and a pleading, earnest voice.

He knew a few things definitely: that Moroni, last of the Nephites, had hidden up unto the Lord the golden plates in the hill of Cumorah; and that the girl who taught him was in some mysterious way the embodiment of all the wonderful things he had ever thought he wanted, of all the strange beauties he had crudely pictured in lonely days along the trail. Here was something he had supposed could come true only in a different world, the kind of world there was in the first book he had ever read, where there had seemed to be no one but good fairies and children that were uncommonly deserving. Yet he had never been able to get clearly into his mind the nature and precise office of the Holy Ghost; nor had he ever become certain how he could bring this wonderful young woman in closer relationship with himself. He felt that to put out his hand toward her—except at certain great moments when he could help her over rough places and feel her golden weight upon his arm—would be to startle her, and then all at once he would awaken from a dream to find her gone. He thought he would feel very badly then, for probably he would never be able to get back into the same dream again. So he was cautious, resolving to make the thing last until it came true of itself.

Once when they followed the stream down, in the late afternoon, he had mused himself so full of the wonder of her that he almost forgot his caution in an amiable impulse to let her share in his feelings.

"You know," he began, "you're like as if I had been trying to think of a word I wanted to say—some fine, big word, a fancy one—but I couldn't think of it. You know how you can't think of the one you want sometimes, only nothing else will do in place of it, and then all at once, when you quit trying to think, it flashes over you. You're like that. I never could think of you, but I just had to because I couldn't get along without it, and then when I didn't expect it you just happened along—the word came along and said itself."

Without speaking she had run ahead to pick the white and blue columbines and pink roses. And he, alarmed at his boldness, fearing she would now be afraid of him, went forward with the deep purpose of showing her a light, careless mood, to convince her that he had meant nothing much.

To this end he told her lively anecdotes, chaste classics of the range calculated to amuse, until they reached the very door of home:—About the British sailor who, having drifted up the Sacramento valley, was lured to mount a cow-pony known to be hysterical; of how he had declared when they picked him up a moment later, "If I'd been aware of the gale I'd have lashed myself to the rigging." Then about the other trusting tenderfoot who was directed to insist at the stable in Santa Fé that they give him a "bucking broncho;" who was promptly accommodated and speedily unseated with much flourish, to the wicked glee of those who had deceived him; and who, when he asked what the horse had done and was told that he had "bucked," had thereupon declared gratefully, "Did he only buck? It's a God's mercy he didn't *broncho* too, or he'd have killed me!"

From this he drifted into the anecdote of old Chief Chew-feather, who became drunk one day and made a nuisance of himself in the streets of Atchison; how he had been driven out of town by Marshal Ed Lanigan, who, mounting his pony, chased him a mile or so, meantime emptying both his six-shooters at the fleeing brave by way of making the exact situation clear even to a clouded mind; and how the alarmed and sobered chief had ridden his own pony to a shadow, never drawing rein until he reached the encampment of his tribe at dusk, to report that "the whites had broken out at Atchison."

He noticed, however, that she was affected to even greater constraint of manner by these sallies, though he laughed heartily himself at each climax as he made it, determined to show her that he had meant absolutely nothing the moment before. He succeeded so little, that he resolved never again to be reckless, if she would only be her old self on the morrow. He would not even tell her, as he had meant to, that looking into her eyes was like looking off under the spruces, where it was dark and yet light.

The little bent man at the house would look at them with a sort of helplessness when they came in, sometimes even forgetting the smile he was wont to wear to hide his hurts. He was impressed anew each time he saw them with the punishing power of such vengeance as was left to the Lord. He could see more than either of the pair before him. The little white-haired boy who had fought him with tooth and nail so long ago, to be not taken from Prudence, had now come back with the might of a man, even the might of a lover, to take her from him when she had become all of his life. He could think of no sharper revenge upon himself or his people. For this cowboy was the spirit incarnate of the oncoming East, thorned on by the Lord to avenge his Church's crime.

Day after day he would lie consuming the little substance left within him in an effort to save himself; to keep by him the child who had become his miser's gold; to keep her respect above all, to have her think him a good man. Yet never a way would open. Here was the boy with the man's might, and they were already lovers, for he knew too well the meaning of all those signs which they themselves but half understood. And he became more miserable day by day, for he saw clearly it was only his selfishness that made him suffer. He had met so many tests, and now he must fail at the last great sacrifice.

Then in the night would come the terrors of the dark, the curses and groans of that always-dying thing behind him. And always now he would see the hand with the silver bracelet at the wrist, flaunting in his face the shivering strands of gold with the crimson patch at the end. Yet even this, because he could see it, was less fearful than the thing he could not see, the thing that crawled or lurched relentlessly behind him, with the snoring sound in its throat, the smell of warm blood and the horrible dripping of it, whose breath he could feel on his neck and whose nerveless hands sometimes fumbled weakly at his shoulder, as it strove to come in front of him.

He sat sleepless in his chair with candles burning for three nights when Follett, late in August, went off to meet a messenger from one of his father's wagon-trains which, he said, was on its way north. Fearful as was the meaning of his presence, he was inexpressibly glad when the Gentile returned to save him from the terrors of the night.

And there was now a new goad of remorse. The evening before Follett's return he had found Prudence in tears after a visit to the village. With a sudden great outrush of pity he had taken her in his arms to comfort her, feeling the selfishness strangely washed from his love, as the sobs convulsed her.

"Come, come, child—tell your father what it is," he had urged her, and when she became a little quiet she had told him.

"Oh, Daddy dear—I've just heard such an awful thing, what they talk of me in Amalon, and of you and my mother—shameful!"

He knew then what was coming; he had wondered indeed, that this talk should be so long in reaching her; but he waited silently, soothing her.

"They say, whoever my mother was, you couldn't have married her—that Christina is your first wife, and the temple records show it. And oh, Daddy, they say it means that I am a child of sin—and shame—and it made me want to kill myself."

Another passion of tears and sobs had overwhelmed her and all but broken down the little man. Yet he controlled himself and soothed her again to quietness.

"It is all wrong, child, all wrong. You are not a child of sin, but a child of love, as rightly born as any in Amalon. Believe me, and pay no heed to that talk."

"They have been saying it for years, and I never knew."

"They say what is not true."

"You were married to my mother, then?"

He waited too long. She divined, clear though his answer was, that he had evaded, or was quibbling in some way.

"You are the daughter of a truly married husband and wife, as truly married as were ever any pair."

And though she knew he had turned her question, she saw that he must have done it for some great reason of his own, and, even in her grief, she would not pain him by asking another. She could feel that he suffered as she did, and he seemed, moreover, to be pitifully and strangely frightened.

When Follett came riding back that evening he saw that Prudence had been troubled. The candle-light showed sadness in her dark eyes and in the weighted corners of her mouth. He was moved to take her in his arms and soothe her as he had seen mothers do with sorry little children. But instead of this he questioned her father sharply when their corn-husk mattresses had been put before either side of the fireplace for the night. The little man told him frankly the cause of her grief. There was something compelling in the other's way of asking questions. When the thing had been made plain, Follett looked at him indignantly.

"Do you mean to say you let her go on thinking that about herself?"

"I told her that her father and mother had been rightly married."

"Didn't she think you were fooling her in some way?"

"I—I can't be sure—"

"She *must* have, or she wouldn't be so down in the mouth now. Why didn't you tell her the truth?"

"If only—if only she could go on thinking I am her father—only a little while—"

Follett spoke with the ring of a sudden resolution in his voice.

"Now I'll tell you one thing, Mister man, something has got to be done by *some one*. I can't do it because I'm tied by a promise, and so I reckon you ought to!"

"Just a little time! Oh, if you only knew how the knives cut me on every side and the fires burn all through me!"

"Well, think of the knives cutting that girl,—making her believe she has to be ashamed of her mother. You go to sleep now, and try to lie quiet; there ain't anything here to hurt you. But I'll tell you one thing,—you've got to toe the mark."

Chapter XXXVIII
The Mission Service in Box
Cañon is Suspended

Follett waited with a new eagerness next day for their walk to the cañon. But Prudence, looking at him with eyes that sorrow was clouding, said that she could not go. He felt a sharp new resentment against the man who was letting her suffer rather than betray himself, and he again resolved that this man must be made to "toe the mark," to "take his needings;" and that, meantime, the deceived girl must be effectually reassured. Something must be said to take away the hurt that was tugging at the corners of her smile to draw them down. To this end he pleaded with her not to deprive him of the day's lesson, especially as the time was now at hand when he must leave. And so ably did he word his appeal to her sense of duty that at last she consented to go.

Once in the cañon, however, where the pines had stored away the cool gloom of the night against the day's heat, she was glad she had come. For, better than being alone with that strange, new hurt, was it to have by her side this friendly young man, who somehow made her feel as if it were right and safe to lean upon him,—despite his unregenerate condition. And presently there, in the zeal of saving his soul, she was almost happy again.

Yet he seemed to-day to be impatient under the teaching, and more than once she felt that he was on the point of interrupting the lesson to some end of his own.

He seemed insufficiently impressed even with the knowledge of astronomy displayed by the prophets of the Book of Mormon, hearing, without a quiver of interest, that when at Joshua's command the sun seemed to stand still upon Gibeon and the moon in the valley of Ajalon, the real facts were that the earth merely paused in its revolutions upon its own axis and about the sun. Without a question he thus heard Ptolemy refuted and the discoveries of Copernicus anticipated two thousand years before that investigator was born. He was indeed deplorably inattentive. She suspected, from the quick glances she gave him, that he had no understanding at all of what she read. Yet in this she did him injustice, for now she came to the passage, "They all did swear unto him that whoso should vary from the assistance which Akish desired should lose his head; and whoso should divulge whatsoever thing Akish should make known unto them should lose his life." This time he sat up.

"There it is again—they don't mind losing their heads. They were sure the fightingest men—don't you think so now?"

As he went on talking she laid the book down and leaned back against the trunk of the big pine under which they sat. He seemed to be saying something that he had been revolving in his mind while she read.

"I'd hate to have you think you been wasting your time on me this summer, but I'm afraid I'm just too downright unsanctified."

"Oh, don't say that!" she cried.

"But I *have* to. I reckon I'm like the red-roan sorrel Ed Harris got for a pinto from old man Beasley. 'They's two bad things about him,' says the old man. 'I'll tell you one now and the other after we swap.' 'All right,' says Ed. 'Well, first, he's hard to catch,' says Beasley. 'That ain't anything,' says Ed,—'just picket him or hobble him with a good side-line.' So then they traded. 'And the other thing,' says the old man, dragging up his cinches on Ed's pinto,—'he ain't any good after you get him caught.' So that's like me. I've been hard to teach all summer, and now I'm not any good after you get me taught."

"Oh, you are! Don't say you're not."

"I couldn't ever join your Church—"

Her face became full of alarm.

"—only for just one thing;—I don't care very much for this having so many wives."

She was relieved at once. "If *that's* all—I don't approve of it myself. You wouldn't have to."

"Oh, that's what you say *now*"—he spoke with an air of shrewdness and suspicion,—"but when I got in you'd throw up my duty to me constant about building up the Kingdom. Oh, I know how it's done! I've heard your preachers talk enough."

"But it *isn't* necessary. I wouldn't—I don't think it would be at all nice of you."

He looked at her with warm sympathy. "You poor ignorant girl! Not to know your own religion! I read in that book there about this marrying business only the other day. Just hand me that one."

She handed him the "Book of Doctrine and Covenants," from which she had occasionally taught him the Lord's word as revealed to Joseph Smith. The revelation on celestial marriage had never been among her selections. He turned to it now.

"Here, right in the very first of it—" and she heard with a sinking heart,—"'Therefore prepare thyself to receive and obey the instructions which I am about to give unto you; for all those who have this law revealed unto them must obey the same; for behold! I reveal unto you a new and everlasting covenant; and if ye abide not that covenant then are ye damned, for no one can reject this covenant and be permitted to enter into my glory.'

"There now!"

"I never read it," she faltered.

"And don't you know they preach in the tabernacle that anybody who rejects polygamy will be damned?"

"My father never preached that."

"Well, he knows it—ask him."

It was proving to be a hard day for her.

"Of course," he continued, "a new member coming into the Church might think at first he could get along without so many wives. He might say, 'Well, now, I'll draw a line in this marrying business. I'll never take more than two or three wives or maybe four.' He might even be so taken up with one young lady that he'd say, 'I won't even marry a second wife—not for some time yet, that is—not for two or three years, till she begins to get kind of houseworn,' But then after he's taken his second, the others would come easy. Say he marries, first time, a tall, slim, dark girl,"—he looked at her musingly while she gazed intently into the stream in front of them.

"—and then say he meets a little chit of a thing, kind of heavy-set like, with this light yellow hair and pretty light blue eyes, that he saw one Sunday at church—"

Her dark face was flushing now in pained wonder.

"—why then it's so easy to keep on and marry others, with the preachers all preaching it from the pulpit."

"But you wouldn't have to."

"No, you wouldn't have to marry any one after the second—after this little blonde—but you'd have to marry her because it says here that you 'shall abide the law or ye shall be damned, saith the Lord God.'"

He pulled himself along the ground closer to her, and went on again in what seemed to be an extremity of doubt.

"Now I don't want to be lost, and yet I don't want to have a whole lot of wives like Brigham or that old coot we see so often on the road. So what am I going to do? I might think I'd get along with three or four, but you never can tell what religion will do to a man when he really gets it."

He reached for her small brown hand that still held the Book of Mormon open on her lap, and took it in both his own. He went on, appealingly:

"Now you try to tell me right—like as if I was your own brother—tell me as a sister. Try to put yourself in the place of the girl I'd marry first—no, don't; it seems more like your sister if I hold it this way—and try to think how she'd feel when I brought home my second. Would that be doing square by her? Wouldn't it sort of get her on the bark? But if I join your Church and don't do that, I might as well be one of those low-down Freewill Baptists or Episcopals. Come now, tell me true, letting on that you're my sister."

She had not looked at him since he began, nor did she now.

"Oh, I don't know—I don't *know*—it's all so mixed! I thought you could be saved without that."

"There's the word of God against me."

"I wouldn't want you to marry that way,—if I were your sister."

"That's right now, try to feel like a sister. You wouldn't want me to have as many wives as those old codgers down there below, would you?"

"No—I'm sure you shouldn't have but one. Oh, you couldn't marry more than one, could you?" She turned her eyes for the first time upon him, and he saw that some inward warmth seemed to be melting them.

"Well, I'd hate to disappoint you if you were my sister, but there's the word of the Lord—"

"Oh, but could you *anyway*, even if you didn't have a sister, and there was no one but *her* to think of?"

He appeared to debate with himself cautiously.

"Well, now, I must say your teaching has taken a powerful hold on me this summer—" he reached under her arm and caught her other hand. "You've been like a sister to me and made me think about these things pretty deep and serious. I don't know if I could get what you've taught me out of my mind or not."

"But how could you *ever* marry another wife?"

"Well, a man don't like to think he's going to the bad place when he dies, all on account of not marrying a few more times. It sort of takes the ambition all out of him."

"Oh, it couldn't be right!"

"Well now, I'll do as you say. Do I forget all these things you've been teaching me, and settle down with one wife,—or do I come into the Kingdom and lash the cinches of my glory good and plenty by marrying whenever I get time to build a new end on the house, like old man Wright does?"

She was silent.

"Like a sister would tell a brother," he urged, with a tighter pressure of her two hands. But this seemed to recall another trouble to her mind.

"I—I'm not fit to be your sister—don't talk of it—you don't know—" Her voice broke, and he had to release her hand. Whereupon he put his own back up against the pine-tree, reached his arm about her, and had her head upon his shoulder.

"There, there now!"

"But you don't know."

"Well, I *do* know—so just you straighten out that face. I do know, I tell you. Now don't cry and I'll fix it all right, I promise you."

"But you don't even know what the trouble is."

"I do—it's about your father and mother—when they were married."

"How did you know?"

"I can't tell you now, but I will soon. Look here, you can believe what I tell you, can't you?"

"Yes, I can do that."

"Well, then, you listen. Your father and mother were married in the right way, and there wasn't a single bit of crookedness about it. I wouldn't tell you if I didn't know and couldn't prove it to you in a little while. Say, there's one of our wagon-trains coming along here toward Salt Lake next Monday. It's coming out of its way on purpose to pick me up. I'll promise to have it proved to you by that time. Now, is that fair? Can you believe me?"

She looked up at him, her face bright again.

"Oh, I *do* believe you! You don't know how glad you make me. It was an awful thing—oh, you are a dear"—and full upon his lips she kissed the astounded young man, holding him fast with an arm about his neck. "You've made me all over new—I was feeling so wretched—and of course

I can't see how you know anything about it, but I know you are telling the truth." Again she kissed him with the utmost cordiality. Then she stood up to arrange her hair, her face full of the joy of this assurance. The young man saw that she had forgotten both him and his religious perplexities, and he did not wish her to be entirely divested of concern for him at this moment.

"But how about me? Here I am, lost if I do and lost if I don't. You better sit down here again and see if there isn't some way I can get that crown of glory."

She sat down by him, instantly sobered from her own joy, and calmly gave him a hand to hold.

"Well, I'll tell you," she said, frankly. "You wait awhile. Don't do anything right away. I'll have to ask father." And then as he reached over to pick up the Book of Mormon,—"No, let's not read any more to-day. Let's sit a little while and only think about things." She was so free from embarrassment that he began to doubt if he had been so very deeply clever, after all, in suggesting the relationship between them. But after she had mused awhile, she seemed to perceive for the first time that he was very earnestly holding both of her hands. She blushed, and suddenly withdrew them. Whereat he was more pleased than when she had passively let them lie. He approached the matter of salvation for himself once more.

"Of course I can wait awhile for you to find out the rights of this thing, but I'm afraid I can't be baptised even if you tell me to be—even if you want me to obey the Lord and marry some pretty little light-complected, yellow-haired thing afterwards—after I'd married my first wife. Fact is, I don't believe I could. Probably I'd care so much for the first one that I'd have blinders on for all the other women in the world. She'd have me tied down with the red ribbon in her hair"—he touched the red ribbon in her own, by way of illustration—"just like I can tie the biggest steer you ever saw with that little silk rag of mine—hold him, two hind legs and one fore, so he can't budge an inch. I'd just like to see some little, short, kind of plump, pretty yellow-haired thing come between us."

For an instant, she looked such warm, almost indignant approval that he believed she was about to express an opinion of her own in the matter, but she stayed silent, looking away instead with a little movement of having swallowed something.

"And you, too, if you were my sister, do you think I'd want you married to a man who'd begin to look around for some one else as soon as he got you? No, sir—you deserve some decent young fellow who'd love you all to pieces day in and day out and never so much as look at this little yellow-haired girl—even if she was almost as pretty as you."

But she was not to be led into rendering any hasty decision which might affect his eternal salvation. Moreover, she was embarrassed and disturbed.

"We must go," she said, rising before he could help her. When they had picked their way down to the mouth of the cañon, he walking behind her, she turned back and said, "Of course you could marry that little yellow-haired girl with the blue eyes first, the one you're thinking so much about—the little short, fat thing with a doll-baby face—"

But he only answered, "Oh, well, if you get me into your Church it wouldn't make a bit of difference whether I took her first or second."

Chapter XXXIX
A Revelation Concerning the
True Order of Marriage

While matters of theology and consanguinity were being debated in Box Cañon, the little bent man down in the first house to the left, in his struggle to free himself, was tightening the meshes of his fate about him. In his harried mind he had formed one great resolution. He believed that a revelation had come to him. It seemed to press upon him as the culmination of all the days of his distress. He could see now that he had felt it years before, when he first met the wife of Elder Tench, the gaunt, gray woman, toiling along the dusty road; and again when he had found the imbecile boy turning upon his tormentors. A hundred times it had quickened within him. And it had gained in force steadily, until to-day, when it was overwhelming him. Now that his flesh was wasted, it seemed that his spirit could see far.

His great discovery was that the revelation upon celestial marriage given to Joseph Smith had been "from beneath,"—a trick of Satan to corrupt them. Not only did it flatly contradict earlier revelations, but the very Book of Mormon itself declared again and again that polygamy was wickedness. Joseph had been duped by the powers of darkness, and all Israel had sinned in consequence. Upon the golden plates delivered to him, concerning the divine source of which there could be no doubt, this order of marriage had been repeatedly condemned and forbidden. But as to the revelation which sanctioned it there could rightly be doubt; for had not Joseph himself once warned them that "some revelations are from God, some from men, and some from the Devil." Either the Book of Mormon was not inspired, or the revelation was not from God, since they were fatally in opposition.

It came to him with the effect of a blinding light, yet seemed to endow him with a new vigour, so that he felt strong and eager to be up, to spread his truth abroad. Some remnant of that old fire of inspiration flamed up within him as he lay on the hard bed in his little room, with the summer scents floating in and the out-of-doors sounds,—a woman's voice calling a child afar off, the lowing of cattle, the rhythmic whetting of a scythe-blade, the echoing strokes of an axe, the mellow fluting of a robin,—all coming to him a little muted, as if he were no longer in the world.

He raised upon his elbow, glowing with the flush of old memories when his heart had been perfect with the Lord; when he had wrought miracles in the face of the people; when he had besought Heaven fearlessly for signs of its favour; when he had dreamed of being a pillar of fire to his people in their march across the desert, and another Lion of the Lord to fight their just battles. The little bent man of sorrows had again become the Lute of the Holy Ghost.

He knew it must be a true revelation. And, while he might not now have strength to preach it as it should be preached, there were other mighty men to spread its tidings. Even his simple announcement of it must work a revolution. Others would see it when he had once declared it. Others would spread it with power until the Saints were again become a purified people. But he would have been the prophet, seer, and revelator, to whom the truth was given, and so his suffering would not have been in vain; perhaps that suffering had been ordained to the end that his vision should be cleared for this truth.

He remembered the day was Saturday, and he began at once to word the phrases in which he would tell his revelation on the morrow. He knew that this must be done tactfully, in spite of its divine source. It would be a momentous thing to the people and to the priesthood. It was conceivable, indeed, that members of the latter might dispute it and argue with him, or even denounce him for a heretic. But only at first; the thing was too simply true to be long questioned. In any event, his duty was plain; with righteousness as the girdle of his loins he must go forth on the morrow and magnify his office in the sight of Heaven.

When the decision had been taken he lay in an ecstasy of anticipation, feeling new pulses in all his frame and the blood warm in his face. It would mean a new dawn for Israel. There would, however, be a vexing difficulty in the matter of the present wives of the Saints. The song of Lorena came in to him now:—

> "I was riding out this morning
>   With my cousin by my side;
> She was telling her intentions
>   For to soon become a bride."

The accent fell upon the first and third syllables with an upward surge of melody that seemed to make the house vibrate. He thought perhaps some of the Saints would find it well to put away all but the one rightful wife, making due provision, of course, for their support. Lorena's never-ending ballad came like the horns that blew before the walls of Jericho, bringing down the ramparts of his old belief. Some of the Saints would doubtless put away the false wives as a penance. He might even bring himself to do it, since, in the light of his wondrous new revelation, it would be obeying the Lord's will.

When Prudence came softly in to him, like a cool little breath of fragrance from the cañon, he smiled up to her with a fulness of delight she had never seen in his face before.

There was a new light in her own eyes, new decisions presaged, a new desire imperfectly suppressed. He stroked her hand as she sat beside him on the bed, wondering if she had at last learned her own secret. But she became grave, and was diverted from her own affairs when she observed him more closely.

"Why, you're sick—you're burning up with fever! You must be covered up at once and have sage tea."

He laughed at her, a free, full laugh, such as she had never heard from him in all the years.

"It's no fever, child. It's new life come to me. I'm strong again. My face burns, but it must be the fire of health. I have a work given to me—God has not wholly put me aside."

"But I believe you *are* sick. Your hands are so hot, and your eyes look so unnatural. You must let me—"

"Now, now—haven't I learned to tell sickness from the glow of a holy purpose?"

"You're sure you are well?"

"Better than for fifteen years."

She let herself be convinced for the moment.

"Then please tell me something. Must a man who comes into our faith, if he is baptised rightly, also marry more than one wife if he is to be saved? Can't he be sure of his glory with one if he loves her—oh, very, *very* much?"

He was moved at first to answer her out of the fulness of his heart, telling her of the wonderful new revelation. But there came the impulse to guard it jealously in his own breast a little longer, to glory secretly in it; half-fearful, too, that some virtue would go out of it should he impart it too soon to another.

"Why do you want to know?"

"Ruel Follett would join our Church if he didn't have to marry more than one wife. If he loved some one very much, I'm afraid he would find it hard to marry another girl—oh, he simply *couldn't*—no matter how pretty she was. He never could do it." Here she pulled one of the scarlet ribbons from her broad hat. She gave a little exclamation of relief as if she had really meant to detach it.

"Tell him to wait a little."

"That's what I did tell him, but it seems hardly right to let him join believing that is necessary. I think some one ought to find out that one wife is all God wants a man ever to have, and to tell Mr. Follett so very plainly. His mind is really open to truth, and you know he might do something reckless—he shouldn't be made to wait too long."

"Tell him to wait till to-morrow. I shall speak of this in meeting then. It will be all right—all right, dear. Everything will be all right!"

"Only I am sure you are sick in spite of what you say. I know how to prove it, too—can you eat?"

"I'm too busy thinking of great things to be hungry."

"There—you would be hungry if you were well."

"I can't tell you how well I am, and as for food—our Elder Brother has been feeding me all day with the bread of truth. Such wonderful new things the Lord has shown me!"

"But you must not get up. Lie still and we will nurse you."

He refused the food she brought him, and refused Lorena's sage tea. He was not to be cajoled into treating as sickness the first real happiness he had felt for years. He lay still until his little room grew shadowy in the dusk, filled with a great reviving hope that the Lord had raised a new prophet to lead Israel out of bondage.

As the night fell, however, the shadows of the room began to trouble him as of old, and he found himself growing hotter and hotter until he burned and gasped and the room seemed about to stifle him. He arose from the bed, wondering that his feet should be so heavy and clumsy, and his knees so weak, when he felt otherwise so strong. His head, too, felt large, and there rang in his ears a singing of incessant quick beats. He made his way to the door, where he heard the voices of Prudence and Follett. It was good to feel the cool night air upon his hot face, and he reassured Prudence, who chided him for leaving his bed.

"When you hear me discourse tomorrow you will see how wrong you were about my being sick," he said. But she saw that he supported himself carefully from the doorway along the wall to the near-by chair, and that he sank into it with every sign of weakness. His eyes, however, were aglow with his secret, and he sat nodding his head over it in a lively way. "Brigham was right," he said, "when he declared that any of us might receive revelations from on high; even the least of us—only we are apt to be deaf to the whispered words until the Lord has scourged us. I have been deaf a long time, but my ears are at last unstopped—who is it coming, dear?"

A tall figure, vague in the dusk, was walking briskly up the path that led in from the road. It proved to be the Wild Ram of the Mountains, freshened by the look of rectitude that the razor gave to his face each Saturday night.

"Evening, Brother Rae—evening, you young folks. Thank you, I will take a chair. You feeling a bit more able than usual, Brother Rae?"

"Much better, Brother Seth. I shall be at meeting tomorrow."

"Glad to hear it, that's right good—you ain't been out for so long. And we want to have a rousing time, too."

"Only we're afraid he has a fever instead of being so well," said Prudence. "He hasn't eaten a thing all day."

"Well, he never did overeat himself, that I knew of," said the Bishop. "Not eating ain't any sign with him. Now it would be with me. I never believed in fasting the flesh. The Spirit of the Lord ain't ever so close to me as after I've had a good meal of victuals,—meat and potatoes and plenty of good sop and a couple of pieces of pie. Then I can unbutton my vest and jest set and set and hear the promptings of the Lord God of Hosts. I know some men ain't that way, but then's the time when I beautify *my* inheritance in Zion the purtiest. And I'm mighty glad Brother Joel can turn out to-morrow. Of course you heard the news?"

"What news, Brother Seth?"

"Brother Brigham gets here at eleven o'clock from New Harmony."

"Brother Brigham *coming?*"

"We're getting the bowery ready down in the square tonight so's to have services out of doors."

"He's coming to-morrow?" The words came from both Prudence and her father.

"Of course he's coming. Ben Hadley brought word over. They'll have a turkey dinner at Beil Wardle's house and then services at two."

The flushed little man with the revelation felt himself grow suddenly cold. He had thought it would be easy to launch his new truth in Amalon and let the news be carried to Brigham. To get up in the very presence of him, in the full gaze of those cold blue eyes, was another matter.

"But it's early for him. He doesn't usually come until after Conference, after it's got cooler."

The Bishop took on the air of a man who does not care to tell quite all that he knows.

"Yes; I suspicion some one's been sending tales to him about a certain young woman's carryings on down here."

He looked sharply at Prudence, who looked at the ground and felt grateful for the dusk. Follett looked hard at them both and was plainly interested. The Bishop spoke again.

"I ain't got no license to say so, but having done that young woman proud by engaging himself to marry her, he might 'a' got annoyed if any one had 'a' told him she was being waited on by a handsome young Gentile, gallivantin' off to cañons day after day—holding hands, too, more than once. Oh, I ain't *saying* anything. Young blood is young blood; mine ain't always been old, and I never blamed the young, but, of course, the needs of the Kingdom is a different matter. Well, I'll have to be getting along now. We're going to put up some of the people at our house, and I've got to fix to bed mother down in the wagon-box again, I reckon. I'll say you'll be with us to-morrow, then, Brother Joel?"

The little bent man's voice had lost much of its life.

"Yes, Brother Seth, if I'm able."

"Well, I hope you are." He arose and looked at the sky. "Looks as if we might have some falling weather. They say it's been moisting quite a bit up Cedar way. Well,—good night, all!"

When he was gone the matter of his visit was not referred to. With some constraint they talked a little while of other things. But as soon as the two men were alone for the night, Follett turned to him, almost fiercely.

"Say, now, what did that old goat-whiskered loon mean by his hintings about Prudence?"

The little man was troubled.

"Well, the fact is, Brigham has meant to marry her."

"You don't mean you'd have let him? Say, I'd hate to feel sorry for holding off on you like I have!"

"No, no, don't think that of me."

"Well, what were you going to do?"

"I hardly knew."

"You better find out."

"I know it—I did find out, to-day. I know, and it will be all right. Trust me. I lost my faith for a moment just now when I heard Brother Brigham was coming to-morrow; but I see how it is,—the Lord has wished to prove me. Now there is all the more reason why I should not flinch. You will see that I shall make it all right to-morrow."

"Well, the time's about up. I've been here over two months now, just because you were so kind of helpless. And one of our wagon-trains will be along here about next Monday. Say, she wouldn't ever have married him, would she?"

"No, she refused at once; she refused to consider it at all."

He was burning again with his fever, and there was something in his eagerness that seemed to overcome Follett's indignation.

"Well, let it go till to-morrow, then. And you try to get some rest now. That's what I'm going to do."

But the little bent man, flushed though he was, felt cold from the night air, and, piling more logs on the fire, he drew his chair close in front of it.

As often as Follett wakened through the night he saw him sitting there, sometimes reading what looked like a little old Bible, sometimes speaking aloud as if seeking to memorise a passage.

The last Follett remembered to have heard was something he seemed to be reading from the little book,—"The Lord is my Shepherd; I shall not want. He maketh me to lie down in green pastures; He leadeth me beside the still waters."

He fell asleep again with a feeling of pity for the little man.

Chapter XL
A Procession, a Pursuit, and a Capture

Follett awoke to find himself superfluous. The women were rushing excitedly through their housework in order to be at hand when the procession of Brigham and his suite should march in. Of Joel Rae he caught but a glimpse through the door of his little room, the face flushed that had a long time been sallow and bloodless. When the door had closed he could hear the voice, now strong again. He seemed to be, as during the night, rehearsing something he meant to say. And later it was plain that he prayed, though he heard nothing more than the high pleading of the voice.

Follett would not have minded these things, but Prudence was gone and no one could tell him where. From Christina of the rock-bound speech he blasted the items that she was wearing "a dress all new" and "a red-ribbon hat." Lorena, too, with all her willingness of speech, knew nothing definite.

"All I know is she fixed herself up like she was going to an evening ball or party. I wish to the lands I'd kep' my complexion the way she does hern. And she had on her best lawn that her pa got her in Salt Lake, the one with the little blue figures in it. She does look sweeter than honey on a rag in a store dress, and that Leghorn hat with the red bow, though what she wanted to start so early for I don't know. The procession can't be along yet, but she might have gone down to march with them, or to help decorate the bowery. I know when I was her age I was always a great hand for getting ready long before any one come, when my mother was making a company for me, putting up my waterfall and curling my beau-catchers on a hot pipe-stem. But, land! I ain't no time to talk with *you*."

Down at the main road he hesitated. To the right he could see where the green mouth of the cañon invited; but to the left lay the village where Prudence doubtless was. He would find her and bring her away. For Follett had determined to toe the mark himself now.

In the one street of Amalon there was the usual Sabbath hush; but above this was an air of dignified festivity. The village in its Sunday best homespun, with here and there a suit of store goods, was holding its breath.

In the bowery a few workers, under the supervision of Bishop Wright, were adding the last touches of decoration. It was a spot of pleasant green in the dusty square—a roof of spruce boughs, with evergreens and flowers garnishing the posts, and a bank of flowers and fruit back of the speaker's stand.

But Prudence was not there, and he wondered with dismay if she had joined the rest of the village and gone out to meet the Prophet. He had seen the last of them going along the dusty road to the north, men and women and little children, hot, excited, and eager. It did not seem like her to be among them, and yet except for those before him working about the bowery, and a few mothers with children in arms, the town was apparently deserted.

But even as he waited, he heard the winding alarm of a bugle, and saw a scurrying of backs in the dusty haze far up the road. The Wild Ram of the Mountains gave a few hurried commands for the very final touches, called off his force from the now completed bowery, and a solitary Gentile was for the moment left to greet the oncoming procession.

Presently, however, from the dark interiors of the log houses came the mothers with babies, a few aged sires too feeble for the march, and such of the remaining housewives as could leave for a little time the dinners they were cooking. They made but a thin line along the little street, and Follett saw at once that Prudence was not among them. He must wait to see if she marched in the approaching procession.

Already the mounted escort was coming into view, four abreast, captained by Elder Wardle, who, with a sash of red and gold slanted across his breast, was riding nervously, as if his seat could be kept only by the most skillful horsemanship, a white mule that he was known to treat with fearless disrespect on days that were not great. Behind the martial Wardle was Peter Peterson, Peter Long Peterson, and Peter Long Peter Peterson, the most martial looking men in Amalon after their leader; and then came a few more fours of proudly mounted Saints.

After this escort, separated by an interval that would let the dust settle a little, came the body of the procession. First a carriage containing the Prophet, portly, strong-faced, easy of manner, as became a giant who felt kindly in his might. By his side was his wife, Amelia, the reigning favourite, who could play the piano and sing "Fair Bingen on the Rhine" with a dash that was said to be superb. Behind this float of honour came other carriages, bearing the Prophet's Counsellors, the Apostles, Chief Bishop, Bishops generally, Elders, Priests, and Deacons, each taking precedence near the Prophet's carriage by seniority of rank or ordination. Along the line of carriages were outriders, bearing proudly aloft banners upon which suitable devices were printed:

"God bless Brigham Young!"

"Hail to Zion's Chief!"

"The Lion of the Lord."

"Welcome to our Mouthpiece of God!"

Behind the last carriage came the citizens in procession, each detachment with its banner. The elderly brethren stepped briskly under "Fathers in Israel"; the elderly sisters gazed proudly aloft to "Mothers in Israel." Then came a company of young men whose banner announced them as "Defenders of Zion." They were followed by a company of maidens led by Matilda Wright, striving to be not too much elated, and whose banner bore the inscription, "Daughters of Zion." At the last came the children, openly set up by the occasion, and big-eyed with importance, the boy who carried their banner, "The Hope of Israel," going with wonderful rigidity, casting not so much as an eye either to right or left.

But Prudence had not been in this triumphal column, nor was she among any of the women who stood with children in their arms, or who rushed to the doors with sleeves rolled up and a long spoon or fork in their hands.

Then all at once a great inspiration came to Follett. When the last dusty little white-dressed girl had trudged solemnly by, and the head of the procession was already winding down the lane that led to Elder Wardle's place, he called himself a fool and turned back. He walked like a man who has suddenly remembered that which he should not have forgotten. And yet he had remembered nothing at all. He had only thought of a possibility, but one that became more plausible with every step; especially when he reached the Rae house and found it deserted. Whenever he thought of his stupidity, which was every score of steps, he would break into a little trot that made the willows along the creek on his left run into a yellowish green blur.

He was breathing hard by the time he had made the last ascent and stood in the cool shade of the comforting pines. He waited until his pulse became slower, wiping his forehead with the blue neckerchief which Prudence had suggested that she liked to see him wear in place of the one of scarlet. When he had cooled and calmed himself a little, he stepped lightly on. Around the big rock he went, over the "down timber" beyond it, up over the rise down which the waters tumbled, and then sharply to the right where their nook was, a call to her already on his lips.

But she was not there. He could see the place at a glance. Nothing below met his eye but the straight red trunks of the pines and the brown carpet beneath them. A jay posed his deep shining blue on a cluster of scarlet sumac, and, cocking his crested head, screamed at him mockingly. The cañon's cool breath fanned him and the pine-tops sighed and sang. At first he was disheartened; but then his eyes caught a gleam of white and red under the pine, touched to movement by a low-swinging breeze.

It was her hat swaying where she had hung it on a broken bough of the tree she liked to lean against. And there was her book; not the book of Mormon, but a secular, frivolous thing called "Leaflets of Memory, an Illuminated Annual for the Year 1847." It was lying on its face, open at the sentimental tale of "Anastasia." He put it down where she had left it. The cañon was narrow and she would hardly leave the waterside for the steep trail. She would be at the upper cascade or in the little park above it, or somewhere between. He crossed the stream, and there in the damp sand was the print of a small heel where she had made a long step from the last stone. He began to hurry again, clambering recklessly over boulders, or through the underbrush where the sides of the stream were steep. When the upper cascade came in sight his heart leaped, for there he caught the fleeting shimmer of a skirt and the gleam of a dark head.

He hurried on, and after a moment's climb had her in full view, standing on the ledge below which the big trout lay. There he saw her turn so that he would have sworn she looked at him. It seemed impossible that she had not seen him; but to his surprise she at once started up the stream, swiftly footing over the rough way, now a little step, now a free leap, grasping a willow to pull herself up an incline, then disappearing around a clump of cedars.

He redoubled his speed over the rocks. When she next came into view, still far ahead, he shouted long and loud. It was almost certain that she must hear; and yet she made no sign. She seemed even to speed ahead the faster for his hail.

Again he sprang forward to cover the distance between them, and again he shouted when the next view of her showed that he was gaining. This time he was sure she heard; but she did not look back, and she very plainly increased her speed.

For an instant he stood aghast at this discovery; then he laughed.

"Well if you *want* a race, you'll get it!"

He was off again along the rough bed of the stream. He shouted no more, but slowly increased the gain he had made upon her. Instead of losing time by climbing up over the bank, he splashed through the water at two places where the little stream was wide and shallow. Then at last he saw that he was closing in upon her. Soon he was near enough to see that she also knew it.

He began at that moment an extended course of marvelling at the ways of woman. For now she had reached the edge of the little open park, and was placidly seating herself on a fallen tree in the grove of quaking aspens. He could not understand this change of manner. And when he reached the opening she again astounded him by greeting him with every manifestation of surprise, from the first nervous start to the pushing up of her dark brows.

"Why," she began, "how did you ever think of coming *here?*"

But he had twice hurried fruitlessly this hot morning and he was not again to be baffled. As he advanced toward her, she regarded him with some apprehension until he stopped a safe six feet away. She had noted certain lines of determination in his face.

"Now what's the use of pretending?—what did you run for?"

"I?—*run?*"

Again the curving black brows went up in frank surprise.

"Yes,—you *run!*"

He took a threatening step forward, and the brows promptly fell to serious intentness of his face.

"What did you do it for?"

She stood up. "What did I do it for?—what did I do *what* for?"

But his eyes were searching her and she had to lower her own. Then she looked up again, and laughed nervously.

"I—I don't know—I couldn't help it." Again she laughed. "And why did you run? How did you think of coming here?"

"I'll tell you how, now I've caught you." He started toward her, but she was quickly backing away into the opening of the little park, still laughing.

"Look out for that blow-down back of you!" he called. In the second that she halted to turn and discover his trick he had caught her by the arm.

"There—I caught you fair—*now* what did you run for?"

"I couldn't help it." Her face was crimson. His own was pale under the tan. They could hear the beating of both their hearts. But with his capture made so boldly he was dumb, knowing not what to say.

The faintest pulling of the imprisoned arm aroused him.

"I'd 'a' followed you till Christmas come if you'd kept on. Clear over the divide and over the whole creation. I never *would* have given you up. I'm never *going* to."

He caught her other wrist and sought to draw her to him.

With head down she came, slowly, yielding yet resisting, with little shudders of terror that was yet a strange delight, with eyes that dared give him but one quick little look, half pleading and half fear. But then after a few tense seconds her struggles were all housed far within his arms; there was no longer play for the faintest of them; and she was strained until she felt her heart rush out to him as she had once felt it go to her dream of a single love, — with the utter abandon of the falling water beside them.

On the opposite side of the park across the half-acre of waving bunch-grass, a many-pronged old buck in his thin red summer coat lay at the edge of the quaking aspens, sunning the velvet of his tender new horns to harden them against approaching combats. He had shrewdly noted that the first comer did not see him; but this second was a creature of action in whose presence it were ill-advised to linger. Noiselessly his hindquarters raised from the ground, and then with a snort of indignation and a mighty, crashing rush he was off through the trees and up the hill. Doubtless the beast cherished a delusion of clever escape from a dangerous foe; but neither of the pair standing so near saw or heard him or would have been conscious of him even had he led past them in wild flight the biggest herd it had ever been his lot to domineer. For these two were lost to all but the wonder of the moment, pushing fearfully on into the glory and sweetness of it.

His voice came to her in a dull murmur, and the sound of the running water came, again like the muffled tinkling of little silver bells in the distance. Both his arms were strong about her, and now her own hands rose in rebellion to meet where the kerchief was knotted at the back of his neck, quite as the hands of the other woman had rebelliously flung down the scarf from the balcony. Then the brim of his hat came down over her hair, and her lips felt his kiss.

They stood so a long time, it seemed to them, in the high grass, amid the white-barked quaking aspens, while a little wind from the dark pines at their side, lowered now to a yearning softness, played over them. They were aroused at last by a squirrel that ran half-way down the trunk of a near-by spruce to bark indignantly at them, believing they menaced his winter's store of spruce cones piled at the foot of the tree. With rattle after rattle his alarm came, until he had the satisfaction of noting an effect.

The young man put the girl away from him to look upon her in the new light that enveloped them both, still holding her hands.

"There's one good thing about your marriages,—they marry you for eternity, don't they? That's for ever—only it isn't long enough, even so—not for me."

"I thought you were never coming."

"But you said"—he saw the futility of it, however, and kissed her instead.

"I was afraid of you all this summer," he said.

"I was afraid of you, too."

"You got over it yesterday all right."

"How?"

"You kissed me."

"Never—what an awful thing to say!"

"But you did—twice—don't you remember?"

"Oh, well, it doesn't matter. If I did it wasn't at all like—like—"

"Like that—"

"No—I didn't think anything about it."

"And now you'll never leave me, and I'll never leave you."

They sat on the fallen tree.

"And to think of that old—"

"Oh, don't talk of it. That's why I ran off here—so I couldn't hear anything about it until he went away."

"Why didn't you tell me you were coming?"

"I didn't think you were so stupid."

"How was I to know where you were coming?"

But now she was reminded of something.

"Tell me one thing—did you ever know a little short fat girl, a blonde that you liked very much?"

"Never!"

"Then what did you talk so much about her for yesterday if you didn't? You'd speak of her every time."

"I didn't think you were so stupid."

"Well, I can't see—"

"You don't need to—we'll call it even."

And so the talk went until the sun had fallen for an hour and they knew it was time to go below.

"We will go to the meeting together," she said, "and then father shall tell Brigham,—tell him—"

"That you're going to marry me. Why don't you say it?"

"That I'm going to marry you, and be your only wife." She nestled under his arm again.

"For time and eternity—that's the way your Church puts it."

Then, not knowing it, they took their last walk down the pine-hung glade. Many times he picked her lightly up to carry her over rough places and was loth to put her down,—having, in truth, to be bribed thereto.

At their usual resting-place she put on her hat with the cherry ribbons, and he, taking off his own, kissed her under it.

And then they were out on the highroad to Amalon, where all was a glaring dusty gray under the high sun, and the ragged rim of the western hills quivered and ran in the heat.

He thought on the way down of how the news would be taken by the little bent man with the fiery eyes. She was thinking how glad she was that young Ammaron Wright had not kissed her that time he tried to at the dance—since kisses were like *that*.

Chapter XLI
The Rise and Fall of a Bent Little Prophet

Down in the village the various dinners of ceremony to the visiting officials were over. An hour had followed of decent rest and informal chat between the visitors and their hosts, touching impartially on matters of general interest; on irrigation, the gift of tongues, the season's crop of peaches, the pouring out of the Spirit abroad, the best mixture of sheep-dip; on many matters not unpleasing to the practical-minded Deity reigning over them.

Then the entire populace of Amalon, in its Sunday best of "valley tan" or store-goods, flocked to the little square and sat expectantly on the benches under the green roof of the bowery, ready to absorb the droppings of the sanctuary.

In due time came Brigham, strolling between Elder Wardle and Bishop Wright, bland, affable, and benignant. On the platform about him sat his Counsellors, the more distinguished of his suite, and the local dignitaries of the Church.

Among these came the little bent man with an unwonted colour in his face, coming in absorbed in thought, shaking hands even with Brigham with something of abstraction in his manner. Prudence and Follett came late, finding seats at the back next to a generous row of the Mrs. Seth Wright.

The hymn to Joseph Smith was given out, and the congregation rose to sing:—

"Unchanged in death, with a Saviour's love,
He pleads their cause in the courts above.

"His home's in the sky, he dwells with the gods,
Far from the rage of furious mobs.

"He died, he died, for those he loved,
He reigns, he reigns, in the realms above.

"Shout, shout, ye Saints! This boon is given,—
We'll meet our martyred seer in heaven."

When they had settled into their seats, the Wild Ram of the Mountains arose and invoked a blessing on those present and upon those who had gone behind the veil; adding a petition that Brigham be increased in his basket and in his store, in wives, flocks, and herds, and in the gifts of the Holy Spirit.

They sang another hymn, and when that was done, the little bent man arose and came hesitatingly forward to the baize-covered table that served as a pulpit. As President of the Stake it was his office to welcome the visitors, and this he did.

There were whisperings in the audience when his appearance was noted. It was the first time he had been seen by many of them in weeks. They whispered that he was failing.

"He ought to be home this minute," was the first Mrs. Wardle's diagnosis to the fifth Mrs. Wardle, behind her hymn-book, "with his feet in a mustard bath and a dose of gamboge and a big brewing of catnip tea. I can tell a fever as far as I can see it."

The words of official welcome spoken, he began his discourse; but in a timid, shuffling manner so unlike his old self that still others whispered of his evident illness. Inside he burned with his purpose, but, with all his resolves, the presence of Brigham left him unnerved. He began by referring to their many adversities since the day when they had first knelt to entreat the mercy of God upon the land. Then he spoke of revelations.

"You must all have had revelations, because they have come even to me. Perhaps you were deaf to the voice, as I have been. Perhaps you have trusted too readily in some revelation that came years ago, supposedly from God—in truth, from the Devil. Perhaps you have been deaf to later revelations meant to warn you of the other's falseness."

He was still uneasy, hesitating, fearful; but he saw interest here and there in the faces before him. Even Brigham, though unseen by the speaker, was looking mildly curious.

"You remember the revelation that came to Joseph in an early day when there was trouble in raising money to print the Book of Mormon,—'Some revelations are from God, some from man, and some from the Devil.' Recalling the many chastenings God has put upon us, may we not have failed to test all our other revelations by this one?"

Deep within he was angry at himself, for he was not speaking with words of fire as he had meant to; he was feeling a shameful cowardice in the presence of the Prophet. He had seen himself once more the Lute of the Holy Ghost, strong and moving; but now he was a poor, low-spoken, hesitating rambler. Nervously he went on, skirting about the edge of his truth as long as he dared, but feeling at last that he must plunge into its icy depths.

"In short, brethren, the Book of Mormon denounces and forbids our plural marriages."

Even this astounding declaration he made without warmth, in tones so low that many did not hear him. Those on the platform heard, however, and now began to view his obvious physical weakness in a new light. Yet he continued, gaining a little in force.

"The declarations on the subject in the Book of Mormon are so worded that we cannot fail to read them as denouncing and forbidding the practise of the Old Testament patriarchs in this matter of the family life."

In rapid succession he cited the passages to which he referred, those concerning David and Solomon and Noah and Ripkalish, who "did not do that which was right in the sight of the Lord, for he did have many wives."

There were murmurings and rustlings among the people now, and on his right he heard Brigham stirring ominously in his chair; but he nerved himself to keep on his feet, feeling he had that to say which should make them hail him as a new prophet when they understood.

"But besides these warnings against the sin there are many early revelations to Joseph himself condemning it."

He cited several of these, feeling the amazement and the alarm grow about him.

"And now against these plain words, given at many times in many places, written on the golden plates in letters that cannot lie, or brought to Joseph by the angel of the Lord, we have only the one revelation on celestial marriage. Read it now in the light of these other revelations and see if it does not too plainly convict itself of having been counterfeited to Joseph by an evil spirit. Such, brethren, has been the revelation that the Lord has given to me again and again until it burns within me, and I must cry it out to you. Try to receive it from me."

There was commotion among the people in front, chairs were moved at his side, and a low voice called to him to sit down. He heard this voice through the ringing that had been in his ears for many days, like the beating of a sea against him, and he felt the strength go suddenly from his knees.

He stumbled weakly back to his chair and sank into it with head bowed, feeling, rather than seeing, the figure of Brigham rise from its seat and step forward with deliberate, unruffled majesty.

As the Prophet faced his people they became quite silent, so that the robins could be heard in the Pettigrew peach-trees across the street. He poured a glass of water from the pitcher on the table, and drank of it slowly. Then, leaning a little forward, resting both his big cushiony hands on the green of the table, the Lion of the Lord began to roar—very softly at first. Slowly the words came, in tones scarce audible, marked indeed almost by the hesitation of the first speaker. But then a difference showed; gradually the tone increased in volume, the words came faster, fluency succeeding hesitation, and now his voice was high and searching, while his easy, masterful gestures laid their old spell upon the people.

"It does not occupy my feelings to curse any individual," he had begun, awkwardly; "in fact, I feel to render all thanks and praise for the discourse to which we have just listened, but I couldn't help saying to myself, 'Oh, dear, Granny! what a long tale our puss has got!'"

An uneasy titter came from the packed square of faces in front of him. He went on with rising power:

"But it is foretold in the Book of Mormon that the Lord will remove the bitter branches, and it's a good thing to find out where the bitter branches are. We can remove them ourselves. We can't expect the Lord to do *all* our dirty work. Now hear it once more, you that need to hear it—and damn all such poor pussyism as sniffles and whines and rejects it! We don't want that scrubby breed here!—Listen, I say. The celestial order of marriage is necessary for our exaltation to the fulness of the Lord's glory in the world eternal. Where much is given much is required. Understand me,—those that reject polygamy will be damned. Hear it now once for all. I will give you to know that God, our Father, has many wives, and so has Jesus Christ, our Elder Brother. Our God and Father in heaven is *a being of tabernacle*, or, in other words, He has a body of parts the same as you and I have. And that God and Father of ours was Adam."

Again there was a stirring below as if a wind swept the people, and the little man in his chair cowered for shame of himself. He had meant to do a great thing; he had thrilled so strongly with it; it had promised to master others as it had mastered him; and now he was shamed by the one true Lion of the Lord. "Hear it now," continued Brigham. "When God, our Father Adam, came into the garden of Eden, he came into it with a celestial body, and brought one of his wives with him,—Eve. He made and organised this world. He is Michael, the Archangel, the Ancient of Days, *about whom holy men have written and spoken.* He is our Father and our God, and the only

God with whom we have to do. I could tell you much more about this; but were I to tell you the whole truth, blasphemy would be nothing to it, in the estimation of the superstitious and over-righteous of mankind. But I will tell you this, that Jesus, our Elder Brother, was begotten in the flesh by the same character that was in the garden of Eden, and who is our Father in Heaven."

A chorus of Amens from the platform greeted this. It was led by the Wild Ram of the Mountains. In his chair the little bent man now cowered lower and lower, one moment praying for strength, the next for death; feeling the blood surge through him like storm waves that would beat him down. If only Heaven would send him one last moment of power to word this truth so that it might prevail. But Brigham was continuing.

"And what of this Elder Brother, Jesus? Did he reject the patriarchal order—like some poor pusillanimous cry-babies among us? No, I say! It will be borne in mind that once on a time there was a marriage in Cana of Galilee; and on a careful reading of that transaction it will be discovered that no less a person than Jesus Christ was married on that occasion. If he was never married his intimacy with Mary and Martha, and the other Mary also, whom Jesus loved, must have been highly unbecoming and improper, to say the best of it. I will venture to say that, if Jesus Christ was now to pass through the most pious countries in Christendom, with a train of women such as used to follow Him, fondling about Him, combing His hair, anointing Him with precious ointments, washing His feet with tears, and wiping them with the hair of their heads,—that, unmarried or even married, He would be mobbed, tarred and feathered, and ridden, not on an ass, but on a rail. Now did He multiply, and did He see His seed? Others may do as they like, but I will not charge our Saviour with neglect or transgression in this or any other duty."

He turned and went to his seat with a last threatening gesture, amid many little sounds of people relaxing from strained positions.

But then, before another could arise, a wonder came upon them. The little man stood up and came quickly forward, a strange new life in his step, a new confidence in his bearing, a curious glow of new strength in his face. Even his stoop had straightened for the moment. For, as he had listened to Brigham's last words, the picture of his vision in the desert had come back,—the cross in the sky, the crucified Saviour upon it, the head in death-agony fallen over upon the shoulder. And then before his eyes had come page after page of that New Testament with a wash of blood across two of them. He felt the new life he had prayed for pouring into his veins, and with it a fierce anger. The one on the cross who had been more than man, who had shirked no sacrifice and loved infinitely, was not thus to be assailed. A panorama of wrong—wrong thinking and wrong doing—extended before his clearing gaze. For once he seemed to see truth in a vision and to feel the power to utter it.

There was silence again as he stood in front of the little table, the faces before him frozen into wonder that he should have either the power or the temerity to answer Brigham. He spoke, and his voice was again rough with force, and high and fearless, a voice many of them recalled from the days when he had not been weak.

"Now I see what we have done. Listen, brethren, for God has not before so plainly said it to any man, and I know my time is short among you. We have gone back to the ages of Hebrew barbarism for our God—to the God of Battles worshipped by a heathen people—a God who loved the reek of blood and the smell of burning flesh. But you shall not—"

He turned squarely and fiercely to the face of Brigham.

"—you shall not confuse that bloody God of Battles with the true Christ, nor yet with the true God of Love that this Christ came to tell us of. Once I believed in Him. I was taught to by your priests. War seemed a righteous thing, for we had been grievously put upon, and I believed the God of Israel should avenge our wrongs as He had avenged those of His older Zion. And hear me now—so long as I believed this, I was no coward; while you, sir—"

A long forefinger was pointed straight at the amazed Brigham.

"—while you, sir, were a craven, contemptible in your cowardice. I would have fought in Echo Cañon to the end, because I believed. But you did not believe, and so you were afraid to fight. And for your cowardice and your wretched lusts your name among all but your ignorant dupes shall become a hissing and a scorn. For mark it well, unless you forsake that heathen God of Battles and preach the divine Christ of the New Testament, you shall come to hold only the ignorant, and them only by keeping them ignorant."

The commotion among the people in front was now all but a panic. On the platform the sires of Israel whispered one to another, while Brigham gazed as if fascinated, driven to admiration for the speaker's power and audacity. For the feverish, fleeting moment, Joel Rae was that veritable Lion of the Lord he had prayed to be, putting upon the people his spell of the old days. Heads were again strained up and forward, and amazed horror was on most of the faces. Far back, Prudence trembled, feeling that she must be away at once, until she felt the firm grasp of Follett's hand. The speaker went on, having turned again to the front.

"Instead of a church you shall become justly hated and despised as a people who foul their homes and dishonour beyond forgiveness the names of wife and mother. Then your punishment shall come upon you as it has already come for this and for other sins. Even now the Gentile is upon us; and mark this truth that God has but now given me to know: we have never been persecuted as a church,—but always as a political body hostile to the government of this nation. Even so, you had no faith. Believing as I believed, I would have fought that nation and died a thousand bloody deaths rather than submit. But you had no faith, and you were so low that you let yourselves be ruled by a coward—and I tell you God *hates* a coward."

Now the old pleading music came into his voice,—the music that had made him the Lute of the Holy Ghost in the Poet's roster of titles.

"O brethren, let me beg you to be good—simply good. Nothing can prevail against you if you are. If you are not, nothing shall avail you,—the power of no priesthood, no signs, ordinances, or rituals. Believe me, I know. Not even the forgiveness of the Father. For I tell you there is a divinity within each of you that you may some day unwittingly affront; and then you shall lie always in hell, for if you cannot forgive yourself, the forgiveness of God will not free you even if it come seventy times seven. I *know*. For fifteen years I have lain in hell for the work this Church did at Mountain Meadows. A cross was put there to the memory of those we slew. Not a day has passed but that cross has been burned and cut into my living heart with a blade of white heat. Now I am going to hell; but I am tired and ready to go. Nor do I go as a coward, as *you* will go—"

Again the long forefinger was flung out to point at Brigham.

"—but I shall go as a fighter to the end. I have not worshipped Mammon, and I have conquered my flesh—conquered it after it had once all but conquered me, so that I had to fight the harder—"

He stopped, waiting as if he were not done, but the spell was broken. The life, indeed, had in the later moments been slowly dying from his words; and, as they lost their fire, scattered voices of protest had been heard; then voices in warning from behind him, and the sound of two or three rising and pushing back their chairs.

Now that he no longer heard his own voice he stood quivering and panic-stricken, the fire out and the pained little smile coming to make his face gentle again. He turned weakly toward Brigham, but the Prophet had risen from his seat and his broad back was rounded toward the speaker. He appeared to be consulting a group of those who stood on the platform, and they who were not of this group had also turned away.

The little bent man tried again to smile, hoping for a friendly glance, perhaps a hand-clasp without words from some one of them. Seeing that he was shunned, he stepped down off the platform at the side, twisting his hat in his long, thin hands in embarrassment. A moment he stood so, turning to look back at the group of priests and Elders around the Prophet, seeking for any sign, even for a glance that should be not unkind. The little pained smile still lighted his face, but no friendly look came from the others. Seeing only the backs turned toward him, he at length straightened out his crumpled hat, still smiling, and slowly put it on his head; as he turned away he pulled the hat farther over his eyes, and then he was off along the dusty street, looking to neither side, still with the little smile that made his face gentle.

But when he had come to the end of the street and was on the road up the hill, the smile died. He seemed all at once to shrink and stoop and fade,—no longer a Lion of the Lord, but a poor, white-faced, horrified little man who had meant in his heart to give a great revelation, and who had succeeded only in uttering blasphemy to the very face of God's prophet.

From below, the little groups of excited people along the street looked up and saw his thin, bent figure alone in the fading sunlight, toiling resolutely upward.

Other groups back in the square talked among themselves, not a few in whispers. A listener among them might have heard such expressions as, "He'll be blood-atoned sure!" — "They'll make a breach upon him!" — "They'll accomplish his decease!" — "He'll be sent over the rim of the basin right quick!" One indignant Saint, with a talent for euphemism, was heard to say, "Brigham will have his spirit disembodied!"

To the priests and Elders on the platform Elder Wardle was saying, "The trouble with him was he was crazy with fever. Why, I'll bet my best set of harness his pulse ain't less than a hundred and twenty this minute."

The others looked at Brigham.

"He's a crazy man, sure enough," assented the Prophet, "but my opinion is he'll stay crazy, and it wouldn't be just the right thing by Israel to let him go on talking before strangers. You see, it *sounds* so almighty sane!"

Back in the crowd Prudence and Follett had lingered a little at the latter's suggestion, for he had caught the drift of the talk. When he had comprehended its meaning they set off up the hill, full of alarm.

At the door Christina met them. They saw she had been crying.

"Where is father, Christina?"

"Himself saddle his horse, and say, 'I go to toe some of those marks.' He say, 'I see you plenty not no more, so good-bye!' He kissed me," she added.

"Which way did he go?"

"So!" She pointed toward the road that led out of the valley to the north.

"I'll go after him," said Follett.

"I'll go with you. Saddle Dandy and Kit—and Christina will have something for you to eat; you've had nothing since morning."

"I reckon I know where we'll have to go," said Follett, as he went for the saddles.

Chapter XLII
The Little Bent Man at the Foot of the Cross

It was dusk when they rode down the hill together. They followed the cañon road to its meeting with the main highway at the northern edge of Amalon. Where the roads joined they passed Bishop Wright, who, with his hat off, turned to stare at them, and to pull at his fringe of whisker in seeming perplexity.

"He must have been on his way to our house," Prudence called.

"With that hair and whiskers," answered Follett, with some irrelevance, "he looks like an old buffalo-bull just before shedding-time."

They rode fast until the night fell, scanning the road ahead for a figure on horseback. When it was quite dark they halted.

"We might pass him," suggested Follett. "He was fairly tuckered out, and he might fall off any minute."

"Shall we go on slowly?" she asked.

"We might miss him in the dark. But the moon will be up in an hour, and then we can go at full speed. We better wait."

"Poor little sorry father! I wish we had gone home sooner."

"He certainly's got more spunk in him than I gave him credit for! He had old Brigham and the rest of them plumb buffaloed for a minute. Oh, he did crack the old bull-whip over them good!"

"Poor little father! Where could he have gone at this hour?"

"I've got an idea he's set out for that cross he's talked so much about—that one up here in the Meadows."

"I've seen it,—where the Indians killed those poor people years ago. But what did he mean by the crime of his Church there?"

"We'll ask him when we find him. And I reckon we'll find him right there if he holds out to ride that far."

He tied her pony to an oak-bush a little off the road, threw Dandy's bridle-rein to the ground to make him stand, and on a shelving rock near by he found her a seat.

"It won't be long, and the horses need a chance to breathe. We've come along at a right smart clip, and Dandy's been getting a regular grass-stomach on him back there."

Side by side they sat, and in the dark and stillness their own great happiness came back to them.

"The first time I liked you very much," she said, after he had kissed her, "was when I saw you were so kind to your horse."

"That's the only way to treat stock. I can gentle any horse I ever saw. Are you sure you care enough for me?"

"Oh, yes, yes, *yes*! It must be enough. It's so much I'm frightened now."

"Will you go away with me?"

"Yes, I want to go away with you."

"Well, you just come out with me,—out of this hole. There's a fine big country out there you don't know anything about. Our home will reach from Corpus Christi to Deadwood, and from the Missouri clear over to Mister Pacific Ocean. We'll have the prairies for our garden, and the high plains will be our front yard, with the buffalo-grass thicker than hair on a dog's back. And, say, I don't know about it, but I believe they have a bigger God out there than you've got in this Salt Lake Basin. Anyway, He acts more like you'd think God ought to act. He isn't so particular about your knowing a lot of signs and grips and passwords and winks. Going to your heaven must be like going into one of those Free Mason lodges,—a little peek-hole in the door, and God shoving the cover back to see if you know the signs. I guess God isn't so trifling as all that,—having, you know, a lot of signs and getting ducked under water three times and all that business. I don't exactly know what His way is, but I'll bet it isn't any way that you'd have to laugh at if you saw it—like as if, now, you saw old man Wright and God making signs to each other through the door, and Wright saying:—

> 'Eeny meeny miny mo!
> Cracky feeny finy fo!'

and God looking in a little book to see if he got all the words right."

"Anyway, I'm glad you weren't baptised, after what Father said to-day."

"You'll be gladder still when you get out there where they got a full-grown man's God."

They talked on of many things, chiefly of the wonder of their love—that each should actually be each and the two have come together—until a full yellow moon came up, seemingly from the farther side of the hill in front of them. When at last its light flooded the road so that it lay off to the north like a broad, gray ribbon flung over the black land, they set out again, galloping side by side mile after mile, scanning sharply the road ahead and its near sides.

Down out of Pine Valley they went, and over more miles of gray alkali desert toward a line of hills low and black in the north.

They came to these, followed the road out of the desert through a narrow gap, and passed into the Mountain Meadows, reining in their horses as they did so.

Before them the Meadows stretched between two ranges of low, rocky hills, narrow at first but widening gradually from the gap through which they had come. But the ground where the long, rich grass had once grown was now barren, gray and ugly in the moonlight, cut into deep gullies and naked of all but a scant growth of sage-brush which the moon was silvering, and a few clumps of shadowy scrub-oak along the base of the hills on either side.

Instinctively they stopped, speaking in low tones. And then there came to them out of the night's silence a strange, weird beating; hollow, muffled, slow, and rhythmic, but penetrating and curiously exciting, like another pulse cunningly playing upon their own to make them beat more rapidly. The girl pulled her horse close in by his, but he reassured her.

"It's Indians—they must be holding the funeral of some chief. But no matter—these Indians aren't any more account than prairie-dogs."

They rode on slowly, the funeral-drum sounding nearer as they went.

Then far up the meadow by the roadside they could see the hard, square lines of the cross in the moonlight. Slower still they went, while the drumbeats became louder, until they seemed to fall upon their own ear-drums.

"Could he have come to this dreadful place?" she asked, almost in a whisper.

"We haven't passed him, that's sure; and I've got a notion he did. I've heard him talk about this cross off and on—it's been a good deal in his mind—and maybe he was a little out of his head. But we'll soon see."

They walked their horses up a little ascent, and the cross stood out more clearly against the sky. They approached it slowly, leaning forward to peer all about it; but the shadows lay heavy at its base, and from a little distance they could distinguish no outline.

But at last they were close by and could pierce the gloom, and there at the foot of the cross, beside the cairn of stones that helped to support it, was a little huddled bit of blackness. It moved as they looked, and they knew the voice that came from it.

"O God, I am tired and ready! Take me and burn me!"

She was off her horse and quickly at his side. Follett, to let them be alone, led the horses to the spring below. It was almost gone now, only the feeblest trickle of a rivulet remaining. The once green meadows had behaved, indeed, as if a curse were put upon them. Hardly had grass grown or water run through it since the day that Israel wrought there. When he had tied the horses he heard Prudence calling him.

"I'm afraid he's delirous," she said, when he reached her side. "He keeps hearing cries and shots, and sees a woman's hair waving before him, and he's afraid of something back of him. What can we do?"

At the foot of the cross the little man was again sounding his endless prayer.

"Bow me, bend me, break me, for I have been soul-proud. Burn me out—"

She knelt by his side, trying to soothe him.

"Father—it's all right—it's Prudence—"

But at her name he uttered a cry with such terror in it that she shuddered and was still. Then he began to mutter incoherently, and she heard her own name repeated many times.

"If that awful beating would only stop," she said to Follett, who had now brought water in the curled brim of his hat. She tried to have the little man drink. He swallowed some of the water from the hat-brim, shivering as he did so.

"We ought to have a fire," she said. Follett began to gather twigs and sage-brush, and presently had a blaze in front of them.

In the light of the fire the little man could see their faces, and he became suddenly coherent, smiling at them in the old way.

"Why have you come so far in the night?" he asked Prudence, taking one of her cool hands between his own that burned.

"But, you poor little father! Why have *you* come, when you should be home in bed? You are burning with fever."

"Yes, yes, dear, but it's over now. This is the end. I came here—to be here—I came to say my last prayer in the body. And they will come to find me here. You must go before they come."

"Who will find you?"

"They from the Church. I didn't mean to do it, but when I was on my feet something forced it out of me. I knew what they would do, but I was ready to die, and I hoped I could awaken some of them."

"But no one shall hurt you."

"Don't tempt me to stay any longer, dear, even if they would let me. Oh, you don't know, you don't know—and that Devil's drumming over there to madden me as on that other night. But it's just—my God, how just!"

"Come away, then. Ruel will find your horse, and we'll ride home."

"It's too late—don't ask me to leave my hell now. It would only follow me. It was this way that night—the night before—the beating got into my blood and hammered on my brain till I didn't know. Prudence, I must tell you—everything—"

He glanced at Follett appealingly, as he had looked at the others when he left the platform that day, beseeching some expression of friendliness.

"Yes, I must tell you—everything." But his face lighted as Follett interrupted him.

"You tell her," said Follett, doggedly, "how you saved her that day and kept her like your own and brought her up to be a good woman—that's what you tell her." The gratitude in the little man's eyes had grown with each word.

"Yes, yes, dear, I have loved you like my own little child, but your father and mother were killed here that day—and I found you and loved you—such a dear, forlorn little girl—will you hate me now?" he broke off anxiously. She had both his hands in her own.

"But why, how *could* I hate you? You are my dear little sorry father—all I've known. I shall always love you."

"That will be good to take with me," he said, smiling again. "It's all I've got to take—it's all I've had since the day I found you. You are good," he said, turning to Follett.

"Oh, shucks!" answered Follett.

A smile of rare contentment played over the little man's face.

In the silence that followed, the funeral-drum came booming in upon them over the ridge, and once they saw an Indian from the encampment standing on top of the hill to look down at their fire. Then the little man spoke again.

"You will go with him," he said to Prudence. "He will take you out of here and back to your mother's people."

"She's going to marry me," said Follett. The little man smiled at this.

"It is right—the Gentile has come to take you away. The Lord is cunning in His vengeance. I felt it must be so when I saw you together."

After this he was so quiet for a time that they thought he was sleeping. But presently he grew restless again, and said to Follett:—

"I want you to have me buried here. Up there to the north, three hundred yards from here on the right, is a dwarf cedar standing alone. Straight over the ridge from that and half-way down the other side is another cedar growing at the foot of a ledge. Below that ledge is a grave. There are stones piled flat, and a cross cut in the one toward the cedar. Make a grave beside that one, and put me in it—just as I am. Remember that—*uncoffined*. It must be that way, remember. There's a little book here in this pocket. Let it stay with me—but surely uncoffined, remember, as—as the rest of them were."

"But, father, why talk so? You are going home with us."

"There, dear, it's all right, and you'll feel kind about me always when you remember me?"

"Don't,—don't talk so."

"If that beating would only stay out of my brain—the thing is crawling behind me again! Oh, no, not yet—not yet! Say this with me, dear:—

"*The Lord is my Shepherd; I shall not want.*

"*He maketh me to lie down in green pastures: he leadeth me beside the still waters.'*"

She said the psalm with him, and he grew quiet again.

"You will go away with your husband, and go at once—" He sat up suddenly from where he had been lying, the light of a new design in his eyes.

"Come,—you will need protection now—I must marry you at once. Surely that will be an office acceptable in the sight of God. And you will remember me better for it—and kinder. Come, Prudence; come, Ruel!"

"But, father, you are sick, and so weak—let us wait."

"It will give me such joy to do it—and this is the last."

She looked at Follett questioningly, but gave him her hand silently when he arose from the ground where he had been sitting.

"He'd like it, and it's what we want,—all simple," he said.

In the light of the fire they stood with hands joined, and the little man, too, got to his feet, helping himself up by the cairn against which he had been leaning.

Then, with the unceasing beats of the funeral-drum in their ears, he made them man and wife.

"Do you, Ruel, take Prudence by the right hand to receive her unto yourself to be your lawful and wedded wife, and you to be her lawful and wedded husband for time and eternity—"

Thus far he had followed the formula of his Church, but now he departed from it with something like defiance coming up in his voice.

"—with a covenant and promise on your part that you will cleave to her and to none other, so help you God, taking never another wife in spite of promise or threat of any priesthood whatsoever, cleaving unto her and her alone with singleness of heart?"

When they had made their responses, and while the drum was beating upon his heart, he pronounced them man and wife, sealing upon them "the blessings of the holy resurrection, with power to come forth in the morning clothed with glory and immortality."

When he had spoken the final words of the ceremony, he seemed to lose himself from weakness, reaching out his hands for support. They helped him down on to the saddle-blanket that Follett had brought, and the latter now went for more wood.

When he came back they were again reciting the psalm that had seemed to quiet the sufferer.

"'Yea, though I walk through the valley of the shadow of death, I will fear no evil: for thou art with me; thy rod and thy staff they comfort me.'"

Follett spread the other saddle-blanket over him. He lay on his side, his face to the fire, one moment saying over the words of the psalm, but the next listening in abject terror to something the others could not hear.

"I wonder you don't hear their screams," he said, in one of these moments; "but their blood is not upon you." Then, after a little:—

"See, it is growing light over there. Now they will soon be here. They will know where I had to come, and they will have a spade." He seemed to be fainting in his last weakness.

Another hour they sat silently beside him. Slowly the dark over the eastern hill lightened to a gray. Then the gray paled until a flush of pink was there, and they could see about them in the chill of the morning.

Then came a silence that startled them all. The drum had stopped, and the night-long vibrations ceased from their ears.

They looked toward the little man with relief, for the drumming had tortured him. But his breathing was shallow and irregular now, and from time to time they could hear a rattle in his throat. His eyes, when he opened them, were looking far off. He was turning restlessly and muttering again. She took his hands and found them cold and moist.

"His fever must have broken," she said, hopefully. The little man opened his eyes to look up at her, and spoke, though absently, and not as if he saw her.

"They will have a spade with them when they come, never fear. And the spot must not be forgotten—three hundred yards north to the dwarf cedar, then straight over the ridge and half-way down, to the other cedar below the sandstone—and uncoffined, with the book here in this pocket where I have it. 'Thou preparest a table before me in the presence of mine enemies: thou anointest my head with oil; my cup runneth over. Surely goodness and mercy shall follow me all the days of my life: and I will dwell in the house of the Lord forever.'"

He started up in terror of something that seemed to be behind him, but fell back, and a moment later was rambling off through some sermon of the bygone year.

"Sometimes, brethren, it has seemed to my inner soul that Christ came not alone to reveal God to man, but to reveal man to God; taking on that human form to reconcile the Father to our sins. Sometimes I have thought He might so well have done this that God would view our sins as we view the faults of our well-loved little children—loving us through all—perhaps touched—even more amused than offended, at our childish stumblings in these blind, twisted paths of right and wrong; knowing at the last He should save the least of us who have been most awkward. But, oh, brethren! beware of the sin for which you cannot win forgiveness from that other God, that spirit of the true Father, fixed forever in the breast of each of you."

The light was coming swiftly. Already their fire had paled, and the embers, but a little before glowing red, seemed now to be only white ashes.

From over the ridge back of them, whence had come the notes of the funeral-drum, an Indian now slouched toward them, drawn by curiosity; stopping to look, then advancing, to stop again.

At length he stood close by them, silent, gazing. Then, as if understanding, he spoke to Follett.

"Big sick—go get big medicine! Then you give chitcup!"

He ran swiftly back, disappearing over the ridge.

The sick man was now delirious again, muttering disjointed texts and bits of old sermons with which the Lute of the Holy Ghost, young and ardent, had once thrilled the Saints.

"'For without shedding of blood there shall be no remission'—'but where are now your prophets which prophesied unto you, saying the King of Babylon shall not come against you nor against this land'—'But I say unto you which hear, Love your enemies, do good to them which hate you, bless them that curse you, and pray for them which despitefully use you.' That is where the stain was,—the bloody stain that held the leaves together—but I tore them apart and read,—"

The Indian who had come to them first now appeared again over the ridge, and with him another. The second was accoutered lavishly with a girdle of brilliant feathers, anklets of shell, and bracelets of silver, his face barred by alternating streaks of vermilion and yellow, a lank braid of his black hair hanging either side of his face, and on his head the horns and painted skull of a buffalo. In one hand was a wand of red-dyed wood with a beaded and quilled amulet at the end. The other down by his side held something they did not at first notice.

The little man was growing weaker each moment, but still muttered as he turned restlessly on the blanket.

"'And as ye would that men should do to you, do ye also to them likewise.'" His quick ear detecting the light step of the approaching Indians, he sat up and grasped Follett's arm.

"What do they want? Let no one come now. Death is here and I am going out to meet it—I am glad to go—so tired!"

Follett, looking up at the two Indians now standing awkwardly by them, said, in a low tone, with a wave of his free arm:

"*Vamose!*"

"Big medicine!" grunted the Indian who had first come to them, pointing to his companion. In an instant this other was before the sick man, chanting and making passes with his wand.

Then, before Follett could rise, the Indian's other hand came up, and they saw, slowly waved before the staring eyes of the little man, a long mass of yellow hair that writhed and ran in little gleaming waves as if it lived. It was tied about the wrist of the Indian with strips of scarlet flannel—tied below a broad silver bracelet that glittered from the bronzed arm.

The face of the sick man had a moment before been tranquil, almost smiling; but now his eyes followed the hair with something of fascination in them. Then a shade of terror darkened the peaceful look, like the shadow of a cloud hurried by the wind over a fair green garden.

But with its passing there came again into his eyes the light of sanity. He gazed at the hair, breathless, still in wonder; and then very slowly there grew over his face the look of an unearthly peace, so that they who were by him deferred the putting aside of the Indian. With eyes wide open, full of a calm they could not understand, he looked and smiled, his wan face flushing again in that last time. Then, reaching suddenly out, his long white fingers tangled themselves feebly in the golden skein, and with a little loving uplift of the eyes he drew it to his breast. A few seconds he held it so, with an eagerness that told of some sweet and mighty relief come to his soul,—some illumination of grace that had seemed to be struck by the first sunrays from that hair into his wondering eyes.

Slowly, then, the little smile faded,—the wistful light of it dying for the last time. The tired head fell suddenly back and the wan lids closed over lifeless eyes.

Still the hand clutched the hair to the quiet heart, the yellow strands curling peacefully through the dead fingers as if in forgiveness. From the look of rest on the still face it was as if, in his years of service and sacrifice, the little man had learned how to forgive his own sin in the flash of those last heart-beats when his soul had rushed out to welcome Death.

Prudence had arisen before the end came and was standing in front of the Indian to motion him away. Follett was glad she did not see the eyes glaze nor the head drop. He leaned forward and gently loosed the limp fingers from the yellow tangle. Then he sprang quickly up and put his arm about Prudence. The two Indians backed off in some dismay. The one who had first come to them spoke again.

"Big medicine! You give some chitcup?"

"No—no! Got no chitcup! *Vamose!*"

They turned silently and trotted back over the ridge.

"Come, sit here close by the fire, dear—no, around this side. It's all over now."

"Oh! Oh! My poor, sorry little father—he was so good to me!" She threw herself on the ground, sobbing.

Follett spread a saddle-blanket over the huddled figure at the foot of the cross. Then he went back to take her in his arms and give her such comfort as he could.

Chapter XLIII
The Gentile Carries off his Spoil

Half an hour later they heard the sound of voices and wheels. Follett looked up and saw a light wagon with four men in it driving into the Meadows from the south. The driver was Seth Wright; the man beside him he knew to be Bishop Snow, the one they called the Entablature of Truth. The two others he had seen in Amalon, but he did not know their names.

He got up and went forward when the wagon stopped, leaning casually on the wheel.

"He's already dead, but you can help me bury him as soon as I get my wife out of the way around that oak-brush—I see you've brought along a spade."

The men in the wagon looked at each other, and then climbed slowly out.

"Now who could 'a' left that there spade in the wagon?" began the Wild Ram of the Mountains, a look of perplexity clouding his ingenuous face.

The Entablature of Truth was less disposed for idle talk.

"Who did you say you'd get out of the way, young man?"

"My wife, Mrs. Ruel Follett."

"Meaning Prudence Rae?"

"Meaning her that was Prudence Rae."

"Oh!"

The ruddy-faced Bishop scanned the horizon with a dreamy, speculative eye, turning at length to his companions.

"We better get to this burying," he said.

"Wait a minute," said Follett.

They saw him go to Prudence, raise her from the ground, put a saddle-blanket over his arm, and lead her slowly up the road around a turn that took them beyond a clump of the oak-brush.

"It won't do!" said Wright, with a meaning glance at the Entablature of Truth, quite as if he had divined his thought.

"I'd like to know why not?" retorted this good man, aggressively.

"Because times has changed; this ain't '57."

"It'll almost do itself," insisted Snow. "What say, Glines?" and he turned to one of the others.

"Looks all right," answered the man addressed. "By heck! but that's a purty saddle he carries!"

"What say, Taggart?"

"For God's sake, no, Bishop! No—I got enough dead faces looking at me now from this place. I'm ha'nted into hell a'ready, like he said he was yesterday. By God! I sometimes a'most think I'll have my ears busted and my eyes put out to git away from the bloody things!"

"Ho! Scared, are you? Well, I'll do it myself. *You* don't need to help."

"Better let well enough alone, Brother Warren!" interposed Wright.

"But it *ain't* well enough! Think of that girl going to a low cuss of a Gentile when Brigham wants her. Why, think of letting such a critter get away, even if Brigham didn't want her!"

"You know they got Brother Brigham under indictment for murder now, account of that Aiken party."

"What of it? He'll get off."

"That he will, but it's because he's Brigham. *You* ain't. You're just a south country Bishop. Don't you know he'd throw you to the Gentile courts as a sop quicker'n a wink if he got a chance,—just like he'll do with old John D. Lee the minute George A. peters out so the chain will be broke between Lee and Brigham?"

"And maybe this cuss has got friends," suggested Glines.

"Who'd know but the girl?" Snow insisted. "And Brother Brigham would fix *her* all right. Is the household of faith to be spoiled?"

"Well, they got a railroad running through it now," said Wright, "and a telegraph, and a lot of soldiers. So don't you count on *me*, Brother Snow, at any stage of it now or afterwards. I got a pretty sizable family that would hate to lose me. Look out! Here he comes."

Follett now came up, speaking in a cheerful manner that nevertheless chilled even the enthusiasm of the good Bishop Snow.

"Now, gentlemen, just by way of friendly advice to you,—like as not I'll be stepping in front of some of you in the next hour. But it isn't going to worry me any, and I'll tell you why. I'd feel awful sad for you all if anything was to happen to me,—if the Injuns got me, or I was took bad with a chill, or a jack-rabbit crept up and bit me to death, or anything. You see, there's a train of twenty-five big J. Murphy wagons will be along here over the San Bernardino trail. They are coming out of their way, almost any time now, on purpose to pick me up. Fact is, my ears have been pricking up all morning to hear the old bull-whips crack. There were thirty-one men in the train when they went down, and there may be more coming back. It's a train of Ezra Calkins, my adopted father. You see, they know I've been here on special business, and I sent word the other day I was about due to finish it, and they wasn't to go through coming back without me. Well, that bull outfit will stop for me—and they'll *get* me or get pay for me. That's their orders. And it isn't a train of women and babies, either. They're such an outrageous rough lot, quick-tempered and all like that, that they wouldn't believe the truth that I had an accident—not if you swore it on a stack of Mormon Bibles topped off by the life of Joe Smith. They'd go right out and make Amalon look like a whole cavayard of razor-hoofed buffaloes had raced back and forth over it. And the rest of the two thousand men on Ezra Calkins's pay-roll would come hanging around pestering you all with Winchesters. They'd make you scratch gravel, sure!

"Now let's get to work. I see you'll be awful careful and tender with me. I'll bet I don't get even a sprained ankle. You folks get him, and I'll show you where he said the place was."

Two hours later Follett came running back to where Prudence lay on the saddle-blanket in the warm morning sun.

"The wagon-train is coming—hear the whips? Now, look here, why don't we go right on with it, in one of the big wagons? They're coming back light, and we can have a J. Murphy that is bigger than a whole lot of houses in this country. You don't want to go back there, do you?"

She shook her head.

"No, it would hurt me to see it now. I should be expecting to see him at every turn. Oh, I couldn't stand that—poor sorry little father!"

"Well, then, leave it all; leave the place to the women, and good riddance, and come off with me. I'll send one of the boys back with a pack-mule for any plunder you want to bring away, and you needn't ever see the place again."

She nestled in his arms, feeling in her grief the comfort of his tenderness.

"Yes, take me away now."

The big whips could be heard plainly, cracking like rifle-shots, and shortly came the creaking and hollow rumbling of the wagons and the cries of the teamsters to their six-mule teams. There were shouts and calls, snatches of song from along the line, then the rattling of harness, and in a cloud of dust the train was beside them, the teamsters sitting with rounded shoulders up under the bowed covers of the big wagons.

A hail came from the rear of the train, and a bronzed and bearded man in a leather jacket cantered up on a small pony.

"Hello there, Rool! I'm whoopin' glad to see you!"

He turned to the driver of the foremost wagon.

"All right, boys! We'll make a layby for noon."

Follett shook hands with him heartily, and turned to Prudence.

"This is my wife, Lew. Prudence, this is Lew Steffins, our wagon-master."

"Shoo, now!—you young cub—married? Well, I'm right glad to see Mrs. Rool Follett—and bless your heart, little girl!"

"Did you stop back there at the settlement?"

"Yes; and they said you'd hit the pike about dark last night, to chase a crazy man. I told them I'd be back with the whackers if I didn't find you. I was afraid some trouble was on, and here you're only married to the sweetest thing that ever—why, she's been crying! Anything wrong?"

"No; never mind now, anyway. We're going on with you, Lew."

"Bully proud to have you. There's that third wagon—"

"Could I ride in that?" asked the girl, looking at the big lumbering conveyance doubtfully.

"It carried six thousands pounds of freight to Los Angeles, little woman," answered Steffins, promptly, "and I wouldn't guess you to heft over one twenty-eight or thirty at the outside. I'll have the box filled in with spruce boughs and a lot of nice bunch-grass, and put some comforts over that, and you'll be all snug and tidy. You won't starve, either, not while there's meat running."

"And say, Lew, she's got some stuff back at that place. Let the extra hand ride back with a packjack and bring it on. She'll tell him what to get."

"Sure! Tom Callahan can go."

"And give us some grub, Lew. I've hardly had a bite since yesterday morning."

An hour later, when the train was nearly ready to start, Follett took his wife to the top of the ridge and showed her, a little way below them, the cedar at the foot of the sandstone ledge. He stayed back, thinking she would wish to be there alone. But when she stood by the new grave she looked up and beckoned to him.

"I wanted you by me," she said, as he reached her side. "I never knew how much he was to me. He wasn't big and strong like other men, but now I see that he was very dear and more than I suspected. He was so quiet and always so kind—I don't remember that he was ever stern with me once. And though he suffered from some great sorrow and from sickness, he never complained. He wouldn't even admit he was sick, and he always tried to smile in that little way he had, so gentle. Poor sorry little father!— and yesterday not one of them would be his friend. It broke my heart to see him there so wistful when they turned their backs on him. Poor little man! And see, here's another grave all grown around with sage and the stones worn smooth; but there's the cross he spoke of. It must be some one that he wanted to lie beside. Poor little sorry father! Oh, you will have to be so much to me!"

The train was under way again. In the box of the big wagon, on a springy couch of spruce boughs and long bunch-grass, Prudence lay at rest, hurt by her grief, yet soothed by her love, her thoughts in a whirl about her.

Follett, mounted on Dandy, rode beside her wagon.

"Better get some sleep yourself, Rool," urged Steffins.

"Can't, Lew. I ain't sleepy. I'm too busy thinking about things, and I have to watch out for my little girl there. You can't tell what these cusses might do."

"There's thirty of us watching out for her now, young fellow."

"There'll be thirty-one till we get out of this neighbourhood, Lew."

He lifted up the wagon-cover softly a little later; and found that she slept. As they rode on, Steffins questioned him.

"Did you make that surround you was going to make, Rool?"

"No, Lew, I couldn't. Two of them was already under, and, honest, I couldn't have got the other one any more than you could have shot your kid that day he up-ended the gravy-dish in your lap."

"Hell!"

"That's right! I hope I never have to kill any one, Lew, no matter *how* much I got a right to. I reckon it always leaves uneasy feelings in a man's mind."

Eight days later a tall, bronzed young man with yellow hair and quick blue eyes, in what an observant British tourist noted in his journal as "the not unpicturesque garb of a border-ruffian," helped a dazed but very pretty young woman on to the rear platform of the Pullman car attached to the east-bound overland express at Ogden.

As they lingered on the platform before the train started they were hailed and loudly cheered, averred the journal of this same Briton, "by a crowd of the outlaw's companions, at least a score and a half of most disreputable-looking wretches, unshaven, roughly dressed, heavily booted, slouch-hatted (they swung their hats in a drunken frenzy), and to this rough ovation the girl, though seemingly a person of some decency, waved her handkerchief and smiled repeatedly, though her face had seemed to be sad and there were tears in her eyes at that very moment."

At this response from the girl, the journal went on to say, the ruffians had redoubled their drunken pandemonium. And as the train pulled away, to the observant tourist's marked relief, the young outlaw on the platform had waved his own hat and shouted as a last message to one "Lew," that he "must not let Dandy get gandered up," nor forget "to tie him to grass."

Later, as the train shrieked its way through Echo Cañon, the observant tourist, with his double-visored plaid cap well over his face, pretending to sleep, overheard the same person across the aisle say to the girl:—

"Now we're on our own property at last. For the next sixty hours we'll be riding across our own front yard—and there aren't any keys and passwords and grips here, either—just a plain Almighty God with no nonsense about Him."

Whereupon had been later added to the journal a note to the effect that Americans are not only quite as prone to vaunt and brag and tell big stories as other explorers had asserted, but that in the West they were ready blasphemers.

Yet the couple minded not the observant tourist, and continued to enlarge and complicate his views of American life to the very bank of the Missouri. Unwittingly, however, for they knew him not nor saw him nor heard him, being occupied with the matter of themselves.

"You'll have to back me up when we get to Springfield," he said to her one late afternoon, when they neared the end of their exciting journey. "I've heard that old Grandpa Corson is mighty peppery. He might take you away from me."

Her eyes came in from the brown rolling of the plain outside to light him with their love; and then, the lamps having not yet been lighted, the head of grace nestled suddenly on its pillow of brawn with only a little tremulous sigh of security for answer.

This brought his arm quickly about her in a protecting clasp, plainly in the sidelong gaze of the now scandalised but not less observant tourist.